THE RETURN OF THE PIRATE

Angélique rushed down to the water's edge and began to undo the fastenings on her dress. A moment later Goldbeard was with her once more.

"What are you trying to do? Are you mad?"

"I shall swim if I have to. I don't care! I shall reach Gouldsboro naked but I shall not stay here. Let me go!"

"You must be mad!" he repeated. "The current is very treacherous and you'll be drowned in the channels."

"I don't care! I'd rather be drowned . . . Let go of me, I say."

"No, I will not let you go."

Bantam Books by Sergeanne Golon
Ask your bookseller for the books you have missed

The Temptation of Angélique

by SERGEANNE GOLON

*Translated from the French
by Marguerite Barnett*

BANTAM BOOKS ·
TORONTO · LONDON
NEW YORK

This low-priced Bantam Book
has been completely reset in a type face
designed for easy reading, and was printed
from new plates. It contains the complete
text of the original hard-cover edition.
NOT ONE WORD HAS BEEN OMITTED.

THE TEMPTATION OF ANGÉLIQUE

*A Bantam Book / published by arrangement with
G. P. Putnam's Sons*

PRINTING HISTORY
Putnam edition published February 1970
*Originally published as La Tentation d'Angélique
in France by Editions Trévise 1969*
Heinemann edition published in England August 1969
Bantam edition / April 1971
2nd printing ...... April 1971   4th printing .... October 1973
3rd printing .... May 1972   5th printing .... July 1976

ISBN 0-553-06392-8

Published simultaneously in the United States and Canada

PRINTED IN THE UNITED STATES OF AMERICA

PRINCIPAL CHARACTERS

Angélique, Countess Peyrac: an aristocratic French lady of the seventeenth century; after an early marriage to the Gascon nobleman, Joffrey de Peyrac, by whom she had two sons, Florimond and Cantor, she becomes separated from her husband whom she believes has been executed for sorcery. She herself regains favour at Court as a result of her second marriage to her cousin Philippe du Plessis-Bellière, who is killed shortly afterwards. In order to escape the King's attentions she flees the country and is captured on the Mediterranean by the Berbers and imprisoned by the Sultan Mulai Ismail at Meknès in North Africa. There she is rescued by her fellow-captive, Colin Paturel, who accompanies her across the desert to Ceuta. She is taken back to France by the King's agents but escapes and leads the people of her native province, Poitou, in their uprising. She is condemned to death and once more obliged to flee France with her youngest child, Honorine, and a party of Huguenot refugees. On reaching America she is reunited with her long-lost husband, Joffrey de Peyrac, and with Florimond and Cantor. Together they survive their first winter in the inland fort of Wapassou, in the mountainous country of Upper Kennebec near the Canadian border. When spring comes they set off down river to visit their settlement of Gouldsboro at the mouth of the Bay of Fundy, then known as Frenchman Bay.

Joffrey de Peyrac: a high-born Frenchman. His great learning and considerable fortune arouses the envy of King Louis XIV, who contrives his ruin and has him condemned as a sorcerer. After many adventures, he is reunited with his family and disembarks on the shores of

Maine where he founds the colony of Gouldsboro. By setting up inland mining communities to exploit the vast mineral resources of the region, he establishes a claim to a large part of the territory of Maine, then known as Acadia, the sovereignty over which was disputed between France and Britain.

Colin Paturel: often referred to as the King of the Slaves at Meknès, Angélique's rescuer from captivity in North Africa. (See p. v)
Florimond and Cantor: Joffrey's and Angèlique's sons, aged 17 and 15 respectively at the time of the action.
Honorine: Angélique's four-year-old illegitimate daughter.
Yann le Couennec: Joffrey de Peyrac's equerry.
Kurt Ritz: a Swiss mercenary in Peyrac's employ.
Rose-Ann: an English child whose life Angélique has saved.
Piksarett: chief of the Patsuikett Indians.

French Canadians:
Baron Saint-Castine: a friend of Peyrac's.
François Maupertuis and Roman de l'Aubignière: trappers.
Adhemar: a buffoon.

Settlers in Gouldsboro:
Gabriel Berne: leader of the Protestant community.
Abigail Berne: his young wife.
Monsieur and Madame Mercelot: paper-makers.
Bertille: their daughter.
Monsieur and Madame Manigault.
Madame Carrère: the innkeeper.

THE
TEMPTATION
OF ANGÉLIQUE

PART ONE
The Dutchman's Trading-post

CHAPTER 1

FROM THE forest rose the sound of an Indian drum, a muffled, rhythmic roll vibrating through the oppressive heat that hung heavily over the trees and the river.

Joffrey de Peyrac and Angélique stood quite still on the river-bank and listened for a moment to the low yet distinct pounding of the drum. It came to them through the branches, in full soft notes, firmly tapped out like the beating of a powerful heart. Nature, sweltering in the steamy haze of a torrid day, was recalling the presence of man in her midst.

Instinctively Angélique caught her husband's hands, as he stood at her side.

'That drum,' she said, 'what is it saying?'

'I don't know. Wait.'

Night had not yet fallen, but the day was drawing to an end. The river lay spread out like a huge sheet of tarnished silver before Angélique and her husband the Comte de Peyrac as they stood at the water's edge, beneath the arching alders.

A little farther on towards the left, a number of canoes made of birch bark caulked with resin had been drawn up on the sandy shore of a small cove to dry out.

The line of the cove curved round, half enclosed by a narrow promontory, while, at its innermost point, the tall black cliffs, crowned with elms and oak, had retained a welcome coolness.

This was the spot they had chosen to pitch camp. They could hear the crackle of branches, snapped off for the building of huts and the lighting of fires, and already a blue pall of smoke was beginning to rise and spread out slowly over the calm waters.

Angélique tossed her head vigorously to drive off a

cloud of buzzing gnats which had suddenly begun to eddy around her. And she tried to shake off at the same time a vague sense of apprehension caused by the throbbing of the drum in the forest.

'That's strange,' she said, almost without thinking. 'There were hardly any braves in the few Abenaki villages we passed on our way down the Kennebec. Only women, children and old men.'

'Yes, all the natives have gone off to the south to sell their furs.'

'It isn't just that. The travelling parties we met on our way south consisted mainly of women. It looks as if it is they who are doing the fur trading. But where are all the men? . . .'

Peyrac threw her a swift, inscrutable glance. He too had asked himself this question, and he, like her, suspected that he knew the answer. The menfolk of the Indian tribes must have gone off to some secret meeting to plan a war. . . . But what war, and against whom?

He hesitated to put his fears into words, and decided it was better to remain silent.

It was a peaceful, carefree hour. For several days now they had journeyed without let or hindrance. The thought of returning to the coast and the more thickly populated areas, filled them all with childish excitement.

'Look!' said Peyrac with a quick gesture, 'that must be what set the drums beating. Visitors!'

Three canoes had rounded the promontory opposite them and were heading into the cove.

From the way they had so suddenly appeared, it looked as if they must have been paddling up the Kennebec instead of slipping downstream like most craft at this time of the year.

With Angélique close behind, Peyrac strode forward to the very edge of the water, where ripples stained with foam were leaving brownish lines on the fine gravel of the shore. He screwed up his eyes a little and scrutinized the newcomers.

The Indians in the three canoes showed every sign of pulling in. They lifted their dripping paddles from the

4

water, then slid overboard to push their canoes in towards the bank.

'At all events these are men, not women,' Peyrac commented.

Then, breaking off abruptly, he grasped Angélique's arm.

In one of the canoes, a dark shape in a black soutane had risen up and then slipped down into the water to make its way to the beach under the willow trees.

'The Jesuit,' murmured Angélique.

A wave of panic swept over her so powerfully that she almost yielded to the impulse to run off and hide in the depths of the forest.

But the Count checked her by laying his fingers on her wrist.

'What have you to fear from a Jesuit, my love?'

'You know what Father d'Orgeval thinks of us. He considers us dangerous usurpers if not agents of the devil.'

'As long as he comes to us only as a visitor, we must keep calm.'

Meanwhile, on the other side of the water, Black Robe had begun to pace swiftly along the bank. His long thin shadow moved across the shimmering emerald reflection of the trees with an alacrity which seemed strangely out of keeping with the heat-wearied landscape, which was already sinking into the mists and torpor of the evening. The figure was that of a young man, brimming over with vitality, a man who went straight for his goal, heedless of all obstacles, refusing even to see them.

He vanished for a moment on reaching the camp, and a heavy silence seemed to settle around the campfires, then they heard the approaching thud of the Spanish soldier's knee-boots, and the tall black shape reappeared just behind him, between the leafy drapery of the willows.

'It's not he,' said Peyrac between his teeth. 'It is not Father d'Orgeval.'

He almost felt disappointed.

The visitor was tall and thin and looked very young. Inasmuch as his Order required a very long novitiate, he could not have been under thirty, and yet he seemed to have all the inconsequential grace of a man ten years younger. His hair and beard were blond and his eyes of an almost colourless blue. His face would have been pale had it not been for the large red patches where the sun, so harsh to people of his complexion, had burned him on the forehead, the cheeks and the nose.

He halted as he caught sight of the Count and his wife, and scrutinized them for a brief moment, standing a few paces off; one of his slender, delicate hands was laid across his chest on the crucifix that hung around his neck from a purple ribbon, while the other clasped his walking stick topped with a silver cross.

Angélique thought him astonishingly distinguished looking, like a knight errant or one of the warrior arch-angels portrayed in stained-glass windows in French churches.

'I am Father Philip de Guérande,' he stated in courteous tones, 'coadjutor of Father Sebastian d'Orgeval. My superior heard that you were travelling down the Kenne-bec, Monsieur de Peyrac, and sent me to present his compliments.'

'Please convey my thanks to him for his kind thought,' Peyrac replied.

He motioned to the Spaniard, who, overwhelmed by the presence of the Jesuit Father, was holding himself almost at attention, to withdraw.

'My apologies for being able to offer you nothing better than the rustic hospitality of an encampment, Father, but I imagine you must be used to this kind of discomfort. Shall we move closer to the fires? The smoke will afford us some protection from the mosquitoes. It was one of your Order, I believe, who said that in America the hair-shirt was superfluous as the mosquitoes and gnats more than adequately fulfilled its function of chastizing the flesh.'

The priest condescended to smile.

'Blessed Father Bréboeuf was indeed responsible for that quip,' he admitted.

They sat down not far from the groups of people who were busy preparing the meal and making ready for the night, but at a certain distance.

Angélique made as if to leave them but Joffrey held her back with a scarcely perceptible pressure of his

6

hand, for he wished her to be present at the interview. So she took her place beside him on a large moss-covered rock. She had already noticed, with a woman's quick intuition, that Father de Guérande was behaving as if he had not noticed her presence.

'May I introduce my wife, the Countess of Peyrac de Morens d'Irristru?' Joffrey went on in the same serenely urbane tones.

The young Jesuit bowed his head in Angélique's direction in a stiff, almost perfunctory gesture, then turned away to gaze over the smooth, gradually darkening surface of the water in whose depths were beginning to appear the scarlet reflections of the numerous camp fires that crackled along the shore.

On the opposite side of the cove, the Indians who had accompanied the priest were preparing their encampment.

Peyrac suggested that they be invited to share the venison and turkey already roasting on the spits, and the salmon caught only an hour before and now baking in the hot ashes, closely wrapped in leaves.

But Father de Guérande shook his head, explaining that the Indians were Kennebas, an unsociable tribe that did not care to mix with strangers.

Angélique suddenly remembered the little English girl, Rose-Ann, who was accompanying them, and she looked around for her but failed to see her. Later she was to learn that Cantor had whisked the child away out of sight as soon as the Jesuit had arrived, and was sitting patiently in some thicket, strumming his guitar to amuse her, until the conversation should come to an end.

'I gather,' continued Father de Guérande, 'that you spent the winter in the depths of the Appalachians. Did you suffer scurvy, or famine? Did you lose any members of your colony? . . .'

'No, not a single man, God be praised!'

The priest raised his eyebrows and gave a surprised little smile.

'How delighted we are to hear you praise God, Monsieur de Peyrac. It has been rumoured that you and your band were scarcely what one might call pious people, indeed, that among your recruits were heretics, men of

7

no particular religious belief, free thinkers, and even head-strong men whom pride had so misled as to indulge in blasphemy and in cursing God—blessed be His Holy Name. . . .'

He waved aside the goblet of cold water and the bowl of roast meat offered him by Yann le Couennec, the young Breton who served as Count Peyrac's equerry.

'What a pity,' thought Angélique irreverently, 'we shan't be able to get at these Jesuits through their stomachs any more. . . . In the old days Father Masserat was more sybaritic.'

'Do take some refreshment, Father,' Peyrac insisted.

But the Jesuit shook his head.

'We ate at noon. That is enough for one day. I eat little, like the Indians. . . . But you did not answer my question, Sir. Do you deliberately recruit your men from among those in rebellion against the authority of the Church?'

'To tell the truth, Father, what I ask above all of those I employ is that they should be skilled in the use of arms, axes and hammers, that they should be capable of withstanding cold, hunger, fatigue, and battle, in a word, adversity, without a word of complaint, that they should remain faithful and obedient to me for as long as they have contracted to work for me, and that they should give of their best in all the tasks I set them. But if they happen to be pious and devout as well, that I do not expressly regard as an obstacle.'

'And yet you have never set up the Cross over any of your settlements.'

Peyrac made no reply.

The sheen on the glittering water, suddenly afire from the light of the setting sun, seemed to kindle a tiny mocking light in his eyes—a light that Angélique knew well—but he remained patient and uncommonly friendly.

The priest persisted in his questioning.

'Do you mean to say that there are men among you whom this sign, this wonderful sign of love, of sacrifice —may God bless it—that this sign, I say, might shock or even antagonize.'

'Possibly.'

8

'And what if there were among your men some—like that young man, for instance, with the frank, open face who offered me food just now—who might, remembering a pious childhood, still feel some affection for the sign of redemption? Would you deliberately deprive them of the succour of their Holy Religion?'

'One is always more or less obliged to forgo something when one undertakes to live in a mixed community, under harsh conditions, and sometimes in very cramped quarters. It is not for me, Father, to remind you how imperfect a thing is human nature, or that mutual concessions are essential if one is to live in harmony.'

'It would seem to me that to give up paying tribute to God and seeking His mercy should be the last concession one should make; that it is indeed a sinful one. Is this not an indication, Monsieur de Peyrac, of the very slender importance you attach to spiritual succour? Works done without the life-giving divine force count for nothing. Works undertaken without sanctifying Grace are null and void. They are empty shells, a mere puff of wind; they are as nought. And this Grace can only be given to those who recognize God as Lord of all their actions, who obey His laws and who offer up to Him, in the prayers they utter every day of their lives, the fruits of all their labours.'

'And yet the Apostle James wrote: "Faith without works is dead. . . ." ' Peyrac straightened his shoulders that had been bowed as if weighed down by his thoughts. From a slit in his leather jerkin he drew forth a cigar made from rolled tobacco leaves which he lit at the burning brand the young Breton lad passed him almost instantaneously before withdrawing discreetly again.

On hearing the Count quote Scripture, Philip de Guérande gave the cold, thin smile of an adversary acknowledging a shrewd thrust. But the smile in no way indicated he had been won over.

Angélique kept silence, gnawing irritably at her little finger nail. Who did this Jesuit think he was, to dare to talk like this to Joffrey de Peyrac? Yet at the same time her convent upbringing came back to her with sudden force, recalling the feeling of painful dependence she had felt as a child before all clergy, particularly Jesuits, who

9

feared nothing, neither King nor Pope. Their Order had been founded to teach and admonish the powerful of this world. She gazed thoughtfully with her wide eyes at that emaciated face, experiencing through the unaccustomed presence of this visitor, in the heart of the American forest, all the ancient fears that belonged to the Old World: the fear of the priest, the possessor of mystical powers. Then she looked again at her husband's face and breathed a sigh of belief. For he was free—and would ever be free of such influences. He was a son of Aquitaine, an heir to a liberal philosophy of existence, handed down through time immemorial from pagan civilizations. He was not of the same essence as her or this Jesuit, both of them irrevocably involved in unshakeable creeds. He escaped this attraction, and because of it she loved him passionately. She heard him reply in measured tones:

'Father, anyone who works for me is free to pray if he so chooses. As for the others, do you not consider that work well done sanctifies men?'

The Jesuit appeared to reflect for a moment then slowly shook his head.

'No, sir, I do not. And I recognize in what you say foolish and dangerous heresies propounded by philosophers who wish to free themselves from dependence upon the Church.

'You are from Aquitaine,' he continued in a different tone. 'Men from your province are both numerous and active in Canada or Acadia. At Pentagouet Baron de Saint-Castine has utterly cleared the English from along the Penobscot river. He has had the chief of the Etchemins baptized, and the Indians of that area treat him like one of themselves.

'Yes, Castine is my neighbour at Gouldsboro. He is a man I know and esteem,' Peyrac replied.

'Now, what other Gascons have we in our colony?' Father de Guérande continued with studied affability. 'Why yes, there is Vauvenart on the St John river . . .'

'A pirate of my ilk!'

'Granted! But he is utterly devoted to the French cause and an excellent friend of the Governor of Acadia, Monsieur de Villedavray. In the north we have Monsieur de Morsac at Cataracoui. Not forgetting of course our dearly beloved Governor Monsieur de Frontenac.'

Peyrac, puffing quietly at his cigar, nodded his agreement. Angélique herself could read nothing from his expression. The evening light falling through the shining leaves of the enormous oaks that overhung the cliff, and filtering through the dense masses of verdure, had taken on a greenish tinge that made their faces look pale, and deepened the shadows. Now a golden sheen lay on the river and the little bay had darkened to the colour of copper. Thanks to the reflection of the sky in the waters, there seemed to be more light about than a little earlier. Soon it would be June, when the evenings encroach upon the kingdom of night, a time of the year when both human beings and animals devote but few hours to sleep.

Someone had thrown big black mushrooms, round and desiccated like cannon balls, on to the fires, where they burned giving off a bitter, woody smell which had the beneficial effect of driving the mosquitoes away, and this smell now mingled with that of tobacco rising from the pipes of the men. The tiny cove was full of mist and goodly fragrance, a cosy refuge beside the Kennebec.

Angélique passed her hand over her brow and from time to time ran her fingers through her heavy, golden hair, drawing it back from her moist temples, in an attempt to enjoy a momentary sensation of coolness, while she unconsciously strove to cast off her anxiety. Her eyes travelled backwards and forwards between the two men with the keenest interest, while her lips remained parted, so closely was she following the conversation. But what she was really listening to was all that lay hidden behind the words they exchanged. Then suddenly Father de Guérande came in to the attack:

'Can you explain to me, Monsieur de Peyrac, by what chance, if you are in no way hostile towards the Church, every single member of your colony in Gouldsboro is a Huguenot?'

'Yes indeed, Father. The chance, to which you refer, was that one day I cast anchor off La Rochelle, just as this handful of Huguenots, destined for the King's prisons, was fleeing from the Dragoons who had been ordered to apprehend them. I took them on board my ship to save them, from what looked to me like certain doom when I saw those musketeers draw their swords. Not knowing what to do with them, once I had them on board, I brought them over to Gouldsboro, so that they could pay for their passages by cultivating my lands.'

'But why did you remove them from the jurisdiction of the King of France?'

'I'm not sure,' Peyrac replied with an offhanded gesture and his habitual sardonic smile. 'Possibly because it is written in the Bible: "Preserve Thou those that are appointed to die!"'

'Are you quoting the Bible?'

'Yes, that phrase occurs in the Holy Scriptures.'

'Dangerously tainted with Judaism, it seems to me.'

'It seems to me to be rather obvious that the Bible is tainted with Judaism,' Peyrac replied, with a burst of laughter.

And to Angélique's surprise Father de Guérande began to laugh too, this time appearing quite relaxed.

'Yes, obviously,' he said, willingly admitting the ineptitude of the dictum he had just uttered, 'but you see, Monsieur, nowadays Holy Scripture is so often mingled in people's minds with the most disturbing heresies, that it is our duty to view with suspicion anyone quoting it recklessly.

'Monsieur de Peyrac, from whom do you hold the charter giving you rights over the lands of the Gouldsboro? From the King of France?'

'No, Father.'

'From whom then? From the English of the Bay of Massachusetts who claim improperly to be the proprietors of these shores?'

Peyrac side-stepped the trap.

"I have made alliance with the Abenakis and the Mohicans.'

'But all those Indians are subjects of the King of France, most of them have been baptized and they should never, under any circumstances, have entered into any such agreement without consulting Monsieur de Frontenac.'

'Go and tell them so then. . . .'

A note of irony was beginning to creep into the conversation. The Count had a way of swathing himself in his own cigar smoke that betrayed his impatience.

'As for my Gouldsboro people, they are not the first Huguenots to set foot on these shores. There was Monsieur de Monts, for instance, who was sent over by King Henry IV.'

'Never mind the past. At this present time here you are without a charter, without a chaplain, without a creed—without the backing of any nation, laying claim to these lands, and you alone already possess more outposts, more trading-posts and a greater number of people than the whole of France, which has held possessions here for a very long time. You alone, quite alone, claim ownership of all this, am I right?'

Peyrac made a gesture that could have been read as acquiescence.

'In your own right,' the Jesuit repeated, his agate eyes suddenly lighting up. 'Pride! pride! that was Lucifer's unpardonable sin. For it is not true that he attempted to be like God; but he did claim to be the source of his own greatness which he attributed to his own intellect. Is that your creed?'

'I would hesitate to associate my own creed with so formidable a figure.'

'You are being evasive, Monsieur. He who sought to achieve Knowledge unaided and to his own glory, what a fate was his! Like the sorcerer's apprentice, he lost control over that Knowledge and brought about the destruction of the Universe.'

'And Lucifer and the wicked angels fell in a shower of stars,' Peyrac murmured. 'And now they and their secrets are mingled with the earth, are become tiny grinning gnomes and goblins that men find in the depths of mines, where they keep watch and guard over gold and other precious metals.

'You must know, Father, for you must undoubtedly have studied the secrets of the Cabbala, what name the Hermetic philosophers gave to the legions of demons made up of these little kobolds, gnomes, and genii of the earth.'

The priest stiffened and threw him a piercing glance

13

that was at once a challenge and the recognition of a fellow initiate.

'I follow you perfectly,' he replied slowly and thoughtfully. 'We all too readily forget that certain names which we have come to accept as part of our everyday language, once served to describe the hordes of the infernal powers. Thus it was that the genii of Water, the undines, formed the legions of the Lustful. Those of the Air, the sylphs, were the legions of Sloth. The spirits of Fire, symbolized by the salamander and the will-o'-the-wisp, were the cohorts of Wrath. And those of the Earth, the gnomes, were known as . . .'

'The Rebels,' Peyrac replied with a smile.

'True sons of the Evil One,' the Jesuit murmured.

Angélique's eyes travelled backwards and forwards in dismay between the two participants in this strange dialogue.

She laid her hand impulsively upon her husband's as a warning to take care.

A warning a protection! To restrain him. . . . Here in the heart of the American forests they were suddenly menaced once more by the very same perils that had beset them in their palace in Toulouse. The Inquisition! And Joffrey de Peyrac was smiling that same sardonic smile accentuated by the scars that had remained on his face.

The Jesuit caught Angélique's eye.

Would he say tomorrow, when he had returned to his Indian mission station: 'Yes, I have seen them! They are indeed as they are reported to be. He is a dangerous man, a subtle man, while she is as lovely and sensual as Eve, with strange, incomparable grace in her every movement . . . ?'

Would he say: 'Yes, I saw them standing by the river, reflected in the blue waters of the Kennebec, standing amid the trees; he was black, hard, and sardonic, and she was dazzling; they leaned the one upon the other, the man and the woman bound by some pact. . .? Ah but what pact could it be?' he would say to Father d'Orgeval with a shudder. . . .

And once again the marsh-fever that so often racked the missionary would set his limbs quivering wretchedly. . . . 'Yes, I saw them, and I spent a long time with them, and I did as you asked me—I sounded the heart of this man. . . . But now I am exhausted.'

'Is it gold you have come to seek?' asked the Jesuit in measured tones. 'Gold you have found! You have come to enslave all these pure, primitive lands to the idolatry of gold.'

'I have never been called an idolater before!' Peyrac replied with a merry guffaw. 'Are you forgetting, Father, that 150 years ago the monk Tritheim taught at Prague that gold represented the soul of the first man?'

'But he also laid down that gold contained in substance Vice and Evil,' the Jesuit replied with alacrity.

'And yet wealth gives power which can serve the Good. Your Order realized that from the time of its foundation, it seems to me, for it is the richest Order in the world.'

As he had already done several times before Father de Guérande changed the subject:

'If you are a Frenchman, why are you not an enemy of the English and the Iroquois who are seeking to destroy New France?' he asked.

'The quarrels between you go back such a long way that it is more than I can manage to take sides. I shall do my best to live on good terms with everyone. And who knows? I might even be able to establish peace.'

'You could do us a great deal of harm,' the young Jesuit replied, in a strained voice, in which Angélique caught a ring of genuine distress. 'Oh why,' he cried, 'why did you not set up the Cross?'

'It is an emblem of conflict.'

'Many a crime has been perpetrated in the name of gold.'

'And in the name of the Cross too,' Peyrac replied looking hard at the priest.

The Jesuit drew himself up to his full height. He was so pale that the sunburned patches looked like raw, bleeding wounds on his chalky face.

In his thin neck, rising above his white bands, the sole adornment of his black soutane, a vein pulsated violently.

'At last I have heard your profession of faith, Monsieur,' came his gruff reply. 'In vain will you protest that your intentions towards us are friendly. Every word that has fallen from your lips was tainted by that abominable spirit of revolt which characterizes the heretics with whom you associate—rejection of the external signs of piety, scepticism about revealed truths, indifference to the triumph of Truth, and little do you care if the very image of the Word made Flesh is wiped off the face of the globe along with the Catholic Church, and if darkness descends on men's souls!'

The Count stood up and laid a hand on the Jesuit's shoulder, a gesture full of indulgence and a kind of compassion.

'Very well!' he said. 'And now, Father, listen to me and make sure you repeat my exact words to the man who sent you here. If you have come to ask me to show no hostility towards you, to help you in time of famine and poverty, that I will do as I have done before since I settled on these shores. But if you have come to ask me to go away along with my Huguenots and my pirates, then I will reply: *No!* And if you have come to ask me to help you to massacre the English and fight the Iroquois as a matter of sheer principle, without any provocation, then I will reply: *No!* I am not one of your men, I owe allegiance to no one. I have no time to waste and I regard it as pointless to transfer the metaphysical wrangles of the Old World to the New.'

'Is that your last word?'

Their glances met.

'No doubt not my last,' Peyrac murmured with a smile.

'Well, it is ours!'

And the Jesuit strode off under the shadow of the trees.

CHAPTER 2

'Is THAT a declaration of war?' Angélique asked, looking up at her husband.

'It looks like it to me.'

16

He smiled and laid a hand on Angélique's hair, stroking it slowly.

'But these are only the preliminaries. We must discuss things with Father d'Orgeval and that I shall try to do. And then . . . well, every day gained is a victory for us. The *Gouldsboro* should be back from Europe by now and I have some small coasting-vessels due from New England which are well armed, and further reinforcements of mercenaries. If necessary I shall sail right up to Quebec with my fleet, but I am determined to face next winter in peace and in strength, that I swear. After all, however hostile and antagonistic towards me they may be, they are only four Jesuits in a territory that is bigger than France and Spain put together.'

Angélique brooded. In spite of Count Peyrac's optimism and reassuring logic, it seemed to her that the battle would be fought on a plane where numbers, arms and men were of little account in comparison with the mysterious, nameless forces pitted against them.

And she sensed that he felt as she did.

'Why, oh why did you talk all that nonsense to him?' she complained.

'What nonsense, my love?'

'All that talk about little demons at the bottom of mines and the theories of some monk or other long ago in Prague. . . .'

'I tried to talk to him in his own terms. He has a fine brain and he's a born scholar. He must have a sheaf of bachelor's and doctor's degrees; his head is stuffed with every scrap of theological and occult science known to this day and age. What on earth does he think he's doing in America? . . . The savages will put paid to him.'

Peyrac, who seemed inwardly cheerful and not at all upset, raised his eyes towards the dark leafy vault, where some invisible bird was flapping its wings. Night had come, deep purple, velvet night, spangled by the firelight from the bivouacs. A voice called through the branches, summoning the company to dinner.

Then in the silence that followed, the bird gave a sudden cry, so close to them that Angélique shuddered.

'An owl,' said Joffrey de Peyrac, 'the sorcerer's bird.'

'Oh! my love, please don't,' she cried, throwing her

arms around him and burying her face in his leather doublet. 'You scare me!'

He laughed softly and, gently yet passionately, stroked her silky hair. He would have liked to say something, to talk about the words that had been exchanged, to bring out the meaning of the conversation they had had with the Jesuit. But suddenly he found it unnecessary to speak, knowing that both he and Angélique had sensed, guessed, and understood exactly the same things at each stage of the dialogue. They both knew that this visit was nothing other than a declaration of war. A means too, perhaps, of obtaining a pretext for war.

With the extraordinary skill characteristic of members of his Order the young Jesuit had forced him to say much more than he had intended. One had to admit that the Jesuits knew how to handle human beings. And they had other weapons too, of a particular kind, whose power Joffrey did not entirely discount.

Almost imperceptibly Joffrey de Peyrac's cheerfulness evaporated and in some inexplicable way he found his anxiety centring upon his wife.

He clasped her closer. Every day, every night, he felt this need to hold her close to him, to encircle her with his arms to reassure himself that she was really there, and that nothing could touch her while the shelter of his arms was about her.

He would have liked to speak to her, but feared that in so doing his own anxiety might be communicated to her, so he decided to remain silent.

All he said was:

'I do miss little Honorine, don't you? . . .'

She nodded her bowed head, drawn closer by the tenderness his remark had inspired. A little later she asked:

'She is safe at Wapassou, isn't she?'

'Yes, my love, she is safe,' he replied.

CHAPTER 3

FATHER DE GUÉRANDE bivouacked for the night with the Indians, and declined to share the white men's meal when an invitation to do so was sent across to him.

He set off at dawn, without bidding farewell, which in a man of his breeding constituted a slight of the first order.

Angélique alone caught sight of him as he carried his pack down the shore on the far side of the water. A handful of Indians were moving lackadaisically around the beached canoes. Early mist hung over the ground up to the height of the trees but was thin enough for her to make out the shapes of people and their reflections. The heavy dew was beginning to glisten in the faint light, while the still invisible sun struggled to overcome the mists of night.

Angélique had slept but little, although their tent was by no means lacking in comfort: if the bed of pine branches strewn with furs was not exactly the softest she had ever slept on, she had known many worse. But the events of the previous evening had left her with a feeling of uneasiness.

Now, enjoying the coolness of early morning, she stood brushing her long hair in front of a small mirror propped up against a branch, telling herself that she must find some means of softening the heart of the Jesuit, of easing the tension that held him as taut as a bow drawn and ready for war.

Thus it was that she caught sight of him preparing for departure, and, after a moment's hesitation, laid down her brush and comb and shook her hair out over her shoulders.

The previous evening, as they talked, a certain question had been constantly on the tip of her tongue, but she had been unable to find the right moment to ask it in the course of such a serious conversation, full of veiled meanings and threatening hints.

19

Now she really wanted to know the answer, so she made up her mind.

Holding up her skirts to avoid contact with the dead ashes and the pots of lard that littered the camp, she picked her way through the customary untidy muddle left by the Indians and followed the path along the edge of the cove; then, disturbing two tawny dogs gnawing at the entrails of a doe, she approached the priest as he was about to set off with his sorry gear.

He had caught sight of her a few moments before emerging from the thinning, golden mist of the morning. The same sheen that dawn had laid upon the leaves, played likewise over her fair, streaming hair.

Father de Guérande was a man of delicate constitution and often, on first rising in the morning, his mind felt dull and empty. Then bit by bit the memory of God came back to him and he would begin to pray. But it always took him a certain time to pick up the thread of his thoughts. Seeing Angélique approach, at first he did not recognize her, and began to ask himself anxiously who this apparition might be.

Then he remembered with a sensation like a stab of pain in his side that it was She, the Countess of Peyrac. She saw quite clearly, in spite of the impassiveness of his expression, his inner start of fear and repulsion, a stiffening of his entire being.

She smiled in an attempt to win an answering smile from the young, stony face. 'Father! Are you leaving us already?'

'My duties oblige me to, Madame.'

'Father, I wanted to ask you one question that has been bothering me.'

'I am listening, Madame.'

'Could you tell me what kinds of plants Father d'Orgeval uses to make his green candles?'

The Jesuit had obviously been prepared for anything but this. So taken aback was he that he quite lost countenance. At first he looked for some hidden meaning in Angélique's words, then when he realized that the matter was indeed a practical, domestic one, he lost his bearings. For an instance he thought she must be making fun of him, and the blood rushed to his face, but he took a hold on himself, and made a desperate attempt to call to mind the details he needed to give a precise answer.

'His green candles?' he muttered.

'People say that the candles are very beautiful,' Angélique went on, 'and give a delightful white light. I understand they are made with some berries the Indians pick in late summer, but if you could tell me at least the name of the bush they grow on—you who know the native tongue so well—I should be most obliged . . .'

'No, I am afraid I can't . . . I have never noticed the candles. . . .'

'The poor man has no practical sense,' she told herself. 'He lives in his own dream world.' But she liked him more thus, rather than when hiding behind the breastplate of a mystical fighter. She glimpsed a point of contact between them.

'It does not matter,' she went on. 'Do not let me delay you, Father.'

He gave her a brief nod.

She watched him climb into the Indian canoe with ease of long custom, bringing in 'neither sand nor stone' as Father Bréboeuf had instructed his missionaries. Father de Guérande's body had bowed to the necessities of primitive life, but his mind would never accept its intolerable disorder. 'The savages will prove too much for him,' Peyrac had said. America would prove too much for him. This long frame with its lean backbone visible through the threadbare black robe, this body would be martyred. They all died a martyr's death.

Father de Guérande glanced one last time towards Angélique, and what he read in her eyes brought a sarcastic smile to his lips.

With an ironical phrase he defended himself against the inexplicable pity which he sensed that she felt for him.

'If you are so anxious to get an answer to the question you asked me, Madame, why not ask it yourself of Father d'Orgeval? . . . Why not go to see him at Norridgewock?'

CHAPTER 4

THREE SMALL craft, their sails billowing in the wind, were making their way down the Kennebec. At the last halt, the baggage had been transferred from the Indian canoes into bigger and more comfortable boats prepared and fitted out by three of Count Peyrac's men who, after wintering at the Dutchman's trading-post, had returned to their duties at a small silver mine the Count had staked the previous year. He had agents and allies everywhere, and a whole network of miners and settlers had grown up imperceptibly under his name in Dawn-East.

Yann, after accompanying Florimond de Peyrac as far as Lake Champlain with Cavelier de la Salle's party, had got back just in time to reoccupy his former position as Count Peyrac's equerry on the journey to the Atlantic. He brought good tidings of Peyrac's elder son, but thought that the expedition to the Mississippi was unlikely to succeed because of the difficult personality of its leader, the Frenchman Cavelier.

The little wooden boat, boasting only a mainsail and a forestay sail, carried scarcely more passengers than the Indian canoes which always seemed miraculously expansible when it came to accommodating numbers, but it was more comfortable.

Yann le Couennec managed the sails while the Count steered with Angélique sitting beside him.

A warm, gusty wind played with her hair, and she felt happy. She felt that a boat drifting downstream was in utter harmony with the very momentum of a man's soul, exemplifying freedom, fluidity, and at the same time control, self-possession, despite an intoxicating sense of temporary liberation from earthly contingencies. The river was very wide and its shores distant and hazy.

She was with Joffrey, her whole being suffused with emotions that were both tranquil and acute. Ever since Wapassou, ever since they had won the battle with the winter, she had ceased to be in a state of conflict. She was happy. No longer could anything disturb the even tenor of her life. All that mattered to her now was the knowledge that he was there beside her, and that she had become worthy of his love. He had told her so, beside the Silver Lake, while the polar dawn crept up over the trees. She was his companion, she was the fulfilment of his great heart and his boundless spirit, she, who knew so little, she who had for so long drifted weak and helpless in a world without haven. Now she was truly his. They had acknowledged the kinship of their spirits, she and this frighteningly virile and pugnacious, exceptional man. They were bound together now, and no one would ever be able to loosen the bonds that held them linked.

She glanced at him occasionally, taking in his image, his tanned, scar-lined face, and his eyebrows drawn together over his half-closed eyes as a protection against the dazzling shimmer of the water. Sitting there beside him like this, without touching him, her knees close to his, without a single gesture passing between them, so intensely did she feel her physical union with him that the colour came and went in her cheeks. Then he would glance at her impenetrably, almost casually.

He noted the smooth line of her profile and the downy curve of her cheek caressed by her wind-blown golden locks. The spring had revitalized her; the lines of her figure were full and rounded, and she had an animal grace that was as apparent in her stillness as in her every gesture.

There were stars in her eyes, and a sparkle on her soft, moist, parted lips.

Then suddenly, as they rounded a sharp bend in the river, a landing place appeared beside a deserted village. An Indian called out something from one of the other boats.

Joffrey de Peyrac pointed towards a line of trees, their colours softened by the heat haze.

'Over there!' he said, 'that's Norridgewock . . . the mission station. . . .'

Angélique's heart began to flutter but she braced her resolution, knowing in her heart that they must not leave the area without meeting Father d'Orgeval face to face and trying by diplomatic means to dispel the misunderstandings and difficulties which had grown up between them.

While the three boats leaned to one side and steered for the shore, she drew towards her the soft leather bag in which she had brought some of her belongings.

It would not be fitting for a member of the French nobility to meet so redoubtable a Jesuit in clothes that appeared casual.

She carefully arranged her hair beneath a starched but becoming coiffe, and completed the effect with her wide felt hat stuck with a red feather. A touch of flamboyance was also a necessity. For had she not been to Versailles and been presented to the King? She needed to remind the proud ecclesiastic of that fact, for he was in the habit of using his connections with the court somewhat freely in order to impress those around him.

Then she slipped on a long-sleeved mantle which she had made for herself at the fort from some blue Limburg cloth, to which she had contrived to add a white lace collar and cuffs.

The boat grounded, and Yann caught hold of a trailing branch and drew it up on the sand.

To save his wife from wetting her shoes and the hem of her dress, Peyrac lifted her and carried her in his arms to the shore, and while so doing gave her a smile of encouragement.

The shore was deserted and hemmed in by sumac trees overhung by huge slender elms. The inhabitants appeared to have abandoned the village several years before, for the whole area was overgrown with a thicket of hawthorn bushes.

One of the Indians informed them that the mission station was farther back from the river.

'We simply must talk things over with that difficult man,' Peyrac grumbled.

'Yes, we must,' Angélique agreed, although she felt highly apprehensive. God would not allow them to leave the area without taking with them a promise of peace.

As they advanced, strung out in single file, along a path that cut through the undergrowth, the smell of the flowering hawthorns accompanied them, heady and delectable.

As they left the river bank behind, the wind dropped, and the heat came down, heavy and breathless. They found the smell of flowers and pollen oppressive, and a kind of febrile agitation took hold of them, a vague nostalgia for they knew not what.

Two of the Spaniards headed the column while two others brought up the rear. They had left some of the armed men to guard the boats.

The path wound its way through the forest full of the growth of spring, narrowing here as it squeezed between clusters of thick bushes, widening there as it passed through a coppice of cherry or hazel trees.

They walked on for nearly an hour, then, when they were in the very thickest part of the forest, they heard the sound of a bell. Its pure limpid notes rang out across the forest in rapid succession.

'It's a chapel bell,' said one of the party, coming to a halt in astonishment. 'It can't be far now.'

And the Wapassou column moved forward again. The smell that hangs around the approaches to a village was beginning to reach them now, a smell of wood smoke and tobacco, of fried fat and boiled maize.

No one came out to meet them, a most surprising fact considering the habitual curiosity of the Red Indian, always avid to witness the most trivial spectacle.

The bell rang again, then fell silent. Then suddenly they came upon the hamlet, which consisted of some twenty rounded wigwams with roofs of elm and birch bark, surrounded by tiny gardens full of ripening gourds and pumpkins growing from long coiling shoots. A few scraggy hens were pecking here and there, but apart from them the village appeared to be deserted.

The visitors walked right down the central avenue in a silence that was almost palpable. . . .

The Spaniards had placed the barrels of their heavy muskets on wooden forks, so as to be ready to fire at the slightest suspicious movement, and their eyes were everywhere at once.

They held the forks in their left hands, while the index fingers of their rights rested on the flintlocks, and they moved forward with the gun butts firmly clasped under their arms.

Thus they made their way slowly through to the far end of the village, where Father d'Orgeval's little chapel was situated.

CHAPTER 5

SURROUNDED BY flowering shrubs that made it look like a street-altar, the chapel was an attractive wooden building, constructed by no mean craftsman. It was widely known that the Jesuit father had built it with his own hands.

There was a bell tower over the main part of the building in which the silver bell hung still vibrating.

In the silence Joffrey de Peyrac stepped forward and opened the door.

Almost immediately they were dazzled by a brilliant, flickering light. Four silver candelabra with flat, circular bases each held innumerable candles that burned with a faint rustling sound giving the impression of some hidden presence. But there was no one inside, only the dancing light from the soft green candles that banished every shadow.

The candelabra stood in pairs on either side of the main altar, and towards this Joffrey de Peyrac and Angélique walked.

Above their heads a lamp shone in a holder of silver-gilt open-work lined with crimson glass. It held a little oil in which trailed a lighted wick.

'The Blessed Sacrament is present,' Angélique murmured, crossing herself.

The Count removed his hat and bowed his head. A fragrant smell filled the air, warmed by the glow of the candles.

On either side of the altar, copes and chasubles hung exposed to view, dazzling in all their silk and gold work, with their embroidered faces of saints and angels, hieratic and sumptuous; 'robes of light' as they were called by the Indians, who greatly envied the priests on their account.

The banner was there too, and for the first time they saw it as it had been described to them, stained with

English blood, with the four red hearts at the corners, and a sword drawn diagonally across the battle-stained silk.

Extremely fine sacred vessels, reliquaries and silver-embroidered corporals were on display beside the tabernacle, above which stood a magnificent silver processional crucifix.

The reliquary was an ancient piece, a gift of the Queen Mother, and consisted of a small coffer fashioned of Fatimite rock crystal encircled by six gold bands studded alternately with pearls and rubies. It was said to contain a splinter of one of the arrows which had killed Saint Sebastian in the second century A.D.

On the altar stone itself lay something difficult to identify until they drew closer and saw that it was a musket. It was a long, glistening, handsome warlike object laid there on the altar, as an offering, in homage—a categorical declaration.

They both gave a shudder, and seemed to hear the prayer which had risen so many times, in this very spot, from the lips of him who owned this weapon:

'Accept, O Lord, in expiation of our sins, the blood we have shed for You. . . .

'The unclean blood of the heretic, the blood of the sacrificed Indians, and my own blood which has been shed for You, for Your glory, for Your greater glory. . . .

'Accept, O Lord, the trials and tribulations of war, so that Justice may reign, and Your enemies be wiped from the face of the earth. Let the idolater who knows You not, the heretic who flouts You, the indifferent man who ignores You, be crushed. Let those alone who serve You have the right to live, may Your Kingdom alone come, and Your name alone be honoured!

'I, Your servant will take up arms and offer my life to Your greater glory, for You are all in all to me.'

This passionate, violent prayer echoed through their hearts, so clearly that Angélique felt a strange dread creep over her.

She understood him. She understood perfectly well that this man should regard God as the one and only being that mattered.

27

Would he fight for his own life? . . . What a mockery! To protect his possessions? How petty!

But for God! What a death, what high stakes!

The blood of the Crusaders, her ancestors, rose to her heart. She understood what kind of spring it was at which the man who had laid this weapon here quenched and intensified turn and turn about his thirst for martyrdom and sacrifice.

She saw him in her mind's eye, with bowed head and closed eyes, far away, remote from his wretched, mortified body. Here he had offered up all the toils of war, the weariness of battle, of massacre, that left the arms broken from striking too often, the lips dry from never having had time to draw breath during the fighting, he had offered up the joys of triumph, the prayers for victory, the sacrifice of pride, giving to the angels and the saints the credit for the strength and valiance of the warriors. . . .

'Musket of the Holy War, faithful servant, keep your vigil at the feet of the King of Kings, until the time comes to ring out for Him!

'Blessed weapon, sanctified and blest a thousand times over, lovely in honour of Him you serve and defend, watch and pray, and let not those that gaze on you prevail against you.

'May those who gaze on you today understand your symbolism and the message that I cry to them on your behalf!'

Anguish gripped Angélique by the throat.

'It's terrible,' she thought. 'He has the angels and the saints on his side, while we . . .'

She glanced distractedly towards the man who stood beside her, her husband, and already an answer had formed in her heart.

'We . . . we have Love and Life . . .'

On the face of Joffrey de Peyrac—the adventurer, the outcast—the dancing light of the candles revealed what looked like expressions of bitterness and mockery.

Yet he was, at this moment, impassive. He did not wish to frighten Angélique, did not wish to give the incident its precise, mystical interpretation; but he too had understood the message of the exposition of the musket.

Such power! Such an admission! Between you and me there will be forever total war.

Between him, the solitary soul, and them, blessed by love, war . . . forever war!

And no doubt out there in the forest, prostrated on the ground, he had a precise image of them within himself, that warrior priest, that Jesuit, could see those who had chosen the delights of this world, the couple standing before the sign of the cross, as they stood, their hands close and ready to grasp one another, as they in fact grasped one another in silence. . . .

Peyrac's warm hand clasped Angélique's cold fingers, then once more he bowed respectfully before the tabernacle, slowly retreating, and led her from the glittering, perfumed chapel, barbarous, mystical, burning, and fiery. . . .

Once outside they had to stop in order to find their bearings once more in the unaccustomed light, to return to the world once more with its white sun, its humming insects and village smells.

The Spaniards remained anxious, on the alert. . . .

'Where is he?' thought Angélique, 'Where is he?'

And she sought him with her eyes beyond the hedges and the trembling trees, limp with the heat, grown pale in the fine, dancing dust.

Count Peyrac gave a signal indicating that the company should set off on the return journey.

When they were about half-way back to the river, rain began to fall gently, murmuring through the trees.

To this sound was added the throbbing of a distant drum.

They quickened their pace and when they reached the boats the river was spattered with the sudden shower and the banks had faded from view.

But it was only a shower, and soon the sun came out once more, brighter than ever across the rain-washed landscape, and the sails filled softly in the wind.

Followed by the flotilla of Indian canoes heading downstream to trade their goods, the boats set off once more and soon the Norridgewock mission station vanished behind a promontory of cedars and huge dark, densely-growing oaks.

CHAPTER 6

AT THEIR next halt, while they were setting up camp, Angélique caught sight of an Indian woman running, carrying something unusual on her head. She sent someone to run after the woman, who, when she had been brought back, readily agreed to show the object in question, which turned out to be a huge wheaten loaf. She had purchased it that very day at the Dutchman's trading-post for six black otter-skins and had also obtained a pint of brandy for two silver foxes. She was on her way back to her camp where she had more furs. She told them that the Dutchman's trading-post did a brisk trade.

The trading-post proclaimed its presence by the appetizing smell of baking bread. The Indians were extremely fond of wheat bread and during the bartering season the trader's assistant was kept constantly busy loading batches of bread into a huge brick oven.

The trading-post was built on an island, in the hope, probably a vain one, that this would save it from suffering the fate of previous establishments which had been founded over the past fifty years round the big village of Houssnock,[1] and which had on many an occasion been pillaged, burnt or razed to the ground on one pretext or another.

Houssnock no longer even merited the title of township. The name alone remained, and a tradition among nomadic tribes heading south to make halt at this point.

From this point on, in fact, where the river became tidal, they were approaching the mouth of the Kennebec, and in spite of the clarity of the water, which flowed calm, vast and powerful between forest-clad banks, there were many reminders of the proximity of the sea.

There was a salty tang in the moisture-laden air, and the Indians of the region, the Wawenokes and Kanibas, instead of covering their bodies with bear fat, plastered

[1] Now the city of Augusta.

themselves from head to foot with the oil of seals, which they call sea-wolves, and which they hunted during the winter months along the shores of the Atlantic. Thus a strong fishy smell mingled with the smell of new bread and the rank odours of piles of skins, creating about the trading-post a powerful symphony of smells, hardly appreciated by those with delicate noses. Angélique had long since ceased to worry about details like these, and the ant-like activity that blackened the river around the island seemed to her a promising sign. It should be possible to find untold treasures of merchandise there.

Once landed on the island, everyone went off bargain hunting. Joffrey de Peyrac was almost immediately approached by someone who appeared to know him and who began to talk to him in a strange tongue.

'Come,' said Angélique to Rose-Ann, the little English girl, 'let us first get something to drink, for I imagine we shall find some good cold beer here. Then we shall go shopping, just like in the Galerie du Palais.'

They were managing quite well together as far as language was concerned, since, over the past few months, Angélique had been practising English with some occasional tuition from Cantor. And in any case her charge was not very talkative; her smooth, pale face, with its rather prominent jaw, wore an expression of dreamy good behaviour far beyond her years. She sometimes had a lost, almost doltish look.

But she was a sweet child: when they had set out from Wapassou she had unhesitatingly left Honorine her doll, the doll which Rose-Ann had skilfully and lovingly hidden in the bodice of her dress lest it should fall into the hands of the Indians when she had been held captive by them and was on the point of dying.

Honorine had been delighted with the gift; with this marvellous toy and her tame bear, she would manage to wait not too impatiently for her mother's return.

But in spite of this fact, Angélique still wished Honorine had accompanied them, for the little creature would so have loved the bustle of the trading-post where the bartering season was in full swing.

The Dutchman, manager and agent of the Massachusetts Bay Company, lorded it over everyone in the middle of the yard, dressed in black petticoat breeches, with billowing, dusty skirts.

At that moment, musket in hand, he was busy measuring a pile of beaver skins. The height of the gun barrel measured forty skins.

The store itself was a modest building, constructed of weather-boards stained with walnut juice.

Angélique and Rose-Ann made their way into a big room, which was adequately lighted by two windows with diamond-shaped leaded panes but sufficiently dim inside to remain cool. In spite of the fact that Indians were perpetually coming and going in and out of the building in order to trade their wares, it remained more or less clean and tidy, which spoke volumes for the drive and organizational powers of the man in charge.

On the right stood a long counter furnished with scales, balances, receptacles, and various measures for the sale of beads and ironmongery.

Above the counter, wooden shelves had been fitted one above the other along some of the walls to hold various wares, among which Angélique had already noted blankets, woollen bonnets, shirts and underlinen, brown and white sugar, spices and biscuits. There were also kegs of peas, beans, prunes, salt pork and smoked fish.

A large brick fireplace surrounded by kitchen utensils held nothing on this very hot day but a low fire over which stood simmering a frugal meal for the storekeeper and his assistants.

A range of beer mugs and pewter goblets stood along the edge of the chimney hood, for the use of customers who wanted to drink the beer that stood in an imposing barrel, open to all, that dominated everything else. Capacious ladles hung from the edge of the barrel, thus enabling people to help themselves as they wished. Part of the room was arranged like a tavern, with two huge wooden tables flanked by wooden stools, and a few upturned barrels to serve as extra seats in case of need or to accommodate solitary drinkers. Groups of men were sitting in this part, swathed in clouds of blue smoke.

When Angélique entered, nobody moved, but heads turned slowly in her direction, and eyes began to glow. After greeting the assembled company she took two pewter goblets from the chimney hood; for she felt an urgent need for some cool beer.

But in order to reach the barrel she had to disturb an Indian chieftain, who, wrapped in his embroidered cloak, sat drowsily puffing away at his pipe at the end of one of the tables.

She addressed him in the Abenaki tongue with all the customary circumlocutions and respect due to his rank, which was manifested by the eagle feathers stuck in the coil of long black hair which he wore plaited at the nape of his neck.

The Indian appeared to awaken from his nebulous dream and sprang to his feet, his eyes grown clear and sparkling. For a moment he examined her in astonishment and delight, then, laying one hand on his heart, held forward his right leg and gave the most impeccable courtly bow.

'Madame, how can you forgive me?' he replied in excellent French. 'Such an apparition was so totally unexpected. Allow me to introduce myself: Jean-Vincent d'Abbadie, Lord of Rasdacq and other places, Baron of Saint-Castine, Lieutenant of the King in his fortress of Pentagouet, for the government of his possessions in Acadia.'

'Baron, I am delighted to meet you. I have heard a great deal about you.'

'And I too, Madame. . . . No, you do not need to tell me who you are. I recognize you, although I have never seen you before. You are the lovely, the most lovely Madame de Peyrac! And although I have heard time and time again how lovely you are, reality far exceeds anything I could ever have conjured up in my imagination. . . . You took me for an Indian? How can I explain my discourtesy? Seeing you suddenly appear before me, realizing in a flash who you were and that you were present before me, I was overcome, petrified, made dumb like those mortals who receive the visit of a goddess moved by some incomprehensible whim to call upon them in their sombre earthly dwellings. For, to tell the truth, Madame, I knew that you were infinitely beautiful, but I did not know that such graciousness and charm went hand in hand with your beauty. Furthermore, what

33

an extraordinary sensation it was to hear the Indian tongue I love so dearly fall from your lips and to see your smile suddenly light up this crude, dismal den! This I shall never forget!'

'And you, Sir, now I know that you are a Gascon!' she replied in a burst of laughter.

'Did you really take me for an Indian?'

'Indeed I did.'

She scanned his copper-coloured face, in which shone two brilliant black pupils, his hair, and his general bearing.

'And like this?' he asked, throwing off the scarlet cloak embroidered with beads and porcupine quills in which he had been wrapped.

He appeared in the blue, gold-braided jerkin of the officers of the regiment of Carignan-Sallières, with its white lace ruffle. But this was the sole item of his regulation uniform; for the rest, he wore high Indian-style leggings and moccasins instead of breeches and knee-boots.

Then he stood, one hand on his hip, with all the haughtiness of a young officer in the King's service.

'What about that? Am I not the perfect courtier from Versailles?'

Angélique shook her head.

'No,' she replied, 'your fine words come too late, Sir. In my eyes you are an Abenaki chieftain.'

'In that case, so be it!' the Baron replied gravely. 'And you are right.'

He bent down to kiss her hand.

This brisk and lively exchange of compliments and courtesies in the French style, had taken place beneath the bold, unblinking gaze of the drinkers in the smoke-filled room. As for the handful of Indians in the warehouse, busy with their bartering, for once they paid not the slightest attention to the scene. One of them was busy counting out needles one by one with a magnet, another testing the blades of jack-knives on the edge of the counter, while a third, stepping back to measure a piece of cloth, bumped into Angélique, and in his displeasure, gave her an unceremonious shove to get out of his way.

'Let us go elsewhere,' the Baron suggested. 'There is a

room next to this one where we can talk in peace and quiet. I shall ask old Joshua Higgins to bring us something to eat. Is this delightful child your daughter?'

'No, she's a little English girl who . . .'

'Ssh!' the young Gascon officer broke in. 'An English girl! . . . If anyone heard that, I would not stake much on her scalp, and certainly nothing on her freedom.'

'But I bought her back officially from the Indians who had captured her,' Angélique protested.

'Your status as a Frenchwoman enables you to do certain things,' Saint-Castine replied, 'but it is well known that Monsieur de Peyrac does not buy back English citizens in order to have them baptized, and this fact is not viewed favourably in high circles. So above all let no one suspect that the child is English.'

'And yet there are foreigners here. Is not the head of this trading-post a Dutchman? And his assistants look as if they came straight from New England.'

'That proves nothing.'

'But they are here, aren't they?'

'For how long? Believe me, play for safety. Ah, my dear Countess,' he exclaimed, kissing the tips of her fingers once again, 'how charming you are, and how exactly you resemble the reputation you have acquired!'

'I thought that the French considered me rather diabolical.'

'That you are,' he retorted. 'Diabolical for those who, like me, are too easily moved by the beauty of women . . . diabolical, too, for those who . . . I mean that you are exactly like your husband . . . whom I admire and who scares me. I must confess that the reason I left my outpost of Pentagouet and travelled across to the Kennebec was to meet him, for I have grave news for him.'

'Has anything gone wrong in Gouldsboro?' Angélique asked, growing pale.

'No, rest assured, it has not. But I imagine that Monsieur de Peyrac is with you; I shall send word to ask him to be so kind as to join us.'

He pushed open a door, but before Angélique, still holding Rose-Ann by the hand, could enter the neighbouring room, someone clattered noisily down into the main room and rushed towards Baron Saint-Castine.

35

It was a French soldier, musket in hand.

'This time, this is it, Lieutenant,' he wailed. 'They are preparing their war cauldrons. . . . There is no mistake about it. It's a smell I would recognize anywhere. Come here, come and smell it!'

He grasped the officer by the sleeve and dragged him outside almost forcibly.

'Smell it! Just smell it!' he went on, lifting up a nose that was both long and turned up at the end, a nose that gave him the look of a fairground entertainer, 'It smells of . . . it smells of maize and boiled dog. Can you really not smell it?'

'There are so many smells,' Saint-Castine replied with a grimace of distaste.

'But it doesn't fool me. When it stinks like that, that means they're all out there in the woods, feasting before setting off to battle. They eat maize and boiled dog to give themselves courage! And they drink water on top of it all,' he added with a look of loathing that made his eyes stand out still farther from his head like those of a startled snail.

This soldier had the face of a real buffoon, and any mountebank who had engaged him to appear on his stage would have been sure of raising a great laugh.

It was a fact that the wind was blowing a sickly smell across the water from the depths of the forest, the smell of Indian feasting.

'It's coming from there, from there, and from there,' the soldier went on, indicating various points, along the left bank of the Kennebec. 'It doesn't fool me!'

What a queer looking man he was, with his ill-fitting blue coat and clutching his gun with alarming awkwardness. He was wearing neither leggings nor moccasins, but heavy shoes which seemed to add still further to his clumsiness, and his thick cotton stockings, inadequately tied beneath the knee, hung down his legs in folds that would hardly have passed as regulation dress.

'Why get into such a state, Adhemar,' said Baron Saint-Castine with feigned solicitude. 'You should never have joined a colonial regiment if you were so frightened of Indian warfare.'

'But I've told you over and over again that it was the

36

recruiting sergeant in France who got me drunk, and I came to again on board the ship,' the man wailed.

At that moment Count Peyrac arrived, in the company of the Dutchman and the Frenchman who had approached him as they landed.

They had heard what Adhemar had said about the war cauldrons.

'I think the lad is right,' said the Frenchman; 'there is much talk of the Abenakis being about to attack those insolent English. Will you be joining them, Castine, with your Etchevemins?' The Baron appeared put out and did not reply, but bowed to the Count who held out his hand to him affectionately.

Then Joffrey de Peyrac introduced his two companions to his wife.

The Dutchman's name was Pieter Boggen.

The other man was Monsieur Bertrand Defour who, with his three brothers, was joint proprietor of a cookhouse on the Isthmus at the far end of Frenchman Bay.

He was a Picard with broad shoulders and heavy features carved from what looked like wood seasoned by the sun, and it was obvious that it had been a very long time since he had last had the opportunity of greeting a pretty woman.

At first he appeared embarrassed, then, pulling himself together, and helped by the courage of his natural simplicity, he gave a low bow.

'This is something we must celebrate,' he said. 'Let's go and have a drink.'

A kind of gasp from behind the group of men made them turn their heads.

Adhemar the soldier had collapsed against the door frame, and was staring hard at Angélique.

'The She-Devil,' he stammered, 'it . . . it's her! You never told me. That was not fair. Why did you not tell me right away, Lieutenant?'

Saint-Castine let out a roar of exasperation.

He seized hold of the man and sent him sprawling head over heels in the dust with a firm, accurately placed kick.

'Damn that imbecile!' he said, panting with fury.

37

'Wherever did you dig up a creature like that?' Peyrac asked.

'Heaven only knows! That's the sort of thing they send you from the recruiting centres in Quebec nowadays. Do they imagine we want soldiers in Canada who spend their whole time sweating with fear?'

'Please do not upset yourself, Monsieur de Saint-Castine,' said Angélique, laying a calming hand on his arm. 'I know what the poor man meant and'—she could not help laughing—'he was so funny with his eyes popping out of his head like that. It was not his fault. Ugly rumours have been going around Canada, rumours I am powerless to combat—and they have terrified him. It is not his fault.'

'So you are not offended, Madame? Truly not?' Saint-Castine insisted, ringing his hands with typically southern exuberance, 'how I curse those imbeciles who, taking advantage of your absence and of the mystery that surrounds your name, have spread these nonsensical and insulting tales.'

'And now that I have come out of the woods it is up to me to do my best to destroy them. That is why I am accompanying my husband down to the sea; for when I return to Wapassou I want the whole of Acadia to be convinced not that I am a saint—heavens, no!—but at least that I am harmless.'

'As for me, I am already convinced of it,' the powerfully built Frenchman Defour affirmed striking his heart with his open hand.

'You are both wonderful friends,' said Angélique with gratitude. And as she put an arm round each of the two men's shoulders, she gave them each one of her enchanting smiles. She knew that she could encompass them both in her friendship: the very aristocratic Baron Saint-Castine and the worthy Picard peasant, made brothers through their common citizenship of this crazy wild land of Acadia. Peyrac watched as she drew them both away towards the door laughing and joking with them as she went.

'You might not believe it, my friends,' she said, 'but it is not altogether displeasing for a woman to be regarded as diabolical. There is something about the notion that suggests a kind of grim homage to some power which has all too often been denied. Poor Adhemar did not deserve so rough a handling. . . . But now I beg you, let us talk of the matter no more, and let us go and have a drink; I am dying of thirst.'

They seated themselves round a table in the second room of the outpost, where they laughed and joked about all kinds of serious matters, which to many others might have appeared dramatic.

The Dutchman recovered, in the company of the French, the innate joviality of the Flemish, and set on the table glasses, tankards and pitchers, beer, rum, brandy, and a flask of Spanish wine, red and burning, that a Caribbean corsair who had wandered into the mouth of the Kennebec by mistake, had recently bartered for some furs.

CHAPTER 7

PEYRAC SAT smiling and listening to the conversation with one ear, his eyes glued to Angélique. He remembered how, in the old days in Toulouse she would captivate all his friends with a single smile and a few words, so that from that moment on they would have given their very lives for her. Once again he discovered all the varied aspects of her feminine character, her quick, vivacious wit, her incomparable elegance of movement and the charm of her repartee, each matured now by a woman's experience of life.

Then suddenly he remembered her as she had been the previous year when she and he had reached this land together, after that strange voyage on board the *Goldsboro* during which they had recognized and discovered each other.

Then she had worn a look of sadness, she had behaved like a woman on the run; it was as if an aura of unhappiness surrounded her.

And now after less than a year she had recovered her gaiety, the zest of a happy woman. This was the effect of love and happiness, in spite of the trials of winter, this was his doing!

He had helped her to come alive once more, and as his eyes met hers he gave her a tender, possessive smile.

The little English girl, pale and silent in the midst of this exuberant crowd, kept on looking from one to another.

Baron Saint-Castine told her the Marquis of Urville, the commanding officer of Gouldsboro, had, with the help of the Huguenots from La Rochelle, held off two ships belonging to the pirate Gold Beard. The thing that had finally turned the tide of victory had been the firing of salvoes of red-hot cannon balls. When the pirate ships found their decks were on fire they had retreated to the far side of the islands, since when they appeared to be lying low, but everyone had to keep on the alert.

The Count asked whether the two ships he was expecting, one from Boston and the other the *Gouldsboro* on its way back from Europe, had yet appeared. But it was still too early in the year. As for the little yacht from Boston which had dropped Kurt Ritz's men at the mouth of the Kennebec, it had been forced to do battle with Gold Beard and had put back into harbour considerably damaged.

'That brigand will have to pay me a hundred times over for that,' Joffrey de Peyrac declared. 'He is losing nothing by waiting, and if he does not let me have my Swiss back alive, I'll have his skin for it; I'll chase him right to the Antipodes.'

Defour said that Frenchman Bay was infested with the worst pirates and filibusters from the tropical seas. Knowing that in the summer months both the French and English in the north were visited by ships from Europe laden with goods, they prowled about the area in the hope of intercepting these, which was less risky than setting upon Spanish galleons. Moreover, their attacks drew the British warships up towards Acadia when they should have been protecting the fishing fleets off Boston or Virginia.

'And in any case, Monsieur le Comte, these Englishmen have no right to be in Frenchman Bay, where they think they can behave exactly as they like.

'You supplied me so generously with provisions last year, Monsieur de Peyrac,' Defour continued, 'when I was about to die of hunger for lack of supplies, that I wanted to do something to repay your generosity. So when I passed the mouth of the Saint John river on my trip along the coast I rounded up all six soldiers who formed the garrison of the little fort of Sainte-Marie, and brought them down here to place them at your disposal.'

'So it is you we have to thank, Defour, for the presence of that yokel in uniform Adhemar!' the Baron exclaimed.

To which the other rejoined:

'He was forced on me. It appears that from Montreal to Quebec, from Lake Superior to Chaleur Bay, everyone keeps passing him on in order to get rid of him. But the others are tough chaps who know how to fight.'

Peyrac laughed, quite delighted.

'Thank you, Defour. I welcome the presence of a few good shots, but what did Monsieur de Vauvenart and the Chevalier de Grandrivière have to say about your theft?'

'They were at Jemseg, waiting for the visit of the Governor of Acadia, Monsieur de Villedavray. That, incidentally, was why I set off across the bay; it seemed more prudent. My brothers can take charge of this nuisance,' he concluded with a great burst of mocking laughter.

'But why did you not drop the soldiers off at Gouldsboro?' asked Castine.

'I was driven right down to the Matinicus Islands by a storm,' the other man replied simply. 'And then I was completely fog-bound for four days. The Gouldsboro harbour channel is not an easy one to navigate, and I might have run into Gold Beard. But we always seem to meet up in the end.'

Peyrac got up to go and see the soldiers and his companions followed.

Angélique stayed behind in the shady room. The Spanish wine was delicious but a little heady. Rose-Ann had drunk some beer and was hungry. Scarcely had Angélique and her young charge had time to convey to one another the fact that they both needed some food in their stomachs, when an amiable old man suddenly appeared and put two plates on the table covered with huge slices of hot bread spread with a preserve made from huckleberries, which the Europeans call bilberries, and which in America cover vast areas of the countryside.

With a smile he urged them to take some refreshment. He had a tiny white beard and his face wore an expression of great kindness. He was austerely dressed in a black doublet and somewhat old-fashioned breeches that puffed out above the knee, and his white pleated collar reminded Angélique of the clothes her grandfather habitually wore in the days when the goffered ruff was still in fashion. He told them his name was Joshua Pilgrim.

When little Rose-Ann had eaten her fill, he sat down beside her and asked her some friendly questions in English.

He seemed very moved when she told him that her parents were called Williams and had come from Biddeford-Sebago.

He told Angélique that Rose-Ann's very own grandparents lived less than thirty miles away on the Androscoggin river, at a place the Indians called Newehewanik, which means land of spring. Some ten years back they had founded a settlement, which had grown and prospered and which was known in English as Brunswick-Falls. They were enterprising folk, these Williamses, always heading farther and farther inland. John Williams, the son, had left Biddeford on Lake Sebago, and had been taken away captive to Canada. But villages on the coast were not much safer when the red tide of Indians poured down from the woods upon the English. Still if you lived along the shore you could always escape to the islands.

As for himself, Joshua, he understood people like the Williamses, for he had never liked cod nor did he enjoy the turbulence of the sea. He preferred reflections on rivers and lakes beneath the trees and the meat of wild turkeys.

He himself had been ten when his father, a merchant from Plymouth on Cape Cod, he founded this trading house as Houssnock. That was why he was known as Joshua Pilgrim, for he had been among the Pilgrim Fathers and as a small child had come ashore from a ship called the *Mayflower* on a deserted stretch of land where half the settlers had perished during the first winter.

After telling his tale in measured and somewhat schoolmasterly tones, the old man went to fetch something from a shelf and came back with a goose quill pen, an ink horn and a sheet of thin birch bark resembling a piece of parchment, on which he began to draw some lines. It was a plan to enable them to find the English trading-post of Brunswick-Falls where Rose-Ann's grandparents, old Benjamin Williams and his wife Sarah, lived.

He went on to explain to Angélique that if they crossed on to the right bank of the Kennebec and went on heading west they would arrive in less than a day.

'That's wonderful,' she cried.

She and her husband had always intended to take the child back to her own people, but there had been difficulties involved. Since they were going to Gouldsboro, that is to say towards the east, they were heading right away from the main Anglo-Saxon community. But the region in which they found themselves at that moment, called Maine by the English, Acadia by the French, was in fact a frontier region whose shifting boundaries were more or less mapped out by the Kennebec, a no-man's land without masters or laws.

And Providence had willed it that their protégée's family should live less than ten leagues from Houssnock. . . .

CHAPTER 8

THAT EVENING, they all returned to the trading-post at the invitation of the Dutchman, who wanted to hold a banquet for his most important visitors, and they first of all discussed ways and means of getting the child back to her grandparents.

Their host brought them maps of the region.

Taking into account detours, trails and hills, they would have to reckon on three days there and back to Houss-

43

nock before heading off towards Gouldsboro with the caravan. But Joffrey de Peyrac soon hit upon another solution. Brunswick-Falls was on the Androscoggin river, which was navigable and swift flowing and would enable them to reach the mouth of the Kennebec in a few hours. So Count Peyrac's expedition would divide into two; one group, the larger, would continue as planned down the Kennebec to the sea where a ship sent by d'Urville was awaiting them, Joffrey de Peyrac and Angélique, accompanied by a few men, would travel across to the English village and, after handing the child over to her family, make their way down the Androscoggin as far as the coast where they would join up with the first group. The whole procedure should not take more than two days.

Having disposed of this matter, they did justice to Pieter Boggen's party. He had made up an old recipe passed on from one person to another wherever there were Dutchmen in the New World, all along the banks of the Hudson from New Amsterdam to Orange.

You took a large pot and poured into it two gallons of the best madeira, three gallons of water, seven pounds of sugar, some oatmeal, some mixed spice, some raisins and some sliced lemons. . . . The mixture was served scalding hot in a huge silver bowl placed in the centre of the table, so that each guest could plunge his silver spoon again and again in the fragrant cordial.

There is nothing better to cheer a man up and dispel gloom.

In addition to the Peyracs and their son the Baron Saint-Castine was there, Monsieur Defour, the corporal of the garrison of Saint John, and the French captain of the filibuster ship from Tortuga with his chaplain.

The Dutchman with his two English Puritan assistants completed the party.

Angélique was the only woman, and her presence and that of the chaplain prevented the party from becoming too rowdy.

But Angélique was determined that they should not regret her being among them and managed to create a happy atmosphere in which each man shone, feeling himself to be the centre of attention. Great bursts of joyous laughter rose up from the trading-post, mingling with the mysterious sounds of the river and the night.

When the party broke up they were all feeling very happy and very friendly. They left the Dutchman on his island and, crossing the river by moonlight, returned to their respective camps or ships.

'I shall come and see you tomorrow,' Baron Saint-Castine whispered to Peyrac. 'I have some important matters to communicate to you. But tonight we must sleep. My head is reeling. Good night to you all.'

And he disappeared into the forest, surrounded by a group of Indians who had suddenly appeared out of the shadows, like so many ghosts, to escort him back.

The sentries were on watch at the camp, having been given strict orders by Peyrac to keep a close guard. For greater security the party was occupying only two huts, so that no one remained alone at night. The Count and his wife had abandoned their own private shelter, for Houssnock attracted the scum of all the forest lands, and there were redskins from everywhere, some of them baptized Indians with their gold crosses and rosary beads among their feathers. This was still very much French Acadia, French Canada, despite the presence of the Dutchman and his English assistants. These were still the woodlands, and throughout the woods of America the French ruled.

CHAPTER 9

'WHAT A pity!' Angélique sighed. . . . 'Could there be anyone more charming than Baron Saint-Castine? And I do so enjoy meeting Frenchmen. . . .'

'Because they dance attendance on you?'

They were neither of them sleepy and Joffrey supported Angélique as she walked somewhat unsteadily along the riverbank.

He stopped and, laying his hand on her cheek, turned her face towards him.

In the golden moonlight she looked all flushed and animated and her eyes seemed to flicker, full of stars.

He smiled, indulgent and tender.

'They think you are beautiful, my love,' he whispered. 'They pay tribute to you . . . I enjoy seeing them at your feet like that. I am not too jealous. They know that you are one of their race, a Frenchwoman, and this makes them proud. And they belong to our race too. Even if we are chased to the ends of the earth and separated from our own people, this fact will always remain. I enjoy meeting my brother Frenchmen too—and reading in their sincere, fearless eyes the admiration they have for you. A crazy, ungovernable race; and we belong to it too, my love. That fact will always remain!'

A willow tree cast a deep shadow beside them, and together they stepped into the darkness, leaving the brilliant light of the moon in favour of this welcome obscurity; then clasping her against him he kissed her gently on the lips. Desire, their familiar yet ever surprising desire, welled up within them, like a living creature between them, hot-blooded, burning and devouring.

But they could not tarry for dawn was about to break, and there was no privacy in the forest. They made their way back slowly, walking as in a trance, enfolded in their desire, with that secret, that tide between them to quicken them, that touch of pain experienced from an impetus cut short but unwilling to die, which spelt regret and complicity in the smiles they exchanged.

Joffrey de Peyrac's hand, resting lightly against her hip, was full of promise to Angélique.

And as for him, the movement of her leg against his brought him torment and delight.

But that would have to wait.

In a few days' time in Gouldsboro, with all the charm and delight of procrastination. How slowly would those hours tick by, swollen with anticipation. . . .

Once again they exchanged a few words with the men on guard.

The huts they had constructed were full of sleeping figures, but Angélique felt too wide awake to join them and chose to remain outside. She sat down alone beside the water, her arms clasped round her knees and her chin resting on them while her eyes strayed over the golden surface of the river.

Delicate wraiths of mist in evanescent streaks.

She was feeling happy and full of a vibrant, impatient energy. Everything had a savour that delighted her. Just as she enjoyed the certainty that she would make love with him, so did she find pleasure in waiting. Their day-to-day existence ordered their lovemaking; they sometimes found themselves forced to live for long days on end completely caught up in their work, far removed from pleasure, then a single look, a single tender note in the voice would set them suddenly afire, make them giddy with the urgent need to be alone.

Then she would sink into the heady darkness, would be submerged by what she in her own mind called 'my golden darkness', and would founder in her oblivion of the world and indeed of life itself.

Thus it was that their love life was so closely interwoven with the fabric of their day-to-day existence that it became at times like the subterranean murmur of a stream, an imperceptible melody, and at others like the great gusts of a storm, dominating everything and isolating them in the centre of the world, enslaving them to its laws, but at the same time, freeing them from every law.

This love life of theirs, strung out along the days, the nights, the months and the seasons, was their shared secret, the leaven of their radiant joy, something she felt constantly afire within her. It was like a gentle weight pressing on her loins, a feeling of faintness about the heart, something which filled her whole being as a child fills its mother's womb, the mystery of the spirit in the tabernacle. Love. . . .

She longed to be back in Gouldsboro which, like Wapassou, was a haven to them. At Gouldsboro there was a great wooden fortress built on the edge of the sea, and the fort contained a huge room with a vast, fur-covered bed. She had slept there with him, and would sleep there again while the stormy seas sent huge clouds of spray up from the rocks and the wind howled through the sloping trees along the promontory. In the shelter of this palace, the lights in the rustic but solid houses of the Huguenots would go out one by one.

47

In the morning everything would be pure and sparkling; with the island glistening like jewels in the bay. She would take a walk on the beach with a group of children following her, wander round the new port, and eat lobster with its salty, delicate tang and savour oysters and other shellfish.

Then she would open up coffers full of wares brought over by ship, and tidy them away, she would put on new, rustling dresses and other adornments, and try out new hair styles. At Gouldsboro there was a full length mirror set in Venetian bronze, where she would see a fresh reflection of herself; what kind of image did she think would appear?

Such was her serenity that she had no fear of finding that she had altered for the worse. She would merely be different. She had acquired the face and appearance she had dreamed of in vain for so many years; the face of a happy and utterly contented woman.

Was this not miraculous? Less than a year before she had staggered onto these shores full of fear. Tense, thin and haggard, with a kind of inner tension and exhaustion, she had staggered across the pink sands of Gouldsboro and almost fallen to her knees like one about to give up the ghost. But Joffrey de Peyrac's arm had sustained her.

All the cruel battles she had had to fight throughout her youth had come to an end there.

And how far away they seemed now, those fifteen years during which she had wandered alone, carrying the entire weight of her existence on her own shoulders. Today she felt younger than she had then, for now she was protected and loved.

A childlike joy occasionally cast its glow over her whole being and an immense confidence had replaced the suspicion—that of a frightened hunted animal—that had lurked within her. For as she had stepped onto that beach a beloved sturdy arm had encircled her. And from that moment on, it had never let her go.

'How young it makes you to be loved,' she thought, 'I used to be old. I was a hundred years old. Always on the alert, aggressive and ready to fight.'

But now, when fear came, it was no longer the same,

blind, irremediable anguish she had felt when she had been struggling against the King and the overpowerful forces leagued against her.

The man in whose shadow she rested today was strong, clear-headed and prudent. He took responsibility for everything without anxiety; he was different from the others. But he knew how to reach them and make them his friends, and she was beginning to realize that the spirit of a single man worthy of the name could move mountains, for the spirit is stronger than matter.

He would triumph over his enemies, over those lurking in the darkness, those who rejected his power. So mighty was he that he would draw them to him through his astonishing wisdom and energy.

The country would find peace, the nations put their houses in order, the forests would be cleared and cities founded and filled with people. Enough of the natural beauties would always remain to give dignity to these new destinies. The New World would be forever rich and admirable, but liberated from fruitless warfare.

Half benumbed by her reverie and the headiness of this spectacular night, Angélique's thoughts clothed themselves in her unusual surroundings, draped themselves in the contained passion of nature, tuned themselves to the tension that lurked everywhere. Nothing could impair her secret jubilation.

Let the unsavoury smell of warlike feasting be wafted over the forest, and the drum beat in the distance like an anxious, impatient heart, everything was still basically simple. She was concerned with these things but they could not reach her.

Standing out in relief against the pale brilliance of the night sky, she could see towards the south-west the little three-masted filibuster rocking at anchor on the bend of the river.

On the other hand, when she looked upstream in the other direction, all was luxuriant blackness, heavy with mist and smoke, intermittently spangled with the red glow of the fires the Indians had lighted in their wigwams.

A fox yelped. A heavy but supple animal scurried

through the grass beside her. It was Cantor's wolverine. For an instance she caught the glimmer of its eyes wide open in the darkness, unconsciously ferocious, they seemed to be asking some question of her.

PART TWO
The English Village

CHAPTER 10

THE FOLLOWING morning Angélique was sitting in the small back room of the trading-post, busy sewing a scarlet cotton dress for Rose-Ann, thinking that her family would like to see her prettily dressed when she arrived rather than looking like a wretched prisoner of 'these abominable French people'.

Through the open window she caught sight of a raft crossing the river. There were three horses on it which Maupertuis, the trapper who worked for Peyrac, had brought up the previous day from the coast. He was accompanied by his son and Cantor.

As soon as they reached the island, the boy ran as fast as his legs could carry him up to the trading-post, which he entered in a state of high excitement.

'Father says that you are to set off straight away for Brunswick-Falls with Maupertuis. He himself is unable to accompany us but I am to go with you as interpreter. We shall link up with him again tomorrow or the next day at the latest at the mouth of the Kennebec, where our boat is already lying at anchor.'

'What a nuisance,' said Angélique, 'I have not quite finished this dress. Now I shan't have time to make the bows for the bodice. Why is your father unable to accompany us?'

'He has to meet some Etchevemin of Mic-Mac chieftain —I am not sure which, on the coast . . . someone Baron Saint-Castine is very anxious to introduce to him. With the Indians you have to take your chances as they come. . . . They are so fickle. So Father thought it best to set off immediately and entrust us with taking the child back to her people. I have already collected your things from the camp on my way here.'

Angélique helped the little English girl to put on her pretty dress and then pinned on the lace collar and cuffs old Joshua had produced from some bale of merchandise.

Then quickly she did her hair again and buckled on the leather belt that held her pistol.

The horses were waiting outside, already saddled and held on a tight reign by Maupertuis and his son. Out of sheer habit Angélique checked harness and saddle and noted the presence of the leather bag she had prepared that morning. Then she enquired of each man how much ammunition he was carrying.

'Well, off we go then!' she decided.

'What about me, what am I to do?' asked Adhemar the soldier, who was sitting outside the door on an up-turned barrel, his musket between his knees.

He had become a general laughing stock, and much fun was had at his expense. Knowing how terrified he was of Angélique, or possibly because he did not know what else to do with him, the corporal from the fort of Saint John had ordered him to serve as Madame de Peyrac's personal guard, so Adhemar, torn. between his superstitious fear and the dictates of military discipline, was suffering the torments of the damned.

Maupertuis cast a pitying glance at him.

'You stay here, old chap!'

'But I can't stay here alone: the place is full of savages!'

'Well come with us then,' Maupertuis replied crossly. 'Your corporal and the others have already gone off with Monsieur de Peyrac.'

'Gone?' stammered the lad, on the brink of tears.

'Well come with us, I tell you. It's perfectly true we can't leave him here alone,' he said with an apologetic glance towards Angélique. 'And he will be an extra gun, in any case.'

They said good-bye to the Dutchman, and on reaching the opposite bank of the river plunged into the semi-darkness of the forest where a fairly clear path led off beneath the trees towards the west.

'Where are we going to?' asked Adhemar.

'To Brunswick-Falls.'

'What's that?'

'An English village.'

'But I don't want to go to any English village! They're enemies!'

'Oh shut up, you silly booby, and get on with it.'

The path was scarcely visible because of the new spring growth, but the horses managed to make their way unerringly along it with that sixth sense animals seem to possess for recognizing paths that men have frequented, in spite of the countless obstacles thrown across their way by bushes and brushwood. Spring had come in all its impudence to overlay the wild winter blackness of the forest with tangles of green shoots; but they were young and flexible and easily pushed aside. The grass was short and soft and the undergrowth full of light. They found the remains of the abandoned village which they had been told to look out for, then plunged into the woods again. Shortly after, they caught sight of the glistening waters of a lake through an avenue of aspen and birch trees; there it lay gleaming in the sun, without a ripple, as smooth as a mirror. By now it was almost noon and the silence deepened, while a kind of torpor settled over everything, filled only with the buzzing of insects.

The child was riding pillion behind Angélique, while Maupertuis and Cantor rode the other two horses. The soldier and the young trapper had little difficulty in following on foot, since in any case the horses were unable to travel faster than walking pace along the path. But they did make it possible for the woman and child to be spared the fatigue of walking.

Adhemar kept on casting nervous glances about him. 'Someone's following us, I tell you.'

They finally called a halt to satisfy him, and he strained an ear to listen.

'It's Wolverine,' said Cantor.

And the animal suddenly appeared in the undergrowth beside them, crouching as if about to spring, its vicious-looking little mouth stretched in a snarl that bared its two white pointed fangs.

Cantor laughed at Adhemar's discomfiture.

'W-whatever is that creature?'

'It's a wolverine that's going to eat you alive.'

'But it's as big as a sheep!' the man wailed.

From that time on he kept turning round to see if Wolverine was following him and the mischevous creature sometimes brushed his legs to make him jump.

'If you imagine it's fun to walk with that on your heels! ...'

They were all greatly amused and little Rose-Ann had never laughed so much.

The forest here was like that on the opposite bank. There were gentle valleys that sloped down to tiny streams and waterfalls, then climbed again on the other side up to stony plateaux covered in pines and stocky cedars cooled by a fragrant breeze, but which soon dropped down again into the frothy greenery of deciduous trees, almost with delight, like plunging into the sea.

After the heat of the day a breeze sprang up that made the leaves tremble and filled the undergrowth with soft murmurs.

They stopped once more to examine the map old Joshua had given them. After passing another abandoned Indian village the route became less clear but Cantor took a bearing with his compass and assured them that if they kept on in the same direction for another two or three hours they would reach their destination.

Although he did not possess Florimond's infallible sense of direction, Cantor, like his elder brother, had a keen sense of observation which prevented him from ever getting lost, and furthermore both of them had been extensively schooled in this matter by their father, who, ever since they were young boys, had made them familiar with the workings of sextant, chronometer and compass.

Angélique had implicit faith in her son, although she could not help regretting that Joffrey de Peyrac had been unable to accompany them, and, as the hours went by, she became more and more at a loss to understand the reasons for such a hasty departure.

Why was Joffrey not there? And how deserted and silent the forest was, and yet at the same time how much noise there was since the wind had risen.

'Did Monsieur de Peyrac not explain to you why he had to make this sudden unexpected journey?' she asked, turning towards the trapper. She knew him less well than the others because he had not spent the winter with them at Wapassou, but she knew that he was loyal and reliable.

'I did not see Monsieur le Comte myself,' the man replied. 'It was Clovis who brought me the message.'

'Clovis?'

A vague feeling of alarm began to grow within her. There was something strange about the whole business. Why had Joffrey not written her a note? It was not like him . . . messages passed from mouth to mouth . . . Clovis? . . . Her horse stumbled against a stone projecting slightly from the ground, and she had to concentrate all her attention on keeping it heading in the right direction.

Through the deep emerald-green tracery of the oak leaves could be seen the massive trunks, branching out into black boughs like candelabra.

It reminded her of the forest of Nieul at the time of the ambushes. . . .

Plunged in her memories, she longed to get out of this deep shade.

'Are we on the right road, Cantor?'

'Yes, yes,' the young man replied with a further glance at his map and compass.

But a little farther on he dismounted and he and Pierre-Joseph, the young half-caste, carefully scrutinized the surroundings. The track disappeared into the undergrowth at this point, yet the two young men insisted that that was the way to go. The trees began to hedge them in more and more until they formed a narrow tunnel which grew darker and darker. On reaching a bend, however, the light grew brighter, marking the end of the tunnel in a patch of sunlight.

But it was at this moment that Maupertuis raised his hand and all of them, even the horses, stopped dead at the signal. Some imperceptible change had taken place, a change which indicated that the deserted forest had become not exactly peopled, but as if inhabited by some other presence.

'Indians!' Adhemar whispered, almost swooning.

'No, Englishmen,' Cantor replied.

A silhouette had risen up against the sunny halo in the gap between the branches, and a more extraordinary sight one would find it hard to imagine.

Hunch-backed, twisted, shod in enormous buckled shoes out of which a pair of skinny calves rose, dressed in a broad-brimmed, incredibly high sugar-loaf hat, a little old man was standing at bay at the exit from the wood. In his two hands he clasped an old blunderbuss with a short, bell-shaped barrel stuffed full of grapeshot, a weapon that would undoubtedly have caused as much damage to the man who fired it as to his victims.

The newcomers were careful to make no move.

'Halt!' shouted the little old man in a high-pitched, penetrating voice. 'If ye be spirits, ye had best be gone, or I fire!'

'You can see that we are no spirits,' Cantor replied in English.

'Just a minute, please.'

The old man raised his antiquated gun and burrowed with one hand in his doublet from which he drew an enormous pair of tortoiseshell-rimmed spectacles, which he placed on his nose thus giving himself the appearance of an elderly owl.

'Yes! I see!' he muttered.

He drew out the end of each syllable with suspicious deliberation.

He came towards the horsemen with little mincing steps, examining Cantor from top to toe and pretending not to see Angélique.

'And who art thou, that speakest in the Yorkshire tongue, like those accursed professors in Boston? Hast thou no fear of wandering in the woods, like an honest Christian? Dost thou not know that ill betides lads and lasses that wander in the woods? They might encounter the Black Man and perform manifold abominations with him. Is it not thou that taunteth me, oh son of Belial the lustful, Prince of the Waters with whom begot thee one witches' sabbath the woman that accompanies thee? I would not be surprised! To boot, thou are too handsome to be of human kind, young man!'

'We are on our way to see Benjamin and Sara Wil-

58

liams,' Cantor replied without excessive surprise, for he had encountered oddities of this kind before among the Boston Illuminati. 'We are escorting their granddaughter Rose-Ann, the daughter of John Williams.'

'Ha! Ha! To Benjamin Williams.'

The old man bent forward to examine the little girl in the red dress, screwing up his piercing eyes behind the thick lenses of his spectacles.

'Dost they say that this child is granddaughter to Williams? Ho! Ho! What a jest! How we shall laugh!'

And he rubbed his hands together in glee as if he had suddenly been told an excellent joke. 'Ha! Ha! I can just imagine it!'

Unobtrusively, his sharp eyes had taken in all the other members of the party: the two trappers with their leather jackets fringed in the Indian style, their belts and coloured Canadian bonnets, and the French soldier behind them in his faded but still recognizable army tunic.

He replaced his gun on his hunched shoulder and stepped aside from the path.

'Well then, pass your way, Frenchmen,' he said, still chuckling to himself. 'Go along then and take old Ben's granddaughter to him. Ha! Ha! I can just imagine the look on Williams's face! Ha! Ha! What a joke! But count ye not on any ransom, for he is a close man. . . .'

Angélique had more or less managed to follow the conversation. Although she had found the old man's English perfectly intelligible, she had gasped almost nothing of what he was trying to convey. Fortunately Cantor kept his serene calm.

'Are we still far from Brunswick,' he asked politely. 'We fear we may have lost our way.'

The man gave a pout and shook his head, as if to say that when people are crazy enough to go walking in the devil's own forest, they should know where they are going and manage without help.

During this conversation another figure had appeared and crept up silently behind the old man. He was a tall Indian with a cold stare, an Abenaki from the Sokoki or Sheepscot region to judge by his sharp profile with its two prominent incisors. He carried a lance in his hand

59

and a bow and quiver of arrows slung across his back. He listened to the conversation with a look of complete indifference.

'Could you really not tell us the way to Brunswick-Falls, worthy old man?' Cantor insisted, unable to think of any further means of persuasion.

But his request, although formulated with every possible courtesy, transformed the face of the old gnome who grimaced in anger and stormed off with a volley of abuse, in which Angélique caught, as he went by, verses from the Bible, curses, prophesies, accusations, and whole sentences of Latin and Greek, all of which conveyed that the people of Brunswick—called Newehewanik by the Indians—were all crazy, ignorant unbelievers, possessed of the devil, and that he, George Shapleigh, would never again set foot in their place.

Cantor persisted in his request with all the guilelessness of youth, and little by little the old man calmed down, growled a bit, launched a few more anathemas, then turning his back on them, set off ahead of them down the path, while his Indian, still silent and expressionless, followed at the end of the line.

'Does this mean that this crazy old coot has decided to show us the way?' Maupertuis growled.

'So it seems,' replied Cantor. 'Let's follow him! We shall soon see where he takes us.'

'Offer him a seat on one of the horses,' Angélique suggested. 'He may be tired.'

Cantor passed on his mother's suggestion, but the old Englishman, without turning round, gesticulated with such vehemence that it was quite clear they had offended him and that in any case, in his eyes, horses were also naturally to be regarded as creatures of the devil.

He pranced swiftly along and, in spite of his heavy shoes it was astonishing to note that he made not the slightest sound and seemed scarcely to touch the ground.

'He is an old medicine-man,' Cantor explained, 'who claims to have combed every forest in America in search of plants and tree bark for his medicine. That alone would explain the suspicion with which his compatriots must view him. For in New England people who go off into the woods are not liked, as he has just told you himself.

But, odd as he is, I think we can trust him to put us on the right road.'

'I don't want to go to these English people and I don't like walking with an unknown Indian at my heels,' Adhemar grumbled through the shadows.

Every time he turned round he caught sight of the dark, stony face and the eyes like pools of black water staring at him. A cold sweat soaked his shirt, as it had often done before during his many moments of fright. He plodded on, stumbling over tree roots.

The little man in the pointed hat bounded on ahead like a dark elf, a 'will-o'-the-wisp in mourning weeds, occasionally vanishing as he entered some shadow then reappearing in a shaft of reddish sunlight falling through a gap in the trees. But throughout all these twistings and turnings of the way, Angélique noticed with impatience that night was falling. The hollows of the ravines were beginning to fill with purple.

As he walked, the old man occasionally turned right round, muttering a few indistinct words, with his arms raised, and his skinny fingers spread as if pointing up at something in the air.

'I am beginning to wonder whether he is not completely insane and whether he has any idea where he is taking us,' Maupertuis said at last, ill at ease. 'These English!'

'It doesn't matter where he takes us so long as he gets us out of this forest,' Angélique replied, her patience exhausted.

Almost immediately, as if in fulfilment of her wish, they emerged onto a vast plateau covered in green grass and strewn with rocky outcrops and juniper trees. An occasional wind-beaten cedar or cluster of black fir trees stood out from the plain like sentinels. Far, far away beyond a ridge of wooded hills and valleys, the eastern sky was like mother-of-pearl, the kind of sky one sees over the sea. It was a long, long way off. A promise. But the wind that blew across the plateau carried a scent that was familiar, indefinable, and full of memories.

After winding its way between the rocks and bushes, the path ran down into a little valley which the night had already filled until no glimmer of light remained.

61

The far slope rose in front of them in a smooth curve whose higher black crest stood out against the pale sky. It was from there that the half-forgotten smell came. The strong, homely smell of a *ploughed field*.

They could see nothing through the darkness, and could only guess at the presence of the rich, damp earth smelling of spring, and its deep ploughed furrows.

Old Shapleigh began to mutter and snigger.

'Yes, here we are! Roger Stoughton still in his field. If he could do away with the night, and the stars, and the sleep that weighs upon his eyelids, how happy would Roger Stoughton be. He would never know a moment of rest. He would labour on, digging, scratching, breaking up the ground, for ever and ever, nor would he rest his hand from toil. His fork would turn and never cease, like the devil's own fork in the depth of hell, for ever and aye.

'But the devil's fork is barren, whereas mine is not, you uncouth old man,' came in reply a sepulchral voice from the ploughed field. 'The devil only uses the tip of his fork on the dregs of men's souls, whereas I bring forth fruit from the earth which the Lord blesses. . . .'

A dim shadow moved towards them.

'And to that end I shall never be able to devote sufficient of the days of my life,' the voice went on as if delivering a lecture, 'I am not like thee, old sorcerer, that fearest not to sully thy soul by consorting with the rude wilderness of nature. Oho! Whom dost thou bring us tonight, spirit of darkness? Whom dost thou bring us from the accursed lands?'

The peasant drew closer, then stopped, and craned his neck towards them.

'The place is rank with Frenchmen and Indians,' he growled. 'Halt! Hold your ground!'

They sensed him raise a gun to his shoulder. During the whole of this monologue, Shapleigh had replied with a volley of sniggers, as if greatly amused. The horses kept shying, upset by this voice that scolded at them out of the darkness. Cantor summoned up his very best English to greet the peasant, introduced little Rose-Ann Williams and, without attempting to hide the fact that they were French, took care to mention his father's name: Count Peyrac of Gouldsboro.

'If you have any connections with Boston or Casco Bay you will surely have heard of Count Peyrac of Gouldsboro. He has commissioned several ships from the New England shipyards.'

Without deigning to reply, the peasant drew closer, and circled round them, sniffing at them like a suspicious dog.

'I see thou still hast this horrid redskin creature skulking at thy heels,' he remarked, still addressing the old medicine man. 'It were better to bring a nest of serpents into a village than a single Indian!'

'If I enter the village, so will he,' the old man replied aggressively.

'And we shall all wake up dead in our beds tomorrow and scalped by those traitors, as happened to the people of Wells, who offered shelter to a wretched Indian woman one stormy night. She showed her redskin sons and grandsons how to get in, opened the gate of the fort to them and the white men were all massacred. For, thus spake the Lord: "Never shall ye forget that the land into which ye enter is a land stained by the uncleanness of the people of that land. . . . Ye shall not give your daughters unto their sons, nor take their daughters unto your sons, and take no thought for their prosperity, neither for their comfort, and thus shall ye grow strong. . . ." Whereas thou, Shapleigh, thou growest weaker with every day that thou hast truck with these Indians. . . .'

After this gloomy biblical language silence reigned once more, and shortly afterwards Angélique realized that this inhabitant of Brunswick-Falls had finally decided to let them pass.

In fact he even went ahead of the little cluster of people and began to climb the hill in front of them. Then as they emerged from the hollow they found themselves once more walking through the brightness of the long-drawn-out spring evening. A guest of wind brought them the smell of stables, and the still distant sounds of cattle being driven home from the fields.

CHAPTER 11

THEN SUDDENLY, against a golden sky streaked with bold russet lines, loomed the shape of a big English farm-house.

The house was isolated and a single lighted window seemed to cast a wary eye over the dark valley from which they had emerged.

As the travellers drew closer they could make out the shape of fenced enclosures. It was a sheep-fold, where the shearing was carried out and cheese made. Several men and women turned round and stared at the three horses that brought the strangers.

The farther they continued down the long track the nearer they seemed to get to the glow of the sunset.

A bend in the path revealed the entire village with its wooden houses rising one above the other up the side of a hill crowned with elms and maple trees.

They overlooked a grassy curve with a stream running though it.

Some washerwomen were coming back from the stream with their wicker baskets, laden with clothes, balanced on their heads, their blue cotton dresses flapping in the wind.

Beyond the stream, the fields rose in gentle slopes up to the forest with its serried ranks of trees.

The path became a road and, after sloping gently downwards, led up between the houses and gardens.

Lighted candles behind the window panes or parch-ment squares dotted the crystal-clear evening air with stars, taking the place of the daylight and giving the peaceful scene a glittering brightness as if strung with precious stones.

And yet, by some mysterious grapevine, when they came to a halt at the other end of the village before an imposing gabled house with an overhanging upper storey, almost all the inhabitants of Brunswick-Falls were gathered behind them, open-mouthed and wide-eyed, a sea of blue and black clothes, astonished faces, white coifs and pointed hats.

As Angélique dismounted and gave a general greeting, the crowd shrank back in alarm with a vague murmur, but when Maupertuis stepped forward and lifted little Rose-Ann to the ground, the murmur swelled to a roar of stupefaction, indignation, and protest and muttered questions and conjectures began to pass from one to another.

'What on earth have I done?' asked Maupertuis in dismay. 'It isn't as if they had never seen a trapper before, is it? And in any case, we are at peace, or so I thought!'

The old apothecary was dancing about like a newly landed fish.

'It's here! It's here!' he kept on repeating impatiently, pointing to the door of the big house. He was full of glee.

He was the first to climb the steps of the wooden porch and push the door open with a firm hand.

'Benjamin and Sarah Williams! I bring you your granddaughter Rose-Ann from Biddeford-Sebago and the Frenchmen who have captured her,' he cried in his sharp, triumphant voice.

For a split second Angélique saw inside the room: there was a brick fireplace at the far end adorned with numerous copper and pewter utensils, and two old people, a man and a woman sitting on either side of the fire, dressed in black, as stiff and formal as portraits; they both wore identical white, starched ruffs, and the woman an imposing lace coif, and both sat very upright in high-backed, carved chairs. An enormous book lay open on the old man's knees, no doubt a Bible, and the woman was spinning flax with a distaff. Close by, at their feet, sat some children and servants dressed in blue, working spinning wheels.

It was only a fleeting vision since at the very mention of the word Frenchmen the two old people leapt to their feet, the Bible and distaff fell unheeded to the floor, and with astonishing agility they seized two guns from the chimneypiece, apparently loaded and ready to fire, and took aim at the new arrivals.

Shapleigh chortled even louder than before and rubbed his hands together, but almost at once the sight of Angélique pushing the little girl before her seemed to create such utter dismay in the old people, even more violent than that caused by the appearance of the French, that their hands began to shake and their weapons suddenly seemed too heavy for their old arms. . . . The gun barrels drooped slowly as if overcome by stupefaction.

'Oh God! God!' the old lady's pale lips muttered.

'Oh Lord!' cried her husband.

Angélique dropped them a curtsy, begged them to forgive her imperfect English, and told them how happy she was to be able to return the child who had been through so terrible an experience, safe and sound into the hands of her grandparents.

"She is your granddaughter, Rose-Ann,' she insisted, for it seemed to her as if they had not yet grasped the fact. 'Are you not going to kiss her?'

Still unsmiling, Benjamin and Sarah Williams looked gloomily down at the child, and together heaved a great sigh.

'Yes, yes indeed,' old Ben said at last, 'yes indeed, we can see that this is Rose-Ann and we would like to kiss her, but first, she must, she really must remove that unspeakable scarlet gown.'

CHAPTER 12

'YOU MIGHT just as well have brought her along stark naked, with the devil's horns in her hair,' Cantor pointed out to his mother a little later.

Realizing what a sad miscalculation she had made, Angélique was full of self-reproach.

'Whatever would they have said if I had had time to make the golden bows for the bodice of that red dress?'

'The mind boggles,' agreed Cantor.

'You have lived in New England, you should have

warned me. I could have spared my fingers, instead of making her a special dress to take her back to such dreadfully puritanical people in.'

'Please forgive me, Mother. . . . But they might equally well have turned out to be a less intolerant sect. Such do exist. And in any case, I thought it would be fun to see their reaction.'

'You are as bad a mischief-maker as that quaint old apothecary, whom they seem to be as chary of as the plague. I wouldn't be surprised if he was looking forward to seeing the effect Rose-Ann's red dress would have on them from the time he first set eyes on it. No doubt that was why he agreed to show us the way.'

All of them including the unfortunate Rose-Ann, had been ushered into a kind of parlour leading off the main room, no doubt to get the child, in her ridiculous and shameful get-up, out of sight of the gaping crowds as quickly as possible, along with the woman who had brought her, whose gaudy and unseemly attire only too clearly indicated the nation and corrupt religion to which she belonged—a Frenchwoman and a Papist!

What strange creatures these Puritans were; one could not help wondering whether they had a heart . . . whether they had any sex. When one saw how cold their family relationships were, it was diffcult to imagine that any act of love could ever have brought their families into existence. And yet Mr and Mrs Williams had numerous progeny, and there were at least two families with their children installed in the big house at Brunswick-Falls. But Angélique was at a loss to understand that no one seemed to be concerned about the fate of John and Margaret Williams who had been taken prisoner by the Indians and carried off to Canada.

The tidings that her daughter-in-law had given birth to a child under appalling difficulties in the Indian forest-lands, had left Mrs Williams cold. And her husband had launched out into a long diatribe to the effect that John and Margaret had received their just desserts for their unbiddableness.

Why had they not stayed at Biddeford-Saco, on the coast, a well-established, God-fearing colony, instead of thinking, in their pride, that they were the Lord's

Anointed, chosen to found their own colony in a wilderness which was as fraught with peril for their souls as for their bodies, and, instead of having the final audacity to call this new settlement, which was the fruit of their pride and indiscipline, by the very same name, Biddeford, as the place in which they had been born? And now they were in Canada and it served them right. He, Ben Williams, had never considered that his son John had the makings of a leader.

He waved aside the details Cantor attempted to provide about the captives, saying that he had already heard all about their capture from Darwin, the husband of his daughter-in-law's sister, who was a somewhat limited young man and who was preparing to re-marry. 'But his wife is not dead,' Angélique tried to explain. 'At least she wasn't when I last saw her at Wapassou. . . .'

But Benjamin Williams was not listening. As far as he was concerned everything that lay to the north of the great woods, those far-off, impenetrable regions where Frenchmen, possessed of the devil, sharpened up their scalping knives in the midst of clouds of incense, might as well be regarded as part of the Next World, and, as a matter of fact, very few English men or women had ever returned from those regions.

'Now tell me honestly for once,' Angélique asked Cantor, 'is there anything about my clothes which could possibly offend them? Am I improperly dressed without realizing it?'

'You should put something across *there*,' said Cantor sententiously, pointing to the low neckline of Angélique's bodice.

They were laughing like a pair of children, watched unsmilingly by poor Rose-Ann, when the serving maids in blue dresses came in carrying a wooden tub hooped with copper bands and a large number of pitchers full of steaming hot water. A tall young man, as solemn as a parson, came to fetch Cantor, who followed him, putting on the same formal, worried expression which was so out of place on fresh young faces.

The maids, on the other hand, attractive girls, their cheeks rosy from work in the fields, seemed far less strait-laced. As soon as they were out of the watchful eye of their old master, they had a smile and a lively sparkle in their eyes as they scrutinized Angélique, whose arrival was a major event in their lives. They examined admiringly every detail of her costume, simple as it was, and followed her every gesture, which did not however prevent them from bustling hither and thither, bringing a cake of soap in a wooden bowl and handing round towels warmed in front of the fire.

Angélique dealt with Rose-Ann first of all. She was no longer surprised that the little English girl had at times seemed a trifle slow witted, when she saw what kind of background she came from. The atmosphere of La Rochelle gave only a faint idea of what it was like.

Nevertheless, when the moment came to dress her again and Angélique went to put on the dark dress that had been put out for her, the timid child rebelled. Her stay among the French, although short, had been her undoing—or at least that is how his Reverence the Pastor would have seen it. For she suddenly and passionately pushed aside the dismal dress, buried her face in Angélique's bosom and burst into tears.

'I want to keep my pretty red dress!' she cried.

And as if to emphasize where she had come by this rebelliousness, she repeated the phrase several times in French, to the great consternation of the servants. That ungodly language on the lips of a Williams, this shameless outburst of temper and wilfulness, this avowed coquettishness, all this was terribly disconcerting, and boded nothing but ill. . . .

'Mistress Williams will never agree to that,' said one of the girls hesitantly.

CHAPTER 13

OLD SARAH WILLIAMS stood very straight, very tall, very thin, regal and imposing, and gazed solemnly down at her granddaughter and at Angélique.

They had gone to fetch her to settle the dispute, and indeed no one could have better summoned up the notion of Justice and Renouncement than this tall woman, Sarah, who, seen close to, was very impressive in her dark clothes, her neck held erect by her pleated ruff.

Her eyelids were big, heavy and bluish, covering dark, slightly protruding eyes which every now and then flashed in her very pale face whose time-worn curves had a touch of majesty.

And one could never forget, looking at her thin, pale hands clasped piously, the speed with which they were still capable of grasping a gun.

Rose-Ann was still crying and Angélique stroked her hair.

'She's only a child,' she pleaded, looking at the intractable old lady. 'It is in a child's nature to like bright things, joyous things, pretty things. . . .'

It was then that she noticed that Mrs Williams was wearing an exquisite Flanders lace bonnet, one of those very inventions of the devil, inducements to the sin of vanity, which old Ben had denounced only a short while previously.

Mrs Williams lowered her heavy eyelids and appeared to reflect. Then she gave a curt order to one of the girls, who returned carrying a folded white garment, which Angélique saw to be a cotton pinafore with a large bib.

With a gesture Mrs Williams indicated that Rose-Ann might put on the offending dress again on condition that she covered up some of its provocative splendour with the pinafore.

Then, turning towards Angélique, she gave her a conspiratorial wink, and the ghost of a sly smile flitted across her tight lips.

Having made these mutual concessions, the Williamses and their guests forgathered again at the table for the evening meal.

Maupertuis and his son had sent to say that they were being entertained by a member of the community with whom they had once had dealings in furs, on a journey they had made to Salem.

Adhemar was wandering like a lost soul along the grassy paths of the colony, followed by a crowd of curious young Puritans who from time to time would put out a timorous finger to touch the blue uniform of a soldier of the King of France, and his musket, slung from one discouraged arm.

'The forest is full of savages,' he wailed, 'I can feel them all around.'

Angélique came out to fetch him.

'But come, Adhemar, we have not met a soul all day! Come in and take some refreshment.'

'And sit amongst those heretics who hate the Virgin Mary? Never!'

So he remained outside the door, squashing mosquitoes on his cheeks and considering the horrors lying in wait for him on all sides in this horrible country—savages, Englishmen. . . . He had even come to feel more secure in the presence of a certain person who was suspected of being a diabolical spirit, but who had at least the merit of being French. And what was more, she spoke to him gently and patiently, this woman they called the She-Devil, instead of being unkind to him. So he would stand guard to defend her since the King's recruiting officers had made a soldier of him and had put a musket in his hands.

Angélique had been given a bowl of warm milk with a beaten egg in it. This simple dish, with its almost forgotten savour, filled her with delight. Then there was boiled turkey with a strong mint sauce to give it some flavour, and corn on the cob. Then they were served a pie with a cover of pastry through which rose the delectable smell of stewed bilberries.

The Englishmen were startled to learn that Count Peyrac and his family had been living in Upper Kennebec, more than 400 miles from the sea. Of course, they were Frenchmen, but the exploit was still regarded as very much out-of-the-way, especially as women and children were involved.

'Is it true that you had to eat your horses?' they kept on asking.

The young men were especially interested in this French gentleman, who was a friend and a delegate of Massachusetts Bay. What were his plans? Was it true that he was trying to make an alliance with the Indians and his French compatriots, in an attempt to put an end to the murderous raids against New England?

Old Benjamin took no part in the discussion. He had of course heard tell of Count Peyrac but preferred not to let his mind dwell on the razzle-tazzle of all the different nations who claimed nowadays to inhabit the county of Maine.

Was it not enough that there was hardly any room left along the shores of Massachusetts? He did not like to think that there were any other people on earth than the members of his little tribe.

He would have preferred to be *alone* with his people, at the dawn of time, or like Noah emerging from the Ark.

He had always fled towards the empty spaces, always tried to imagine that they alone were able to praise their Creator, 'the well-beloved flock, the elect of God to His greater glory', but the world always caught up with him and reminded him that the Creator must needs share out his gifts among innumerable uninteresting and ungrateful peoples.

Angélique, who saw at a glance in the Patriarch a roving leader of men—she only had to look at his long, bold, inquisitive nose above his white beard, and his intolerant eyes—asked herself why he was so angry with his son for having wanted to follow the independent example of his father, by leaving Biddeford-Saco to settle at Biddeford-Sebago. But this was one of those classic mysteries in the relationship between father and son that have existed since the world began. Human failings show through the toughest and most saintly of shells, and Angélique began to feel the first promptings of affection and sympathy towards these intransigent, upright people.

Cheered by the excellent meal, she began to sense a certain comradely warmth that bound together these people with their sombre clothes and principles.

But once these principles had been decreed and loudly proclaimed, more human feelings reasserted themselves.

Rose-Ann had kept her red dress, and Angélique, although a Frenchwoman and a Papist, had nevertheless been accorded the honours of the family table.

Cantor's presence intrigued them. This young man with the bright eyes seemed to belong neither here, nor to any other specific place.

The English accepted him unanimously on account of his excellent English and his knowledge of Boston; then, remembering that he too was French and a Papist, they drew back. Every man present, old Benjamin, his sons and sons-in-law, examined him curiously from beneath their churlish brows, questioning him, making him talk, and carefully considering each of his answers.

Towards the end of the meal the door opened and in came a huge fat-bellied man, whose appearance threw an immediate chill on the jovial, friendly atmosphere which had gradually been built up.

The two grandparents immediately put on their most rigid expressions.

It was the Reverend Thomas Patridge. The fact that nature had made him an Irishman and endowed him with a full-blooded constitution, over and above the normal difficulties that all men experience in their attempts to achieve the virtues of mildness, humility and chastity, had made it possible for him to achieve the moral rectitude which made him one of the most outstanding ministers of religion of his time only by means of a far-ranging and fastidious scholarship, a constant denunciation of other men's sins, and frequent outbursts—like jets of steam forcing up the lid of a saucepan—of a righteous and devastating anger. In addition to all that, he had read Cicero, Terence, Ovid and Virgil, spoke Latin, and knew Hebrew.

He glowered at the assembled company, stopping when his eyes reached Angélique with a reaction of feigned shock as if the sight of her was worse than he could ever have imagined, glanced sadly and contemptuously at Rose-Ann who was unashamedly covering herself with bilberries, then wrapped himself about in his huge, long Genevese cape, as if to insulate himself from so much wickedness.

'I see, Ben,' he began in a sepulchral voice, 'I see that wisdom has not come to you in your old age—you have introduced Jesuits and Papists here, you have the temerity to welcome at your table the living image of the woman

73

who precipitated the dread fall of the human race, Eve, flaunting her irresponsibility and her seductive wiles! You dare to welcome into the bosom of your God-fearing family a child who can bring you nothing but shame and confusion. And, last but not least, you dare to welcome him who met with the Black Man in the forest and signed with his own blood the infamous book held out to him by Satan himself, from whence he derives his impunity to travel the Pagan paths, but which should bar him for ever more from crossing the threshold of any pious home. . . .'

'Art thou speaking of me, Pastor?' old Shapleigh interrupted, raising his nose from his bowl.

'Yes, you, you fool!' the pastor thundered. 'You who without care for your soul have dared to dabble in magic to satisfy your shameful curiosity.

'I, whom the Lord has granted spiritual insight that can read deep into the secret of men's consciences, it is not difficult for me to see that diabolical spark glistening in your eyes. .. . .'

'And I, Pastor, I read in thy bloodshot eye—and although the blood is not infernal it is nonetheless thick and a danger to thy health, I can read that one day thou willst find thyself struck down by some violent outburst of temper if thou takest not care. . . .'

And the old 'medicine-man' stood up and walked over to the outraged minister with a knowing expression on his face, forcing the man to bend forward so that he could examine the whites of his eyes.

'I would not urge thee to be bled,' he said. 'There would be no end to the task. But I have in my bag a few herbs that I sought out thanks to my shameful curiosity, which, if thou followest my treatment, will enable thee to rave and rant as often as thou feelest the need without risk to thy health.

'Get thee to bed, Pastor. I will attend thee, and in order to keep the demons away I will burn some coriander and fennel seeds.'

That was the end of the pastor's outbursts for that particular evening.

CHAPTER 14

THE ROUGH-HEWN beams smelt of honey, and a few bunches of dried flowers had been hung up in the nooks and corners between them.

Angélique wakened for the first time that night. The shriek of a nightjar filled the star-spangled darkness. Its two-note cry incessantly repeated was like the creaking of a spinning wheel, now close, now dying away. She got up and, leaning her two hands on the edge of the window, peered out into the forest. She knew that the people of New England have said that the cry of the nightjar, with its two monotonous notes, says: 'Weep! Weep! poor William!' ever since an early settler called William discovered the massacre of his wife and children. He had thought he heard the nightjar's cry during the previous night, but it had been Indians hiding in the undergrowth signalling to one another as they closed in on the white man's cabin.

Then suddenly the cry ceased; a shadow crossed the night sky—two wide pointed wings, a long, rounded tail, a soft, silent flight broken by sudden darts this way and that and a glimpse of a single, luminous red eye. The nightjar was on the hunt.

A multitude of crickets, grasshoppers and frogs filled the night with their noisy chirping and croaking, while from the forest came the scent of wild animals, the fragrance of wild strawberries and thyme, the stale smell of cow-byre and mud.

Angélique got back into the tall oak bed. Its twirly-whirly bed-posts supported a frilled canopy but the chintz curtains remained undrawn on this hot June night.

The linen sheets, woven by Sarah Williams with her own hands, had the same fresh smell of flowers as the room.

A wooden trestle bed had been pulled out from under the big bed and a mattress laid on it. Rose-Ann was sleeping in it for this last night.

Angélique fell asleep again almost immediately.

When she opened her eyes again, the sky was greyish-green above the dark, harmonious line of elms on the hillside, and the song of the hermit-thrush, sweet and solemn, had replaced the plaintive cry of the nightjar. The smell of garden flowers and lilac bushes against the shingle-board walls was driving out the emanations of the night and the forest.

Marrows and pumpkins, growing in the grass at the foot of the houses in the shelter of their own coiling leaves, shone as if painted in the heavy morning dew.

The smell of lilac in the gardens had a wonderful freshness in the dew-drenched air.

Once again Angélique rested her elbows on the edge of the little window. One by one the quaint shapes of the wooden houses began to emerge from the morning mists, their hipped roofs showing their broken and irregular surfaces, and an occasional angle sloping almost down to the ground. With their gable-ends, their overhanging upper storeys, their huge, solid brick chimneys rising straight up through the centre of the roof ridge, they were very like miniature Elizabethan manor houses. Most of them had been built in white pine which took on a silvery glow in the growing light.

Some of the barns were built of rough-hewn logs, thatched with straw, but the general effect of the village was one of prosperity and neatness.

Candles began to glow behind the little diamond-shaped leaded panes of the unshuttered windows. The whole impression was one of cosy comfort born of care and attention lavished on the details of life, and of the value placed on time, which must never be wasted. Life in these isolated valley communities seemed to be made up of these minute but essential details. Colourful gardens must be planted, less for the delight of the eye and the heart than because they must be stocked with a wealth of medicinal, edible and aromatic plants.

Angélique, surprised and captivated by it all, found herself wondering what kind of people these Englishmen were, who had grown accustomed to count on none but themselves, whose first thought on waking was of prayer. How different they were from the people she was accustomed to live with. Driven to the shores of America by their passionate and unshakeable resolve to pray after their own fashion, and by the necessity of finding a piece of land where they could do so, they had brought with them a God in their own image who forbade playgoing, music, cards and scarlet dresses, in fact anything that was not Work or Worship.

The integrity of productive work well done was the fountainhead of their exaltation and pleasure in life. Their sense of perfection was their joy and the tranquility of their home-life was their substitute for sensuality.

But their theology, having eliminated the saints and the angels, left them with nothing but demons, which they saw on every hand. They knew the full hierarchied order of them from the little genii with pointed nails that pierced their sacks of grain, right up to the dread principalities and powers of darkness with their cabalistic names.

And yet the beauty of the land to which the Lord had led them pleaded on the side of the angels.

Torn thus between gentleness and violence, between the lilac and the thorn, between ambition and renunciation, they felt justified only to live with a constant preoccupation about their last end.

Even so their minds did not dwell sufficiently on that fact, or such at least was the view of the Reverend Patridge, urged by him with much vehemence in his sermon on every Sunday.

As she leaned out of her window, Angélique was surprised to see the day bleak with no accompanying sign of activity in the village. No one left his house, apart from a few women going to fetch water from the river, which they did in a leisurely manner.

It was in fact Sunday. Sunday! For the Catholics too, as she was reminded by the snivelling of Adhemar beneath her window.

'Today is the Feast of Saint Anthony of Padua, Madame.'

'May he help you to find your head again and the courage you have lost!' Angélique replied, referring to the fact that Saint Anthony is reputed to help people find lost items of property.

But Adhemar did not think this funny.

'It's an important feast-day in Canada, Madame. And here I am, instead of taking part in a fine procession in a good, holy French town, here I am, at the back of beyond, surrounded by the very heretics who crucified Our Lord. I shall be punished, for sure! Something is going to happen, I feel it. . . .'

'Hold your peace,' whispered Angélique, 'and put away your rosary beads. The Protestants don't like such things.'

But Adhemar went on clutching convulsively at his rosary, muttering prayers begging for the protection of Our Lady and the Saints, and followed everywhere he went by a throng of little Puritans, never breathing a word, their shoes shining even brighter today, wide-eyed beneath their round hats or black bonnets.

The fact that it was Sunday, which was something the French had stupidly not foreseen, quite upset their plans to depart.

Everything came to a halt. It was out of the question to busy oneself for a journey—the whole village would have been scandalized.

Old Shapleigh, as he strode through the village with his pack and his blunderbuss on his shoulder, accompanied by his Indian and evidently heading for the forest, was followed by scowls and black looks, murmurs and even some threatening gestures. But he showed not the slightest concern, and went off sniggering and sardonic as always. Angélique envied him his independence of mind.

The old man had inspired her with the same admiration she had once felt for the remarkable Savary. His concern had been *science* and he had long since set at nought the prejudices of his co-religionists that in any way interfered with the pursuit of his dominating interest. When, as he walked through the forest, he began to dance about waving his pale, tapering fingers, it was because he had noticed some flowers and buds among the leaves, which he was pointing out to himself, naming them with their Latin names and noting the place where they grew.

Had not Angélique behaved just like this when she went looking for simples in the woods around Wapassou?

Old Shapleigh and she had recognized in each other a

kindred spirit, and she was sad to see him set off and vanish with his Indian into the shady ravine that led to the Androscoggin river.

A bell began to ring on the hillside, and the faithful set off in the direction of the meeting-house, a fortified building that stood above the village among the elms. The meeting house served not only as their church, but as the centre of their civic affairs as well.

Built of planks, it was indistinguishable from the other houses except for a small pointed belfry and the fact that it was square in shape. It served also as a fortress and, in the event of an Indian raid, the villagers could shelter there; two culverins were housed in the upper storey and their black muzzles, visible through the loop-holes, framed the bell tower, a symbol of peace and prayer.

Here, after the manner of the New England Fathers, the people of Brunswick-Falls came to hold their assemblies, praise the Lord, read the Bible, attend to the business of the colony, admonish and be admonished, condemn their neighbour and be condemned, God having his part to play in all these tasks.

Angélique felt some hesitation in following this austere company, for a remnant of her former Catholic education made her feel a certain embarrassment at the idea of entering a heretic church. It was a mortal sin, an incalculable danger to the soul of the faithful. A reflex with its roots in her impressionable childhood years.

'Shall I put on my red dress,' little Rose-Ann asked.

As she walked up towards the church with the child, Angélique could see that the inhabitants of Brunswick-Falls seemed to have relaxed their strict rules about clothes in honour of the Lord.

Even if there were no other red dresses like the one she had made for Rose-Ann, there were pink, white and blue ones to be seen amongst the little girls. There were lace bonnets, satin ribbons, broad-brimmed hats with tall black coifs, adorned with silver buckles or feathers, which the women wore over their bonnets with their narrow, embroidered turned-back edges. Lace bonnets were an English fashion, but a very becoming and practical one, and Angélique herself often wore one on her wanderings in America.

There was a quiet elegance about them in harmony with the discreet pale wooden houses, surrounded with lilac bushes, and the softness of the flax-blue sky.

It was a lovely Sunday in Newehewanik—the land of the spring.

As Angélique passed, the villagers smiled kindly at her and nodded their heads, and seeing her making towards the church, they followed close behind, pleased that she was to be their guest that morning.

Cantor joined his mother.

'I feel that we must not refer to our departure, it would not be fitting,' Angélique told him. 'But your father's ship is waiting for us at the mouth of the Kennebec, this evening, or tomorrow at the latest. . . .

'I think we could take our leave after the service. Today the animals have remained in the field with a single shepherd to look after them. The calves were allowed to suckle from their mothers, so as to make it unnecessary to do any milking. It's a day of rest for everyone. But I saw Maupertuis a little while ago, leading our horses down to the river. He said he was going to let them graze there while he and his son kept an eye on them, and that he would bring them back towards noon. Then we can set off, even though it will mean camping in the forest tonight.'

On arriving at the open square before the meeting house they found a platform with a kind of wooden stand on it pierced by three holes, the middle one bigger than the other two. That was the hole for the head, Cantor explained, whereas the other two merely held a man's wrists. This was the famous pillory in which miscreants were held on public view. The barbarous contraption had a notice board beside it on which were written the name of the occupant and the reason for his punishment.

The penal equipment of the little Puritan colony consisted of this pillory and a whipping-post.

Fortunately, this morning the pillory was empty, although the Reverend Patridge intimated in his sermon that in all probability it would shortly be occupied.

Seated among the faithful, who remained motionless

as wax figures, Angélique learned that the fashionable costumes that she had noticed that morning were not the result of any lawful desire to honour the Lord's Day, but rather of a kind of madness which seemed suddenly to have assailed the minister's unruly flock. Some brainstorm from abroad. . . . One had not to look far to see from whence it came, since it originated in a semi-oriental religion whose corruption down the centuries had only narrowly failed—under the crook of leaders vowed to the service of the devil—had only just failed to draw the entire human race to its doom. There followed a catalogue of historical figures in which the Popes Clement and Alexander rubbed shoulders with Astaroth, Asmodeus and Belial. Angélique understood enough English to make out that the ranting pastor was referring to the present Pope as anti-Christ in one breath and Beelzebub in the next, and thought he was laying it on rather thick.

It all reminded her of her youth, and the squabbles she and the other children used to have with the Huguenot peasant boys, and of the heretic farms in Poitou, which were pointed out with reprobation, their people living apart from the Catholic communities, with their solitary tombs beside a cypress tree.

Thomas Patridge reminded them that the attributes of graciousness were fleeting.

He thundered against hair worn too long, either by the men or the women. Too much brushing, immodest curls. These things were damnable, idolatrous.

'Berthos! Berthos!' he shouted.

One wondered which demon he was invoking now, but it was only the sexton he was calling to order, instructing him to go and wake up some impudent man who had fallen asleep in spite of the shouting.

Berthos, a gnome with a pudding-basin haircut, sprang up and made for the sleeper with his long switch that sported a doe's foot and a feather, and hit him violently on the head with it. The feather fulfilled the same purpose with the ladies, but somewhat more delicately, for this he would twiddle beneath their noses if an overlengthy sermon made them feel drowsy.

'Miserable sinners! Miserable sinners!' the minister went on in his lugubrious tones, 'You remind me in your obliviousness of the men of Laish who, according to the Bible, took no thought for their safety and their defence while their enemies the children of Dan were whetting their knives and preparing to slay them. But they went on laughing, and dancing, thinking that they had no enemies in all the world, for they refused to see what was going on, and took no precautions against it.'

'I'm sorry, but I protest,' old Benjamin Williams interrupted, sitting bolt upright, 'pray do not suggest that I have no care for my peoples' safety! I have just sent a message to the Massachusetts Government to ask their Honours to be good enough to send us eight or ten strong, watchful men to protect us during the harvest period. . . .'

'It is too late!' bellowed the minister, furious at this interruption. 'When the soul is not sanctified, all man's precautions are set at nought. Amen, amen I say unto you: by harvest time you will be no more. Even by the morrow, perhaps, yea even before the night, how many of you may not already be dead! The Indians are all about us in the forest, ready to attack! I can see them, I can hear them sharpening up their scalping knives, yes, I can see scarlet blood glistening on their hands, your blood . . . and yours,' he shouted, suddenly pointing towards some of the congregation, who grew pale. By now everyone was terror-stricken.

Next to Angélique sat a frail little old lady, called Elizabeth Pidgeon, whose job it was to instruct the girls of the village; she was shaking with fear from head to toe.

'For scarlet is not the colour of joy,' Thomas Patridge declaimed in a lugubrious voice, staring hard at Angélique, 'it is the colour of calamity and you have brought it amongst us, senseless people that you are! Soon you will hear the voice of the Almighty ring out from the heavens above saying: "Thou has preferred the pleasures of this world to the joys of looking on My face. Wherefore get thee gone, get thee forever out of my sight!" And you will plunge down into the darkness of Hell, there to dwell forever in the bottomless, black abyss, forever . . . forever, and ever and ever!'

Everyone was shuddering. They came out hesitantly

onto the sun-drenched square, pursued by the echo of that implacable, sepulchral voice.

'Forever! . . . Forever, and ever, and ever!'

CHAPTER 15

'WE'LL NEVER hear the end of that red dress,' Angélique grumbled.

The serenity of the Sunday meal accompanied by readings from the Bible could not entirely dispel the uncomfortable feeling left by the pastor's sermon. After lunch Angélique spent some time in the kitchen garden, examining the various herbs and crushing sprigs between her fingers to identify them by their smell. The sultry air was full of the busy hum of bees. She suddenly felt an intense desire to see Joffrey again. The world seemed empty and his presence in her in this English village struck her as odd, intolerable, like wondering in a dream what one is doing in a certain place and realizing that something strange is going on, something inexplicable.

'Whatever is Maupertuis thinking of?' she called across to Cantor. 'Just look! the sun is going down, and still he has not come back from the forest with the horses!'

'I'll go and see,' Cantor shouted back, and immediately set off at a brisk walk towards the opposite end of the village.

She watched him make his way towards the trees that formed a green screen all round the village. She was about to call him back, to shout: 'No, Cantor, don't go! Cantor, my son, don't go into the forest.' But he had already vanished round a bend in the path which led to the sheepfold and the farthest house in the village before the forest. So she went back into Benjamin's house, climbed the stairs, closed her leather bag in haste, picked up her pistols, threw her cloak over her shoulders, put on her hat, and went down again. Some of the serving maids were sitting beside the windows, doing nothing, dreaming or praying. Not wishing to disturb their meditation, she passed them by and went on out into the grassy

83

village street, with little Rose-Ann running behind her in her red dress.

'Oh, don't go away, dear lady,' the child murmured in her clumsy French as she caught up with Angélique.

'My darling, I *must* leave now,' Angélique replied without slowing her step. 'I am very late already. I do not know how you spend your Sunday here, but I should already have reached the coast where there is a ship waiting for me. It is so late already that we shall not get there before dawn. . . .'

With touching affection and solicitude, the little English girl tried to take her bag from her and carry it, and together they climbed the hill and followed the bend in the path before coming in sight of the last houses in the village, the smallest and poorest, built of logs and roofed with grasses and bark, then, in the distance the last house of all, the big sheep farm. Before reaching it they still had to pass a barn in which maize was stored, where the Frenchmen had spent the night and where Adhemar must now have sought refuge to sleep off his fears. Then there was the cottage of the school-teacher, Miss Pidgeon, surrounded by a tangle of flowers, and standing alone at some distance from the solid sheepfold with its gable end and its wind-vane—a handsome building set in the midst of well-fenced pasture lands. Beyond came the ravine up from which they had climbed the previous night, with a few ploughed fields running down the slope, then the domain of trees, rushing waters and steep rock faces—the forest.

In Miss Pidgeon's garden, suddenly appeared the stately figure of Mrs Williams in the midst of the hollyhocks, from which her nimble fingers were busy plucking the spent flowers. She beckoned imperiously to Angélique, who put down her bag and walked towards the old lady to bid her goody-bye.

'Just look at these hollyhocks,' said Mrs Williams. 'Do they have to suffer just because it's the Lord's day? I have been taken to task once again by our pastor, but I silenced him. We have had our fill for today. . . .'

She pointed her index finger, which was covered with a leather glove, towards the little house behind her.

'He's in there now, haranguing Elizabeth about her latter end, the poor creature!'

And her nimble hands resumed their task, while her sharp eyes beneath their heavy eyelids darted a quick glance at Angélique, and the corners of her severe lips lifted in the ghost of a smile.

'Perhaps they will put me in the pillory,' she said. 'And they will write on the board, "For excessive fondness for hollyhocks"!'

Angélique looked at her, a little taken aback, with a trace of a smile on her lips too. Ever since the previous day, when she had first found herself face to face with this forbidding old lady, the latter had seemed to take a certain pleasure in suddenly revealing certain unexpected sides of her character. Angélique no longer knew what to make of her, and now wondered whether Mrs Williams was making fun of her, joking, trying to provoke her, or whether she, Angélique, had failed to understand the English words. The idea crossed her mind that the worthy Puritan lady might conceivably have a slight partiality to some strong liquor, gin perhaps or rum, which might at times put her in a facetious mood, but she quickly dismissed this thought as incongruous, monstrous. No, it was something else, a kind of tipsiness it well might be, but unconscious, stemming from some very pure source.

Then, standing in front of this stately woman, who stood solid and severe like a rock, a good head taller than herself, yet who would suddenly burst forth into lighthearted independence, Angélique felt the same sense of unreality that she had experienced earlier on, a feeling of doubt as to whether she was really there, a sensation that everything about her was fluid, and that earth was slipping from under her feet. A feeling that she was about to wake up but could not. . . .

But it was nothing. Nature stood still, heavy with the scent of flowers and the hum of bees.

Sarah Williams came out from among the hollyhocks, letting her fingers glide lovingly across their stems, with their tight clumps of green, pink and pure white.

'Now they are happy,' she murmured.

She pushed open the gate and advanced towards

Angélique, removing her glove as she did so and placing it in a large pocket hanging from her belt that contained several small gardening tools. As she did so her eyes never left the face of the stranger who the day before had brought her back her little granddaughter.

'Did you ever meet King Louis XIV in France?' she asked. 'Did you ever speak to him? Yes, I feel sure you did. You still have the glow of the Sun. Ah! you French-women, how graceful you are! Walk a bit, will you,' she asked with a gesture to indicate Angélique should move away from her, 'walk over there for me. . . .'

The strange smile at the corners of her mouth grew more marked, as if some inner gaiety were about to burst forth.

"I too am becoming very much of a child. I love things that are bright, graceful and fresh. . . .'

Angélique walked a few steps as the old woman had asked her, then turned round. Her expression was quizzical but yet, although she was quite unaware of the fact, had something childlike about it. Old Sarah Williams fascinated her. Standing there in the middle of the path —the single path that did duty as footpath, street and road, leading right through the village from the forest to the meeting-house up on the hill—in the shade of the great elms, the greenish tint from whose leaves made her waxen cheeks look even more sallow than usual, the tall Englishwoman with one hand on her hip held herself so erect, her neck was so long and elegant above her little starched ruff, that any queen might have envied her her bearing. Her slender waist, drawn in by tight stays, merged below into fuller curves emphasized by a farthingale, a kind of padded roll of black velvet worn like a belt around the hips. Such had been the fashion at the beginning of the century, and Angélique had seen her mother and her aunts dressed in this way. But her black mantle, gathered up over a dark purple under-skirt, was worn shorter than in those days, and, as she held it in a little against her waist with one hand, Mrs Williams showed no concern at revealing that she wore riding boots, likewise black but daintily made, which must have been much more comfortable for moving about the wet fields and paths.

'How beautiful she must have been,' thought Angélique. Perhaps she would be like her one day. . . . She could see herself wearing boots like those, and striding briskly over her domain. People would stand slightly in awe of her, and she would be full. of self-confidence, free, her heart bursting with joy at the mere sight of a meadow full of flowers or a small child taking its first steps. She would in all probability be less stiff, less severe. But was Mrs Williams really so severe? . . . She was coming towards her now, and her face with its heavy, somewhat drooping but harmonious lines, was lit up by the emerald glow from the undergrowth and bore an expression of unforgettable contentment. She stopped beside Angélique, and her expression suddenly changed.

'Can you not smell the smell of red men?' she asked puckering her dark brows and resuming her haughty, forbidding expression once more.

There was horror and repulsion in her voice.

'Can you not smell it?'

'No, truly, I can't,' Angélique replied.

But she shuddered in spite of herself. And yet it seemed to her that she had never known the air so full of perfume as on the hillside where the fragrance of honeysuckle and creeper mingled with garden smells dominated by the scent of lilac and honey.

'I smell that smell often, too often,' said Sarah Williams, shaking her head as if in self-reproach. 'I can always smell it, it pervades my whole life. It haunts me. And yet it is a long time since Benjamin and I have had to use our gun to defend our home against those red serpents.'

'When I was a child . . . and later again when we lived in that cabin near Wells. . . .'

She broke off, with a shake of her head, unwilling to dwell on memories of fear and fighting, all so similar.

'There, there was the sea. . . . As a last resort you could escape that way. But here, there is no sea. . . .'

They walked on a few steps more.

'Is it not beautiful here?' she inquired, her voice losing its sense of urgency.

Little Rose-Ann was kneeling in the grass picking coral-shaded columbines.

'Newehewanik,' the old woman murmured.

'Land of Spring,' said Angélique.

'You know that, do you?' the Englishwoman asked, glancing swiftly at Angélique.

Once again her intensely black eyes beneath their veined lids stared fixedly at Angélique the stranger, the Frenchwoman, as if trying to read in her, to guess at some answer, some explanation.

'So you love America, do you?' she said. 'And yet you are so young. . . .'

'I am not as young as all that,' Angélique protested. 'My elder son is seventeen and . . .'

Old Sarah interrupted her with a burst of laughter, the first time Angélique had seen her laugh, a thin, spontaneous laugh, almost like a little girl, that showed her long, slightly horsey but perfect, healthy teeth.

'Oh yes, you are young,' she repeated. 'You have not lived, my dear!'

'Oh no?'

Angélique was almost angry. It was true that Mrs Williams must have been some twenty-five years older than Angélique, and thus entitled to show a certain condescension, but Angélique considered that her own life had been neither so short nor so lacking in interest that she could be said to have seen nothing of it. . . .

'Your life is just beginning!' Mrs Williams affirmed in a voice that brooked no reply. 'It has only just started!'

'Really?'

'How charming you sound when you say that? Ah, you Frenchwomen, how lucky you are! You are like a flame beginning to sparkle and grow, full of self-confidence, in a dark world that holds no terrors for you! Only now are you beginning to live; can you not feel it? When one is a very young woman, one has to bear the burden of building one's life, of proving oneself.

'A crushing burden! And one is all alone. . . . Once one ceases to be a child, is there anyone more solitary than a young woman? . . . But when you reach forty or fifty, then you can begin to live! One has done with proving oneself; that is all over. One becomes as free as a child again, one finds oneself. . . . I think I never was so happy as the day when I realized that my youth had gone, had gone at last,' she sighed. 'Suddenly my soul grew light, my heart warmer and more responsive, and my eyes were opened on the world. God himself seemed to have grown friendly. I was still alone, but I had grown used to that. I bought two of the prettiest lace coifs I could find from a pedlar who came to the village, and neither the wrath of the pastor nor Ben's reproofs have managed to prevent me from wearing them ever since.'

She laughed again, a mischievous laugh, and touched Angélique's cheek as she would have that of a child. Angélique had forgotten that she must be off! The sun seemed to be standing still in the sky, lying like a huge full-blown flower, still bright yellow, on a bed of tiny, white, downy clouds just above the horizon.

She was listening to Mrs Williams, who took her by the arm as they walked slowly together towards the village. Most of the houses were still half-hidden by the turn in the path and the slope of the ground, by a crystalline mist which seemed to be rising from them, fed by the stream that ran along below the houses.

'You love this land, don't you. Madame?' Mrs Williams went on. 'That is a sign of breeding. It is so beautiful. I have not got to know it as much as I would have liked, but you, you will get to know it better than I. When I was young, I hated the wretched, dangerous life we led on these shores. I wanted to go to London, about which we were told by sailors and our elders. I left there when I was six, and I still remember its jostling spires, and its narrow lanes crowded with creaking coaches. As a girl I used to dream of escaping, of going back to the old world, and the fear of damnation was the only thing that stopped me doing so. No,' she said as if replying to some remark Angélique had made, 'no, I was not pretty in my youth. I am beautiful *now*, because I have reached my fulfilment. But when I was young I was too thin, too tall, dull, pale, really unattractive. I have always been grateful to Ben for agreeing to marry me in exchange for a plot of ground and a fishing sloop he wanted from my father. The value of his own lands with their little creek became enhanced because they were next to ours. It was a wonderful opportunity for him. He was bound to marry me, and he didn't hesitate.'

She winked an eye at Angélique.

'And he never regretted it either, as far as I know.'

She laughed softly.

'But in those days I would not even have brought a glimmer to the eye of the pirates who used to come ashore near by to trade the rum and cloth they had plundered in the Caribbean for some of our fresh food. They were gentlemen of fortune, often Frenchmen. I can still see their tanned buccaneer's faces, and their clothes that looked so outlandish next to our dark dresses with their white collars. They would never have dreamed of harming us for we were as poor as Job. They were delighted to encounter white men along this wild stretch of coastland, and to eat the fruit and vegetables we grew. There they were, a godless and lawless lot, and we with our exaggerated piety, and yet there was kinship between us, we were all marooned on the edge of the earth.

'Now there are far too many people along the coast and far too many ships of ill repute in the bay. So we chose to get away, to live in the frontier lands. . . .

'I surprise you, my child, with these tales, these admissions . . . but you must remember your God is less terrifying than ours. When we grow old, either we become mad, or spiteful, or we become witches, or else we just do as we please. Then everything grows calm, and nothing really matters any more!'

She shook her coif once more in a gesture of defiance, then of approbation and serenity.

Yesterday evening she had been so stiff, so implacably distant, and yet today she had shown such delicacy, almost humility!

Once again it crossed Angélique's mind that the worthy Puritan lady might have some hidden weakness for an equally well hidden flask of plum-brandy or gin; but she immediately dismissed this doubt, for her heart was moved by the sudden confidences the old lady had made as if in a dream.

She was later to relive this touching scene and understand its significance. . . .

Fate pausing in its inexorable march, but its course already set, was prompting a woman who was approaching her final hour to spontaneous, almost thoughtless gestures—stirrings, one might say, of the soul, the expression of an ardent heart, a heart that had ever been warm and loving beneath the rigid exterior imposed by her uncompromising religious beliefs.

Old Sarah turned towards Angélique and, taking her face between her two long, white hands, she lifted it towards her, looking down at it with motherly intensity.

'May this land of America shower blessings upon you, my dear child,' she said softly and with great solemnity, 'and I beg you . . . I beg you, save it from destruction!' Her hands slipped away and she examined them as if she herself had been quite overcome by her own gesture and words.

She stiffened, and her face grew as cold as marble once more while her piercing black eyes fixed themselves on the vast expanse of sky that lay like a huge inverted shell over the valley.

'What is happening?' she murmured. She stopped to listen, then set off once more. They walked several paces in silence, then Mrs Williams halted again, and suddenly grasped Angélique's wrists so hard that she made her jump.

'Listen!' said the Englishwoman, her voice sounded quite different: clear, precise, and icy cold.

Then they heard a confused, distant sound coming to them through the evening air.

An unidentifiable, inarticulate sound like the roaring of the sea, or of the wind, above which rang out a distant, feeble, high pitched shriek:

'Abenakis! Abenakis!'

Hastily, Sarah Williams drew Angélique away towards the bend in the road that hid the rest of the village from their sight. It looked calm, deserted and asleep.

But the roaring sound was growing louder, thousands of hooting voices above which could still be heard the desperate cry of a handful of villagers who had begun to run like terror-stricken rats between the houses.

'The Abenakis! The Abenakis!'

Angélique looked back towards the fields, and a terrifying spectacle met her eyes. It was what she had feared, what she had sensed, what she had been unwilling to believe! An army of half-naked Indians, brandishing tomahawks and cutlasses, was pouring out of the forest; like so many ants driven from their nest, in a matter of a few seconds the Indians had completely covered the fields in the valley, and were spreading out in a dark, moving tide, a thick, red flood, a tidal wave that broke across the countryside, with its death cry going before it:

'You-ou-ou-ou! You-ou-ou-ou!'

The tide of Indians reached the stream, swept over it, reached the near side, began to climb up the hill and came to the first of the houses.

A woman in a blue dress ran up the slope towards them, staggering as if drunk, her mouth a black hole in her blanched face as she shouted at them.

'The Abenakis!'

An unseen something struck her between the shoulders; she gave a kind of hiccough and fell face down on the ground.

'Benjamin!' Sarah Williams cried. 'Benjamin! He is all alone up there in the house.'

'Stop!'

Angélique tried to hold the old woman back but she broke away and ran straight ahead towards the house, fearing her aged husband might be taken by surprise, as he dozed over his Bible.

Sarah had got only a hundred yards when Angélique saw an Indian leap from the undergrowth, catch up with her in a few lithe strides, and strike the old woman down with a single blow from his tomahawk. Then, bending over her, he seized her coif and her hair and, with a flick of his wrist, scalped her. Angélique shuddered as she turned to make her escape.

'Run!' she shouted to Rose-Ann pointing towards the sheepfold: 'Over there near the forest, run quick!'

She herself ran as fast as her legs would carry her. As she reached Miss Pidgeon's garden, she stopped to pick up the bag she had left there, flung open the gate and dashed into the house where the Reverend Patridge and the old maid were still deep in their discussion on the last end of man.

'The savages! . . . They are coming! . . .'

She was so breathless, she could no longer find the right English words, and tried in vain to explain.

'The savages!' she repeated in French. 'The Abenakis . . ; they are coming . . . take refuge in the sheep farm. . . .'

It had already occurred to her that this solid looking farm, apparently fortified, could well sustain a siege and make feasible some kind of defence.

In a crisis, spontaneity as well as experience and habit count. Angélique saw the corpulent Thomas Patridge leap to his feet, pick up little Miss Pidgeon in her arms like a doll, bound across the garden and race without further ado towards the suggested place of shelter.

Angélique was about to follow them, but changed her mind and, hiding behind the house door, she loaded her two pistols, kept one of them in her hand, then went outside again.

Fortunately this particular part of the village was still deserted. The woman who had fallen at the bend of the road after climbing the hill still lay motionless, with an arrow between her shoulder blades.

This area, hidden from the other houses by the slope and the bend in the road, had not yet claimed the attention of the Indians, apart from the one who had scalped Mistress Williams and who had then gone off in another direction.

The noise coming from the other parts was deafening and horrible, but here all was still silent, a kind of agonized, febrile waiting. Even the birds were silent.

Still running, Angélique managed to reach the barn where the maize was stored.

There was Adhemar asleep!

'Get up! The Indians are here! Run! Run to the sheep farm! Take your musket with you!'

As he fled in terror, she seized Maupertuis's guns and powder horns which were hanging from a hook.

She was trying feverishly to load the gun, scraping her fingers as she did so, when something suddenly came tumbling down behind her and she saw an Abenaki Indian, who had entered the barn by the roof and was now slithering down a huge pile of maize. She swung round, still clutching the musket by the barrel, and struck the redskin across the temple with the butt. He fell to the ground and she made her escape.

The shady path was still deserted as she began to run down it. Then she heard someone running behind her, and, glancing over her shoulder, saw that it was an Indian—whether it was the one she had stunned or another, she knew not—who was gaining on her fast and holding his hatchet erect.

His feet made almost no sound on the grass, and Angélique could not stop to take aim. Her only hope of escape was to run as fast as she could and she felt as if her feet were no longer touching the ground.

At last she reached the courtyard of the sheep farm and leapt behind a farm wagon. The Indian's hatchet rang against the wood and the sharp metal wedge buried itself in the wagon. Doing her utmost to control her breathing, Angélique took aim and fired at the redskin at point-blank range. He fell across the gateway, his two hands clutching his powder-blackened breast.

A few strides more and she had reached the threshold of the house where the door was opened to her even before she had time to knock. They closed it again immediately and barred it with two solid oak battens.

CHAPTER 16

IN ADDITION to the parson and Miss Pidgeon, the French soldier Adhemar and little Rose-Ann, the other occupants of the farmhouse were Samuel Corwin, the owner, and his household—his wife and three children, two young hands employed by him and a servant girl—old Jos Carter, a neighbour, and a couple by the name of Stoughton together with their baby, who had also been visiting the Corwins at the time of the attack.

There was no weeping or wailing; American farmers had perforce become inured to battle and bloodshed. The womenfolk were already busy swabbing out the barrels of the guns taken down from over the hearth.

Samuel Corwin had positioned his gun in one of the many loop-holes with which the house was provided, as was usual in New England houses, especially those built in the early days. Through another hole, the occupants were keeping watch on what was going on outside, and they had seen the Countess of Peyrac strike down the Indian pursuing her.

They threw her a swift, grim glance as she came in: she had brought more guns, she was like the others, efficient and diligent. The minister had thrown his frock-coat over a bench and stood in his shirt sleeves preparing powder charges, his lips drawn back over his strong, prominent teeth. He was waiting for a gun to be made available to him, so Angélique handed him Maupertuis's musket and herself took Adhemar's, as he was trembling like a leaf.

One of the children began to cry and someone spoke softly to it to silence it.

In the vicinity of the house all was quiet. All that could be heard was a distant roaring noise like the sound of the sea, which from time to time rose to a crescendo as the massacre proceeded.

Then there came a series of dull booms, and Angélique remembered the small cannons in the fortified church. One could only hope that some of the villagers had managed to take refuge within its walls.

'The Lord will protect His own,' the pastor muttered, 'for they are even as His army.'

At once someone gesticulated furiously to him to keep quiet.

A small band of Indians were running along the path, torch in hand. They seemed to have come from the direction of the ravine and did not stop.

A child began to cry again, whereon Angélique suddenly had an idea; she went over to one of the huge empty cauldrons used for cheese-making, and suggested to Rose-Ann and three of the smallest children that they might like to hide inside it. It would be like being in a nest, she said, and they must not move.

She half closed the lid. In their hiding place the children would be less liable to panic and run less risk of being knocked over by the combatants.

Then she returned to her observation post.

There were some redskins standing by the fence; they

95

had noticed the body of one of their fellows sprawled across the path.

There were four of them talking and glancing towards the house. In the red glow of the sunset, their faces, daubed with war paint, were a terrifying sight, and Angélique, crowded into this confined space with the white men, all of whose lives were at peril, felt the dread of the redskins growing upon her, and her flesh began to creep.

The Indians pushed open the gate and advanced across the yard, crouching slightly like wild animals, full of mystery and terror.

'Fire!' ordered Corwin quietly.

A volley of shots rang out, and when the smoke had dispersed they saw three of the Abenakis writhing in their death throes on the ground, while the fourth was making good his escape.

Then there came a general onslaught, savages coming up from out of the ravine behind the house in a great tide that soon seemed to rise around them on all sides. The brown bodies grew more and more numerous, and their whoops mingled with the detonations of the guns.

The besieged party went on firing automatically, handing the discharged guns back to the women and catching up a loaded weapon, while brushes were drawn quickly through the burning hot barrels, and feverish hands tipped up the powder flasks, snapped the flintlocks into position to the accompaniment of sharp clicks that punctuated the thunder of the gunfire, and the howling and shrieking outside. Smoke stung their parched throats, and the sweat running down their faces had a bitter taste at the corners of their open lips through which their breath came in hoarse gasps.

Angélique dropped her musket. No more ammunition! She picked up her pistols, loaded them, filled her pockets with small-calibre bullets, stuffed as many as she could into her mouth to have them as handy as possible, then tied her powder horn and box of Turkish primer to her belt so as not to waste a single movement with them either.

There was a rending sound in the roof and an Indian slithered to the floor at the far end of the room, landing beside Pastor Patridge, who struck him down with his gun butt. But a second redskin was hard on the heels of the first and brought down his tomahawk on the Reverend Thomas's far from fragile skull. His knees gave beneath him and the redskin, seizing him by the hair, had just begun to run his knife across his forehead in a broad incision when he received the charge of Angélique's pistol full in the chest.

As the Indians continued to pour in through the roof, the English backed away towards the great chimney breast, where Angélique tipped the heavy wooden table on its side and pushed it across one corner of the room so as to constitute a rampart, behind which they all took refuge. She was to ask herself later where she had found the strength to do it. The frenzy of battle lent her superhuman power, intensified by a literal fury at the thought that she had allowed herself to be trapped so stupidly in this village of foreign settlers, in which she might well lose her life.

From their point of refuge, the settlers continued to fire in two directions: towards the far end of the room where the attackers kept leaping in from the roof, and towards the door, which was beginning to give way beneath the blows of Indian hatchets.

It was sheer slaughter and thanks to this deadly crossfire the whites with desperation and firearms on their side almost won the day. But their ammunition was running out, and Corwin, struck just below the shoulder blade by a hatchet, collapsed with a cry.

With a snake-like wriggle, one of the Indians slithered between the wall and the side of the table and, seizing a woman by her skirt, pulled her towards him. She fought back like one possessed and dropped the powder horn she was holding.

Over the top of the table old Carter was stunning anyone who came within striking distance of his gun butt. But as he raised his arms to bring down the weapon yet again, the blade of a hunting knife was slid treacherously between his ribs. He staggered and doubled up, like a straw-filled puppet with dangling arms.

Then suddenly, like a circus acrobat performing a trick, someone at the back of the room leapt into the air, passed right over the heads of the rest, legs spread wide like a dancer, and landed among the Englishmen, behind them in fact, on the other side of the table.

It was the Sagamore Piksarett, chief of the Patsuiketts and the most renowned warrior of Acadia.

Angélique heard his mocking voice behind her, and a hand seized her violently by the nape of the neck.

'You are my prisoner,' said the Patsuikett in triumphal tones.

Angélique dropped her now useless pistols and seized him with both hands by his long tresses tied with fox feet.

Because she knew him, because his weasly face with its wicked eyes was familiar to her, she no longer felt any fear and even ceased to consider him and his horde of Indians as enemies. They were Abenakis, and she knew their tongue and was familiar with their strange, primitive thought processes. She turned her head sharply to one side and spat out the two bullets she still had in her mouth.

'Was it to capture me that you took this village?' she shouted at the Indian, still clinging to his hair. 'It was Black Robe that ordered you to, wasn't it?'

And her green eyes pierced him with such a devastating glance that he stood transfixed. It was not the first time that Sagamore Piksarett and the white woman from the Upper Kennebec had met.

She had been marked out as his enemy! But what woman had ever dared to grasp him thus by his ceremonial tresses and look him so boldly in the face while death hung over her head.

Once she had stood between him and the Iroquois with the same look on her face. She knew no fear.

'You are my prisoner,' he repeated fiercely.

'I accept that I am your prisoner, but you shall not kill me nor hand me over to Black Robe, because I am a Frenchwoman, and because I gave you my cloak in which to wrap the bones of your ancestors.'[1]

All about them the shouting and the throes of battle continued and reached their paroxysm. The fighting was now hand to hand. But the end soon came, and the

[1] See *The Countess Angélique.*

shouts of rage, horror and defiance gradually died down, giving place to a panting silence through which the groans of the wounded soon began to make themselves heard.

Carter had been scalped, but the other Europeans were alive, for the Abenakis were above all interested in the ransom they could secure by their capture. The Reverend Patridge, after struggling free from the mountain of bodies beneath which he had been buried, stood swaying on his feet between two braves, his face covered with blood.

An agonized cry rent the air: 'Help me, Madame, or I am a dead man!'

It was Adhemar, who had been pulled out from under some piece of furniture.

'Don't kill him!' cried Angélique. 'Can't you see that he's a French soldier?'

It was certainly not obvious.

Angélique was quite beside herself, obsessed with the idea that she must escape from this trap into which she had so foolishly blundered. The tragic absurdity of the situation made her extremely angry and heightened her defensive reflexes.

For the past few moments one single thought had come to dominate all others in her mind. *She knew these Indians.* And this was how she would escape the trap that had been set for her. They were wild beasts, but wild beasts could be tamed. In the desert of the Maghreb, Colin Paturel had talked to the lions and won them to his will. . . . She began to realize that Piksarett's war party were separate from the other Indians and had attacked from the opposite direction, and that the battle around the farm had no connection with the rest of the fighting.

Piksarett hesitated. Some of the things Angélique had said puzzled him. 'I am a Frenchwoman!' He had been taught to fight the English. Moreover, he would never forget the magnificent cloak which she had given him for his ancestors.

'Have you been baptized?' he asked.

'Of course I have,' she cried in exasperation, crossing herself several times and calling on the Virgin Mary.

Through the shattered door Angélique thought she glimpsed the familiar figure of a Canadian trapper. She rushed forward, recognized him and called desperately to him.

'Monsieur de L'Aubignière!'

It was Three-Fingers from Trois Rivières. Hearing her shout, he turned and came back towards her. When it came to fighting, he scorned the white man's weapons. In his hands he held a polished wooden tomahawk and a small Indian hatchet whose razor-sharp blade was red with blood. His blue eyes shone in his powder-blackened, blood-stained face, and there was more blood on his deerskin clothing and on a row of scalps slung from his multicoloured belt.

How could she ever make contact with this man? How could she ever circumvent him? He was an incorruptible knight, a warrior of God, his mind possessed, like those of Maudreuil, de Loménie, and Arreboust, with his dream of vengeance, salvation and paradise. . . .

But he did recognize her.

'Madame de Peyrac!' he exclaimed. 'What are you doing here among these damned heretics? Woe betide you!'

He entered the devastated house which the Abenakis, having gathered together their prisoners, were looting.

She seized him too by the collar of his jerkin.

'Black Robe,' she cried, 'I am sure I saw Black Robe across the prairie with his standard. . . . It was Father d'Orgeval who led you into battle, wasn't it? He knew he would find me in this village!'

She was stating facts rather than asking questions, and he stared dumbfounded at her, with open mouth.

He tried to find a reply, an excuse:

'You killed Pont-Briand,' he replied at last, 'and you and your husband are turning Acadia upside down with your alliances. We had to lay our hands on you. . . .'

So that was it.

Joffrey! Joffrey!

They were going to kidnap and carry off as a prisoner the wife of the formidable gentleman from Wapassou who had already made his mastery felt in the land of Acadia.

They would take her to Quebec, and put pressure on Joffrey through her. She would never see him again.

'Maupertuis?' she asked breathlessly.

'We have taken both him and his son and put them under arrest. They are both Canadians of New France, and on a day like this, they should be among their brothers.'

'Did they take part in the attack with you?'

'No. Their case will be tried in Quebec. They have served the enemies of New France. . . .'

How could she win him over? He was fanatical, uncompromising, credulous, cunning, greedy, unstable, believed in miracles, saints, in the cause of God and the King of France, and the supremacy of the Jesuits. A second Michael the Archangel. He was not interested in her. He had his orders. And he had to redeem himself in the eyes of his all-powerful superiors.

'Do you think that after this Count Peyrac, my husband, is going to help you sell your beaver skins in New England,' she shouted at him through her teeth. 'Don't forget that he has advanced you a thousand pounds and has promised you double that if you make a profit. . . .'

'Hush!' he said growing pale and looking about him.

'Get me out of this, or I shall shout the truth about you from the housetops of Quebec.'

'Let us not quarrel,' he whispered, 'we can still sort things out. We are some distance from the rest of the village. I have not seen you. . . .'

Then, turning towards Piksarett, he went on:

'Let this woman go, Sagamore! She is not an English woman and her capture would bring us bad luck.'

Piksarett stretched out his red, oily hand and laid it on Angélique's shoulder.

'She is my prisoner,' he repeated in tones that brooked no reply.

'So be it,' said Angélique feverishly, 'I am your prisoner, I do gainsay that. You can follow me wherever you like, I shall not object. But you shall not take me to Quebec. . . . What would you do with me there? They would not want to buy me from you since I have already been baptized. So take me to Gouldsboro, where my

101

husband will pay you handsomely, any ransom you care to ask.'

It was a spine-chilling game of poker. These wild beasts must be tamed, perplexed, persuaded. But she knew them. The most absurd arguments sprang to her mind, but it was precisely these that worked on these furtive, devious minds. It was out of the question to deny Piksarett's rights over her, for he would have immediately struck her down with a blow of his tomahawk just to assert them, but she knew him to be free, capricious, and absolutely independent of his Canadian allies; inasmuch as he was now deprived of the glory of having obtained another soul for his dear French friends' paradise, since she was already baptized, he had begun to hesitate, and to doubt the importance of his capture. She must win him over before any other Frenchman, who knew what was to be gained by Madame de Peyrac's capture—perhaps even the dreaded Jesuit himself—appeared round the bend in the road. Since de L'Aubignière, by good fortune, was an accomplice. . . .

Burning brands began to fall on their heads as they spoke, for Piksarett's Abenakis, poking about with their torches in their search for plunder, had set the farmhouse on fire.

'Come along! Come along,' Angélique urged the people, pushing them outside. She helped up some of the English who were either wounded or stunned, then added: 'Good heavens, the children!'

She ran back into the house, raised the lid of the cauldron and lifted the children out one by one, dumb with fright. The revelation of this incongruous hiding place caused general hilarity among the Indians, who doubled up with mirth, slapping their thighs and pointing at the spectacle.

The heat was becoming unbearable; a beam crackled and half collapsed in a shower of sparks.

Everyone ran out into the yard, clambering over dead bodies and débris.

The sight of the trees so close, and of the shady forest ravine, spurred Angélique's desire to flee. Every second counted.

'Let me go down to the sea, Sagamore,' she said to Piksarett, 'or your ancestors will be angry with you for showing me so little consideration. They know that my personal spirits do not deserve to be treated lightly. You would be making a grave mistake were you to take me to Quebec. On the other hand, you will have no cause to regret coming with me.'

The tall Abenaki's tormented expression reflected the conflict of his mind, but Angélique gave him no time to disentangle his thoughts.

'Make sure that we are not followed. Report that I was not in the village,' she said to Three-Fingers, who was also confused by the speed of events and Angélique's authoritative tone. 'We shall show you our gratitude. Do you know where my son Cantor is? Did you capture him?'

'I swear to you by the Blessed Sacrament that we never set eyes on him.'

'Off we go then,' she said. 'I am going. Come on! Come on!'

'Hold a minute!' exclaimed Piksarett, seeing that she was gathering together the English survivors from the farm. 'These people belong to my braves. . . .'

'Well, let them come too. But only the masters of the captives.'

Three lumbering feathered giants leapt forward shouting, but a sharp word from Piksarett stopped them in their tracks.

Angélique paused only to pick up one of the children, to drag one of the women with her and give a shove to the huge figure of Thomas Patridge who staggered off, blinded with his own blood.

'Adhemar, come here! Hold this boy's hand and don't let him go, whatever you do. Bear up, Miss Pidgeon!'

She scrambled down the slope, turning her back on the ravaged, burning village, dragging them off to freedom as so often before, in La Rochelle, in Poitou, and even earlier, back in the dark days of her childhood, fleeing, ever fleeing with a flock of outcasts she had snatched from the jaws of death.

That evening the soul of old Sarah walked with her as she plunged ever deeper into the forest and was swallowed up in the silence of the dark trees with the English survivors from Brunswick-Falls.

With them came Piksarett and the three Indians who considered the English people as their chattels. They loped along behind them keeping a certain distance back. There was no attempt to catch them up.

Angélique knew this, she sensed it, and as they all got farther from the doomed village, she began to fear the Indians less, realizing that they had lost much of their warlike, hysterical tension.

The English were mystified by Angélique's conduct, and kept glancing back and complaining that the savages were pursuing them.

'You have nothing to fear,' Angélique replied. 'There are only four of them now instead of a hundred. And I am with you. They will not harm you any more. I know them. Fear nothing. All you have to do is keep on walking.'

Piksarett's thoughts were now as clear to her as if she had formed them herself with a savage's brain.

He was childish and loved anything original, novel, unusual. He was superstitious too and Angélique's personal spirits both intrigued and frightened him.

Full of curiosity, he followed close behind her, holding his impatient braves back with a word, fascinated to know what was going to happen now, and what was the nature of those cunning, fleeting, indomitable spirits he had seen dancing in the green flashes of the white woman's eyes.

Farther on the calm waters of the Audroscoggin river shone through the branches below them. Some canoes had been drawn up on the bank; they climbed into them and began to glide downstream towards the sea.

CHAPTER 17

IT WAS night. . . . At the foot of the waterfall, in the darkness lit fitfully by the fireflies, in the warm darkness filled with the croaking of frogs and the smell of burning, the Europeans snatched a brief rest. Huddled one against the other close to the birch-bark canoes, shivering in spite of the warmth, some prayed while others moaned softly.

There they awaited the dawn.

Among those whom Angélique had brought from the burning farm were farmer Stoughton, his wife and baby, and the entire Corwin family. Corwin's two farm-hands and his servant girl had also managed to follow.

Rose-Ann huddled close to Angélique, while Adhemar sat on her other side, and would gladly have done the same; as it was he stayed as close to her as he possibly could.

'They are up there,' he whispered. 'From the moment I first set foot in this land of savages, I just knew I would lose my scalp one day!'

Frail little Miss Pidgeon had not suffered a scratch and it was she who had led the Reverend Patridge, who, for the time being had become little better than a body with no head, for not only had he been blinded with blood but he was barely conscious and managed to remain on his feet only by sheer force of habit and because such big-framed men are incapable of falling to the ground unless actually dead. As soon as she had been able to do so, the kindly teacher had washed his face for him and bound her shawl around his forehead. Then finally, when they reached the boats. Angélique had managed to open her bag in which she kept a sachet of yellow powder, an iron salt that Joffrey had given her, which had the property of favouring the clotting of blood, and by this means she had succeeded in stopping the bleeding.

Although half-scalped, the pastor would no doubt only be left with an ugly scar across his forehead, which admittedly would do nothing to make his looks any less disconcerting than they had been.

He was sleeping heavily and the grating sound of his laboured breathing filled the intervals of silence. Beneath the bandaging, the whole of one side of his face was swollen and had gone blue. It was just as well that it was dark, for nature had not favoured him in the first place and now he looked absolutely hideous.

A little girl was standing rigidly erect, and crying, her face showing white in the darkness.

'You must sleep, Mary, try to sleep,' Angélique said softly in English, 'you must try to sleep.'

'I can't,' the little girl wailed. 'The savages are watching me.'

All four of them were sitting up above the waterfall, four Abenakis, one of them the mighty Piksarett, and they sat looking down into the darkness in which their wretched prisoners were huddled together.

In the glow of the small campfire one could make out their copper-coloured faces and flashing snake-like eyes.

They had continued to follow the whites, watching them with considerable fascination and curiosity, but they had made no attempt to attack them. They were perfectly calm now and were smoking and talking together. What was going to happen? What would these unknown spirits that lived in the white woman from Wapassou think of next? What action would her personal spirits dictate? Glances were exchanged across the leaping waters of the fall.

Angélique did her best to reassure her protégées.

'They will do us no further harm. We must get them down to the coast and there my husband, Count Peyrac, will know exactly how to treat them, how to flatter them, and will offer them handsome gifts in exchange for our lives and our freedom.'

They stared at her, dumbstruck, sensing in their cold, exaggeratedly puritanical minds that she too was of a different species from them, a little frightening, even a little repugnant to them. This excessively beautiful white woman, who was able to converse with the Indians in their own language, seemed to have the capacity of getting inside their cruel, dark pagan minds in order to tame and subjugate them the more effectively.

They were aware of what she was, and both feared and despised her, somewhat as they did old Shapleigh, while realizing at the same time that they owed her their lives, and certainly their liberty.

It was because of her indecent familiarity with these savages, because of the easy way she spoke to them, because of the vehement harangues in that hated pagan

106

tongue that tripped so lightly off those beautiful lips, that they had seen the mood of the Indians change, had seen their own lives spared and had been able to make their escape through the woods, far from the site of the massacre, under the very eyes of the Indians.

They were conscious of this miracle and of the necessity for remaining under her protection, reassured by the very sound of her voice, and they did their best to excuse her strange ways, by reminding themselves that after all she was French. . . .

Sometime in the middle of the night Angélique climbed up to where the savages sat above the waterfall to ask them quite straightforwardly whether they had a piece of bear fat or some seal oil that she could use to cover the burns of little nine-year-old Sammy Corwin, for they were causing him a great deal of pain.

The Indians bustled about and soon produced a moose bladder containing some precious seal oil, which had an unpleasant smell but was pure and wholesome.

'Do not forget, oh woman, that that boy belongs to me,' one of the braves said to her. 'But take good care of him, for tomorrow I shall take him with me back to my tribe.'

'That boy belongs to his father and mother,' Angélique replied. 'We shall buy him from you.'

'But I laid my hand on him in battle . . . and I want a white child in my wigwam.'

'I shall not let you take him away,' Angélique replied with unshakeable calm.

Then she added to appease the man's anger:

'I shall give you many other things, so that you shall not lack your share of the booty . . . tomorrow we will hold council.'

Apart from this incident, the night passed uneventfully. They heard no more of the massacre. As they were making their escape they had glimpsed, at a bend in the river, a distant red glow, as Brunswick-Falls, the frontier village, burnt to the ground.

They crouched there, their minds blank, seeking refuge in the darkness.

As the grey dawn began to creep up the sky, something came slithering down the slope, weaving through the grass and brushwood as it came, and there stood Wolverine, baring his teeth in what on this occasion looked like a welcoming grin. Cantor followed hard on his tracks, carrying a sleeping English child in his arms, a little boy of three with his thumb in his mouth.

'I found him standing beside his mother who had been scalped,' he explained. 'The woman kept on saying to him: "Don't be frightened, I promise they won't hurt you." When she saw me pick him up she closed her eyes at last and died.'

'That's Rebecca Turner's son,' said Jane Stoughton. 'Poor child! His father was killed last year.'

They fell silent as the four Indians moved towards them. They showed no sign of aggression. Isolated as they were from the rest of the war party, and perplexed by the attitude of these strange prisoners upon whom they seemed unable to impose their right of possession, their mood had changed.

The man who had claimed the Corwin boy walked towards Cantor and held out his hands towards the sleeping child.

'Give him to me,' he said. 'Give him to me. It has always been my desire to have a white child in my wigwam, and your mother will never allow me to take the child I captured at Newehewanik. Give me this child, for he has neither father nor mother nor family nor village. What would you do with him? I shall take him away and bring him up as a hunter and a warrior, and I shall make him happy. Children lead a happy life in our wigwams.'

His expression was entreating, almost pitiable.

Piksarett had had to convince the man during the night, not without a certain slyness, that Angélique would never allow him to take possession of his young captive, little Samuel, and that were he to defy her in this, she would change him into a moose for the rest of his life.

Torn between his fear of so sad a fate and the desire to vindicate his rights, he reckoned that an acceptable solution could be arrived at if he were prepared to take the little orphan Cantor had saved.

Angélique cast an anxious, questioning glance at her son.

'What do you think, Cantor?'

For her part, she really did not know which was the right decision to take. It broke her heart to think of this little white boy being carried off into the depths of the forest; on the other hand, a certain sense of fairness, and prudence as well, inclined her to agree to the humble request of the Abenaki brave. She had hoodwinked them, had put them off sufficiently often since the previous day, and if she were to dispute too much with them over their spoils, they might suddenly lose patience with her.

'What do you think, Cantor?'

'Well,' the young man began with a shrug, 'we know that white children are not unhappy among the Indians. Perhaps it would be better to let this one go as he has not any family anyway, than all have our skulls split.'

The voice of wisdom had spoken through his lips.

Angélique remembered the wails of despair of the little Canadian boy, de L'Aubignière's nephew, when, on the occasion of an exchange, they had sought to remove him for his Iroquois foster parents.[1]

White children were not unhappy among the Indians.

She turned questioningly towards the English. Mistress Corwin sat clutching her son passionately to her, realizing that his fate hung in the balance, while the others made it obvious that in the present circumstances the fate of the little Turner boy was a matter of relative indifference to them. Had the Reverend Patridge been fully conscious, he might well have protested in the name of the child's eternal salvation, but was still in a dazed condition.

It was better that the orphan boy should go rather than the Corwins' boy should be snatched from them, as the whole family had, by good fortune, been saved.

'Give the boy to him,' Angélique said softly to Cantor.

Realizing that he had prevailed, the redskin cut a few capers and made a great show of gratitude.

Then he held out his great hands and gently picked

[1] See *The Countess Angélique.*

up the child who looked fearlessly up into the gaudily painted face that loomed over him.

Delighted at having obtained what he had set his heart on, a white child for his wigwam, the brave took his leave of them, and, after exchanging a few words with his companions went off, lovingly clasping the heretic child against his bear-tooth necklace and his crucifix, feeling that he had saved him from the barbarities of his own people and that he would teach him the true way of life of the True Men.

Cantor related how, after leaving them to search for Maupertuis and the horses, he had noticed some suspicious-looking shapes moving between the trees.

Pursued by some of the braves, he had only succeeded in shaking them off by leading them a considerable distance in the direction of the plateau.

Returning a long way round, he had heard the sound of the battle, and had begun to approach the village with the utmost care, as he had no intention of allowing himself to be used as a hostage by falling into the hands of the Canadians.

Thus it was that he had witnessed the departure of the English captives northwards, and not seeing his mother among them, had deduced that she had managed to make her escape.

'Did it not occur to you that I might have had my throat cut or been scalped?'

'Oh, no!' Cantor replied, as if the thought had never crossed his head.

He had wandered round the burning ruins of Brunswick village and had encountered Three-Fingers from Trois Rivières, from whom he had learned that Madame de Peyrac was safe and heading in the direction of the Bay of Sagadahoc, with a handful of survivors.

The incident with the child seemed to have proved that for the present anyway the Indians were allowing Angélique a certain latitude when it came to making decisions that concerned them all. However odd the situation might be only a few hours after their assault on the English village, it was perfectly consistent with the fickle mentality of the redskins.

Through sheer force of personality Angélique had

taken them off in a different direction from that intended, and they had almost begun to forget why they had been fighting the previous day, what they were doing here with her and a handful of stupid Englishmen, and were now concerned only to know how this adventure on which she had launched them would turn out.

Piksarett nevertheless saw fit to recall certain essential principles.

'Don't forget that you are my prisoner,' he broke in, pointing his finger at the nape of Angélique's neck.

'I know, I know, I have already told you that I accept that. Am I in any way preventing you from staying close to me? Ask your companions if they think I look like a prisoner trying to escape?'

Perplexed by the subtlety of her argument in which he sensed there was something fishy but also comical, Piksarett leaned his head on one side in order to think better and his slanting eyes sparkled with delight while his two companions noisily made known their opinions to him.

'In Gouldsboro you will even be able to sell me back to my own husband,' Angélique explained. 'He is a very wealthy man and I am sure that he will not hesitate to deal generously with you. At least, I hope not,' she went on, letting her face fall suddenly, to the great amusement of the three Indians.

At the idea that Angélique's husband might be obliged to buy back his own wife their mirth knew no bounds.

There certainly was much entertainment to be had from following the white woman from the Upper Kennebec and the English people she had taken in tow.

It was a well-known fact that no animal exceeded the Yenngli (the English) in clumsiness, and these particular Yenngli made even more clumsy than usual through fear and their wounds, floundered along, sprawling on the ground at almost every step, and capsized canoes on the slightest provocation.

'Oh! These Yenngli! They will make us die of laughter,' the Indians kept on saying, going into contortions of mirth. Then, to make clear that they were the masters, they would suddenly add:

'Get along with you! Go on! Walk, you English! You

111

have killed our missionaries, burned our huts, jeered at our beliefs. Unless you are baptized by the Black Robes, you are nothing to us, not even palefaces, although their pagan ancestors were gods!'

Kept on the move by all this chatter, the wretched party reached the Bay of Sagadahoc two days later at the meeting-point of the mouths of the Androscoggin and the Kennebec.

The mist blotted out the horizon of the estuary but, mingling with the sea fog from the shore, they could still smell a suspicious whiff of fire.

Angélique climbed briskly up a small hill. There was not a sail in sight. She could see no trace of a ship on the grey horizon.

Angélique knew instinctively that the bay was deserted. No vessel was lying out there at anchor keeping a lookout for signs of a human presence on the shore, before coming in to take them on board.

There was no sign of the *Rochelais*, a small yacht flying a red pennant, with Le Gall waiting to welcome her on board, or even Joffrey!

No familiar presence. No one at the agreed rendezvous.

A thin drizzle had begun to fall, and Angélique leaned against the trunk of a pine tree. The whole place smelled of death, of the wilderness. On her left, she saw a billowing mushroom cloud of black smoke rising into the sky; it came from the direction of Sheepscot, an English settlement she had been told lay at the mouth of the Androscoggin, where she had intended to leave the survivors of Brunswick village before going on board the *Rochelais*.

But it now looked as if Sheepscot too had been burned down and no longer existed.

An overwhelming feeling of distress swept over Angélique and she felt her strength ebbing away. She turned round and saw that Piksarett was observing her. She must not show him that she was frightened. But she could not go on.

'They are not there,' she told him, almost despairingly.

'Whom were you expecting?'

Then she explained that her husband, the lord of Wapassou and Gouldsboro, should have been there with

112

a ship to meet them. He would have taken them all to Gouldsboro, where he, Piksarett, would have been given the most beautiful beads on the earth, and would have drunk the very best firewater in the world. . . .

The redskin shook his head sadly and seemed genuinely to share her disappointment and anxiety. He looked around him uneasily.

Meanwhile Cantor and the English were climbing the hill more slowly, followed by the other two Indians.

They sat down wearily under the pine-trees to shelter from the rain, and Angélique explained the situation to them. The three Indians began an excited discussion.

'They say that the Sheepscot Indians are their worst enemies,' Angélique explained to the English people. 'They come from the north they are Wonolancets.'

She was not surprised, knowing that Indians were perpetually at war among themselves, which meant that if they strayed only a short distance from home, they could find themselves in enemy territory where they risked their lives unless they were in large numbers and armed.

'It makes no difference,' said Stoughton gloomily, 'whether they are Sheepscot or Wonolancets, it is all the same to us. They can scalp us just the same. Why have we bothered to come as far as this? We shall all be dead soon.'

The silent coastline seemed to conceal a hidden menace. From behind every curtain of trees, every promontory, they expected to see Indians rush out with raised tomahawks, and now Piksarett and his men seemed just as ill at ease as their prisoners.

Angélique made an effort to get on top of her fear. 'No! No! This time, I am not going to give way,' she said, clenching her fists, not quite sure whom it was she was defying.

First of all, she decided, they must leave this stretch of the coast, where the Indian war was bursting into open flames again and attempt at all costs to reach Gouldsboro. There might be other villages farther along and other boats available.

Gouldsboro! Joffrey de Peyrac's territory. Their own domain! Their refuge. But Gouldsboro was so far away!

There was not a single sail in the estuary.

A few hours earlier, not yet twenty-four hours back, old Sarah Williams had taken Angélique's face in her hands and had said to her: 'America! America! You must save it!'

This had been her last message, a trifle wild, perhaps, for death had already been there, lurking in the bushes, about to strike her down. Was it the same kind of anxiety that Angélique felt now as the desolate evening closed in on them with the scent of seaweed, mist, and slaughter?

'Hi!' said Piksarett, laying a hand upon her shoulder.

And he pointed to two human shapes climbing up the slope from the shore.

She had a moment of hope but then saw, from his pointed hat, that it was the old medicine-man John Shapleigh and his Indian.

They all ran to meet him to see if he had any news, and he told them that he had just come from the beach, and that over yonder the Indians had burned everything. A ship? Had there been a ship? No.

Those inhabitants who had escaped scalping or being taken prisoner had taken refuge among the islands in their boats.

Seeing the despair of the unfortunate refugees from Brunswick-Falls, finally, not without great hesitation and many grimaces, and also because Angélique sought his advice, he suggested that he might lead them to a hut he owned about ten miles away on Casco Bay, where they could rest and be cared for.

In spite of the discomfort of spending a misty night in the open, most of them, including Angélique herself, felt hesitant to leave the agreed meeting place. The ship from Gouldsboro might have been delayed, and might well turn up in a few hours' time, or at dawn on the following morning.

The matter was settled by the sudden appearance of a group of about ten Sheepscot Indians at the edge of the wood.

As if by magic. Piksarett and his braves melted from sight. Angélique wondered whether she had exchanged one Indian escort for another less amenable, but fortunately Shapleigh and his companion were on good terms with the newcomers. Old Shapleigh, a medicine-man accepted as on a par with their best jugglers, was greatly respected in the region where he had been practising for over thirty years. His influence with the Indians enabled him to extend his protection to Angélique and her companions, and the Sheepscot Indians were even so obliging as to suggest that they might watch out for the possible arrival of any ships at this point of the coast. They carefully noted the description of the *Rochelais* and promised, should they see it, to direct it on to Maquoit Point where old Shapleigh had his cabin.

CHAPTER 18

JOFFREY DE PEYRAC gave a start of surprise.

'What? What did you say?'

He had just been informed that Madame de Peyrac had set off without him for the village of Brunswick-Falls with her son to take the little English girl back to her family.

This piece of information had been given him quite casually by Jacques Vignot, who had joined the Count on Cape Small, near Popham, where he had gone some two days earlier with Baron Saint-Castine.

Packing-cases containing wares for barter, that had been held up for lack of ships to transport them, had just arrived from Houssnock, escorted by the carpenter and one soldier.

'But which day was it that Madame La Comtesse took this strange decision?'

'Just a few hours after your own departure, Sir, the very same day. . . .'

'Did she not receive my message telling her that I might be away for several days and asking her to wait patiently for me at the Dutchman's trading-post?'

The two men did not know. What a reckless thing to have done! thought Peyrac. With all these rumours of war about. The Dutchman's post was by way of being a fortified encampment, where she would have run no risk. But to set off into the interior of the country, almost unescorted. . . .

'With whom did they go?'

'With the two Maupertuis.'

'What an extraordinary idea! She must have been crazy!' he exclaimed in anger.

He swore at Angélique inwardly, finding it hard to overcome a profound sense of anxiety about her that had suddenly swept over him.

She must be crazy, she must indeed! It was inconceivable. She had behaved completely irresponsibly! When he saw her again, he would have some pretty hard things to say to her, for he must make her understand that in spite of their privileged position the region would not be safe for a long time to come, especially to the west of the Kennebec.

He began to calculate. Three days had elapsed since he himself had set off towards the coast and Angélique, apparently at the same moment, had set off for the frontier town. . . . But where could she possibly be now?

It was raining, and mist hung over the bay, loud with the murmur of the rising tides as its swift-flowing currents swept around the half-submerged islands.

It was on account of these equinoxial tides that many of the Europeans and Indians who should have come to the rendezvous by way of the sea, had been delayed.

The great Tarratine chief Mateconando wanted everybody to be present, so while they waited they had begun their preliminary discussions. On the Sunday, Baron Saint-Castine's chaplain, a Recollect Friar with a thick beard and a face even more tanned than that of a pirate, had said Mass.

Then at last on the Tuesday, that same morning, the entire population of what was known more precisely, amid the myriad convolutions of the coastline, as the lesser gulf of Maine, had met together in one spot. The last of the packing-cases of presents had just arrived and the ceremony was about to begin.

It was then that Peyrac heard of Angélique's escapade.

Where would she be by now? Had she gone back to Houssnock? Or had she, in accordance with the plan they had previously discussed, travelled down the Androscoggin, one of the branches of the Kennebec estuary, to Merry Meeting Bay where Corentin Le Gall was to wait for them with the *Rochelais?*

In his uncertainty, he decided to send for his equerry Yann le Couennec.

He instructed him first to take a good meal, then to check the condition of his weapons and his shoes and to prepare himself to set off post haste.

Then he sat down and scribbled a brief note while one of the Spanish soldiers of his guard deferentially held his inkhorn for him.

When Yann presented himself ready to set off, he handed him the note but added his own special instructions.

If Yann found Madame de Peyrac at the Dutchman's trading-post, they should all pack up and join him here. If, on the other hand, she had not yet returned from Brunswick-Falls, he, Yann, should set off there himself, and should find Madame de Peyrac at all costs, wherever she was, and bring her back to Gouldsboro by the quickest route.

With these strict instructions, the man set off. Peyrac was obliged to make a considerable effort to put out of his mind his acute anxiety about Angélique, and to concentrate his full attention on the meeting which was about to take place; for, at the summons of Baron Saint-Castine, all these little people had come from far off, often at no small danger, just to meet him.

In addition to the Indians from all the principal tribes of the area, a few scattered white men, ignoring their differences of nationality or the antagonisms of their countries of origin, had decided to come together and hold council around the French nobleman from Gouldsboro.

There were English traders from Pemaquid, from Croton, from Oyster River, Wiscasset, Thomaston, Woolwich, Saint George, Nevagan, in all about twenty Englishmen who traded in small, scattered outposts along the fiords of Muscongus Bay, the Damariscotta river and the mouth of the Kennebec. And their neighbouring enemies had also come, with whom, when they were not actually killing one another, they would exchange household goods and milk from a few rare cows: Frenchmen from Acadia, settlers and fishermen, a Dumaresque or a Galatin from Swans Island, where they bred sheep, grew flowers and potatoes side by side with the direct descendants of Adam Winthrop from Boston, Dutchmen sent over by Campden and even an elderly, hoary Scot from Monhegan Island, the proud Island of the Sea with its granite cliffs, the most isolated of the whole bay—he was a MacGregor who had come over with his three sons and whose tartan plaids floated across there in the gusty wind at the far end of the headland.

The State of Massachusetts had expressly recommended that the English and the Dutch should get in touch with Count Peyrac if one day they were to find that they needed protection in their far-flung outposts along this wild coast of Maine, infested as it was with Frenchmen and bloodthirsty Indians, an area people must be a bit mad to venture into.

The Acadians in their turn followed the lead of Baron Saint-Castine.

The Scots did exactly as they fancied.

In brief, there were all sorts there.

Once again, as he thought of Angélique, Peyrac cursed women, whose caprices, often charming but more often than not ill-timed, brought nothing but trouble and complications to men's undertakings.

Then, pulling himself together, he went to meet his guests, surrounded by his Spanish guards in their steel breastplates and morions.

Baron Saint-Castine accompanied him, and the great chief Mateconando came towards him in his most magnificent robe of doeskin embroidered with shells and porcupine quills. His long oily hair, greased with seal oil, was surmounted by a flat, round hat of black satin with a narrow brim, decorated with a white ostrich feather that must have been at least a hundred years old.

One of his ancestors had been given this feather by Verrazano himself, the Florentine explorer, in the service of the French King Francis I. When he had passed this way with his one-hundred-and-fifty-ton ship, he had been one of the first to name this land Arcadie on account of

118

the beauty of its trees. The name, in a slightly altered form, had subsequently been retained.

Fixed to this sixteenth-century nobleman's hat, the lily-white ostrich feather, showing only traces of yellow, bore witness to the care with which the Indians, dirty and careless in their habits as they generally were, had preserved this relic.

The greatest of all chieftains wore it only on the most solemn occasions.

Joffrey de Peyrac gave the Tarratine chief a damascene sword of gold and silver, some decorated cases of razors, scissors and knives, and ten strings of shiny blue glass beads each about six feet long, in exchange for which the Indian presented him with some mother-of-pearl shells and a handful of amethysts, a symbolic gesture of friendship.

'I know you have no greed for furs, and seek only for our alliance.'

'You see,' Saint-Castine had explained to Peyrac, 'I want my Indians to stop fighting, otherwise in a few decades they will have been wiped out.'

The great Tarratine chieftain laid an affectionate hand on Baron Saint-Castine and looked at him with admiration.

Saint-Castine was a man of average height, perhaps even on the short side; but was incredibly strong, agile, hardy, quick-witted and sensitive, and he had won the devotion of all the coastal tribes.

'I shall make him my son-in-law,' Mateconando confided in Peyrac, 'and later on he will succeed me as chief of the Etchemins and the Mic-Macs.'

CHAPTER 19

'ANGÉLIQUE! . . . Pray heaven nothing has happened to her! I should have taken her with me. Saint-Castine caught me unprepared. I ought never to leave her on her own, by day or by night, not for a moment. . . . My precious, my crazy love. . . . She has been independent for too long. As soon as she is left alone, she feels the need to be free again. . . . I must make her understand the dangers that surround us. I shall have to be stern this time. . . . But now I must put aside these worries. . . . I must concentrate my mind. . . . I must not disappoint all these people who have come to meet me. I realize what young Saint-Castine is asking me in their name. What a remarkable lad! He sees things as they are, but he knows his limits. . . . What is he asking of me? To perform a task which is surely impracticable . . . to follow a path beset with pitfalls. . . .'

Such were Count Peyrac's thoughts as he sat on the thick grass in front of the bark hut that had been erected for him.

Once all the ceremonial, the feasting and smoking were over, he had left the others, saying that he wished to be alone for a few hours, and had sat smoking, staring out at the headland on which an occasional larger wave sent up a white plume of foam.

The ocean battered the tree-clad shore, sending clouds of spray among the fir trees, the cedars, the oaks and the giant copper beeches, and occasionally, when the wind changed, there came blowing from the undergrowth a sweet smell of hyacinth and wild strawberries.

Joffrey de Peyrac beckoned to Juan Fernandez, the tall hidalgo who commanded his guard, and asked him to fetch the French baron, feeling that he would prefer to chat with the enthusiastic Gascon on his favourite topic rather than remain alone; for the thought of Angélique kept on coming back to his mind with a nagging sense of apprehension which prevented him from arriving at any useful conclusion.

Baron Saint-Castine joined him with alacrity and sat down beside him. In accordance with the traditions of the country he drew out his pipe from the folds of his cloak and began to smoke too. Then he started to talk, but the conversation was almost entirely a monologue. presenting his whole world, with its dreams, its projects and its perils. . . .

The rain had stopped, but the mist still hung about and the camp fires seemed to tremble through it like huge red orchids in full bloom, stretching out along the coast, and each light was doubled by a halo.

As dusk fell the roar of the sea grew deeper, mingling with the cry of birds flocking up the estuary. They were Jaeger gulls, with long brown wings like those of swallows, and predatory beaks.

'There must have been a storm at sea,' the baron said as his eyes followed their flight. 'Those little pirates only seek shelter on land when the sea is too stormy for them to settle on it.'

He took a deep breath and, smelling the fragrance from the forest, heaved a deep sigh. Summer was drawing near, and in those parts summer meant trouble of the very worst kind.

'This is the time of year when the cod-fishing boats of all nations invade our shores,' he said, 'along with buccaneers from Santo Domingo. A plague upon the thieves! They run less risk by holding up our poor ships bringing provisions over from France to our settlements in Acadia than they do by attacking the Spaniards. And God only knows there are few enough of these ships, and yet they still have to be seized under our very noses. A filthy breed, these Jamaican filibusters!'

'Gold Beard?'

'I have not encountered him yet.'

'I think I heard talk of him when I was in the Caribbean,' Peyrac went on, puckering his brow in an effort to remember. 'On my last trip out there. The gentlemen of fortune spoke of him as a good sailor, and a leader of men. . . . He would have done better to remain in the West Indies.'

'Rumour has it that he is a French pirate who has recently acquired letters of marque in France from some rich society founded for the purpose of fighting French Huguenots wherever encountered. That would explain his attack upon your people at Gouldsboro, and it also sounds like the sort of thing our administration in Paris would do. The last time I was over there I saw that advancement depended more and more on religious zeal, which is making our task in Acadia particularly complicated. . . .'

'Do you mean that people ought to remember that the original founders were Protestants?'

'And that the most Catholic Champlain was originally only cartographer to Pierre de Gaust, Lord of Monts, a notorious Huguenot.'

They exchanged smiles, delighted to feel that they understood one another as readily in all matters.

'That was a long time ago,' said Saint-Castine.

'And it's growing longer and longer. . . . I am interested in what you have to tell me, Baron, and am beginning to understand why this particular pirate should be so set on attacking Gouldsboro in spite of its well hidden position. If this is some holy mission of his, how did he hear about Gouldsboro?'

'News travels fast. In these parts there are not more than three Frenchmen in every hundred leagues, but at least one of them will be a spy for the King . . . and the Jesuits.'

'Be careful, my boy.'

'You laugh? But it doesn't make me laugh. I want to live in peace here with my Etchemins and my Mic-Macs. Those people from Paris and the privateers in their pay have no right to come to these parts. They don't belong to the Bay.

'The Bay? Give me the Basques any day, who hunt whales, or the fishermen from Saint-Malo who make our coasts stink with their dried cod. They at least have a right to be in Acadia. They were coming here five hundred years ago. . . . But their brandy and their orgies with the Indian girls. . . . What a disaster!. . . . On the whole I think I even prefer the ships that come up from Boston, for at least we can barter with them for hardware and cloth. But there are too many of them, far too many of their ships.'

He made a sweeping gesture that encompassed the whole horizon.

'Hundreds of them . . . hundreds of English ships, everywhere, everywhere. Well armed, well equipped. And there's Salem down there, their great drying centre, and their pitch, their tar, their turpentine, their raw hides, and their whalebone and seal and whale-oil— eighty to a hundred thousand hundredweight of oil a year they make—it stinks, but it pays. And I'm expected to hold on to French Acadia . . . to keep it for the King with my four cannons, my wooden fortress that measures sixty feet by twenty, and to compete with the English on the fishing grounds with my fifteen longboats. . . .'

'But you are not as poor as all that,' said Peyrac. 'They say that you are doing very well in the fur trade.'

'Oh yes, I am already well off myself, that I grant. But that is my business, and the reason why I want to be rich is to help my Indians, to make them more stable, to help them to prosper. The Etchemins make up the largest block of my tribes but I also have Mic-Macs of the Tarratine tribe. They are Souriquois of Canada, the same as those that inhabit Casco Bay, related to the Mohicans. I can speak all their dialects, five or six— Etchemins, Wawenoks, Penebscots, Kanibas, Tarratines, they're my men, the best of all the Abenakis. And it's on their account that I want to be rich, in order to care for them, to civilize them and protect them. . . . Yes, protect them, crazy, splendid fighters that they are!'

He puffed away for a while at his pipe, then once more stretched his arm out towards the foam-fringed darkness, towards the west.

'Now, out there, in Casco Bay, I own an island which I wrested from the English not long ago. And not just to get rid of them, but because there was a legend attached to the island. It lies near the mouth of the Presumpscot near Portland, towards the south of Casco Bay, and from time immemorial has been regarded by the Mohicans, the Souriquois and the Etchemins as the site of an ancient paradise, for they have a saying which goes: "If you have once slept on that island, you will never be the same man again." But it had been in the hands of English farmers for several generations, and the Indians were unhappy not to be able to meet there to hold their ancestral feasts, when the heat of August makes the inland areas intolerable. So I took it and handed it over to the Indians.

'What joy! What delight! What celebrations we had! But if peace is not maintained, what is the point of all these efforts?'

'Do you think that peace is in danger?'

'Not only do I think so, I am certain of it. And that is why I was in such a hurry for you to meet Mateconando. Yes, since the Treaty of Breda things have been going more or less all right. But the peace is about to be broken. Father d'Orgeval, that paladin of the days of yore, has mobilized the Abenakis of the north and west who are men of the forest and almost as formidable as the Iroquois. And as for the great Piksarett, their chief, the most devout Christian ever produced by a missionary, who can be expected to cope with him? He is terrible! . . . Monsieur de Peyrac, war is imminent.

'Father d'Orgeval wants war and he has prepared well for it. I am sure that he came here with orders and directives from the King of France himself, to rekindle the conflict against the English. This would suit our sovereign, it appears, and one must admit that this Jesuit is the most formidable politician who has yet set foot in these lands. I know that he has sent one of his priests, Father Maraicher de Vernon, on a secret mission to New England, right down to Maryland, to seek some pretext to break the truce, and no doubt Father d'Orgeval is only awaiting his return before unleashing his offensive. A short while ago I received a visit from Father de Guérande who had come to ask me to join their crusade with my friendly tribes. I dodged giving a straight answer. I know I am a French nobleman, an officer, and a fighting man, but . . .'

He suddenly closed his eyes as if in pain.

'I can't bear to see any more of it.'

'Of what?'

'The holocaust, the slaughter, the endless massacre of my brothers, the unforgivable extinction of their race.'

When Saint-Castine spoke of his brothers Peyrac knew that he was referring to the Indians.

'You see, it is so easy to involve them in war: they are so quickly roused and so easy to deceive. You know as I do, six, that the strongest of all passions among the redskins is an implacable hatred of their enemies and above all of their friend's enemies—that is their code of honour. It is not in their nature to live peaceably, but I have seen too many die already of those I loved, and to what end?

'You can understand what I can tell no one else. . . .

'We are too far from the sun here. You understand what I mean? We cannot, from this distance, do anything to enlighten the King. We are forgotten, we are alone. The Administration only remembers us when the time comes to collect its dividends on fur trading or to ask us to send troops against the English on behalf of the Jesuits and their holy wars. But it is not true that we belong to France. No one belongs to anyone out here in Acadia. All these islands, these peninsulas, all these hidden coves are inhabited by free men. Whether French, English, Dutch, Scandinavian, fishermen or traders, we are all in the same boat—furs and cod, barter and coastal trade. We are the people of Frenchman Bay, the people of the Atlantic coast . . . we share the same interests, and the same needs. We ought to come together under your aegis!'

'Why mine?'

'Because there is only you,' Saint-Castine replied with ardour. 'You alone are strong, invulnerable, you are with everyone and yet remain detached. How shall I put it? We know you are friendly with the English, and yet I am certain that, were you to go to Quebec, you would have all the fine people there eating out of your hand. And even. . . . You see, we Canadians are no doubt brave and shrewd, but we lack something that you possess— political judgment. Face to face with a man like Father d'Orgeval we count for little. You alone can stand up to him.'

'The Jesuits are a very powerful order, the most powerful of all, in fact,' Peyrac replied in tones devoid of emotion.

'But . . . so are you!'

Joffrey de Peyrac turned his head to look at his companion. His thin, youthful face was dominated by his flashing eyes ringed with blue that gave him a slightly effeminate look, which possibly explained why he was thought to look like an Indian; for there is sometimes something sexually ambiguous in the lines of their beardless faces. In his case, it was the refinement of an ancient unconquerable race, made up of a mixture of Iberians and Moors, and, perhaps of remote Asiatic ancestors. The same kind of mixed blood flowed in Peyrac's veins too, and he owed his height, unusual in a Gascon, to his mother's English ancestry.

Baron Saint-Castine looked anxiously at the older man. 'We are ready to rally beneath your standard, Monsieur de Peyrac. . . .'

Peyrac went on looking at him, summing him up as if he did not hear what he said. So a whole nation was looking to him, finding its expression in this young voice with the musical lilt of the accent of Guyenne, their native province.

'Believe me, believe me,' the voice repeated, 'if the fighting continues and constantly flares up anew, it will be the destruction of us all.'

'And the first to go down will be the most vulnerable, our Indians, our friends, our brothers, our relatives . . . yes, our relatives, for every man here in Acadia has a father-in-law, brothers-in-law, sisters-in-law, or cousins out there in the forest. We are tied to them by the ties of the blood of the Indian women we have loved and married. And I myself am soon to marry Matilda, my little Indian princess. What a treasure the child is, Monsieur. . . .

'But they will all die unless we protect them from their own warlike impulses. For one day the English will grow tired of being endlessly slaughtered. The English along our coasts certainly don't like war, and they are slow to be excited. The one thing they hate is sin, and it will take many more scalps slung from the belts of the Abenakis before they are persuaded to take up arms. But then, God protect us! They are slow to move but when once they make up their minds to it they fight as they till the ground . . . heavily, methodically, without passion or hatred, let me tell you, but as if it were a duty, a religious duty. They will sweep clean the land the Lord has given them. They will exterminate my Etchemins and my Souriquois to the last man, just as they exterminated the Pequots forty years ago and the Narragansetts not long since . . . to the last man, I tell you, to the very last man!'

He was almost shouting.

'Naturally I have tried to explain all this to the people in Quebec, but I've had enough of that! They say that

126

the English are cowards and that we must hurl them
into the sea, and sweep the American coastline clear of
all its heretical, protestant vermin. . . . This may be true.
The English are cowards, but they are a tenacious people
and thirty times as numerous as we Canadians; fear can
make them terrible, treacherous and cunning . . . I know
these Englishmen, I have had plenty to do with them, I
have scalped enough of them in battle. No, no one can
reproach me for having been a bad French officer, I
have more than a hundred English scalps drying on the
walls of my fortress at Pentagouet, scalps that I collected, together with my Indians, in fights with the
settlements along the Bay. Two years ago we almost
reached Boston: if only our King had sent us just one
warship, we could have conquered that. But he does
absolutely nothing to help "his" French Acadia. . . .'

He stopped, quite out of breath.

Then he continued, pleading touchingly:

'You will help, won't you, Monsieur? You will help
me to save my Indians?'

Count Peyrac had leaned his head on his hand, hiding
his eyes.

It seemed to him that never had he wished so acutely
for Angélique's presence beside him.

If only she were here! If only he could feel her close
to him. A gentle, merciful feminine presence, silent, deeply silent as she knew so well how to be on occasion, in a
subtle mysterious way that was hers and hers alone.

How understanding was her silence! How compassionate, and shrewd too. The very presence of his wife
seemed to atone for every crime and every horror that
had been mentioned.

He raised his head, looking destiny straight in the
eye.

'All right!' he said. 'I will help you.'

CHAPTER 20

THE FOG hung so thickly over the estuary that the piercing cries of the gulls were muffled, and came to them

through the swirling mists like the uneasy wailing of souls in torment.

On his way back to Houssnock, Joffrey de Peyrac was about to part company with Saint-Castine, when they caught sight of a ship sailing ghost-like up the Kennebec. Driven indolently along by a sluggish wind, the vessel passed close to them with a silky whispering sound. She was a small trader or privateer of about one hundred and twenty to one hundred and fifty tons and her mainmast, from which flew an orange-coloured pennant, was scarcely taller than the pointed tops of the ancient oaks that lined the river bank. She slid past and disappeared like a dream, but a little later, through the mist, they heard the noise of an anchor chain being paid out. The ship was heaving to, and someone made his way towards them along the roughly marked path beside the water. It was a sailor wearing a red-and-white striped jersey and a belt with a cutlass.

'Would one of you gentlemen be Monsieur de Peyrac?'

'I am.'

The sailor pushed his woollen cap back a little in a cursory gesture of greeting.

'A message for you from a vessel we spoke to in the bay off Seguin Island just before we entered the Dresden current.

'If we happen to meet you, they said, it was a yacht called the *Rochelais*. Madame de Peyrac was on board and sent a message that she was joining your Lordship at Gouldsboro.'

'Ah good,' Peyrac exclaimed, greatly relieved. 'When did this happen?'

'Yesterday, just before sundown.'

It was now Wednesday. So, he told himself, Angélique must have successfully completed her rash expedition to Brunswick-Falls. The *Rochelais,* which had been cruising in those waters, must have taken her on board, and no doubt there were special reasons connected with cargo or winds that had obliged the captain, Corentin Le Gall, to set off again.

Reassured about the fate of his wife and son, the Count was no longer worried about his own possible delay. He would find some other means to make his way swiftly to his lands at Gouldsboro. Not for a moment did he suspect the man they had met of lying, for such deceit is a rare thing among seafaring men.

'Come back via Pentagouet with me,' Baron Saint-Castine suggested. 'The land route is probably still muddy and cluttered with branches snapped off by the thaw, but it will still be quicker than going by sea, if your choice is between waiting for a good ship or making do with the boats you left at Houssnock, which would certainly take their time.'

'A good idea,' Peyrac agreed. 'Hi there, you!'

He called out to the sailor, whose outline was beginning to disappear into the mist.

'Here's something for you,' Peyrac said, handing him a fistful of pearls.

The sailor gave a start and stared open-mouthed at Peyrac.

'Pink pearls, "lambis" pearls. From the Caribbean. . . .'

'Yes. I expect you will find a use for them. They don't come most people's way.'

The man seemed embarrassed by the magnificence of the gift.

'Thank you, my lord,' he stammered at last. Then he gave several quick little bows and, still looking at Peyrac, suddenly began to look frightened, and took his leave of them as if taking flight.

And this was why, when Angélique reached the coast at Sabadahoc, she had found the bay deserted.

CHAPTER 21

GEORGE SHAPLEIGH's home on Maquoit Bay was nothing more than a decrepit long-and-bark cabin, battered by the wind and standing on the tip of a promontory with leaning cedar trees.

The fence enclosing the property scarcely merited the name of palisade, but Angélique and her English companions had taken nearly a day to cover the three leagues that separated the Androscoggin river from this long narrow peninsula, and the proffered shelter was welcome.

129

A fat old Indian woman who lived there and was perhaps the mother of the Indian accompanying the old medicine man gave them some pumpkin mash to eat, followed by clams, large shellfish with delicious, pinkish flesh, of a similar variety to those found in Brittany. The hut also contained large quantities of herbal remedies—powders, herbs and balms, in boxes made of bark—which enabled Angélique to set about the task of treating the sick and wounded.

Although the woods had been spangled with the silvery flowers of the trientala, the star-flower, growing thick amid the tender grass, and in spite of the gentle cooing of doves and wood-pigeons, the march had tried them sorely. The poor English had had to be sustained and encouraged, for they were worn out, jaded, wounded and terrified. While they feared an encounter with evil spirits as they crossed the marshlands, Angélique was far more anxious about the possibility of suddenly running into more shrieking painted savages with raised hatchets.

Twenty corpses stretched out in a flower-strewn valley, their skulls covered in blood, left to the circling birds of prey, would not mean much in that spring when almost three thousand warriors set out to attack the New England settlements, devastated more than fifty of them and massacred several hundred settlers. . . .

Fields of iridescent flowers, downy dogwood, coral-red columbines twisting on their slender stems in the shade of the monumental oaks, for centuries to come the banks of the lovely Androscoggin river would tell their terrible tale.

Here they had reached the sea, and beyond the headland lay Casco Bay with its innumerable islands.

The sea crept in everywhere, in among the rocks and the trees, and they could smell the tang of salt and seaweed in the brisk wind while the barking of seals along the beaches mingled with the deep roar of the surf.

Around the log hut was a small field planted with maize, pumpkins and beans, and at the edge of the cliff, beneath a clump of stocky willow trees some beehives were beginning to come to life.

For two days they waited for sight of a sail. Then a

130

Sheepscot Indian, a friend of Shapleigh's, who came by, said that no paleface ship had been sighted in the direction of Sabadahoc.

What was the *Rochelais* doing? Where was Joffrey? Angélique was beginning to grow impatient, and in her mind's eye she began to envisage a horde of Abenakis to the east of the Kennebec, swarming down towards Gouldsboro.

What if Baron Saint-Castine had lured Joffrey de Peyrac into a trap? No, that was impossible. Joffrey would have suspected something. . . . But had not her own instinct failed her and found her strangely off guard? Had she not made fun of poor Adhemar when he cried out in despair 'They are preparing their war cauldrons! Who are they going to kill?'

Adhemar seemed to have completely taken leave of his senses. He mumbled prayers over his rosary beads and stared about him with a lost look. And once again, he was right. On this solitary headland in this remote region, they were as isolated and as abandoned as if they had been on a desert island, yet their isolation did not entirely protect them from prowling savages who took a fancy to their scalps.

At any other time, the able-bodied among them might well have attempted to make their way on foot to some other settlement along the English coast of Maine, which was dotted with small villages, and there find a ship. But at that time, most of these wooden hamlets were in flames, and to head west would have been tantamount to walking straight towards the redskin knives. It was better to keep clear, to let themselves be forgotten, wretched pale-skinned creatures stranded on this horrible, cruel coast of a wild unruly continent. At least they had a roof over their heads, medicines for the sick, vegetables, shell-fish and sea foods to feed their hunger, and a semblance of a fence to give them the illusion of safety. But their total lack of weapons worried Angélique; for, apart from old Shapleigh's blunderbuss with its limited supply of ammunition, all they had was Adhemar's musket with neither gunpowder nor bullets, a few cutlasses and their personal knives.

The sun had come out again, and Angélique entrusted

Cantor with the task of watching the horizon for any sail which might be seen playing hide-and-seek among the islands, and which might possibly come close enough to them for them to be able to send some signal. But every ship they saw seemed to be heading in some other direction. With their white or brown sails billowing out over the brilliant blue waters, these vessels, totally unresponsive to any sound or gesture they might make, seemed from this great distance to behave in a human way and to show a degree of indifference that made their hearts ache.

In spite of his fear of the local tribes, Piksarett of the Abenakis had continued to keep his prisoners, as he still considered them, under intermittent surveillance. In fact he seemed rather to be looking after them, for during their trek down to the coast he had even put in an appearance to carry an exhausted child.

Then, when they were in the hut, he came and set down before them a calabash full of some wild root plants much appreciated by the English, who called them potatoes. Baked in hot ashes they were extremely tasty, less sugary than sweet potatoes or artichokes. He also brought them sweet smelling lichens and a huge salmon, which he grilled himself on a stick.

When the three savages appeared, with the giant Indian in the lead, the poor Brunswick-Falls folk started back hastily, for the Patsuiketts' belts were hung with drying scalps recently acquired from their relatives and friends. After exchanging a few words, Piksarett and his acolytes went off into the woods, but often when Angélique went outside to scan the horizon, she would see Piksarett and his two red companions on the other side of the fiord, perched in the treetops, watching something or other in the bay. They would wave to her and shout jokes, of which she only caught a mere scrap of phrases, but which she sensed were intended to be friendly.

One had to get used to the free and easy ways of the savages, and their rapidly changing moods, which had both a dangerous and a reassuring side, and one had to try to live with them as one might with wild animals, which can be tamed only by the ascendancy and force of character of the tamer. For the time being she had nothing to fear from them.

But should she once appear to falter, then indeed she would have everything to fear.

Piksarett had introduced her to his two braves, whose names were very easy to remember—Tenouienant, which means he-who-is-knowledgeable, he-who-is-skilled-in-business, and Ouaouenouroue, that is to say, he-who-is-as-cunning-as-a-dog-in-hunting.

On the whole she preferred to call them by their baptismal names, which they had told her with considerable pride—Michael and Jerome. These names, with their mild, pious associations, could scarcely have been more incongruous, applied to these men with painted faces—red encircling the left eye, symbol of the first wound, white around the other for clairvoyance, a dreadful black line across the forehead to frighten the enemy, a blue chin, the finger of the Great Spirit, and so on—surmounted and encircled by a wild bush of hair mingled with feathers, furs, rosary beads and medals.

Their bare chests tattooed and painted, their leather loincloths flapping in the wind often barefooted, smeared with grease, hung about with weapons, they would come towards her when she called them.

'Michael! Jerome!'

And she held in her laughter, suddenly touched at the sight of them.

Their language had a dreadfully difficult accent, which it was almost impossible to pick up, almost an English accent! It was precisely on account of his rather ridiculous title, Piksarett, chief of the Patsuiketts, that she had never managed to take him quite seriously. But, as he explained, even that was not the full story. Originally, on account of his happy nature he had been called Piouerlet, that is to say, he-who-understands-jokes, but his warlike exploits had caused his name to evolve towards Pikasou'rett, in other words, the terrible one, which the French pronounced Piksarett to make things easier.

So Piksarett it was!

Ever since the day when she had stood between him and the wounded Iroquois and had given him, in exchange for his enemy's life, her dawn-coloured cloak, the adventure of their strange friendship had begun, an alliance that supplied material for the gossip of the day, that startled, scandalized, disturbed and infuriated.

Angélique did not yet know the part that Piksarett would play in her life over the next few weeks, but she felt no fear of him.

He sometimes assumed a thoughtful expression and seemed to be replying to some unspoken question.

'Yes,' he would state, 'we had decided to deal with the Englishmen, but then the Frenchmen came back, and how could I disappoint those who had baptized me?'

Then, running his hand over his necklace of medallions and crosses, he went on:

'Baptism has been a good thing for us Wonolancets, whereas it was bad for the Hurons: they nearly all either died of smallpox or were massacred by the Iroquois. But we, we are Wonolancets, and that is different!'

Old Shapleigh talked a great deal to Angélique too. He had discovered how much she knew about plants, was only too happy to teach her more and argued with her when she did not share his particular beliefs. After examining the medicines she carried in her travelling bag, he reproached her for using belladonna, the devil's herb, because it had grown in the garden of Hecate.

On the other hand he was particularly fond of southernwood, 'a magnificent herb under the influence of Mercury and worthy of higher esteem than it receives.'

For the planets and their powers were also enclosed in these boxes, and he claimed that a piece of copper, a sprig of vervain and a dove were all 'Venusian'.

And about the blessed thistle he would say:

'That is a herb of Mars, who, under the sign of Aries, cures venereal diseases, out of antipathy for Venus who causes them. I sell a lot of it to seafaring men. They come and ask me for it under the pretext that they have plague on board, but I know what that means. . . .'

And then, suddenly becoming genuinely scientific once more, he would give a Latin name to almost every herb he knew, and among all his wizard spells at the bottom of an old chest, she found a copy of the *Herbatum virtutibus* of Aemilius Maces, and one of the remarkable *Regimen sanitatis salerno*—veritable treasures!

Two days passed thus. They were like shipwrecked people, uncertain what fate held in store for them.

Towards the south-west, when the air was clear, they could just make out the curving line of the coast, from which puffs of grey rose, slowly merging with the hazy atmosphere that hung over the bay, pink and blue and milky white, like fine procelain. . . .

The grey patches marked the location of fires kindled by Indian torches. . . .

Freeport, Yarmouth, all the neighbouring villages were in flames; Portland itself was threatened.

All that was far away, too far for them to descry the masses of people fleeing for their lives across the bay. Tall sails appeared and disappeared, like so many white wings mingled with those of the endlessly wheeling seagulls, cormorants and petrels.

There were so many birds that in spite of the dazzling June light, a sudden twilight would descend as thousands of wings swept in great waves across the sky, attracted this way and that by schools of cod, herring, tunny and mackerel, that had come to spawn in the waters of the great Massachusetts Bay which lies like a cornucopia open at one end to the Atlantic Ocean and closed at the other by the prosperous and terrible French Bay,[1] famous for its monstrous tides.

During their third day on Maquoit Point, Cantor said to his mother:

'If by tomorrow no ship or boat has cast anchor in this accursed place, I shall set off on foot, and follow the coast eastwards. If I can keep out of sight of the Indians and find a canoe here and there in which to cross channels and deltas, I should eventually reach Gouldsboro. By going alone, I shall attract less attention than if we travelled as a party.'

'Won't it take you days and days to complete an expediton of this kind?'

'I can walk as fast as any Indian.'

So she agreed to his plan, although she felt most ap-

[1] The present Bay of Fundy.

135

prehensive about his parting from them. She found comfort in the vigour of his youth, which had adapted itself to meet the unexpected contingencies of American life.

Something had to be done; they could not wait on indefinitely for some problematic help to turn up.

That evening, she continued to keep watch, aided by the brightness of the evening sky.

Screeching birds came to rest upon the waters in the estuaries of the many rivers. The soft, impalpable mist began to clear. Casco Bay was sinking to rest in dazzling serenity. The sea, flecked with gold, held up its island like jewels, refulgent with many-tinted gleams—burnt topaz, sulphur blue, jet black. There were three hundred and sixty-five of them, so it was said, as many as there were days in the year.

The brightness faded again. The gold lost its lustre. The sea turned chill and wan, and little by little the land and its meandering shores melted into impenetrable darkness. The smell of the bay rose towards them, borne on the harsh wind. The entire landscape seemed to be made of brass and bronze.

Over towards the east, at Harpswell Point, just after the sun had disappeared, Angélique glimpsed a ship. It looked as if made of gold as it was caught in the last rays of the setting sun. And then almost immediately she found she could see it no more.

'Did it have a giant shin-bone on its prow?' cried the old medicine-man. "I wager it was furling its sails, before returning to port. I know it. That was the ghost ship that appears at Harpswell Point whenever some calamity is about to befall him—or her—who sees it. And the port for which it is bound is—Death.'

'It was certainly not furling its sails,' rejoined Angélique crossly.

And young Cantor, seeing that she was upset by the old wizard's words, gave her a knowing wink by way of reassurance.

PART THREE
The Pirate Ship

CHAPTER 22

THE FOLLOWING morning very early, Angélique, being unable to sleep, went down among the rocks laid bare by low tide to gather shells. On a nearby beach the colony of seals, apparently in a state of high excitement, were giving vent to piercing cries that echoed round the coves.

Angélique went across to have a look at them, for normally they were peaceable animals. Clumsy and ungainly on land, their dark, glistening bodies looked delightfully supple when seen in the sparkling waters at sunset.

That morning, as she drew near, she discovered the cause of their unrest. Two or three of the seals lay dead, already shrouded by clouds of wheeling, screeching sea birds. They had been brutally bludgeoned to death, and their fellows, the giant bulls, lords of the beach, were trying angrily to drive off the greedy, feathered assailants.

As Angélique took in the scene she gave a start of fear, for the massacre was the work of human hands. MEN MUST HAVE BEEN HERE. . . .

And they were not Indians, for the latter hunted seals only during the month of January, in other words in the winter season.

Angélique gazed around the creek. A ship, probably the one which Shapleigh had called a ghost ship, must have moored there during the night in the misty darkness.

She climbed back up the slope.

The sun had not yet appeared, for it was hidden behind a bank of cloud on the horizon, but the sky was a pristine blue, pure and calm.

Then a tang came to her through the fresh air, the tang

139

of burning grasses, different from that of the smoke rising from the small stone chimney on the hut. Swift and light-footed, gliding instinctively behind the bushes and pine-trees, she made her way along the edge of the promontory that overhung the fiord.

The smell of smoke, the smoke of green wood and damp grass, was growing stronger.

Peering out from among the trees Angélique caught sight of the tip of a mast with a sail furled round it. A ship lay at anchor there, hidden by one of the many curves and bends in the long stretch of water that made its way inland. And the smoke rose up, lazily spreading out below where she stood, accompanied by a murmur of voices. Angélique lay down on the ground and crept forward to the edge of the cliff, but was unable to see those who had set up camp below her on the narrow strip of pebbles edged with seaweed. Only their voices appeared closer and she caught snatches of French and Portuguese spoken in rough coarse tones.

On the other hand, she could now see the whole of the ship which was, in fact, a mere sloop.

Back at the hut, she called the children inside. Now that they had recovered from the weariness of the march, they had begun to play with a little horsehair ball.

'There are men camped down at the creek,' she told Cantor. 'They have a boat which would take at least eight or ten of us, but I am not sure they would be generous enough to give us passage.'

She felt little faith in men who were capable of the needless slaughter of innocent animals which they did not even bother to pick up.

Cantor in his turn set off to take a look at the place Angélique pointed out to him and return saying that he had seen 'them', that there were five or six of them, no more, and that they belonged to the piratical rag, tag and bobtail that haunted the North American coastline during the summer in search of booty, no doubt less valuable but correspondingly less hard to acquire than that of the Spanish vessels.

'We need that boat,' Angélique insisted, 'if only to fetch help.'

She addressed her words mainly to Cantor and to Stoughton—the only other able-bodied man in any state to help her reach a decision.

The pastor was only half-conscious, suffering as he was from a high fever. Corwin was injured, and in great pain, and required all his powers of concentration to keep from swearing in the presence of the pastor. The two farm-hands, burly, taciturn men, were prepared to tackle anything requiring muscle but were useless when it came to offering advice. Old Shapleigh was dissociating himself from his guests, saying that he must leave them that evening or the following day to go off into the forest, as it would soon be the night when wild vervain must be picked.

And as for Adhemar, he has no sense of responsibility.

Only Stoughton remained, a farmer, who, though lacking in imagination, was courageous, and Cantor, son of a nobleman, whose short life had already been rich in experience. In her son, Angélique placed her trust in the wisdom of early adolescence, a period of development which combines instinctive prudence, a sense of one's own powers and the boldness of manly courage.

Cantor undertook to capture the sloop under the buccaneers' very eyes, and to sail it round to the other side of the promontory, where the rest of the company would embark.

At this point in the discussion Angélique stood up and went across to open the door, realizing immediately what it was that had attracted her attention outside.

The cry of a nightjar could be heard, repeated over and over again, a deep throated, insistent cry.

Piksarett was calling her.

She ran to the edge of the headland and there, on the opposite shore, at the top of a black oak, she caught sight of the Indian who, halfhidden amidst the leafy boughs, was making frantic gestures in her direction, pointing to something just below where she stood.

She looked down towards the shore and her blood ran cold, for there were men, clambering up towards her, pulling themselves up by tufts of juniper and the stunted pines that grew in the fissures of the cliff face.

Beyond any doubt, they were the pirates from the

sloop, and when one of them, realizing that they had been detected, raised his villainous countenance and looked up at her, she saw that he held a knife between his teeth.

They too must have discovered that they had neighbours on this lonely shore, and, inveterate pillagers that they were, they were on their way to take them by surprise.

But seeing that their surprise attack had been discovered, they cursed abominably and began to scramble more rapidly up the cliff.

Angélique's eyes lighted on the beehives beside her. Before running away, she seized one of them, and just as the filibusters reached the edge of the plateau, she hurled the hive and its buzzing contents at them.

The object struck them full in the face and they immediately began to yell and scream in the most terrifying way. She did not wait to watch them trying to beat off the black cloud of infuriated bees.

As she ran, she drew out her well-sharpened knife—a wise precaution, for the bandits had split up into two groups.

A sniggering, clown-like figure sprang up between her and John Shapleigh's dwelling. He was dressed in tawdry finery and wore a three-cornered hat with scarlet ostrich feathers. He was brandishing a cudgel.

He must either have been tipsy or have thought that from a woman he had nothing to fear, for he made a rush at her, and, as she ducked to one side to avoid his stick as it whistled through the air, he tripped and literally impaled himself on the sharp blade she had held out in front of her as her only means of defence.

The man gave a hoarse cry and for a brief moment she smelt on her face the foul breath of a rum drinker with rotten teeth. His hands ceased to clutch her, and he almost pulled her over as he fell. Chilled with horror, she thrust him aside and saw him collapse at her feet, his hands clutching at his belly, while his rheumy eyes wore an expression of utter astonishment.

Angélique was prudent enough to take no further interest in the man's fate. She raced back to Shapleigh's hut and fastened the gate of the shaky palisade.

CHAPTER 23

'HE'S LOSING his guts!'

The lugubrious cry rang through the clear air of the June evening and echoed over Casco Bay.

'He's losing his guts!'

Out there behind the bushes man was calling to man, and the besieged English and French heard the cry from their carefully barricaded hut.

The day so disastrously begun was drawing to a close with the contestants more or less equally matched. Angélique and the English on one side, admittedly with few weapons, but very much on their guard behind the shelter of their log walls, and the pirates on the other, ferocious and aggressive, but terribly stung and saddled in addition with a wounded man whose guts were spilling out of him.

Unfortunately for Angélique and her companions the pirates had taken refuge by a stream close to the house in order to bathe their swollen bee-stung faces and limbs. From this vantage point, they could prevent anyone from leaving the hut, and alternately shouted abuse and moaned. They were hidden from sight but their presence could be sensed behind a screen of trees, from which direction came the sound of their lamentations.

When the night had fallen, their wails, sighs and cries of pain filled the air at regular intervals, and what with the baying of the seals down on the beach, the noise was enough to set one's hair on end.

Soon moonlight flooded the scene; the sea turned to silver and the whole flotilla of inky black islands seemed to be about to set sail for some distant white horizon.

Towards the middle of the night, Angélique climbed on a stool and lifted a tile off the roof so that she could look outside and obtain a general view of the situation.

'Listen to me down there, you sailors!' she called in French, in a loud, clear voice.

She saw the shadowy figures of the pirates move.

'Now listen to me; we can come to terms. I have

143

medicines here to ease your suffering. I can dress the wounds of the injured man. . . .

'Come forward to within two fathoms of the house and throw down your arms. We do not seek your death, we only want to save our own lives and to borrow your boat. In exchange for this, your injuries will be attended to,'

At first silence was their only reply, but it was shortly followed by the muffled sound of whispering that mingled with the gusty wind.

'We shall attend to your wounds,' Angélique repeated. 'Otherwise you will die. Bee stings are certain death, and if your wounded friend receives no attention, that will be the end of him.'

'You're telling us! The end of him. . . . He's losing his guts, he's had it,' a thick voice muttered out of the darkness.

'It won't do him any good, that's certain. Now be sensible. Throw down your arms, as I said, and I will take care of you.'

Coming to them through the night, her gentle womanly voice seemed reassuring, as if it came from heaven itself.

But the pirates did not give in at once. They held out till dawn.

'Hi there, woman!' someone shouted, 'we are coming.'

There was a clang of steel from behind the bushes and a heavy figure staggered out, laden with an array of cutlasses, knives, boarding swords, an axe, and a small pistol.

All of which he laid down a few paces from the palisade.

Angélique, covered by old Shapleigh's blunderbuses and by Cantor holding the musket, walked towards the man. He was almost blinded by the swelling from the bee stings that covered his entire face, while the skin of his neck, his shoulders, his arms and his hands was puffy and tight.

Shapleigh pushed his tall puritan hat back on his head and circled round the man sniggering and sniffing merrily.

'I see . . . I see! The pumpkin seems to be just ripe!'

'Have mercy on me!' the man begged.

144

His shirt, darkened with old bloodstains, and his short cotton breeches that left his hairy knees uncovered, were the typical get-up of an authentic buccaneer.

His belt, from which hung sheaths for knives of every conceivable size, at present empty, but very numerous, indicated beyond any shadow of doubt that he was one of those men who hunted, killed and cut up wild pig and wild oxen on the islands of the Caribbean, then, after curing their flesh, sold it to revictual passing ships. They were ocean butchers, in fact, one could even call them traders, no worse than the rest, but driven to piracy and war by the conquering Spaniards who would tolerate no presence other than their own in the American archipelagos.

His companions behind the clump of trees were in still worse shape than he. A puny, sickly-looking ship's boy looked as if he was about to die, the Portuguese with the olive skin looked very much like a cabbage and the last man, a rather swarthy fellow, looked like a gourd. As for the man who had been wounded . . .

Angélique lifted the filthy rag that had been thrown over him, and a gasp of horror and alarm went up from the bystanders. Angélique herself had to fight back the wave of nausea that swept over her.

The gaping wound was at least fifteen inches long, through which protruded a considerable length of extruded intestine, that had the appearance of a writhing nest of serpents, twisting and squirming spasmodically, a nightmare vision of the entrails of a man with his belly split open!

Everybody stood motionless, glued to the ground, except Piksarett, who had suddenly appeared and was examining the horrible sight with amused curiosity.

Almost immediately Angélique sensed that it was an outside chance, and the wounded man, who had not fainted but on the contrary seemed clear-headed and vaguely mocking in his manner was watching her every move from bright eyes beneath his bushy eyebrows. In spite of his waxen hue and his drawn features, Angélique could see none of the signs of death on his ugly, drunken face. It seemed extraordinary, but the man looked determined to live. The stab had not perforated

145

the gut, otherwise he would undoubtedly have died shortly afterwards.

It was he who spoke first, in a muffled voice, as he attempted to suppress a grimace:

'Yes, my lady! For a dirty trick that one takes a bit of beating, eh? Real Gippo stuff, I calls it, and I know what I'm talking about. Now you will have to sew it all up for me again.'

He must have been mulling it over during his long night of agony, and had gradually convinced himself that it might be possible. A funny little chap, not lacking in intelligence, although he was undoubtedly a prime scoundrel. He was the leader or captain of the rascally five. It did not take more than a glance at him and his companions to see what kind of men they were. The scum of the sea! Angélique looked first at the man's face, which reflected a diabolical vitality, then at the monstrous hernia with its putrid smell around which blowflies had already begun to buzz.

'All right,' she decided, 'we'll see what we can do.'

CHAPTER 24

'I'VE SEEN worse,' she kept on telling herself as she hastily laid out a few instruments from her bag on a piece of board in the hut.

That was not absolutely correct, although she had been obliged during the winter at Wapassou, to carry out what amounted to regular operations of increasing diversity and complexity. The extraordinary skill of her slender, nimble fingers, that seemed to possess a life of their own, the sure, instinctive movements of her healing hands, had encouraged her to perform experiments which in that country and at that time could only be called bold.

For example, when spring came she had nursed an Indian chief whose back had been gashed by the horn of a moose, and had made her first attempt to join the two edges of the wound with a few stitches. The wound had healed with astonishing rapidity.

Her reputation had spread, and at Houssnock a horde of redskins had descended on her, asking for treatment from the paleface lady of the Silver Lake.

She had chosen the finest needles available from the stock they used for trading, and Monsieur Jonas, with the skilled fingers of a watchmaker, had given them a slightly curved shape, which Angélique considered preferable for this kind of delicate work. She congratulated herself on having saved her precious traveling bag from all the recent disasters. It was wonderful. She found in it all kinds of things that she needed—a sachet containing a handful of crushed acacia pods, a powder rich in medicinal tannin which she kept to make poultices that might prevent poisonous humours from spreading through the body once the wound was closed. There was not enough of it, and she showed the acacia powder to Piksarett who, after examining it and sniffing at it, gave an understanding smile and dashed off towards the forest.

'You see to the ship with one of the Englishmen,' Angélique ordered Cantor. 'Make sure that it is ready to sail with part of our company. Keep on your guard and stay well armed, although these poor brutes don't look to me as if they could do much harm for the moment.'

Elizabeth Pidgeon timidly offered to help Angélique, but Angélique thought it better to send her to attend to the unfortunate victims of the bees. With the Reverend Patridge's head to dress as well, the old maid had plenty to do, and, bearing in mind the new situation, she chose from among the pirates' weapons the sword with the least jagged edge, and, tucking it bravely into her belt, trotted off to the hut where Shapleigh was beginning to dispense his remedies to the accompaniment of a great display of mirth.

Beneath the tree beside the wounded man, Angélique took a flat stone, brushed it clean, and laid out on it her needle case, her tweezers, reed clips and birch funnel, a flask of very strong brandy, a pair of scissors, and some lint, which she kept clean and white in an oilcloth bag.

There was no need to move the man, for the stream

ran hard by, and she rekindled a little fire, and placed a small earthenware pot on it with a little water in the bottom, to which she added the acacia-pod powder.

Piksarett returned with handfuls of green pods, Angélique took one of them, bit into it, and pulled a wry face as she spat out the green, astringent sap. Although it had an extremely unpleasant taste, it had still not acquired the full flavour of mature tannin, which had a metallic, inky taste and possessed the invaluable property of closing wounds, helping them to heal, preventing them from going dangerously septic and finally, by its tonic and vivifying power, preventing the suppuration that made all wounds, even healthy ones, take so long to heal. These green pods would be less efficacious.

'We shall have to make do with these.'

She was about to put them on to boil when Piksarett stopped her.

'Let Maktera do it,' he said. And he pointed to the old Indian woman, Shapleigh's servant or companion. She seemed to know the properties of the plant and, crouching down beside the fire, began to chew the pods, before spreading them out on large leaves to serve as poultices. Angélique did not interfere, for she knew— the old sorcerer from Beaver Camp near Wapassou had taught her—that prepared in this way the remedy would be most effective.

Then she returned to her patient, whose eyes, still wide open, shone with both hope and fear as he saw her kneel beside him, her face framed by the gold of her hair bearing an expression of such concentrated resolution that the old buccaneer felt himself grow weak, and his villainous countenance assumed an almost pathetic look.

'Easy now, my beauty,' he whispered, and his voice seemed to have grown weaker. 'Before you start, we'd better have a chat, you and me. If you managed to patch me up, and I find myself on an even keel again, you aren't a-going to take all our arms away fom us and make us hand over our old tub, are you? They're all that swine Gold Beard allowed us to try and keep body and soul together with in this damned wilderness. You wouldn't want to be even worse than him, now would you?'

'Gold Beard,' said Angélique, pricking up her ears. 'Are you members of his crew?'

'We were. . . . That son-of-a-bitch put us ashore here without even enough powder to protect ourselves against wild animals, savages and people like you lot along the coast; all wreckers, every man-jack of you. . . .'

'Stop talking now,' said Angélique, preserving a calm front, 'you are too talkative for a man at death's door. We'll talk about all this later.'

The man had worn himself out, and his waxen skin seemed to have shrunk back into the hollows of the bones of his face, giving it the appearance of a death mask, with a red circle round his protruding eyes.

But it was precisely his red-ringed eyelids that indicated his ultimate capacity to survive. 'He will live' she thought, and her lips tightened. She would think about Gold Beard later.

'It is too early to lay down conditions, sirrah,' she continued aloud. 'We shall do whatever we choose with your weapons and your boat, and you will be lucky if you live.'

'In any case . . . it'll take days . . . to patch . . . the old tub . . . up,' the man whispered, unwilling to give in.

'And you too, it will take days to patch you up, you blockhead. And now, my lad, save what strength you have, and keep quiet.'

And she laid her hand on the slack flesh of his brow that was sticky with sweat.

She deliberated whether to give him a calming potion, based on the very belladonna that Shapleigh did not like. Nothing was going to be strong enough to overcome the dreadful pain of the operation.

'A good strong toddy,' the man moaned, 'give me a good strong toddy, burning hot, with half a lemon in it, let me have a last toddy. . . .'

'Not a bad idea,' Angélique remarked, 'it will help him to get over the shock. This filibuster is so completely steeped in rum that it may be his salvation. . . . Hi, you rascal there,' she called to one of the buccaneers who was still able to walk and who had made his way towards them, 'you wouldn't have a pint of rum by you, would you?'

The man nodded as far as his painful swellings allowed him, and, accompanied by one of the Englishmen, made his way down to the camp on the shore and returned with a black glass flask with a long neck, half full of the best West Indian rum, if the smell that filled the air when Angélique uncorked the bottle was anything to go by.

'Here you are,' she said. 'Drink that, my lad, as much as you can, until the sky begins to spin round you like a top.'

Because she was suddenly talking to him in this familiar way he realized that things had become very serious.

'It's going to hurt,' he moaned, then added with a desperate glance:

'Is there anyone to hear my confession in this godforsaken hole?'

'I can,' Piksarett replied, falling to his knees. 'I am chief catechist to Black Robe and chief of all the Abenaki tribe. The Lord has chosen me to administer the sacraments of baptism and absolution.'

'Jesus Christ, a savage, that takes the biscuit or I must be barmy!' the wounded man exclaimed, and lost consciousness, either from shock or from exertion.

'It's better this way,' said Angélique.

'I'll clean the wound,' she thought, 'with warm water and some essence of belladonna.'

She picked up a small piece of bark shaped like a funnel which enabled her to direct the thin stream of water from the calabash held by Piksarett onto the wound, as she leaned over the gaping hole.

At the very first touch, light as it was, the wounded man shuddered and tried to sit up, but Stoughton's strong hands held him back.

Angélique laid the tall buccaneer across his comrade's thighs, while Shapleigh's Indian held his ankles. Finding the position uncomfortable, the wounded man half regained consciousness and begged them to lift his head so that he could swallow a few more swigs of rum, then, in a state of semi-consciousness, he allowed them to tie his wrists to two stakes driven into the ground.

150

Angélique rolled some lint into a ball, placed it between his teeth, and supported the nape of his neck on a bundle of straw, while she checked that he could breathe easily through his nose.

The old English doctor was kneeling on his other side; he had doffed his big hat and the wind stirred his curly, white locks. Without needing to be told what she wanted, he seized the reed clips and placed the first of them in position preparatory to drawing the edge of the wound together. It was almost impossible to join them completely in this way, but Angélique, in one abrupt, resolute movement, drove her needle into the flesh which in spite of its flabby appearance, was extremely tough and resistant, and held the skin together with her fingers while with an imperceptible flick of the wrist that required uncommon strength and dexterity, she drew the waxed thread through and tied it in a knot. She worked swiftly and rhythmically, never hesitating, leaning over the man, completely still save for the inexorable movement of her two deft hands. Old John followed her movements, helping her with clips or with his fingers when the thrust of the tortured flesh forced the clips apart.

The wretched martyr lay prostrate but his whole body was continually shaken by troublesome twitching movements, and from time to time a terrible cry broke through the gag, a cry that sounded as if it would be his last. Then the coiling mass of guts, slimy and incessantly moving, would project again, threatening to burst out, and she would have to push them back inside as if smothering some animal. The loops, white and purple in colour, kept on oozing out through the slightest gap, forming innumerable hernias, and Angélique was in constant fear lest one of these should burst or become perforated, which she realized would be fatal. But the gut held good, and finally the last knot was tied.

The man looked as if he were dead.

Angélique took the tannin poultices handed to her by the Indian woman, covered the whole of his belly with them, and bound him up tightly with the strips of cloth she had laid under his back before beginning the operation.

Bound up tight like this, all old Blockhead had to do

151

was to get used to his intestines being in their proper place again, and it was to be hoped that they would make up their minds to stay put.

Angélique stood up, her back nearly broken. She had been working for over an hour.

She went and washed her hands in the stream, then came back and tidied her things away.

She could hear the sound of a mallet coming from the creek. The boat would be ready to sail well before its wretched captain.

Angélique de Peyrac lifted the wounded man's eyelid and listened to his heart. He was alive. Then, as she looked at him from the tip of his filthy feet covered with corns, to his unkempt shock of hair, she felt a pang of sympathy for this miserable outcast of society whose wretched life she had saved.

CHAPTER 25

THERE WAS not room for everyone, especially not the sick and wounded, on board the pirate sloop after it had been rendered seaworthy again. Choosing who should remain and who should leave inevitably involved conflicts of conscience, and once again Angélique was obliged to give a lead.

It was obvious that Cantor, who was a skilled sailor, should captain the boat as far as Gouldsboro. Stoughton and Corwin, who had grown up beside the sea, would man the ship and it seemed right that their entire families should go with them. Their hired hands did not want to be parted from them; they would die of fear, they said, without their masters, and would not know what to do with themselves. These people alone were enough to fill the boat, and there was no question of taking on board those who were sick enough to need to lie down. From the outset Angélique had realized that she would have to stay behind with them, and never had her sense of responsibility cost her so dear. But how could she leave these dying people to their fate; the hulking parson Patridge no more than the bee-stung pirates and the surgical case, who was beginning miraculously to heal. Cantor protested vehemently, appalled at the idea of leaving his mother behind in such wretched and dangerous company.

'But you do realize, don't you,' she told him, 'that we cannot take any of these sick people on board. They would interfere with the sailing of the ship, would require care that we were unable to give them on board, and might well die at sea.'

'Well, let them stay here with old Shapleigh to look after them.'

'Shapleigh has told me that he must go off to the forest one of these nights, and that he cannot put off his journey because of the moon. I think that above all he does not want to remain alone with these dregs of the Caribbean . . .'

'And what about you, wouldn't you be exposing yourself to great danger in their company?'

'I can look after myself. And in any case, they all as sick as dogs.'

'Not all of them. One of them is much stronger already, and I don't like the look of him.'

'Well then, here is the answer. You take him on board, and Corwin and Stoughton can keep an eye on him until you can put him ashore on some island in Casco Bay. Then make as fast as you can for Gouldsboro. With a good wind, I might even see you back here in the *Rochelais* in less than a week. Nothing very dreadful could happen to me in that time . . .'

She was trying to convince herself, and Cantor finally agreed that there was no other solution possible.

The sooner they set sail, the sooner the whole family would be reunited, safe and sound inside the walls of Gouldsboro, which they thought of as a haven of peace and the end of all their worries. At Gouldsboro there were arms, money, men, and ships . . .

Now only eight of them remained on the promontory overlooking Maquoit Bay.

It was two days since the pirate sloop, all sails set, and expertly steered by Cantor, had glided out of the creek and, bowing like a seagull before the wind, disappeared behind the farthest islands.

It had borne away with it the Corwin and Stoughton families together with their servants, little Rose-Ann and the least unwell of the pirates, whom they would get ride of on one of the islands at the earliest opportunity. He had spoken at great length in his lingo to his companions before setting off, but a close watch would be kept on him.

Little Sammy Corwin, his burns still not properly healed, had stayed behind, as had the Reverend Thomas, who was too weak to travel, and Miss Pidgeon, who had elected to remain with her pastor. As for Adhemar, he had at first wanted to go, but his fear of the sea and of the English had eventually prevailed and, all things considered, he had thought it preferable to remain with Angélique, having come to the conclusion that, whether for diabolical reasons or not, she must possess some kind of protective power. So Angélique set him the task of fetching wood, water and shellfish, and of fanning the sick men, who were tormented by mosquitoes. In fact the sloop would have been quite unable to accommodate anyone else, and it had taken all Wolverine's wild impudence, swimming out frantically like a fat otter in the wake of the boat, to force Cantor to find room for him on board.

Angélique felt herself bound to the fretful carcass of her surgical case, who seemed bent on remaining alive and whose name was Aristide Beaumarchand, or so one of his friends had told her. (The name meant handsome merchant, which Angélique considered highly inappropriate. Blockhead or Slitbelly were names that suited him better.)

That morning the Reverend Patridge opened his eyes, remarked on the fact that it was Sunday, and asked for his Bible so that he would prepare his sermon. They thought he was delirious with fever, and tried to calm him, but he ranted and raved and was so insistent about it being Sunday, the Lord's Day, that there was no choice but to accept that Sunday it was.

A whole week had gone by since the attack on the English village.

Angélique still entertained the hope that some of Joffrey de Peyrac's ships were cruising in the mouth of the Kennebec. Cantor had undertaken to find one. But, he said, if he could not, he could be in Gouldsboro in under two days and would send help from there. A good, big, solid ship, protected by heavy cannon, a ship in which they would be able to rest as they crossed the open sea and return home quite free of anxiety.

How wonderful!

But two days had already elapsed without any sign of a sail on the horizon.

Elizabeth Pidgeon was reading to the pastor from the Bible in a quavering voice, while two of the sick buccaneers listened with suspicious, arrogant expressions. They had to be nursed, but no one was in a hurry to see them get better. The third, the tallest and strongest, spent his time between Slitbelly's bedside and that of his other two comrades lying in the hut, holding long confabulations in some more or less inaudible lingua franca. He was looking better. He was a huge, heavy fellow of unprepossessing appearance.

'Keep an eye on him,' Angélique told Adhemar. 'Otherwise he may manage to retrieve one of his knives and stick it in our backs.'

The man showed genuine solicitude for the surgical case.

'He's my brother,' he said.

'He doesn't look like you,' Angélique commented, comparing the giant standing before her with the puny form lying under the covers.

'We are brothers of the Barbary Coast. We have exchanged blood and shared our spoils for nearly fifteen years.'

And he added with a grin made the more hideous by the puffiness of his bee-stung face:

'Pr'aps that's why I've decided not to cut your throat . . . because you saved Aristide's life . . .'

She had to sit up with the latter at night. She had fixed up a piece of canvas over him, as a protection, less against the sun, which the tree shaded him from, than from the dew that fell nightly, and from sudden occasional showers, or even from flying spray which the wind blew in their direction at high tide.

She watched over him, determined, attentive, astonished to see the doomed man beginning to recover, and so fascinated by the possibility of success, that there were times when she almost began to like poor Aristide.

The very evening of the operation he had opened his eyes, called for tobacco, and asked for a toddy 'with a whole lemon on it . . . which I want you to peel for me, Hyacinth.'

Although he did not get his toddy and lemon, which she replaced with a well-strained fish broth, he nevertheless progressed by leaps and bounds.

And on that famous Sunday, when pastor Thomas showed signs of improvement, she said to the man:

'Now I am going to help you to sit up.'

"To sit up, do you want to kill me?"

'No, but we must keep your blood moving to stop it thickening. And I forbid you to speak to me so familiarly, now that you are out of danger.'

'Good gracious! What a woman!'

'Come and give me a hand, Barbary butcher.'

Together they took hold of the man under the arms, heaved him up and supported him in a sitting position. He was deathly pale and covered in sweat.

'Brandy! Brandy!'

'Adhemar, bring me the flagon.'

When he had taken a drink, he seemed better; she propped him up against a pile of sacks covered with pelts and gazed at him with an air of satisfaction.

He wiped his damp brow. Angélique had shaved off his vermin-infested beard and now he looked as harmless as any little grocer, henpecked by his wife and pestered by his creditors.

'I'm no match for Gold Beard any more,' he wailed. 'And that's a fact . . .'

She helped him to lie down again, and later, when he had had a rest, she said:

"Tell me about Gold Beard, and about this talk I hear among your friends of my being born from Satan's thigh.'

'Oh, it's nothing to do with me,' he said defensively. 'Do you know who I am?'

'Not very well, but Gold Beard does. You are the French woman from Gouldsboro who people do say is a witch and in cahoots with a magician who makes gold out of shells.'

'Why not out of rum while you're at it?' Angélique retaliated, keeping a straight face. 'That would just suit you, wouldn't it?'

'Well, that's how the gossip goes among the sailors we met in Frenchman Bay. Sailors must trust one another, you know.'

'Sailors? You are more like pirates than sailors. In any case sailors don't use your lingo.'

'You can talk for the two of us if you like,' Slitbelly replied with an air of injured dignity, 'but you can't say that of Gold Beard. Now there's a gentleman for you, believe you me! And what's more, he's the best sailor on the surface of the globe. And you can believe me when I say so, because apart from that, you saw how he treated us, that son-of-a-bitch, casting us adrift, abandoning us like maroons, virtually without supplies or arms in this savage-infested hole. He told us we dishonoured his ship.'

The Portuguese pirate, now somewhat less huffy, happened to be near by and agreed wtih the invalid:

'Yes, I have known Gold Beard even longer than you, chief, since we were in Goa and the West Indies. I quarrelled with him over this Gouldsboro business, but I shall always be sorry I did.'

Angélique kept on running her fingers through her hair, for the wind was blowing it over her eyes and she had to keep pushing it back.

She tried to gather her thoughts together, but the deafening wind distracted her and she found it impossible to think straight.

'Do you mean to say that you knew who I was and that *I was here*, when Gold Beard put you down in the creek?'

'No, that we didn't know,' Beaumarchand replied. 'That was luck, that was. Luck that tips the wink to likely lads such as us when we find ourselves in a mess. It's not the first time luck has got us out of a spot of bother

157

by the skin of our teeth, and that's a fact, ain't it Hyacinth?'

'But how did you know I was here?' she insisted impatiently.

'Well, it's like this here, you see. When we realized there were people up on the cliff we climbed up and listened, and then we cottoned on that it was you, the Frenchwoman from Gouldsboro, the Countess of Peyrac, and that you were with a crowd of English. Then, we thought our luck was in, see?'

'What do you mean, your luck?'

'Well, what Gold Beard had said, o'course—that he had orders respecting Count and Countess Peyrac, and that he had to be killed and she must be captured . . .'

'Is that all? Orders from whom?'

Angélique's heart was thudding in her breast. Her drunken patient had this to be said for him, that he was as garrulous as a magpie and forever swigging at the bottle, with the result that he chatted on without rhyme or reason.

CHAPTER 26

A TWIST of the lips indicated that he did not know the answer to that question.

'It was since he went to Paris before his last campaign in the Caribbean. To get his papers signed by the minister. You went with him, didn't you, Lopez?'

The Portuguese sailor nodded.

'And who was it that had to be killed?' Angélique insisted.

'The man you're with, the Count, the man who makes gold out of shells.'

'You had to kill him! And was that why you tried to take me prisoner . . .?'

'Gawd a'mighty! Put yourself in our place. And now that you have slit me open and sewn me up again, I know you *must* be a witch, and that's a fact.'

And he gave her a wink—although whether it was

158

meant to be a sly or a nasty one she could not tell—accompanied by a sardonic, noiseless chuckle.

'Then why did your captain put you ashore here?' she asked.

'We fell out about the sharing out of the spoil; but that is no woman's business, even if she is a witch,' Aristide replied haughtily.

'More likely because you were out of place in his crew, if he's the gentleman you say he is,' Angélique rejoined.

It had not taken a second glance at the five pirates to see that they were scum—the kind of men Joffrey de Peyrac had had to hang from the mast-head during his last voyage.

Stung to the quick, the man took refuge in a dignified silence.

'What was your Gold Beard going to do in Gouldsboro?' Angélique persisted.

The wounded man could not keep up his huffish silence for long.

'Come off it, don't be daft! Seize his lands of course!'

Angélique stared back in astonishment.

'No need to open your peepers like a couple of plates with whiskers, my beauty. I already told you that Mister Gold Beard is a privateer who has all the right credentials from the minister, his company in Paris, and even from the Government of Tortuga. And, what is more'
—the wounded man held up his finger portentously—
'and, what is more, he obtained and bought as a concession from the King of France, all the land that lies between the tip of the Blue Mountains and Gouldsboro Bay.'

'Now I understand!' Angélique exclaimed.

'It is an idea he's always had in his head, Gold Beard, 'spite of him being a sailor. He always wanted to settle with some of his companions on some piece of land somewhere and grow French wheat. That was how we came to fall out with him, me and Lopez. You see, I have a mind to knock about the world until I end up feeding the sharks, and I was the one in the right of it. Gold Beard, clever as he is and for all the King's backing, he found out just where his big ideas of colonization got him. Red hot cannon balls below the waterline, that's what them Gouldsboro folk gave him. Hard as nails they are. Our poor *Heart of Mary* . . .'

'What's that?'

'The name of our ship.'

Angélique made the mental note that the more villainous the intentions of pirates the more anxious they seemed to choose a pious name for their ship, no doubt in the hope of obtaining protection, or forgiveness from the powers above.

'Did your master really not know that those coastal lands were already owned by someone and that there were settlers living there?'

'We were told that there were women there. White women, not Indians. So you see, damn me, that was just the job. We were going to grab the land and start off with a wife apiece. What you call a real colony! But there was nothing doing! Red hot cannon balls, like I said, and when we tried to set foot on shore the beggars hacked us to bits. The ship was beginning to list, and caught on fire, and all we could do was to beat it for the islands like a lot of cowards. So much for my precious Gold Beard and his silly visions of grandeur, his charter under his arm and his plan to plough the land —and the women—so much for all that . . .'

He gave a raucous laugh that terminated in a fit of coughing.

'You mustn't cough,' said Angélique severely.

She made sure that his wound had not been stretched.

A dreadful, low scoundrel, this man Aristide, but if he was telling the truth, she had received some most valuable information.

She trembled at the thought that had not the Huguenots in Gouldsboro sprung so valiantly to their defence, her women friends from La Rochelle might well have fallen into the hands of these wretches.

'No, Gold Beard is not what you think,' the sick man went on, his voice weaker but still determined, as if he had followed her thoughts. 'He has the regular credentials, the King's support as a privateer sailing under the fleur-de-lys, and princes to lend him money, he has it all, I tell you. He treated me rough, but on board his ship, we had nothing to complain about. He's a gentleman I tell you, that Gold Beard. And as for our daily ration of brandy, we got that every day just like on the King's ships. We were quite something, I tell you . . . You wouldn't have a bit of cheese, would you, m'lady?'

'Cheese? Are you mad! Go to sleep!' Angélique replied. And she pulled his covers up to his chin, tucked him in and wiped his weak mouth.

'Poor old Blockhead! You aren't worth the rope to hang you with.'

And in spite of the coldness of these shores, the barking seals, and the dark banks of fir trees standing black along the edge of the beaches, as she looked at him she thought of the pirates she had encountered in the Mediterranean with its motley population of adventurers of all races, and she felt the old fascination and fear . . .

Back in Brunswick-Falls, Mrs Williams had told her that in the old days even the toughest of these gentlemen of adventure who used to cast anchor off the poor villages of the New England settlers would never have harmed anyone, but those days were gone. Better living standards and increased wealth along the American coastline now attracted the looters.

The whole coastline needed to be cleaned up, policed, and an end put to the anarchy that everywhere prevailed. And she saw in her mind's eye the tall silhouette of Joffrey, trusty and reliable, as if involved with everything that was life and action. He appeared to her as the male principle of a new world.

Oh, my love! They had said that he must be killed . . . He would not allow himself to be killed.

But what with the re-kindled Indian war that was sending terrified populations scurrying across the bays and island, that had reopened the issue of alliances with distant kingdoms, the task looked like being a complex one, and any predatory vessels would be sure to find their fill of spoils. By what tangle of chance or design had she herself been driven here, whereas only a few days earlier she had left Fort Wapassou thinking she would make her way unimpeded to their lands at Gouldsboro?

'Lopez,' she said, breaking off her reverie, 'you were

in Paris with this Gold Beard when he went to have his papers signed, and no doubt to obtain money to fit out his ship. Which lord was his patron? Who were the owners or his partners? Can you tell me any of their names?'

But the Portuguese shook his head.

'No . . . I was only there as his valet. Sometimes other valets would bring messages. There was also . . .'

He appeared to be thinking.

'I don't know his name. But if ever you meet a tall ship's captain with a port wine stain there, a purple mark'—he lifted his hand to his brow—'watch out, your enemies are not far off. One good turn deserves another—after all, witch or no, you did save my mate. . .'

CHAPTER 27

AND NOW evening was falling once more over Casco Bay, trailing a long orange glow out towards the west where the land slopes down in a long curve, plunging suddenly to the south in a vast caressing sweep round a land of myriad inlets and islands that fill the vast blue circle of sea, into which, drawn along by the northern currents, come swimming the blue and silver shoals of fish.

These are the breeding grounds of fish from all over the world, the junction of the great warm and cold ocean currents teeming with their vast reserves of plankton that attract fish, offering a never-ending supply for fishermen the world over since the dawn of time.

Men from Saint-Malo used to come here in their sloops many centuries before Christopher Columbus discovered the West Indies.

During the spring months, the sea was alive with white sails, like the full-blown petals of giant waterlilies.

The darker it got, the more clearly could Angélique pick out the glow of fires shining through the dark expanse, far away and flickering like stars.

'He don't drink,' Aristide muttered beside her . . . 'What do you think of a sailor who don't drink?'

'Who are you talking about, my lad?'

'That dratted Gold Beard . . . He don't drink except when he has a woman. And that's not often. Almost as if he didn't like women . . . nor drinking. Yet he's a terrible man. When we captured Portobello he made the monks from the monastery of San Antonio walk in front of his men as a shield, and the Spaniards in the garrison were in tears as they fired on them.'

Angélique shuddered.

'The man must be a fiend.'

'No, not as much as you might think. Prayers are always said on board his ship, and anyone unruly gets sent up into the split-sail crow's-nest to say the rosary twenty times.'

Angélique, ill at ease, imagined she saw the blood-thirsty pirate's golden beard floating in the darkness. The mere thought that such a man's ship had lain at anchor for a whole night at the foot of the promontory when he had come to disembark his mutineers, made her flesh creep.

'He'll be back, you'll see,' the wounded man moaned.

Angélique was shaken by a second shudder and the howling of the wind in the cedars had a sinister sound to her ears as a sudden flash of summer lightning lit up the horizon.

'Go to sleep, my friend.'

She drew the folds of her cloak about her, for she intended to sit with him until the middle of the night, after which the other buccaneer, his blood brother, would take over. He was huddled up before the fire too, a giant of a man, his head sunk between his shoulders, and she could hear him scratching at his unkempt beard to relieve the itching of his tormented skin.

As she sat thinking of a thousand different things with her head turned towards the stars, she did not notice that he was staring at her with glistening eyes. Now that he was beginning to recover, he found himself experiencing strange sensations when he looked at this woman. Motionless as a statue in her black cloak, her face emerging from above it like a patch of moonlight, there was always one golden curl that kept straying across her cheek until she brushed it back with her hand. This single

163

movement conjured up the full richness of her hidden beauty in all its vigorous curves, which he so admired.

'Now me, I'm not like Gold Beard,' he said softly. 'I like women.'

And he cleared his throat.

'Don't you occasionally allow yourself a bit of fun, m'lady?'

She turned her head slowly towards the huge fellow.

'With people of your kind? No, my boy.'

'What is it about people of my kind that you don't like?'

'A face like a pumpkin far too ugly for anyone to want to kiss it.'

'It ain't necessary to kiss if you don't care for that,' came his conciliatory reply. 'There are other things we could do.'

'You stay right where you are,' she rapped out, seeing him about to move towards her. 'I've slit open many a man for less than that. As for you, I wouldn't bother to sew you up again, either.'

'You're a hard nut, aren't you,' he growled, frenziedly scratching at himself again. 'It's a good opportunity I'm offering you. We are all alone, we have plenty of time. Hyacinth is my name . . . Hyacinth Boulanger. Do you really not feel like it?'

'No I don't, if you don't mind. Prudence dictates, Hyacinth,' she went on somewhat flippantly, so as not to antagonize him. 'Sailors marooned on beaches are not always in the pink of health. Just by looking at you I'd be prepared to wager that you're rotten with pox to the very marrow of your bones.'

'No I'm not, that's not true, I swear it,' the pirate exclaimed in outraged tones. 'The reason why I look the way I do is on account of your damned beehives that you hurled at our heads.'

Then Aristide growled:

'Stop fighting over my head as if I were already a stiff.'

Silence fell once more.

Angélique told herself that there was nothing to get agitated about. She had seen worse. But in the state of latent anxiety she was in, the desire this sinister individual felt for her in the middle of this lugubrious night along this weather-beaten, deserted coastline filled her with a sense of uneasiness and almost unbearable horror. Her nerves were so on edge that she felt an almost irresistible longing to run away as fast as her legs would carry her. But she forced herself to sit still and to appear indifferent so that the man would not guess that she was afraid. Then she chose the first suitable opportunity to get up, told the buccaneer to keep an eye on the fire and on his blood brother, and walked back to the cabin.

Miss Pidgeon, leaning over the glowing embers, looked like some tiny witch busy preparing her potions.

Angélique bent down over the boy Sammy, touched his warm brow, felt his bandages, then after smiling at the old maid, went outside again and sat down behind the hut beside the Indian woman Maktara.

The half moon was just emerging from the clouds. It was a night when no one could sleep. The rapid chirping of the crickets was like a high-pitched, syncopated accompaniment to the mingled music of the wind and the sea.

The old medicine-man appeared, wrapped in his flowing cloak which covered everything between his collar and the brim of his hat except the big round lenses of his spectacles across which the moonlight suddenly darted in two pointed shafts of light. His Indian followed him like a shadow, likewise enveloped in his red blanket, holding the blunderbuss cradled in his arms.

'This time,' said Shapleigh, 'I really am off to pick the wild vervain, the sacred herb, the sorcerer's weed; Juno's tear, a drop of Mercury's blood, the joy of simples. It must be picked near the rising of Sirius, when neither the sun nor the moon are above the horizon to witness the act, and hard by the night when the signs are in conjunction. I can wait no more . . . I have left you two charges of gunpowder for your musket and something to drug your patients with to render them less dangerous . . . Keep a sharp eye open on the ruffians!'

She replied softly in English: 'Thank you, Mr Shapleigh.'

He took a few steps, then turned round to listen to the soft, strange voice that had murmured in the night: 'Thank you, Mr Shapleigh.'

He looked at her. By the light of the moon Angélique's green eyes were almost unbearably brilliant.

His toothless mouth stretched in a sardonic grin.

'Are you off to the Witches' Sabbath?' he asked. 'Will you ride your broomstick tonight? It's tonight or never for a woman like you. With this moon you will meet the devil with the goose's legs. . . . Do you not have the wand painted with the Sabbath Salve? You know the recipe? A hundred ounces of lard or human fat, five of hashish, half a handful of flowers of hemp, the same of poppy flowers, a pinch of hellebore root, and some crushed sunflower seed . . .'

As he spoke in English she did not grasp the meaning of what he was saying, but he repeated the formula in Latin, and she gave a start of fear.

The old Indian woman, broad and heavy, accompanied Shapleigh along the peninsula as far as the edge of the forest, then made her slow solemn way back. Angélique asked herself what part this Maktara played in the life of the mad old Englishman, for Indian women only very rarely became servants. Had she been his squaw? That would help to explain the way his compatriots had ostracized him, for they considered all contact with the redskins degrading.

Angélique was later to hear the story of this strange couple who lived on the extreme point of Maquoit Bay, the tale of a young Indian girl, the last survivor of the exterminated tribe of the Pequots who, forty years earlier, had been sold as a slave in the market-square of Boston. She had been bought on behalf of his masters by a young English apprentice, recently arrived from England with his apothecary's diploma in his pocket. Holding her by a rope he had set off dragging the girl behind him, and it was then, as he looked at her slender doe-like body, and her eyes as black as shaded pools of water, that he had found himself in the grip of that obscure passion for good and for madness that haunts every son of Shakespeare.

So, instead of returning home he had walked straight off into the forest. This was how the two of them had become outcasts together.

CHAPTER 28

OVER THE brown shining plain of the rocks laid bare by the tide, a man came leaping through the remaining pools of water.

As he drew closer, Angélique recognized Yann le Couennec, the Breton from Wapassou, her husband's equerry.

She ran to meet him, wild with joy, and threw her arms about him.

'Yann, my dear Yann! How pleased I am to see you! Monsieur le Comte ... where is he?'

'I am on my own,' the young Breton replied.

Then, seeing the disappointment on Angélique's face, he went on:

'When Monsieur le Comte heard that you had set off for the English village, he gave me orders to find you, at all costs. I have been following in your tracks for a week now, from Houssnock to Brunswick-Falls, then all down the Androscoggin.'

He drew a letter from his jacket.

'Monsieur le Comte asked me to give you this.'

She grasped the note eagerly, delighted to have something of his in her hands, but resisted the temptation to kiss the note before breaking the seal.

She hoped it would contain some proposal from Joffrey for a meeting somewhere along the coast, or would announce his arrival in spite of all signs to the contrary. But it only contained a few rather abrupt lines: 'If this message reaches you at Brunswick-Falls, return with Yann to Peter Boggen's trading post. If you are already back at Houssnock, wait patiently for me there. But try, please try, to do nothing reckless or impulsive.'

The tone of the letter—it was almost as if there were some repressed animosity between the lines—disconcerted Angélique. She suddenly felt chilled to the marrow.

The worthy Yann, guessing from her expression that his master's letter must have been lacking in cordiality—

he had noticed that when Joffrey de Peyrac had handed him the letter he had looked extremely angry—tried as tactfully as possible to tone down its effect.

'Monsieur le Comte was very anxious about you, on account of the rumours of war that were going about . . .'

'But . . .' she said.

One thing Yann had said had struck her: 'When Monsieur le Comte heard that you had set out for the English village . . .' but was it not he who had sent her there? She tried hard to call to mind the circumstances of her departure. It had been nearly two weeks ago and the details were beginning to become blurred and vague.

'Monsieur le Comte was quite right too,' Yann commented. "There was real trouble to the west of the Kennebec. The whole red ant-heap is swarming under the trees, tomahawk and torch in hand.

'Nothing but ashes and blackened beams, and corpses and wheeling crows. . . . Luckily there were still a few savages looting at Newehewanik, and they told me that you had set off south with Piksarett, and not north with the other captives. After that I was frightened I might be taken for an Englishman, especially as my hair is on the sandy side like theirs. I had to keep on hiding . . .'

She looked at his haggard, bearded, weary face and regained possession of herself once more.

'But you must be exhausted, my poor friend! You probably haven't even managed to eat properly on the way . . . Come and have some refreshment!'

Yann was there, bringing with him the presence of her people, her faithful friends, of the warm circle of Wapassou, and it was with an immeasurable nostalgia that she conjured up the picture of the fort in those distant forest lands, so rustic, and Honorine . . .

It all seemed already like something from another world.

For something had happened to break the magic circle, the circle of love . . . the chalk circle of the ancient Celtic legends.

The evening was drawing in. Angélique found herself assailed by her old fears. The sound of the sea spoke of her former solitude, of the exhausting battle she had had

to wage as a woman alone, the endless struggle to survive the snares of greedy men, a struggle from which
she had seen no release, no matter which way she turned;
and particularly because of the sound of the sea, and its
harsh breath, coupled with the voices of the pirates—she
thought of the Mediterranean where she had found herself entirely alone, pursued like a hunted animal.

But she soon managed to overcome this moment of
weakness, for the happiness of the past months had
strengthened her.

She felt that she had succeeded in overcoming the
obstacles that had stood in the way of the full blossoming
of her personality, and that now she was gradually at-
taining that inner tranquillity of mind that was the prerogative of her years and one of its greatest attractions.
Sure of herself, sure of the love in which she could take
refuge and seek rest, the world now appeared less hostile
and easier to bend to her will.

She must just persevere a little longer and this trying
time would come to an end. Everything would return
to normal once more.

She sought an opportunity for further conversation
with Yann, for his open face revealed his astonishment
at finding her in the company of these gallows-birds.
But whether by chance or as a result of some minor plot
she never had a moment alone with him all evening, for
the others monopolized him. Although Boulanger and
Beaumarchand did their utmost to welcome him as one
of them, Count Peyrac's equerry found it impossible to
overcome his repulsion for them.

'Eat up, lad,' Hyacinth urged him cordially, serving
him a brimming ladleful of soup, and doing his best to
give his hideously sinister, swollen face an expression of
welcome.

Yann thanked him politely, but remained tense, and
from time to time attempted to catch Angélique's eye
in the hope of some unspoken explanation.

That night they dined on turtle soup, which Hyacinth
had himself put on to simmer. Now turtle soup was the
buccaneers' speciality and it had to be admitted that
this particular specimen was especially delicious, for,
like many other pirates, Hyacinth was an excellent cook.

'I can feel the life flowing back into me,' Aristide said with a smack of the tongue.

'We'll soon have you hopping about like a rabbit,' Angélique agreed as she tucked him up for the night.

By now she had the impression that she was no longer keeping watch over him—rather that he and his companions were watching her.

She nevertheless managed to draw apart with Yann in order to explain the strange company she was in.

'The captain of their ship abandoned them on the coast, probably for insubordination. They are no danger as long as they are sick . . . that is, for the time being. But I am anxious for Monsieur de Peyrac to come for us as soon as possible. Cantor must have reached Gouldsboro by now . . . Have you any ammunition?'

He had used up what he had in hunting animals to keep alive. All that remained was a little gunpowder at the bottom of his powder horn.

Angélique loaded the musket and laid it beside her.

The heat was unbearable, and the night breeze off the sea did nothing to dispel the feeling of oppression.

As was her custom, Angélique sat down under the tree not far from the sick man. A strange lethargy began to steal over her and soon she found it hard to keep her eyes open.

The last thing she saw was the half moon emerging from the clouds, as its long, golden shimmer suddenly spread across the silent bay, leaping over the black mounds of the scattered islands.

'That's my moon,' Angélique thought vaguely, 'the moon that makes me amorous . . .' For she knew that she was more easily roused on the night when the moon billowed like a lateen sail across the sky.

Then she fell fast asleep, and had a most disturbing dream; she was surrounded by a crowd of people whose faces she could not make out, for they stood out like so many black shadows against an ice-pink sky.

She gave a sudden shudder. This was no dream, for her eyes were open. SHE WAS SURROUNDED BY A CROWD OF PEOPLE. She could see their dark heavy shapes moving slowly about her, and the sky was pink, for dawn was rising over Casco Bay.

Angélique made to get up. Her body felt like lead. She ran her hand mechanically over her face.

Then she noticed Yann a short distance from her; he was standing, tied to a tree, well and truly bound, his lips tight with fury.

There was Aristide Beaumarchand, sitting up, supported by two unknown sailors, greedily swigging the contents of a fresh bottle of rum.

'So there you are, my pretty one,' he said with a titter. 'It's our turn to have the upper hand now . . .'

A voice said:

'Shut up, you old numbskull, no self-respecting gentleman of adventure would insult his vanquished enemy . . . especially when that enemy is a lovely lady.'

Angélique looked up at the man who had spoken. He seemed young, attractive, and well dressed, as if he had once been a page, to judge by his smile and his manners.

'And who are you?' she asked in a toneless voice.

He raised his broad-brimmed hat with its red feather and bowed gallantly.

'I am François de Barssempuy.'

Then with a second deep bow, his hand on his heart, he added:

'Lieutenant to Captain Gold Beard.'

CHAPTER 29

IT WAS then that she saw that there was a ship lying at anchor in the bay at the foot of the promontory.

The first thing that struck her was that it was a very handsome ship, although on the short side and somewhat old-fashioned, with its high poop and forecastle, whose brilliantly coloured ornaments glittered in the dawn light.

It was an argosy rather than a ship, a vessel of considerable dignity, that rocked gently as a boat was lowered from its side into the still waters in which the reflection of the anchor chain formed a sharp angle where it touched the surface . . . 'Ha ha!' laughed Hyacinth, 'turtle soup makes one sleep, doesn't it, especially when a little something is added . . . I had the pick of all your little bottles . . .'

Suddenly Angélique felt wide awake again. She grasped what had happened. She leapt nimbly to her feet and in a flash had hurled herself at Beaumarchand, seizing him by the shoulders and shaking him as if he were a plum tree.

'You wretch! I sewed your belly up for you and you have betrayed me to Gold Beard!'

It took four of them to tear her off while he, badly shaken, was as waxen as a candle and running with sweat.

'It's all going to burst open again!' he moaned, clutching at his stomach.

'And I hope it does,' Angélique replied, furiously.

'Hold onto her,' he begged the others. 'You saw what she did to me? A woman who shakes a sick man about like that, deserves no pity.'

'Idiot!' Angélique shouted at him, and with a gesture that brooked no retort she freed herself from the hands that held her, saying as she did so:

'Take your hands off me!'

Breathing rapidly she stood glowering at Aristide, who was not feeling in good fettle.

He was no Adonis, with his body shrunken within his ill-fitting clothes.

'You are a loathsome creep,' she shouted contemptuously at him, 'the most despicable person I ever met. I could gladly spit on you . . .'

'Get her knife,' he begged.

'Let any man dare to come near me,' said Angélique, stepping back, one hand on her dagger.

And the circle of flabbergasted men looked at her as if she were some apparition, with her dazzling hair all blown about by the wind and her pale green eyes that seemed to mirror the sea.

'Madame,' Monsieur de Barssempuy said with great courtesy, 'I'm afraid I must ask you for your weapon.'

'Come and get it.'

'Be careful, Lieutenant!' called Aristide, 'she knows how to use it. That was what ripped me open.'

'And she hurled beehives at our heads,' the buccaneer

called Hyacinth added, standing prudently out of range, 'and we still have faces like pumpkins.'

The men looked at him and burst out laughing.

'She's dangerous, I tell you!' Hyacinth yelled indignantly. 'She's a witch, is that woman, you know she is. They told us so in the Bay.'

But the men only laughed the louder.

Angélique sensed that most of them thought pretty poorly of these wretched deserters who had betrayed her so ignominiously.

She pretended to lose interest in the wretched pair and turned to Barssempuy, who at least was a Frenchman and a nobleman to all appearances.

'How did they manage to betray me like this?' she asked, walking up to the man with complete unconcern. 'That wretch had been terribly wounded, and the others were not much better. And we were watching them all the time. How could they have told you that I was here?'

'It was Martinez,' the young man replied. 'He disembarked on one of the islands in the Bay where we were caulking the ship and he told us where you were.'

Martinez? . . . the fifth pirate who had left with Cantor and the English? A troublesome fellow whom they had intended to disembark somewhere before leaving Casco Bay. So it had been easy for the cunning wretch to get them to put him down somewhere on an island where he knew his erstwhile companions were resting and cleaning the hull of their vessel.

As bearer of the information that the Countess of Peyrac could be taken prisoner without difficulty a few miles away, the mutineer was certain of a warm welcome.

And all the time that Angélique had been wearing herself out nursing this evil wretch he, although a desperately sick man, had managed to find enough breath to plot and scheme this piece of double-dealing, this backhanded blow of which she was now the victim.

The arrival of Yann could scarcely have suited them, but he was alone.

Warned no doubt by distant signals of the arrival of their accomplices, the night before they were due to land, the men had put a sleeping-draught into the soup.

She look round. Where were Adhemar, the old Indian woman, and the four English people who had escaped the massacre? A certain amount of noise from the beach led her to think that they had probably already been taken on board as prisoners.

And what about Piksarett? She looked hard in the direction of the forest, but the forest was mute, motionless, and offered her no reprieve. Before her lay the sea, with its horizon tipped by a wisp of mauve mist, and the mouth of the little bay of Maquoit, with its brightly painted ship lying at anchor, as the pink of dawn grew paler, merging little by little into the colourless light of day.

Angélique had regained her composure and her mind was working feverishly. She asked herself what advantages there were in having fallen in with French privateers. The Caribbean buccaneers owed their allegiance half to the French and half to the English. English pirates might well not have bothered about her and would have left her in peace on her rock, but with her compatriots at least she had the advantage of being able to talk things over.

This man Gold Beard, so be it! He wanted war. He was taking her prisoner no doubt to use her as a hostage against Joffrey de Peyrac! So be it! But he would hear her out! He would come to regret this foray of his . . . No matter what kind of man he turned out to be, she felt quite sure that she could win over.

Gold Beard! A man calculated to frighten the name of a swashbuckler, a braggart who thought that the disguise made the man! Not very clever, in all likelihood, but possibly more civilized and more approachable than many of his kind.

Angélique noticed that the members of the crew surrounding her were better dressed and cleaner than she would have expected, which led her to think that she might be able to come to some kind of understanding with their master. Of course, they were dressed in a somewhat showy and flamboyant manner, like most sailors who, freed from all ties and with pockets full of gold, lead a gay life, unable to resist the temptation of strutting about in borrowed plumes. Within every man

174

who suffers no constraint lies a bragging child. But there was nothing in their manner that she could have regarded as really coarse or disreputable, and she now understood better why the five scoundrels she had found had been set ashore as undesirables on some deserted strand.

All this took Angélique only a few seconds to register, long enough for her heart to regain its normal rhythm and for her to make her plans.

'This Gold Beard, your captain, where is he?'

'He is coming towards us now, Madame.'

François de Barssempuy pointed to the boat that had left the ship's side and was being rowed towards them.

Standing in the prow was a man of giant stature. Seen against the light his figure stood out as a huge black silhouette, and his features could not be perceived—only that he was bearded and long-haired like a Viking, and had a kind of golden, bristling halo all round his head. He wore a sleeved doublet with broad revers sewn with gold braid, and a broad shoulderbelt laden with weapons; his riding boots reached to mid-thigh, emphasizing the strong lines of his robust legs. Standing thus outlined against the dazzling backcloth of the bay, he seemed to Angélique to be a veritable giant.

As they came within a few fathoms of the shore, he suddenly donned a large felt hat with yellow and green parrot feathers, that he had been holding in his hand.

Angélique felt a sudden pang of apprehension. Would the captain in fact be more civilized and reassuring than his crew?

Taking advantage of the fact that everyone seemed to be looking at the new arrival, she sidled imperceptibly closer to Yann, where he stood tied to his tree.

'Get ready,' she whispered. 'I'm going to cut your bonds with my knife. When this man Gold Beard lands, everyone will be busy looking at him and will move forwards to meet him. Run off into the forest as fast as you can . . . Run! Run! Go and warn Monsieur de Peyrac and tell him not to worry too much about me. I will do my best to keep the pirate in these waters until help arrives . . .'

She spoke in the Indian way, almost without moving her lips, and kept her gaze fixed in the direction of the boat.

It seemed to her that Gold Beard must be a redoubtable captain with a considerable hold over his men, for they all kept their eyes firmly fixed on him and straightened their ranks.

The moment he slipped into the water and began to wade heavily towards the shore, Angélique slipped her knife round behind the tree between Yann's wrists, and with a single cut severed his bonds.

In complete silence, broken only by the sudden screeching of gulls that sent a thrill of anxiety through her heart, the pirate advanced towards the promontory.

In an attempt to draw the others away from Yann, Angélique stepped forward boldly.

Yann bounded off like a wild hare, jumping over bushes, leaping over clefts and hollows, slipping between the tree trunks of the pine woods, scaling rocks as he gradually climbed higher and higher. Using the light from the bay seen through the trees to guide him, he made his way round the inlet until he had reached the other side of the fiord.

Then, panting for breath, he stopped, certain that he had not been followed. When he had got his breath back he made his way towards the edge of the cliff to see where he was.

From this vantage point he could see the whole sweep of the bay, the ship lying at anchor and the beach black with people.

His eyes sought out Madame de Peyrac, but, unable to see her, he leaned still farther out, clutching at the root of a stunted tree growing from the extreme edge of the cliff.

Then he saw ... HE SAW ...

His jaw fell, as he gazed in open-eyed surprise, for Yann the sailor, who had seen quite a lot in the course of a harsh life, suddenly felt the world fall to pieces round him as in some cataclysm.

Gold Beard was standing there on the beach with a woman in his arms. A woman who stood looking up at him as if transfigured.

That woman was none other than the wife of Count Peyrac!

There, surrounded by all those men, immobile and almost as astonished as Yann up on his cliff, Gold Beard and Angélique stood gazing at one another, passionately embracing and kissing in front of everyone exactly like two long separated lovers . . . EXACTLY LIKE TWO LONG SEPARATED LOVERS.

CHAPTER 30

'COLIN!' she said.

The room on board his ship to which he had taken her was cool, and through the open poop windows could be seen the sparkling waters of the bay and the dancing reflection of an island.

The ship was still riding at anchor. Silent, drowsy with the heat of the day, it rocked gently, dreamily, and there was no sound but the splashing of wavelets against the hull. The *Heart of Mary* seemed suddenly deserted, its only two remaining occupants being these whom Destiny had brought so dramatically face to face.

'Colin! Colin!' she repeated in a dreamy voice.

Angélique was gazing at him with half-open lips. She had still not recovered properly from the violent emotional shock composed of mingled surprise, consternation, and intense delight she had felt as this giant of a man had climbed up from the water's edge and she had suddenly recognized . . . yes, those broad shoulders, those blue eyes, then, when he saw her, the indescribable expression, the start of surprise that had stopped him in his tracks. She had run towards him. Colin! Colin! My dear friend of the desert!

In the narrow confines of the cabin the huge frame of the man now known as Gold Beard dominated everything else.

He stood facing her in silence.

It was very hot. He removed his cross-belt and laid it on the table, then took off his doublet. Three pistols and a small axe hung from his cross-belt, and she remembered

177

the pain she had felt when he had clasped her to him against all this weaponry. But at the time he had bent down and laid his lips on hers, which had been a spontaneous, violent and delicious sensation.

Now that the frantic excitement of the moment was dying away, she had begun to see him better as the pirate he had become, and regretted the impulse that had thrown her into his arms.

The white collar of his shirt open on his massive chest and the white sleeves rolled up on his powerful arms stood out as bright splashes of light among the oppressive shadows . . .

The last time she had seen him had been at Ceuta,[1] the Spanish city in a Saracen land.

Four—no five—years had passed since then, and now they were in America.

Angélique was beginning to get her bearings again, to take in what was happening. That morning in the anxious light of dawn she had awaited Gold Beard, a redoubtable pirate, an enemy . . . and the man who had come was Colin Paturel, her companion, her friend . . . her lover of old. A shattering surprise!

But it was true. Somewhat crazy but true. For is it not in the nature of all adventurers, all mariners to do just that: to meet at every point on the globe to which ships are drawn across the seas.

It was chance—of a kind about which she had never even thought—that had brought her face to face with the man in whose company she had escaped from Meknès, with whom she had fled from Barbary . . . But that was on the other side of the globe, and a long time ago. Neither of them knew what the other had been doing in the years since.

That tall, silent presence, similar to and yet different from the one she had remembered, made her more acutely aware of the reality of that time, as if the years had suddenly begun to fill the confined space of the cabin with a heavy, slightly turbid water that held them apart. And now they were growing more distant from each other, recrossing the barrier of time. Time was resuming

[1] See *Angélique and the Sultan*.

its shape, and once more becoming a palpable element.

Angélique rested her chin on her hands and forced herself to smile in an attempt to dispel the confusion that had brought fire to her cheeks and made her eyes over bright.

'So it's you,' she said . . . 'You my dear friend Colin, in the person of the corsair Gold Beard about whom I have heard so much . . . I must confess it was the last thing I was expecting . . . I had not the slightest inkling . . .'

She broke off because he moved. He drew up a stool and sat down to face her, across the table, his arms folded, leaning forward, head sunk slightly into his shoulders as he looked at her unwaveringly with his blue, thoughtful eyes.

And beneath this gaze she knew not what to say, aware that he sought and found each familiar feature, as she herself in this weather-beaten face with its golden beard, in this broad forehead crossed by three pale lines that looked like scars beneath his tousled Norman hair, rediscovered, scarcely changed, a familiar, reassuring and beloved face. No doubt an illusion, for during the past years had he not become a criminal?

But she could not help seeing him as he had bent over her when fear had set her trembling. And beneath his incisive glance, she knew that she was holding up to him the face of the woman she had become and that the light from the open windows was casting a pearly sheen over her hair. The features of a woman who did not seek to hide them, full of pride and self-knowledge, with that imperial seal that maturity set upon them; there was a greater purity of line, greater harmony in the bone structure, the line of the nose, the brows, the curve of the mouth, a greater softness, shadow and mystery in her sea-blue gaze, and a perfection in the fulfilment of her whole being that radiated from her and that had been responsible for the enslavement of Pont-Briand to the point of madness.

CHAPTER 31

AFTER A long pause he said:

'It's astounding! You are even more beautiful than I remembered you.

'And yet,' he went on, 'that memory, God knows how it has haunted me!'

Angélique shook her head in denial.

'There is nothing very miraculous about my being more beautiful today than the poor wreck I was then . . . And my hair has gone almost white, look.'

He nodded.

'I remember . . . It began to go white as we made our way through the desert . . . Too much pain . . . Too much suffering . . . poor child! Poor courageous child . . .'

She recognized his voice with its hint of peasant accent and that trace of paternal teasing in its deep tones that had so moved her in days gone by. She did not want to feel moved like this, to be unable to find the words she sought.

And her gesture of passing her hand across her forehead, gracefully but a little sadly, to brush back a lock of her golden hair, made him sigh deeply.

Angélique would have preferred to give the whole incident a lighter tone, to talk and joke with him. She felt as if Colin Paturel's glance penetrated to her innermost depths, overwhelming her, paralysing her.

He had always been serious, and did not easily laugh. But today he seemed still more grave, with a heavy inscrutability that might well mask sadness and cunning.

'So you know that I am Count Peyrac's wife?' she resumed, to break the silence.

'Yes, indeed I do . . . That is why I am here. To capture you, for I have an account to settle with the Lord of Gouldsboro, Count Peyrac.'

A smile lit up his features, suddenly giving his rough features a look of gentleness.

'But were I to say that I expected to find you under this name, it would be a lie,' he said. 'And you are here, you, whom I have dreamed of night and day for so many years.'

Angélique began to feel that she was losing her grip on the situation. She realized that the past few days, spent at the extreme tip of a wind-beaten peninsula hoping against hope to be rescued, had worn down her resistance, and that she now found herself defenceless when faced with a situation whose demands exceeded her powers.

'But you are Gold Beard,' she exclaimed as if to protect herself from herself. 'You are no longer Colin Paturel . . . You have become a criminal.'

'No, good heavens no, what a notion!' he replied in surprise, but remaining completely calm.

'I am a corsair in the King's name, and I have valid documents to this effect.'

'Was it true that you drew the Spaniards' fire on to the monks when you took Portobello?'

'Oh! That was another story. They had been sent to us by the Governor, thinking that their pious prayers would make us agree to terms, but treachery is always treachery, whether disguised by a monk's robes or not. We had come to vanquish the Spaniard, and vanquish him we did. The Spaniards are not like us people from the North, and they never will be like us. They have too much Moorish blood in their veins . . . And that's not the end of it . . . The cruelty they practise in the name of Christ, that I cannot stand. The day we made those monks walk ahead of us, there were ten pyres burning on the hills, ten fires lighted at the orders of those pious monks—*autas-da-fé* being held as sacrifice for victory, with hundreds of Indians burning at the stake, because they had refused to work in the gold mines or to the converted . . .

'Crueller than Moors and greedier than Christians— that's the Spaniards. A frightening mixture of rapacity and fanaticism . . . No, I have not the slightest remorse at having made those monks act as a shield to us in Portobello. It is true, and I have to admit it, my sweet, that I am no longer the good Christian I used to be . . . When I left Ceuta on the *Bonaventure*, I went first to the East Indies.

'There it fell to my lot to save the life of the daughter of the Great Mogul who had been captured by pirates, and the riches he showered upon me as a mark of gratitude made me a wealthy man. Then, by way of the Pacific islands I made my way to Peru, then to New Granada, and finally to the Antilles, where, after fighting with that great English commander, Captain Morgan, against the Spaniards—I was with him in Panama—I followed him to Jamaica where he is Governor. With the money from the Great Mogul and the booty I had won I fitted out a ship as a privateer. That was last year. Yes, I admit it, after my days in Morocco I have ceased to be a good Christian. I've found I could only pray to the Virginia Mary because she was a woman and made me think of you. I know that that was not right either, but I felt that the heart of the Virgin is indulgent to poor men, that she understands everything and especially matters of that kind. So that was why, as soon as I found myself the owner of a ship, I called it the *Heart of Mary*.'

He carefully drew off his leather gloves and laid his two bare hands, palms uppermost, in front of her on the table.

'Do you see,' he said, 'can you see the marks of the nails? They are still there . . .'

She lowered her gaze from his face and saw the purple marks left by the nails that had crucified him. One day at Meknès, the Sultan Moulay Ismael had had him nailed to the New Gate at the entrance to the town, and if he had not died, it was only because nothing could lay low Colin Paturel, the King of the Slaves.

'There was a time when seafaring folk began to call me the Crucified,' he continued. 'I said I would kill anyone who gave me this name, and I had some gloves made. For I knew that I was unworthy of bearing so blessed a name. But I am not a criminal either, only a seaman who, after much fighting, and much plundering, has managed to become his own master . . . to obtain his freedom, in other words. We alone know that that means more than life.'

He had spoken for a long time. And Angélique's heart had begun to grow calmer and she felt grateful to him for enabling her to take possession of herself once more. The heat outside seemed less trying.

'His own master,' he repeated. 'After twelve years of slavery, and many more of servitude under the orders of captains not worth the rope to hang them with, that is something to delight the heart of man.'

His hands moved towards Angélique's, enveloping them but without clasping them.

'Do you remember,' he asked, 'do you remember Meknès?'

She shook her head and drew her hands away, holding them against herself in a gesture of refusal.

'No, hardly at all, I don't want to remember. Everything is different now. We are in another land now, Colin, and I am the wife of Count Peyrac . . .'

'Yes, yes, I know,' he said with the same faint smile, 'you have already said that.'

But she could see that the statement meant nothing to him, that she would always remain in his eyes that solitary, hunted slave-girl whom he had once taken under his protection, his companion in flight, his beloved child of the desert whom he had carried on his back, whom he had possessed on the bare, rocky ground of the Rif and tasted in her the most wondrous delights of love.

And then she suddenly remembered that she had borne Colin's child in her womb, and a pang shot through her, as poignant as the pain she had felt on losing the child.

Her eyelids drooped and in spite of herself her head fell back as she relived that demented carriage drive that had carried her off, a prisoner of the King, across the roads of France, then the accident, the terrible shock, the pain, and the blood that had begun to flow . . . At that time she had been abandoned by everyone; in a swift moment of reminiscence she had asked herself, wild-eyed, how she had ever managed to escape the crushing pincers of the French Kings' ban and begin a new life once more. It seemed unbelievable.

The man who sat watching her saw, fleeting across this disturbingly beautiful face, a reflection of pain and distress never revealed . . . never avowed. Those secret sorrows that women keep to themselves, for men would never understand . . .

The sunlight, now growing pink, gave to Angélique's golden face, with the long shadow of her eyelashes spread across her cheeks, an unearthly beauty, and brought back marvellous memories that had haunted him day and night, memories of this woman asleep beside him, or swooning with pleasure in his arms.

He half stood up and leaned across towards her.

'What is it, my lamb? Are you unwell?'

'It's nothing,' she replied softly.

Colin's deep, troubled voice, so reminiscent of the past, stirred her to the very depths, but this time it was a gentler movement like that of a child within her, and she recognized the feeling, the sweet wave of physical desire that this man's presence made her feel in spite of herself.

'I am so tired,' she murmured. 'All those days waiting by the sea, looking after that miserable wretch . . . what was his name now?'

And she ran the palms of her hands nervously over her brow and cheeks, avoiding his gaze.

He stood up straight, came round the table and stood before her. He looked gigantic under this low ceiling. The Herculean figure, all muscle and bone, of Moulay Ismael's strongest slave had, over the course of his seafaring years, filled out with flesh which gave this giant, whom none had ever managed to beat or bend to their will, an impressive stature, square shoulders, a powerful round neck, the brow of a bull and a chest as broad as a shield.

'Rest,' he said gently, 'I will have you sent some refreshment. You must rest, then you will feel better and we can talk.'

His tone remained calm and assured, a tone that reassured, that relieved her anxiety. But she sensed that he had reached some implacable decision about her and she threw him an almost supplicating look.

A tremor ran through him and his jaws clenched.

She hoped that he would leave her, but suddenly he was kneeling down, and she felt his hot hand grasp her ankle in a grip that nothing could release, as his fingers lifted the hem of her dress up towards her bare knee.

He laid bare her pearly white leg upon which was revealed the twisting bluish furrow of the old scar.

'It's there,' he cried with contained rapture, 'it is still there, the mark of the serpent.' Then leaning down, he suddenly laid his burning lips on the blue scar.

Then almost as swiftly he released her and, with a glance full of passionate longing, left the room.

CHAPTER 32

SHE REMAINED alone, but the burning sensation of his kiss on the ancient wound that Colin's knife had made so many years ago to save her when she had been bitten by a snake, still remained, and, where his fingers had encircled her ankle, the sensation remained with her, like a tight steel band.

She saw the pink mark of his fingers gradually begin to fade.

He had always been so; this man, this gentle, peace-loving, courageous man who did not know his own strength! He had often hurt people unintentionally, under the stress of emotion, and as he made love to her he had sometimes frightened her, even made her groan, so weak and fragile had she felt in his arms, a creature he could so easily have crushed through inadvertence. Whenever he became aware of his unintentional violence, he would implore: 'Forgive me . . . I am a brute, am I not? Tell me I am, tell me I am a brute,' to which she would reply laughing: 'No you aren't; didn't you feel you made me happy?'

Angélique was shaken by a violent trembling and began to pace up and down the narrow cabin, unable to overcome the sensations that tormented her. The heat was unbearable and the evening light had become orange, sulphur-coloured.

Her dress stuck to her shoulder-blades and she felt a tremendous need to change her clothes, and to feel some cool water trickling over her.

Caught off her guard that morning by the pirates, she had been barefooted when captured. And barefooted she had gone down to the beach to where Gold Beard awaited her—how tightly he had clasped her to him!—and she was still barefooted as she strode up and down the wooden floor boards. She went over to the window and shook out her hair in the hope of feeling the freshness of the sea breeze, but the air was still and heavy, with a smell of melted pitch. The sailors were still busy caulking and filling the timbers of the ship . . . She felt overpowered at the thought that chance had brought her face to face with a lover from her past life whom she had not realized had made so vivid an impression on her heart. And once again her heart gave a lurch as she felt the sweet wave of desire sweep over her at the recollection of his deep voice saying: 'What is it, my lamb? Are you unwell? . . .'

Simple words, but words which had always moved her to the very depths. Like his possession of her, primitive, but total, so full of power that she submitted to it rather than shared it.

It swept over her, like a wave breaking on top of her, taking her breath away, the drive and ardour of the gigantic Norman, freed from all restraint as soon as her eyes said yes. Her body was revisited by forgotten sensations, the extraordinary delight of that desert love-making.

He had always been terribly impatient to possess her. He wanted her right away. He would lay her down on the sand and enter her immediately, without a word of love, without a caress. And yet she had never been offended by his way with her, for every time she had been aware, in the thrust of his powerful loins, in his inexorable invasion of her, of the drive of a strength that was prodigious, but serene and generous, a boundless and almost mystical giving of his entire being. He may have been heedless of her, but not of the act itself. A celebrant lost in love, celebrating the offering, the union, the joy of mankind on earth.

Was it sacrilegious to think that Colin Paturel made love as he did everything else, with faith, piety, strength and violence?

She sometimes thought she would die of his embraces, for her exhausted body was too weakened by privation to be able to bear his raptures and respond to them, and yet this lovemaking had taught her the delights of submission, the savour of being nothing, nothing more than a proffered cup from which he drank his fill, nothing but flesh to provoke his pleasure, nothing but a body, a female body, abandoned and forgotten beneath him, but from which he drew such utter ecstasy.

Abnegation, abdication, which would suddenly find their recompense in an unpredictable flash, at that moment when she sank into oblivion, just as the virile attack was reaching its climax and snatching her from the void, dragging her back to life with a cry of awakening, a cry of rebirth, of renewal, a cry that rose from her innermost depths as she writhed in the ultimate spasm.

She still remembered that irrepressible convulsion as a dazzling wave that radiated in a torrent of sensation through her body, half dead and yet still capable of the pleasure that is the source of all life.

Like the bud that bursts forth suddenly in the light of spring.

By this stirring of her vitals she recognized the strength of life.

'I am alive, I am alive,' she kept on repeating to herself. With his blind passion he seemed to have wrested her from the sleep of death into which she had been sinking, her blood stirred again in her veins, and she wondered at this precious miracle, as, wide-eyed, she looked up at Colin's face, close to hers, with its blue, limpid eyes like pools of clear water, and his shadowy mouth glimpsed between the hairs of his golden beard as his panting breath gently brushed her face.

Yes, Colin had not only saved her life: he had given her back life and taught her to love life and not merely survive. And it was essentially thanks to him that she had had the courage and strength to find her husband and children again.

Oh! why now did the movement of the sea and the sound of the tide rushing into the narrow channels along the coast, why did all this have to conjure up so vividly visions of the past? In the woods of Wapassou she would have forgotten Colin.

'I must get out of here,' she told herself, beginning to panic.

She ran to the door and tried to open it. But it had been bolted. Then she noticed her travelling bag on the floor, and a tray of food on a table, some grilled salmon with boiled golden corn, a bowl of salad, and a glass dish containing some slices of preserved citron and pineapple. The wine in the flagon seemed of good quality and the water in the jug was cold.

While she had been day-dreaming someone must have come in and left all this, and her thoughts had been so far away that she had not noticed.

She did not touch the food but drank some water.

She opened her bag and noticed that half her things were missing, and this made her impatient. She would go and ask Colin to send those good-for-nothing sailors of his back on land to fetch all her things.

He would do as she bade him. He was her slave. She was the only person who mattered to him. She had seen this as soon as their eyes had met and they had recognized one another.

The only thing he wanted on earth was her, still her, always her. And she had just been restored to him . . .

How could she escape him? How could she escape from herself?

She was on the point of banging on the door and calling loudly, when she changed her mind. No, she did not want to see Colin. The mere thought of the way he looked at her threw her into a state of extreme agitation and she began to feel that things were too much for her.

If only Joffrey would come quickly to fetch her.

'I do hope that Yann hurries!'

She looked outside. The day was drawing to a close. The sun had disappeared behind a bank of cloud from which came the occasional flash of summer lightning, while the rocking of the ship, still riding at anchor, was becoming more pronounced.

Angélique removed her clothes and poured the cold water from the jug over the nape of her neck, letting it run the full length of her body. This made her feel better, and she slipped on a fine lawn shift. She continued to pace up and down the little room, now grown quite dark, like a pale, agitated ghost. The short shift felt pleasant and light on her feverish body and she became aware of the pleasant sensation of a light breeze playing around her bare legs, a still uncertain breeze that had at last sprung up, ruffling the crests of the waves before falling again.

'There is a storm brewing . . . That is why the ship is still lying at anchor and has not sailed,' she thought. Colin must have sensed the approach of a storm.

She picked up the piece of printed calico spread over the bunk, wrapped herself in it and lay down. She wanted to sleep.

But myriad thoughts crowded in her brain. Why had Gold Beard wanted to take her prisoner? What were these title deeds he held to land at Gouldsboro? Why had Joffrey sent her to the English village? She would think all this out later, later!

The thunder burst upon them with a dull roar, awakening echoes on the nearby land. But the following rumble already seemed farther off.

The storm is farther out at sea. . . .

The rocking motion of the ship was bearing her away, plunging her into a sweet torpor. Colin . . . Long ago . . . in the desert . . .

He only kissed her afterwards, after his body had satisfied its urgent hunger. He only caressed her afterwards . . . Their kisses were gentle, hesitant and cautious, for their lips were cracked through lack of water and the burning rays of the sun, and would often bleed . . . A thrill ran through her and her body tensed at the memory of Colin's cracked, dry lips on hers, Colin's lips exploring her body . . .

She turned over violently. Then, with nerves at breaking-point, through sheer exhaustion she fell into a deep sleep.

CHAPTER 33

'No, COLIN, not that, I beg you not that . . .'
Gold Beard's arms, Colin's muscular arms were lifting

189

her irresistibly, raising her up towards him, and, clasped to his firm naked chest she felt Colin's fingers, there between her breasts, grasping the edge of the fine lawn shift and pulling until the veil was rent without effort in a single wrench, as silent as the dimness of a mist. Colin's hand were on her loins, on her hips, taking hold of her, familiarizing himself once again with her. The man's hand insinuating itself between her legs, there, in that place set apart where the skin is as soft a satin, moving still higher in a caress that seemed never to end.

'No, Colin, not that, I beg you . . . I beg you!'

Black night surrounded her, shot with a glimmer of bronze.

The man had placed a candle on the table behind him, but for Angélique, naked and swooning in Colin's arms, all was night. He was like night himself, a vast abyss of night, a dark shape, leaning over her entirely enveloping her in his obscure untamed passion. And as he clasped her to him, still tenaciously caressing her, his mouth sought her lips as she tried to escape him, rolling her head from side to side in a final attempt to resist him.

'My little girl, my little girl!' he whispered, trying to appease her.

This was what he used to call her.

At last he managed to overcome her resistance and she felt his soft, cool lips through the tickling warmth of his beard as they took hold of hers.

Then he remained completely motionless, her head held rigid by his encircling steely arm, and made no attempt to force the barrier of her closed lips. And little by little it was she herself who sought to awaken, to move, and grasp the secret of the man's mouth that lay like a seal upon hers, bidding it come to life, soliciting a response, and finally feeling the lips part. Then she in turn capitulated with a kind of avid, dumb cry, overwhelmed by a sudden hunger, and gave herself up to the mysterious, intimate approach of the kiss.

Unspoken, giddy dialogue, a quest more subtle, more delicate than total possession, hesitant curiosity, recognition, avowal, discovery, a striking spark, its crackling ever renewed, stirring desire and tenderness in the blood, as the sun burst forth in the head, an endless contact, thirst never slaked, the paradisial taste of oblivion, delicious pulp to stave off hunger, response, response, each time more tender, more total, until the body so desired is nothing more than an immense, impatient offering, a feast of love duly prepared for the celebration of the rites.

Colin's sheer power pushed her down, tilting her back until she was pinned, powerless, to the bed.

'No, Colin! . . . please, my love, not that . . . Have pity on me, I can't . . . I can't . . . resist you any more.'

Colin's knees had begun to force their way between her tightly joined legs, trying to part them with one firm thrust, a single, unremitting pressure . . .

Then Angélique cried out in protest, almost without hearing it herself:

'If you do, I will hate you! By God, I would hate you, Colin!'

He froze, thunderstruck, listening to the echo of her cry as it cut into him like a blade.

A long minute dragged by in silence, while the flickering flame of the candle cast shadows on the wall, those eternal shadows of human nights, confused shadows, everlastingly reshaped since time immemorial, the shadows of a man and a woman intertwined in love . . .

With a firm twist of her body Angélique freed herself from the imprisoning band of Colin's powerful arms and leapt in such haste and folly from her bunk that she almost tipped the table over, knocking the candle to the floor, where it went out.

She had drawn with her the piece of calico in which she had wrapped herself before going to sleep, and now feverishly wrapped it round her again, while she tried, giving herself many a hard knock in the process, to place the table as a rampart between Colin and herself.

She could not see him, for the darkness was absolute. Outside the night was moonless, a night of cloud and trailing mists.

But she sensed that the man had gathered himself together again like an animal about to spring.

'Angélique! Angélique!' Colin's voice came to her through the darkness, and his cry not only told of the anguish of frustrated desire but also spoke of heart-rending despair.

'Angélique!'

He moved forward, staggering, arms outstretched, and stumbled into the table.

'Be quiet!' said Angélique softly, through clenched teeth, 'and go away. I cannot give myself to you, Colin, I am Count Peyrac's wife.'

'Peyrac!' murmured Colin's hoarse voice, and she had the impression he was about to die, 'Peyrac, that outlaw, that gentleman of adventure, playing the prince and the king on the Acadian coast . . .'

'I am his wife!'

'You married him the way all the sluts who knock about the Antilles marry . . . for his gold, for his ships, for the jewels he decked you out in, because he fed you . . . didn't you? What rock did you discover him on? You were knocking about the world looking for a rich corsair, weren't you? And he offered you emeralds and pearls . . . didn't he? Now be honest?'

'I owe you no explanation. I am his wife, and I married him before God.'

'Fiddlesticks! . . . these things are easily forgotten!'

'Don't blaspheme, Colin!'

'I too can offer you emeralds and pearls . . . I could be as rich as him . . . Do you love him?'

'It's not your business whether I love him or not!' she cried in despair. 'I am HIS WIFE and I don't intend to spend my life breaking solemn oaths.'

He flinched, and she added quickly:

'We cannot do that, Colin . . . it's out of the question! That's over . . . You would destroy my life . . .'

His voice was dull as he asked:

'Is it true that you would hate me?'

'Yes, I would! I should hate you. I should hate even the memory of you, even the past . . . You would have become the cause of my unhappiness, my worst enemy . . . the instrument of my worst transgression . . . I should hate myself. I would rather you killed me right now . . . Kill me! Kill me rather than that . . .'

Colin's breath rasped like the bellows of a forge, as if he was in his death agony.

'Leave me alone! Leave me, Colin!'

She spoke softly, but the contained violence of her words gave each one the strength and cutting edge of a sharp dagger.

'I cannot leave you,' he breathed, 'you belong to me. You belong to me in all my dreams. And now that you are here before me, I will not give you up. Otherwise what would be the point of my having found you again? What would be the meaning of the chance that put you in my path again? . . . I have missed you too much by night and by day . . . I have suffered too much from the memory of you to give you up now . . . I must have you.'

'Then kill me; Kill me right away.'

The heavy darkness was filled with the sound of their broken breathing. And Angélique felt herself faltering as she clung to the table, as the ship rocked back and forth in a giddy, immeasurable movement, a blind vertigo in which her fear of her own weakness was added to her fear of what might happen if ever this inescapable 'thing' which she sensed was returning, ever took place . . . And it was true that at that moment she would have preferred to die.

When she heard Colin move and felt that he was drawing closer, a noiseless cry rose from her innermost depths, a cry such as she had never uttered within her, a cry she did not recognize as an appeal for help to something stronger than her own weakness, something more lucid, more merciful . . .

Then little by little she realized that all had grown still about her, that peace had returned, and she sensed an emptiness, as she realized that once again she was alone.

Colin had left her, Colin had gone.

CHAPTER 34

IT WAS a very cruel moment for her, a moment of confusion, of despair, in which the eternal child in woman took the upper hand with all its illogicality, its regrets, its unwillingness to face reality, a moment in which her tormented body and distracted mind struggled in the grasp of an unbearable dilemma. She felt as if she ached to the very tips of her fingers, ached so that she could scream.

Finally her nerves began to calm down and she groped around in vain for the candle. It must have rolled away into some corner, but a glimmering of milky white light came from the moon, slipping between two clouds, and Angélique staggered as if drunk across to the little balcony outside the french windows and leaned against the gilded balustrade.

There she rested her weight on her elbows, and drew a series of deep breaths.

The moon was shining now. The sky, just dappled with clouds, spread out over her head like a pearly shell, filled with the endless roar of the surf and the nostalgic, rather lugubrious cry of the seals along the beaches.

Angélique's eyes strayed, without dwelling on any one thing, but her senses gradually grew calmer, and as a full realization of the terrible danger she had run was borne in on her, her legs almost gave way under her.

'I almost did it,' she told herself, breaking out into a cold sweat.

Then, as the seconds passed, elemental fear crushed and utterly destroyed the dazzling, delightful mirage of temptation.

'If I had done it. . .!'

At that very moment, she told herself, she would have been like one dead . . . like . . . she could no longer find words to describe the sensation of ravishment and total destruction she would have felt, if . . .

Henceforth she would know that desire must be rated among the most terrible of terrestrial cataclysms, equal in force to tidal waves, cyclones, and earthquakes, something that defied reason, that trampled human weakness irresistibly beneath blind physical force.

How had she found the strength to escape him? Horror-struck, she bit her fingers, staring before her into the yawning gulf.

How could I have?

She touched her lips.

194

'And that kiss . . . I should never . . . I should never have kissed Colin in that way.'

Her tongue against his tongue.

She dropped her face into her hands.

'Unpardonable! Unpardonable! . . .'

Joffrey!

She felt a superstitious fear at calling upon him, as if he were standing there behind her, staring at her with piercing eyes.

'It was Joffrey who taught me the delights of kissing, it was he who gave me back my taste for it. And I love . . . I so love those endless kisses we share, I could spend my life clasped to his heart, my arms around his neck, and my mouth on his. . . . He knows I could. How could I have come so close to betraying him. It is because I am parted from him that I am weak . . .'

Never is a woman more vulnerable than when she feels the need for consolation in her beloved's absence. Men should be aware of this; husbands should know it.

With her discovery that the turmoil she had felt had stemmed from the unbearable emptiness she felt at being alone, far from him, little by little Angélique began to absolve herself from guilt.

'He should never leave me alone . . . and in any case, was it so serious? Even supposing I had? An embrace? . . . Would that really have parted me from him? It is so little. . . . Like drinking when one is thirsty. There is no harm in drinking. . . . If that is all that is involved when we women are deceived, why all the fuss? A passing desire, a sudden longing . . . so little, in truth. In future I shall be more indulgent when men misbehave. What if Joffrey one day . . . with another woman? . . . No, I couldn't bear it . . . I should die. . . . Yes, now I know that it is very serious! Forgive me . . . Why is it that so accidental an act should, ever since the world was created, bring such tragedy in its wake? The spirit is willing but the flesh is weak! Oh-yes, how true!

'Why should I have felt with Colin, who is almost a stranger to me, so irresistible a temptation? . . . Is love so physical a thing? Joffrey, in his usual cynical way, tells me it is when he wants to tease me. Love is a question of waves of mutual attraction that emanate from the skin. . . . No, not only that! But possibly one of the fundamental conditions? In the past there were some men with whom I found it not, of course, disagreeable, but I knew that there was something missing. The thing I felt from the start with Joffrey, even when he frightened me. . . .

And with Colin? . . . There has always been something more with him, something I could not explain. . . . With Desgrez too, perhaps. And, now that I think of it, it seems strange, the fat captain at the Chatelet, could I have brought myself to 'pay' him thus to save Cantor's life if. . . . My memory of him is not as unpleasant as all that. . . . But with the King? In that case I understand better. . . . There was something lacking. . . . Something missing, that strange, weird recognition between flesh and flesh, that exists between certain people without any evident reason

'Whatever it is exists between Colin and me—and there lies the danger—I must never be alone with him.'

Dreamily, as the ship rose and fell, she let her thoughts wander through the moonlight, and saw in her mind's eye a procession of all the men she had ever known, all so different, among whom suddenly, and without her knowing why, she caught sight of the frank, open face of Count Lomenie-Chambord and the distant, noble figure, hieratic yet forbearing, of the Abbot of Nieul.[1]

CHAPTER 35

THERE WAS a man trying to hide as he clung to the woodwork beneath the balustrade.

For some moments Angélique had broken off her wandering thoughts about the inconsequence and illogicality of the human race in matters of love, and her memories and comparison, in order to observe him.

Her attention caught by a slight noise, she had leaned forward and caught sight of the shadow of a man with hair unkempt and clothes in ribbons, clinging to what

[1] See *Angélique in Revolt.*

were known as the 'galleries', projecting ornaments encircling the two floors of the poop-castle.

'Hi! you,' she whispered, 'what are you doing there?'

Seeing himself discovered, the man slithered away to one side and she caught sight of him again a little lower down, this time clinging to the mouldings around the great plaque painted with the allegory of the Heart of Mary surrounded by angels.

The mysterious arobat gave her a menacing look that nevertheless held a note of supplication.

There were raw, bleeding patches round his wrists.

Angélique understood. Gold Beard's ship had prisoners on board. And this must be one of them trying to escape.

She signalled to him that she had understood and backed away out of sight.

Realizing that she would not raise the alarm, the man took courage and she felt a jerk as he left the ship and heard him dive into the water.

When she looked again all was calm. She sought him in the water beside the ship but he had already surfaced some way off in the shadow of an island and had begun to swim away.

A terrible nostalgia gripped Angélique. She too wanted to get away, to flee this ship in which she felt trapped by her own weakness. Tomorrow Colin would be there again.

'I must leave this ship at all costs,' she told herself, 'at all costs. . . .'

CHAPTER 36

AT THE foot of Mount Desert flows a cool, shady stream, whose limpid waters taste of clay. Pierre du Guast de Monts drank of this water when he came in 1604 to found the first European colony in North America. He was a rich Huguenot nobleman, to whom his friend Henry IV of France, had given the title of Viceroy of the Atlantic Coast of the New World. The geographer Samuel Champlain accompanied him, as did the poet Lescarbot who sang of 'the sweet waters of Acadia'.

Of that first settlement nothing remains but a rotting, half-fallen cross set up by Father Biard the Jesuit, and an old chapel with a silver bell that tinkles in the wind, and is occasionally rung by inquisitive and anxious Redskin children of the Cadillac tribe.[1] An ancient Indian track finishes there, a track leading from the north, crossing lakes and forests from the distant Mount Katthedin, then from rock to rock and across a short stretch of sea before coming to an end on Mount Desert Island.

That particular spring, the green grass and tender birch shoots had lured back the herds of lowing bison, sombre, ancestral, gigantic bovine creatures with obstinate looking heads and velvety withers.

Seen as dark masses through the golden leaves, they seemed fearsome but they were in fact peaceable bucolic creatures.

The forest Indians hunted them very little, for they preferred fallow-deer, stags and roe-deer. So the herd of bison which was busy that morning cropping the tall grass at the foot of the mountain showed no anxiety when their delicate nostrils sniffed a passing group of men up wind.

Joffrey de Peyrac, accompanied by Roland d'Urville, the Norman, Gilles Vanereick, the filibuster from Dunkirk, and Erasmus Baure, the Recollect Father, having left his chebec in the shelter of the harbour on the eastern side of the island, had set off to climb the mountain. This, the highest point in the area, lay less than a league across the sea from Gouldsboro, and was a peak over fifteen hundred feet in height, composed of huge twin domes of pink granite.

Once through the foliated zone that foamed greenly around the foot of the mountain, all vegetation disappeared save the dark tufts of a few stunted pines and, growing almost flat out of the bare, flesh-coloured rock, a few glossy bilberry bushes and a carpet of dwarf

---

[1] During the following century, after one of their great chiefs had distinguished himself in the Franco-English war, the mountain was renamed Mount Cadillac.

In modern times the name of this great Indian chieftain was also given to a make of motorcar.

rhododendrons that spread out across the rounded, worn curves of the mountain forming sumptuous carpets of purple and pink.

The close, whispering wind grew more and more cutting and icy as they climbed higher.

The four men, with their escort of sailors, carrying the muskets, climbed, swift and light-footed, without following any particular path. The huge slabs of pinkish or purplish granite were sufficient guide, drawing them up towards the summit like the shallow steps of a well-worn stairway.

In every crevice, every fissure where the wind had blown a handful of arable soil, grew a thousand tiny, precious flowers: white and yellow stonecrop, and various saxifrages delicately spotting the vast expanses of bare rock with patches of intricate embroidery.

Caring little for so much prettiness mingled with such wild grandeur, Count Peyrac pressed on with his head down, anxious to reach the top before some unpredictable mist came down and masked the horizon.

To examine the extensive panorama that would be revealed from the top, to count every island and scrutinize every inlet and promontory, this was his purpose in climbing this mountain.

Every moment mattered. The days were flying past in the hurly-burly of the active season, in the confusion of awakening when the land and its creatures fling themselves ravenously into the tide of summer.

The Indians were coming down to the coast to barter their goods, white men were arriving for the fishing, men felled timber, planted seed, and did business; and great whirlwinds of activity swept them all along in the feverish hustle and bustle of a too short season.

One event followed hard upon another. Ten days earlier, after parting company from his young ally Baron Castine at Pentagouet on the Penobscot, Count Peyrac had set off eastwards towards Gouldsboro.

He had lingered a little on the way, for his route lay along a still somewhat inaccessible track, that ran close to a couple of small mines of his that worked silver and sylvanite, an ore in which gold occurs in a black, and therefore invisible form. There he stopped, and had a look at the work going on, and brought cheer to the miners who had spent the winter there, left Clovis as foreman, and set off again. A little father on he found Saint-Castine's chaplain, a Recollect Father called Baure, with a message from the Baron.

Thus it was that he learnt of the massacres in the west. The Abenakis had unearthed their war hatchet and were lying waste the English colonies in Maine down towards Boston.

'I am managing to keep hold on my tribes,' Saint-Castine wrote. 'So no one will move in our part of the country. I have sent messages to the English traders in Pemaquid and Wiscasset, my neighbours, telling them there is no need for alarm on this occasion and to remain where they are.

'Nevertheless, they have taken refuge on Newagan Island with supplies of food and ammunition. But I am willing to vouch that, with your help, peace will be maintained in our territories.'

Then Peyrac had reached Gouldsboro.

There he learned at one and the same moment that Angélique had not reached Gouldsboro after going on board the *Rochelais* in Sabadahoc Bay, as the unknown sailor had told him she had, but that his son Cantor, after sailing a sloop full of English refugees as far as Gouldsboro, had just set off again in the *Rochelais* with its captain Le Gall, to fetch Angélique from Casco Bay, where she had remained, it was said, with the sick and wounded.

Feeling both reassured about his wife's fate and annoyed by these setbacks, these endless to-ings and fro-ings and the incomprehensible behaviour of one and all, Joffrey de Peyrac wondered whether he should not set off after his son, but in view of the feverish agitation that gripped his coastal colony, he decided that he had better bide his time.

His meeting with the man of the 'lambis' pearls along the Kennebec, the man from the ship with the orange flag, still continued to nag at his mind. Who were those people who had lied to him? Perhaps they had just misheard something shouted to them through the fog, from one ship to another?

He would have to wait for Angélique to return with Le Gall in order to sort out the mess. The main thing was that Angélique was safe and sound. And yet he would not feel completely easy until he held her in his arms.

Now all this had taken place four days earlier, and as he climbed hastily up the side of the Desert Mountain, perhaps one motive for his haste was a secret hope that he might be the first to see a reassuring sail in the distance.

Behind him his two companions exchanged banter snatched away by the gusty wind. Gilles Vanereick, a Frenchman by nationality, a Protestant converted to Catholicism, a merry, earthy servant of the King of France who nevertheless preferred to serve him from afar, was wearing a yellow satin doublet with buttons fashioned out of genuine pistoles, plum-coloured silk breeches and green pleated hose. He wore a printed calico scarf round his forehead beneath a hat decked with parrot feathers, and a sash of the same floral print round his slightly protruding abdomen. Agile and alert in spite of his girth, he had the reputation of being a devastating fighter and of never having been wounded. The only scar he bore was a mark on the back of his hand made by the hand-guard of his boarding sword, the result of prolonged use of the weapon, 'day and night', as he said, 'day and night!'

A northerner, from the Low Countries that were for so long subject to Charles V and his descendants, he had dark eyes and a curling, black moustache in the Spanish style superimposed on his good natured, Flemish sensuality.

Count Peyrac had become friendly with him in the Caribbean, and Vanereick had decided to pay him a visit in his northern colony, the time of the year, he reckoned, being too hard for a small-time filibuster from Saint Christopher with all the Spaniards about.

He had arrived at the same time as the *Gouldsboro*, under the command of Erickson, upon its return from Europe.

The *Gouldsboro* was carrying craftsmen and a few Huguenot refugees, whereas the corsair ship had on board more or less dark-skinned women, among them a Hispano-Indian half-caste of great beauty, who was Vanereick's mistress. No sooner had she disembarked than she began to dance on the beach to the clicking of the castanets and to the considerable displeasure of Messrs Manigault and Berne, who were responsible for discipline in the port and the morals of their little Protestant community.

The night of the summer solstice had been marked by some rather violent affrays, and although Joffrey de Peyrac's presence had prevented things from getting out of hand, d'Urville the Governor said he had had enough of all these madmen and wanted to resign.

The day after that eventful midsummer night, Peyrac took them up the mountain to cheer them up a bit. And he too felt the need to get away for a while in order to get his bearings. He hoped that a kindly wind would enable him to see from the summit, however far away, the sail of the ship bringing Angélique back to him.

Then he had another idea concerning the suspicious vessel that they had encountered on the banks of the Kennebec, the ship whose orange flag he had seen flying above the tree tops. He wanted to test his hypothesis.

Behind him, the small group of his subordinates, lieutenants and friends, were busy chatting together as they clambered nimbly up the large slabs of pink granite.

D'Urville was busy asking Vanereick what had driven him, a filibuster from the Antilles, to try his luck in Massachusetts Bay and Frenchman Bay. And Vanereick made no secret of his reasons.

'I am too small a fish for those enormous Spanish galleons one meets nowadays in the Caribbean, six hundred tons and armed to the teeth, with a veritable pack of other vessels to escort them. On the other hand I could trade with Monsieur de Peyrac: sugar, molasses, rum, cotton, in exchange for dried cod and timber for masts . . . and we might even join forces to attack some enemy ships.'

'We shall see . . .' Peyrac replied. 'Meanwhile refit your ship, refresh yourselves in our domains, do as you like, in short. It occurs to me that you might indeed be of assistance to me shortly against Gold Beard, the pirate you must have heard speak of in Jamaica.'

Now they were on the crest of the mountain. The wind cutting like a knife blade across the bare top of Mount Desert assailed them with such violence that they had difficulty in keeping their feet. Vanereick was the first to capitulate, saying that he was used to warm lands, and, chilled to the marrow, he took shelter on the less exposed side of the mountain behind a rocky outcrop. Roland d'Urville soon joined him there, clinging to his felt hat with both hands. Father Erasmus Baure faced the wind long enough to say an Our Father and a Hail Mary, then decided he had had enough, as did Vanereick's sailors.

Enrico Enzi, who was escorting Peyrac, remained stoical, as yellow as a quince, swathed in the Arab style sashes and turbans that made up his habitual Maltese garb.

'Get away with you,' the Count said to him, 'go and shelter somewhere.' He remained alone at the top of Mount Desert, braced against the force of the incessant wind, unable to take his eyes off the panorama spread out beneath him.

There, inscribed in hieroglyphics of land and water, lay all the charm, the vastness and the complexity of a land coming to life in its full vigour, a land with an endless reserve of rare sights to offer.

On all sides lay the sea, pushing its way into the land; on all sides lay the land stretching out in peninsulas and promontories across the blue mottled surface of the turbulent ocean, but which, seen from so high, looked soft and smooth as satin. Islands crowned with ebony-coloured pines, islands dim with the greenish gold of birch trees in their spring growth.

At the far end of the bay he could see an area completely made up of pink and red rocks breaking through the ironstone rock face, ancient ironstone that had turned almost mauve from the compression of vast glaciers in the remote past.

In the gravel of the moraine of rivers younger than the ironstone could be found the pre-historic remains of fur-covered elephants with tusks shaped like hunting horns. Granite surfaces had been rounded by the pressure of the ice and sudden sheer cliffs bore witness to sudden subsidence, as they stood reflecting the starkness of their open wounds in the deep waters of the roadsteads.

And the bays, the islands, the rivers made hazardous by tidal bores, up which one could only sail at high tide, with their endless mists and storms, beaches peopled with seals, forest-covered banks swarming with fur-bearing animals, where you can see black bears catching fish with their paws at the edge of the waves, and Indians swarming everywhere in the hope of trading their furs with visiting ships; all this vast area around Frenchman Bay, like a miniature Mediterranean, its shores new and not ancient, here beaches pink or white, or tinged with blue, even on occasion raspberry red, this desert, this paradise, this witch's cauldron, that narrows as one goes farther up, deeper and deeper into darkness and mist, with the surf roaring all round one, until the very tip of Frenchman Bay is reached, where the four Defours brothers, Marcelline-la-Belle and her ten children, Gontran-le-Jeune, brother-in-law to old Nicolas Parys, and a handful of others flounder about in the Chignecto marshes, selling their baskets of peat to the highest bidding ship, while Father Jean Rousse hurls imprecations at them for their wild, godless lives, this tiny section of the American continent—although gigantic to the wretched creature trying to establish himself on it—already had a history in its image—unknown, cruel and dispersed over vast expanses and the abysses of lost horizons, a history filled with sadness and pain.[1]

Joffrey de Peyrac looked down at the oval-shaped sheltered harbour of the island and saw the tiny shape of his chebec with its long, sharp lines.

The boat had been built to his own specification at Kittery in New England, already quite an old seaport, on the Piscataqua river in the state of Massachusetts. What remained now, he wondered, of that busy naval

---

[1] Apart from the fighting that took place during the Franco-English war, the history of Acadia was marked, in the years 1620–1640, by bloody rivalry between two Frenchmen, Charles Latour and Pierre d'Aulnay, which assumed truly tragic proportions.

shipyard? Ashes, possibly? The Indian wars, flaring once more, would cause incalculable upheaval for them all.

The birds began to circle noisily up towards the heights, announcing the arrival of one of the lords and masters of the region—fog. . . .

Joffrey de Peyrac closed his spyglass and rejoined his companions, who were making the best of the icy conditions with their collars pulled about their noses.

He sat down beside them, wrapped about in his huge cloak. The savage wind laid flat the multicoloured feathers in their hats, and the fog suddenly bore down upon them in silence, rolling its smoke-like waves round the pink flanks of the mountain, wrapped them about and engulfed them in its mystery. So heavily did its breath fall upon them, that the wind had dropped, and fled away with a whisper, and for a while, all was calm, and the white men, alone in an invisible universe, sat as it were in the clouds, above a world that had vanished utterly.

'Well, Monsieur d'Urville, it appears that you are about to hand me your resignation as Governor of Gouldsboro?' said Peyrac.

The gentleman from Normandy blushed, then grew pale and looked at the Count as if he thought he must possess the unnerving faculty of reading men's most hidden thoughts. Yet there was in fact nothing very sinister in this piece of guesswork, for a few days earlier, Peyrac had seen him tearing his hair out over the difficulties facing his administration.

There were too many people in Gouldsboro now, he said. What with the Huguenots, the miners, the pirates and sailors of all nationalities, he could make neither head nor tail of them all, not that he had ever been much good at it anyway. Where had the good old days gone when, as almost the only man in charge of this deserted region, he had been able to devote himself to the lucrative business of fur trading with the Indians and the rare ship that risked entering the harbour, still undeveloped in those days and difficult of access.

But now it was like a continental fair and he, d'Urville, a Norman gentleman from Cape Cotentin, no longer even had time to bestow his favours on his lovely Indian wife, the daughter of the local Abenaki-Kakou chieftain, nor to go off, under the pretext of visiting some distant French or English neighbour, to enjoy for a change the pleasures of sailing on the choppy ocean.

'My lord,' he cried, 'pray do not think that I no longer wish to serve you. I shall always be there to obey your orders and help you as best I can, to attack your enemies, and protect your domains at cannon point, nay, even at sword point, to command your soldiers, your sailors, but I have to admit that I am not equipped to deal with situations that involve the Saints, the Devil and the Scriptures. Your Huguenots are hard-working, courageous, capable, industrious and devilish good merchants ... but devilish troublemakers too. They will turn Gouldsboro into a very well-ordered city, but we shall never hear the end of their gas and gab, for we shall never know what laws we are supposed to be following. Whatever was done to them in La Rochelle, those people have been, as it were, mutilated so that they no longer feel themselves subjects of the King of France. Let just one Frenchman come among them with a medallion of the Blessed Virgin about his neck and they begin to kick up a shindy and refuse even to allow him to take on fresh water from their place. We got on quite well with one another this winter, and spent many hours chatting round the fire during the stormy season. I am a bit of an unbeliever myself—begging your pardon, Father—and ran little risk of offending them with my paternosters. And we fought well together when we had to against that pirate Gold Beard. But it is precisely because I know them too well now that I do not feel I am enough of a diplomat to keep the balance between the extraordinary mixture of religions and nationalities and all those pirates as well.'

Joffrey de Peyrac was silent. He was thinking of his friend Captain Jason, the persecuted Huguenot who had been broken in to the Latin temperament on the Mediterranean, a man who would have done wonders in the position that d'Urville was relinquishing. But Jason was dead and so was that admirable scholar the Arab doctor Abd-el-Medrat who might also have helped him in his task. D'Urville, merry and shrewd man that he was, was not abandoning the task out of cowardliness, or even laziness, although a life led under conditions of such complete freedom had bred in him a certain propensity for taking things easy.

The youngest son of his family, he had received no kind of professional training beyond being taught to hold a sword and ride a horse, and, scarce knowing how to read, he was aware of his own shortcomings. He had killed a man in a duel and had fled to America to save his neck from the block under the laws brought in by Cardinal Richelieu. Nothing short of this would have dragged him here, for he had no conception of any kind of life beyond that of the Paris taverns and gambling dens. Fortunately for him he came from the Cotentin pèninsula, that snail's horn that stands out from the French coast to peer across at England, almost an island in the solitude of its wild coastlines, copses and its sandy wastes.

Brought up in an old castle on the Cap de la Hague, d'Urville loved and understood the sea that had cradled him in his youth. Today he could do wonders by keeping a tight hold on the little fleet of ships at Gouldsboro, swelled every year by new additions, but Joffrey de Peyrac also realized the necessity of taking from his shoulders burdens he considered beyond him.

'And how about you, Monsieur Vanereick, if you have wearied of venturing out against the Spaniards, would you be tempted by the honours of Viceroy in these latitudes?'

'Possibly! . . . But only when I acquire a wooden leg. I think I would prefer even that to selling turnips and coconuts in the streets of Tortuga. . . . But joking apart, my coffers are not yet full enough. And one must be rich to impress a population that is a mixture of adventurers and Huguenots. I have already sown scandal among the latter with my Ines. Have you seen Ines?'

'I have seen Ines.'

'Is she not enchanting?'

'She is indeed enchanting.'

'You see I could not possibly give that charming creature up yet. But later . . . it seems an interesting idea. . . . There you have Morgan, the greatest pirate and plunderer of our time, and today he is Governor of Jamaica, and I can assure you that he does not trifle with law and order there, and even princes bare their heads to him. . . . I feel I am that sort of a man too. Less stupid than I look, you know!'

'That is indeed why I had no hesitation in making you such a proposition. . . .'

'And I am honoured by it, indeed I am, my dear Count. . . . But later, later! You see, I have not yet sown my wild oats, even if I have left it a bit late in the day!'

CHAPTER 37

THE FOG began to clear and Joffrey de Peyrac stood up and made his way back to the summit platform.

'Are you hoping to catch a glimpse of Gold Beard, lurking in some corner?' d'Urville asked him.

'Possibly.'

What was he looking for precisely, what did he hope to discover in that labyrinth of water and trees spread out at his feet? It was less a process of logical deduction than a shrewd sixth sense, that had led him to the top of this vantage point.

The man with the 'lambis' pearls . . . the man to whom he had given those pink pearls on the banks of the Kennebec, the man who had lied to him, had he been one of Gold Beard's accomplices? And that mysterious ship, had it been the pirate's? And why had someone twice tried to mislead him about what had happened to Angélique?

Were these 'mistakes' just a matter of chance? He did not believe it. It was a rare thing at sea to find messages sent by word of mouth not transmitted with complete accuracy. For the brotherhood that exists between sailors, their very soul and hopes, demand that this should be so. . . . So why these sudden repeated deceptions? What new danger lay in that direction?

A final gust of wind swept across the bay, clearing the last of the fog as far as the horizon. The clear bluish white sky hovered over the sea like a wing, like a hollow, sonorous shell lined with mother-of-pearl.

Joffrey had to fight his way forward, step by step, leaning against the wind, as if against some contrary force, struggling forward to reach the edge of the plateau, where he stretched out full length to give less of a hold to the wind.

With his spyglass glued to his eye, he systematically examined the island-studded waters.

Here he saw a ship lying at anchor, there a fishing boat, there a flotilla of Indians crossing the straits, there two cod-fishing sloops, and farther off in the lee of an island the cod-fishing boats themselves.

Their crews had gone ashore, and he could see smoke rising as they caulked, cooked food or smoked meat.

As he proceeded with his inspection, he felt the jagged edges of the granite pressing into his chest, causing him a feeling of pain and oppression.

Would he find what he had come to seek on this bare wind-swept mountain?

Out towards the west, just beginning to appear through gaps in the cloud, the chain of the Blue Mountains stood out against the sky, such a vivid blue that the bay beneath them had been given the same name: Blue Hill Bay.

Was it behind there, somewhere, that Angélique was in danger?

'Angélique! Angélique! My life!'

As he lay clutching the bare rock, he called to her in a burst of feeling that yearned to cross those fathomless distances. She had suddenly become a distant, faceless entity, but still warm and infinitely alive and attractive in her uniquely charming way.

'Angélique! Angélique! My life!'

With a whistle, the wind lashed all around him, and seemed to be hissing cruelly:

'He will separate you! You will see! You will see!'

The prediction made by Pont-Briand, the man he had killed for having desired Angélique, whistled in his ears: 'He will separate you . . . you will see!'

Overcome by a sudden sense of anguish, he unconsciously lifted his hand to his breast, then, on second thoughts, he went on:

'But what have I to fear? Tomorrow, or the day after at the latest, she will be here. . . . Angélique is no longer a young, helpless inexperienced woman. More than once she has proved to me that life could not cast her down. She could cope with anything, has she not just proved this again—God only knows how!—by managing to escape from that strange ambush at Brunswick-Falls? . . . Yes, she truly is of warrior and knightly stock, my dauntless one! It is almost as if danger makes her stronger, more efficient, more lucid . . . even lovelier . . . as if her incredible vitality thrived on it! . . . Angélique! Angélique! . . . We shall win through, shan't we, my love? Both of us. . . . Wherever you are, I know we shall soon be together again. . . .'

He gave a start. While he had been thinking, his wandering gaze had chanced to light on an unusual detail among the maze of islands—an orange flag flying from a mast top, half hidden among the trees of one of the islands. He lay motionless for a long time like a hunter sighting game his eye riveted to his spyglass. Then he got up, pondering on what he had seen.

He had found what he had come to seek at the top of Mount Desert.

CHAPTER 38

'MY LORD! My lord!'

Just as Count Peyrac's chebec was rounding Schoodic Point a voice hailed him from a French cod-fisher that was sailing under the lee a few cables away.

Standing at the poop-rail he recognized Yann le Couennec, whom he had sent from Popham to find Angélique.

Shortly afterwards, when the two ships had cast anchor off the Gouldsboro wharfs, the Count hastened to join Yann.

'Speak, man! Speak up quick!'

Yann was not wearing his customary cheerful expression and Joffrey de Peyrac felt his heart grow tense with apprehension.

'Did you find Madame la Comtesse? Why is she not with you? Did you pass the *Rochelais*?'

The unfortunate Yann bowed his head. No, he had not passed the *Rochelais*. Yes, he had managed to join Madame la Comtesse, after crossing the area round the mouth of the Androscoggin which had been burnt and pillaged by the Indians, and had found her stranded at Casco Bay.

'I know all that. . . . Cantor told us as much. He has gone off to fetch them.'

'But alas! It is already too late!' Yann almost wept. 'Cantor will find her gone, for Gold Beard has taken Madame de Peyrac prisoner as a hostage.' And he added hurriedly, to attentuate the effect of this disturbing news, that he did not consider Madame la Comtesse to be in danger. She knew how to look after herself and this particular pirate seemed to have a respectable-looking crew. She herself had had sufficient coolness to help him to escape in time, so that he, Yann, could make known what had happened to her.

And he told them of the circumstances of his escape.

'I ran for it, and fortunately they did not give chase. For a whole day I followed the line of the coast, then as I approached a creek that evening I had the good fortune to discover this French cod-fisher moored there. Its crew had put in to fetch water, and they took me on board and agreed to go out of their way in order to get me here as soon as possible.'

Joffrey de Peyrac had gone deathly white and was clenching his fists.

'Gold Beard! It's always that bandit! I shall pursue him to the death! He already captured the chief of my mercenaries last month, and now he has my wife! What outrageous impudence!'

He thought anxiously of Le Gall and Cantor who must by now have reached the agreed rendezvous only to find it deserted or—worse—still occupied by those dangerous, seafaring brigands. Discovering that his mother was now in their hands, might not Cantor be tempted to embark on some premature act of war? But no! The lad was more prudent than that! In the Mediterranean he had learned all the tricks of the corsair's trade, and would undoubtedly be content to keep a close watch on Gold Beard's ship while trying to contact his father.

Unfortunately the *Gouldsboro* would not be in any condition to give chase and do battle for two days. By working on her all night they might possibly be able to put out in her the following evening accompanied by the chebec, to which they would add two cannons, and Vanereick's ship. They would have to hope that the pirate would be sufficiently intimated by this show of force to be willing to parley.

Then Joffrey de Peyrac swung round and strode back to Yann.

'What else is there that you have not dared tell me? . . . What are you hiding?'

His piercing eyes were riveted to Yann's who, terrified, shook his head in emphatic denial.

'No . . . my lord, I swear it. . . . I swear to you on the image of the Virgin and Saint Anne . . . I have told you everything. . . . Why? . . . What do you think I am hiding? . . .'

'Has something happened to her? She is wounded, isn't she? . . . Or sick? . . . Speak. . . .'

'No, my lord, I would never hide such a disaster from you. . . . Madame de Peyrac is in fact in excellent health. . . . It is she who is looking after all the others. . . . She remained there precisely because of the sick and wounded. . . . She even sewed up the belly of one of those foul creatures, the one who betrayed her. . . .'

'Yes, I know that too. . . .'

Peyrac's keen eyes scrutinized the open face of his sailor who during the past winter had become a companion and friend. No Iroquois had ever made him tremble, nor indeed had the prospect of famine. But now Yann was trembling. Peyrac put his arm round the young man's shoulders.

'What's wrong?'

And Yann felt as if he was about to burst into tears like a child. He bowed his head.

'I have walked a long way,' he murmured. 'And it

wasn't easy to keep out of the way of the savages on the warpath.'

'That's true. . . . Go and get some rest. There is a kind of inn below the fort, run by Madame Carrère and her daughters. The food is good and as from today they are offering claret which has just arrived from Europe. Go and get your strength back again and be ready to set out with me tomorrow if the weather is favourable.'

Count Peyrac and Roland d'Urville summoned Manigault, Berne, Pastor Beaucaire and the chief Huguenot notables to one of the rooms in the fort that served as a council chamber; they asked Vanereick and his lieutenant to attend, likewise Erikson the captain of the *Gouldsboro*, and Father Baure was also present.

Don Juan Alvarez, the commander of the small Spanish guard, stood behind the Count, a dark, forbidding figure watching over his safety.

Joffrey de Peyrac gave them a brief account of recent events. The fact that his wife, Countess Peyrac, had fallen into the hands of their enemy, made it necessary for them to observe the utmost caution. After years in the Caribbean they knew the ways of these gentlemen of fortune and Gilles Vanereick would bear him out when he said that Madame de Peyrac ran no risk of ill-treatment as long as she had any value as a hostage. Never had any great lady taken prisoner, whether she be Spanish French or Portuguese, had cause to complain of her gaolers, while she awaited the payment of the generous ransom that would set her free once more. It had even been said that some of them, especially when the pirate was a man of prepossessing appearance, were in no particular hurry to see the end of their captivity. But it was also known that, should they be hunted down, brought to battle, run aground, or disappointed in their hopes of ransom, some of these ruthless brutes did not hesitate to carry out their threats to their hostages.

They must also bear in mind the fact that, if attacked, Gouldsboro would have only land defences. Accordingly, before the departure of the expedition ammunition must be shared out to everyone.

At this point, the Spanish sentry poked a frightened

head in a black steel helmet round the door and called out:

'Excelencia, someone is asking for you.'

'Who is it?'

'*Un hombre.*'

'Send him in!'

A man, well built and heavily bearded, dressed only in a pair of tattered sailor's trousers, soaking wet, appeared on the threshold.

'Kurt Ritz!' exclaimed Peyrac.

The newcomer was Gold Beard's 'other' hostage, the Swiss mercenary whom Peyrac had engaged as a recruiting officer during a visit to Maryland. The inhabitants of Gouldsboro also recognized him, for he had come ashore among them in May with the soldiers he had recruited for Count Peyrac. He had been about to set off inland when one evening he had been taken by surprise somewhere along the shore by some of Gold Beard's men who had been lying in wait among the islands preparatory to laying siege to Gouldsboro. This had been shortly before the decisive battle that had forced the pirate to take flight, and it was feared that Kurt Ritz might have been made to pay for this defeat. But here he was, apparently in good health, although obviously tired from a long journey.

Peyrac grasped him cordially by the shoulders.

'*Grüs Gott! Wie geht es mit Ihnen, lieber Herr?* I was worried about you.'

'I managed at last to make my escape from that damned boat, and that damned pirate, my lord.'

'When was that?'

'Just about three days ago.'

'Three days,' Peyrac repeated thoughtfully. 'Was that when Gold Beard's ship was lying to the north of Casco Bay, near Maquoit Point?'

'Monsieur, you must have second sight! That was indeed the name I heard mentioned by members of the crew. We cast anchor there at dawn. . . . There was a great deal of coming and going between the ship and the land, a certain amount of confusion. Towards the evening I noticed that the cabin in which I was being held had not been properly locked. The boy who brought

214

me my miserable rations had forgotten to padlock the door, so I waited till dead of night then slipped outside. I was right at the stern under the poop-deck and the whole place seemed deserted. I could see fires burning along the beach, and it looked as if the crew was making merry on the shore. There was no moon, so I climbed up the poop and clambered onto the rear deck. Then by clinging to the mouldings, I clambered down as far as the balcony of the main stateroom, and from there I dived and managed to reach a nearby island. I waited until I was sure that no one had given the alarm, then picked out another island farther off and chanced my luck, although I am not much of a swimmer. By dawn I had reached it. There were some English refugees on the west side, but I did not mingle with them, I waited over on the east side where there were cliffs. During the day I saw some Indian canoes go by, Tarratines, Sebagos, and Etchemins, heading north with scalps hanging at their belts. I signalled to them and showed them the crucifix I wear round my neck. We are Catholics, you know, in the upper Rhone Valley. They took me on board with them and dropped me somewhere near the mouth of the Penobscot. Then I walked day and night and, rather than go round each fiord, I swam across several of them, and nearly got swept away by the currents at high tide. . . . But anyway, here I am.'

'God be praised!' Peyrac exclaimed. 'Monsieur Berne, you wouldn't have a flagon of good wine by you, would you, to cheer the greatest sea-water swimmer of the Waldstaette?'[1]

'Indeed I have.'

And from a console-table Master Berne drew a flagon of claret and a pewter goblet.

The man drained the wine at a single draught. The salt water had made him thirsty, but he had eaten nothing and the strong wine went to his head and sent the blood rushing to his face.

'Ah! *Es schmeckt prima. Ein feiner Wein!*' The waves have knocked me about so much that my head is spinning.'

[1] The old name for the earliest of the Swiss cantons — the Forest States.

'You were lucky,' someone said. 'The equinoctial gales were threatening but did not arrive.'

The Swiss poured himself a second drink and seemed greatly cheered.

'Have you still got my good halberd?' he asked, 'I did not have it with me when I was walking among the rocks and those confounded wretches set upon me.'

'It is still in the arm-rack,' Manigault replied, pointing to the row of hooks along the wall supporting lances of different sizes among which stood a longer pike topped with the admirable steel thistle flower of the Swiss weapon, whose elegant ironwork has for so long disguised its deadly efficacy in the hands of a Swiss—its hooked blade for seizing and hauling in, its sharp cutting edge for severing heads, and its tapering point to pierce bellies and hearts.

Kurt Ritz grasped his pike with a sigh.

'Ah! Here it is at last! How many miserable weeks I have spent biting my nails in frustration on board that ship! And what has happened to my men?'

'They are at Fort Wapassou.'

As they looked at him it occurred to them all that he must have made his escape on the day that Angélique de Peyrac was taken prisoner by Gold Beard. Had he seen her? Had he caught sight of the Count's wife? An indefinable sense of foreboding held them back, as indeed it held back Peyrac himself, from questioning him on this point.

'Did they ill-treat you at all?' Peyrac asked him hesitantly.

'Oh no! Gold Beard is no ruffian and he is a good Christian. His men held prayers every morning and evening up on deck. But he is out for your blood, Monsieur le Comte, for he says that the lands of Maine where you have established yourself belong to him and that he and his men have come over to found a colony. .... The women of Gouldsboro were promised to him and his men, for he was told that they were ransportees.'

'What insolence!' Manigault exclaimed.

'So he was very much surprised by the defence we put up, and he only captured me to have an opening for negotiations with you, for he is as stubborn as a mule. After these gentlemen here had fired red-hot cannon balls at him, he went off to repair his ships on an island in Casco Bay, but he will be back.'

Kurt Ritz had another drink. By now he was beginning to feel in splendid fettle.

'Oh! I could tell you a great deal about Gold Beard. I talked to the sailors and also to Gold Beard himself, for he is a rough, but honest man, yes, honest. Seen from a distance, he frightens people, but his intentions are honourable. And there's a woman in all this . . . his mistress. . . . It was she who joined him at Maquoit Point. It was she who must have engineered the whole thing for she looks a regular hussy. One of those women who will tot up figures on a sheet of parchment without a single mistake, fill their money bags, and send a chap off to war to fill them yet again. But they've got what it takes to pay for it, the jades. As lovely as Venus and intelligent too. Any man who wouldn't willingly give his life for them, must love neither life nor love. Gold Beard's mistress is that kind of woman . . . and lovely too. . . . The whole ship was seething with excitement at the sight of her coming on board. She's a Frenchwoman. She had been waiting there for him, at Maquoit. Her eyes are like pools of water bubbling from the rock, and her hair is like a sunbeam. It was thanks to her that I was able to make my escape that night, for Gold Beard had given every man three pints of rum to celebrate the occasion . . . and as for him. . . .'

Kurt Ritz threw back his head in a silent laugh, then downed another glass of wine.

'Him. . . . I would never have thought it. . . . He's crazy about her. . . . I saw them through the cracks in the boards of my cabin, as they crossed the poop-deck; he was holding her arm and looking at her . . . looking at her. . . .'

The wine was going to his head and he babbled on, not the least surprised at their silence, in no way disconcerted that he saw them, as through a mist, standing rooted to the ground, without a smile, their faces hard and frozen.

'And the woman's name?' snapped the Count, his voice seeming to come from some cotton-wool universe, muffled

217

and far away. Every man present was seized with panic and a desperate desire to run away. Kurt Ritz's head rocked from side to side.

'*Weiss nicht!* All I know is that she is French . . . and that she's beautiful, that I do know! And that he's got her under his skin, has Gold Beard, fit to bust. . . . I SAW THEM. . . . That night in the stateroom, through the poop window. . . . The window was open. . . . I had climbed down that far so I glanced in. . . . There was a candle burning on the table and I saw them. . . . The woman was naked in Gold Beard's arms . . . the body of a goddess . . . with her hair spread out over her shoulders. . . . In the sunlight I had thought her hair was golden but there I saw it was the colour of moonlight. . . . A sheet of silvery gold . . . like a fairy. . . . There was something about that woman which is like no one else, something marvellous. . . . I can quite understand his being crazy about her, that pirate. I didn't dare to dive because of the open window. . . . Even people making love may have sharp ears . . . and Gold Beard is a captain, always on the alert. . . . I had to wait a while. . . .'

He talked on and on. By now he was quite drunk and went on without showing the slightest astonishment at the crushing silence that surrounded him, without realizing that there was anything odd about his being allowed to go on in this way, describing and dwelling on every detail of the love scene.

He went on, his head wagging from side to side:

'Where does she come from, this woman? I don't know. She met him over there. . . . Her name . . . wait a minute, I think it's coming back to me. While he was making love to her I heard him call her "Angélique! Angélique!" It's a name that suits her.'

There was a terrible silence then suddenly Kurt Ritz's halberd slid from his fingers, and he staggered back until he found himself leaning against the wall, suddenly sober again, his face deathly white and his eyes starting out of his head as he stared at Peyrac.

'Don't kill me, Monsieur!'

And yet not a soul had moved. Not even Count Peyrac, who stood there as erect and immutable as ever. But it was the terrible black look in his eyes in which Kurt Ritz had seen the flash of death. As a man familiar with the battlefield, he had known that death was upon him, and now, completely sober, without understanding why, he looked at Peyrac and knew that he was in mortal danger.

At the same moment with a horrified prescience, he realized that every one of the participants in what was for him an incomprehensible drama, all those who stood there like ghosts in an unearthly silence, would have rather been deaf, dumb, blind, or six feet under ground, than have to live through this moment between those four walls.

He swallowed hard.

'What is the matter, gentlemen?' He groaned. 'What have I said?'

'Nothing!'

The word fell like a cleaver from Peyrac's lips.

Once again his master's voice seemed to come from another world.

'Nothing for you to reproach yourself with, Ritz. . . . Come now, you need rest. . . . In a few days' time you will have to rejoin your men in the Appalachians at Fort Wapassou.'

The man staggered across to the door and when he had gone the others hastened to take their leave in silence, each man bowing low to the master of Gouldsboro as he went, as they would have done when taking leave of the King of France.

Once outside, they donned their hats and went off home in silence, All except Gilles Vanereick who drew d'Urville to one side and said: 'Please explain. . . .'

CHAPTER 39

THEN JOFFREY DE PEYRAC turned to Juan Fernandez.

'Send Yann le Couennec to me here.'

When Yann entered the council chamber, the Count was alone, bending over a map which he appeared to be studying with care.

His thick hair, with its trace of silver at the temples,

half hid his face, as he pored over the map, and his lowered eyelids veiled his gaze.

But when he stood up and his glance fell on Yann, the lad gave a shudder, conscious of anxiety coiling within him like a cold snake.

'What is the matter? What is the matter with my master?' he thought. 'Is he ill, is he wounded, has he received some blow? . . . It is as if he had received some inner blow . . . a death blow.'

Joffrey de Peyrac went round the table and came towards Yann, appearing so calm and walking so straight that Yann began to think he must have been mistaken.

'No, there is nothing wrong. . . . What will I imagine next? . . .'

Joffrey examined him with penetrating attention. Yann was of medium height and reached to Joffrey's shoulder, a well set up young man, with a lively, bold expression, who still looked younger than his thirty years, although his eventful life had made an old campaigner of him, a man ready for anything. But where Joffrey de Peyrac was concerned, that French Celtic face would never hold any secrets, for he could read it like an open book.

'And now, Yann,' he said softly, 'tell me what it was you did not dare say before.'

The Breton paled and took a step back, as he searched his head for vain denials. Terrified, he knew there was no escape, for he had already seen Joffrey de Peyrac at work once he had set himself a goal, once he had determined to discover the truth about something his diabolical sixth sense had revealed to him. He was like a hunter who never lost the scent until his quarry was brought to bay.

'What is the matter with you? What is it that you are unable to tell me? Do you think I cannot see how disturbed you are? Tell me, what happened? It was something that happened at Maquoit, wasn't it, where you left the Countess? What was it you saw, what was it you happened on that could have upset you as much as this?'

'But . . . I didn't'—Yann gave a helpless shrug—'I told you everything that happened, my lord.'

'It was there, wasn't it? Answer me, it happened over there?'

The poor lad nodded, then let his face fall into his hands.

'What did you see? What was it? Was it before you made your escape? . . .'

Yann shook his head in misery.

'Well, was it after you ran off? You told me you ran away. You were running, and you turned round, and you saw something. . . . That's it, isn't it? Something strange, something inconceivable.'

How could he have guessed? It was diabolical. Yann was beginning to falter.

'What was it you saw?' the implacable voice repeated. 'What was it you saw when you looked back at the beach where you had left her? What did you see?'

Then suddenly Yann felt a hand clamp down like a vice on the back of his neck, a terrible hand that gripped him as if it would snap him in two.

'Now tell me,' came the voice, soft and menacing.

Then, realizing that the young man was suffocating and had turned purple in the face, the Count relaxed his grip in an effort to control himself, and a poignant gentleness vibrated in his persuasive voice.

'Tell me, my boy . . . I beg you!'

Then Yann's resistance broke, and he fell to his knees, clutching at Joffrey de Peyrac's doublet with the distraught gesture of a blind man.

'Forgive me, my lord. Forgive me!'

'Tell me about it. . . .'

'I was running . . . I was running . . . I had made my escape just as Gold Beard reached the shore . . . taking advantage of the fact that everyone was looking at him. . . . Madame la Comtesse had suggested I should choose that moment. . . . I ran, I ran, and then I turned round to see if I was being followed. . . . I turned towards the beach. . . .'

He looked up at Peyrac in agony.

'She was in his arms, Monsieur!' he cried, clutching the Count as if he himself was being struck these terrible blows. 'She was in Gold Beard's arms . . . and they were kissing, oh! forgive me, my lord, kill me. . . . They were kissing one another like lovers . . . like long-separated lovers. . . .'

PART FOUR
Jack Merwin's Sloop

CHAPTER 40

THREE DAYS before all this, to the north of Casco Bay, a ship on the sea. One ship among so many others. But the sea is so vast and the islands so numerous that the ship seemed to be alone as it crept along like a hunted animal, constantly in peril of the treachery of current and rock. Keeling over to the leeward she would round a promontory, melt into the shadow of a cliff, reappear in the sunshine, sometimes escorted by the scent of flower-strewn shores, sometimes rising and dipping in salt-laden squalls.

Human forms could be seen along the beaches of the islands, waving their arms as they ran along, shouting. There were boats and bigger ships hidden in the creeks, some tacking as they sailed or fished on the far side of some rock, while others only appeared after the ship had gone by.

It was for ever alone amid the labyrinth of those three hundred and sixty-five islands in Casco Bay. From Maquoit Point, the ship had followed the coastline southwards.

The last part of the night had left Angélique exhausted, after trying to devise a thousand and one ways to escape from Colin.

That morning he had come into her cabin. She had slept but little and felt weary and heavy-hearted, but determined to make him set her free.

But he had anticipated her request.

'Follow me, Madame,' he had bade her coldly.

He was calm and distant, still imposing, with all his weapons slung about him, and she followed him out onto the deck. Some of the crew were loitering about, ostensibly performing their usual morning duties, but above all trying to catch a glimpse of Gold Beard's prisoner, and Angélique saw a boat lying up against the hull of the ship, pitching up and down with a straw bollard to protect it from collisions.

It was an English sloop, one of those big boats that constantly plied from bay to bay, from village to village between New York and Pemaquid or still farther. Its master, a powerfully-built, gloomy-looking man, must have been hailed that morning by the French filibusters of the *Heart of Mary*, and no one knew precisely what his views were concerning the booty with which they were busy filling his sloop. But, accustomed as he was to navigation in these waters, he must have learnt that it was prudent to show circumspection when dealing with undesirable visitors from the Caribbean. Angélique leaned forward and saw a large number of passengers on board the sloop, among whom she recognized the Revered Patridge's bulldog-like face, that of the devoted little Miss Pidgeon, young Sammy Stoughton, and Adhemar, whose wails of protest filled the particularly limpid air of that wistaria-coloured dawn.

'Well! Falling into the hands of pirates now! It certainly looks as if I collect disaster. . . .'

The wooden bar across the gang-port had been removed and a rope ladder hung from the opening.

'So that's that!' Colin remarked in a stifled voice, standing close to her and speaking to her alone, 'We had better part, had we not, my dear? The skipper of this boat tells me he is sailing to Penobscot. So if the wind is good and he cuts straight across east-north-east, you will be there in four days at the outside. . . .'

For all his efforts and his good intention, he could not help addressing her in the familiar form; and she realized that every time he felt her close to him it would be as it had been in the desert, when he was the only one in the world to look upon her and to take her in his arms. . . .

She looked up at him in an attempt to make him understand what she felt—friendship and gratitude.

She was overjoyed at the thought that within four days she might be with Joffrey again, and her nightmare over.

She would be able to breathe again and straighten out

226

her thoughts. Once back with her husband again, re-assured by his beloved voice, so sweet to her ears, she would try to sort things out. They would talk things over together. . . .

Colin's face contorted in pain at the dazzling smile she gave him.

'Ah! You love him, I can see . . .' he murmured.

But she scarcely heard him.

She knew she must not give way to emotion and that she must escape as soon as possible.

She must seize this present opportunity before he changed his mind. Already, because she recognized how characteristic was this open, generous gesture he was making in releasing her, she felt an indefinable sense of regret grip her heart.

She took her bag from one of the sailors and threw it unceremoniously across her shoulders.

She was still barefoot, but what did it matter! What did one need shoes for on the slippery deck of a sloop? At the last moment she almost enquired after Slit-Belly, the man she had operated on, but resisted the temptation, for she did not wish to lose a single second. She refused help from a man who offered to assist her down the rope ladder, and called out gaily: 'Thanks all the same, friend, but I've knocked about the Mediterranean, you know.'

Colin laid his hand on her shoulder, unable to contain himself as the moment came to see her go. He stared intently at her and, with his astonishingly clear blue eyes that still looked almost childishly youthful in his heavily-lined and tough-looking face framed in the pale hair and beard which he had tried to turn into a symbol of fear, he tried to take in everything about her. He seemed to be attempting to hold her image fast as one does a ghost, a phantasmagoria of the mind, as if she were not completely real. And yet she had the feeling that he was not only thinking of his passion for her, but of something still more urgent, more outward, something even more serious that preoccupied him. Twice he seemed on the point of speaking.

'Take care,' he whispered at last, 'take care, my lamb

. . . there are people who wish you no good! . . . No good at all! . . .'

—Then he let her go, and she made her way swiftly down the rope ladder, arriving near the prow just as the captain pushed off from the ship with a shove of his boathook, heedless of the fact that Angélique stumbled and almost fell into the water.

Nonetheless she gave him a cordial greeting in English, to which his only response was a glance as expressionless as that of a dead fish. Another Puritan, no doubt, who considered any young, laughing and . . . tousled woman the very incarnation of the Devil!

Angélique sat down happily beside Adhemar and Sammy while a young ship's boy with tow-coloured hair unfurled the jib and the boom-and-gaff mainsail and the captain rowed his craft away from the corsair ship to pick up the wind.

And thus it was that this little sloop, the *White Bud*, began to tack back and forth among the islands of Casco Bay, sailing in solitude from one wave crest to another, like a lovely wheeling bird.

There were three other passengers on board the boat which had rescued Angélique, her French soldier and her English refugees.

There was a pedlar from the colony of Connecticut, a little black boy acting as his assistant and . . . a bear. It was this bear that Angélique noticed first, her glance irresistibly drawn towards a wise, appreciative and amused expression she felt light upon her, although unable to determine whence it came.

It was the bear. She suddenly caught sight of it, lying beneath the false after-deck where it had made its den. With its sharp nose between its paws, it stared at her with tiny shining eyes. The pedlar immediately introduced the bear to her:

'Mr Willoughby. . . . Believe me, milady, I could not wish for a better friend than this animal.'

His own name was Elias Kempton, and in less than an hour Angélique knew everything about him. Born in Massachusetts, he had set out from the little colony of Newton at the age of eight with his parents and about a hundred of the other inhabitants. Led by their pastor

Thomas Hooker, a man of liberal views who disliked the harsh oligarchy of the Puritans, they had made their way through the forest until they came to a river with broad, calm expanses of grey water, the Connecticut. On its banks they had founded Hartford, where before there had been nothing but a small Dutch fur-trading post. Now it was a pleasant town, godly and gay, that made its living from the sea. It was not easy to till the land on the banks of a river like the Connecticut, for the current constantly tempted you down towards the river mouth, towards more fertile soil . . . so at the age of twenty Elias had set off with a bag filled with wares and his bear, Mr Willoughby, had followed him.

'I brought him up and we have never been separated since.'

He told them how the bear would accompany him on all his journeys, which occasionally gave rise to complications, but it helped to create a relaxed and happy atmosphere with his clients, who were generally slow to part with their shekels. The bear could dance and perform a few tricks, but he was best of all at wrestling. The strongest lads in the villages used to take him on, and he was a good sport and always gave them a chance, but eventually a friendly, almost casual swipe of one paw would send the young fighting cocks reeling.

'Willoughby . . .' said the Reverend Patridge thoughtfully, 'but I think I knew a pastor of that name somewhere near Watertown.'

'Very likely,' the pedlar admitted. 'My friend here looked so like that worthy clergyman, who used both to terrify me and amuse me when I was young, that I gave him his name.'

'A decided slight,' Thomas Patridge replied sharply, deeply offended. Then he continued, in a threatening tone: 'You could find yourself in serious trouble. . . .'

'Connecticut is not Massachusetts, saving your pardon, Reverend. Our people are more liberal in their outlook and enjoy a good laugh.'

'It's a land of taverns,' growled the pastor, 'rum drinkers from birth.'

'But we do have our own constitution and we do not travel on Sundays to please the Lord.'

Looking pleased with himself Elias Kempton drew from his pockets twists of tobacco, pictures, lace, and some small watches. He had everything imaginable to catch the interest of the settlers in the farthest flung outposts in the land—or rather their wives—and as he had coasted round every smallest inlet of every bay in the region, he knew better than anyone what could be found in this or that place, what was lacking in some other, what would bring a sparkle to some young girl's eyes, and a disdainful pout to the lips of another, what would enchant some child or some grandfather, or bring the radiance of pure joy to the humblest lob cabin in the form of some treasured or useful object.

He said he was making for Bartlett Island to the east of the Penobscot, in search of the woollen cloth dyed a particularly brilliant shade of indigo or red for which the place was famous. For there the sheep grazed on a hundred different varieties of flowers and the inhabitants of the island bartered catechu with the ships from the Caribbean.

'But that island must be close to Gouldsboro,' Angélique remarked, resolved to go and make some purchases there herself.

Elias Kempton knew Gouldsboro from hearsay, but had never done business there, as his usual class of customers, settlers' wives, had hitherto been lacking in those parts.

'Oh there are women there now, and I shall be your first customer,' Angélique assured him.

Delighted, the pedlar fell to his knees, but only to measure her feet there and then, for he was also an itinerant shoemaker and promised he would make her a marvellous pair of shoes of the softest leather, with laces tipped with copper to protect them from wear. Up in the north on Fox Island, there was a solitary old Scot who tanned the most supple skins for him. Provided, of course, that he found all those English folk alive, for they might well have been scalped by the Indians meanwhile.

Taciturn and disdainful of the passengers, the captain gave his full attention to the management of his craft. Once again it fell to the agreeable pedlar to inform his new companions that the aforesaid skipper answered to the name of Jack Merwin. He had discovered him in New York, and, although a moody man, he was a remarkable pilot.

And it was indeed true that Jack Merwin steered his boat among the shining, perilous currents and over the foam-crested ocean shelves with an easy, deft skill, which to the trained eye bordered on the miraculous.

Apart from a few manœuvres with the jib which he instructed the boy to carry out, he managed the boat alone, handling both the tiller and the big square mainsail, sometimes holding the sheet taut with his big toe.

If the weather stayed fair the passage with him promised to be a fast one. But after some hours Angélique was alarmed to see that the boat was still heading obstinately south. She questioned the captain, but he pretended not to understand her imperfect English. Then the Reverend Patridge solemnly enjoined him to reply when he was spoken to. He condescended to mutter out of the corner of his mouth, his eyes turned in another direction, that to get out of this maze of blasted islands in Casco Bay without losing your boat or your life, the quickest route was to head down towards Portland, and to pick up the current that ran between Peaks Island and Cushing Island, the latter of which was known as the White Hat. Until the White Hat was sighted, he concluded, they must follow the coast southwards. Young Sammy opened his eyes wide in an attempt to catch sight of this famous White Hat.

Shocked by the lack of respect shown him by the English salt, in spite of his being a clergyman, the Reverend Thomas began to eye the man with suspicion, muttering something or other about his probably being a Virginian, that all the members of that colony were jail-birds and other riff-raff, and just because they had grown rich with their Virginian tobacco there was no call for them to bring their godless ways up to Massachusetts Bay. And so he went on in an aside, to relate the history of Virginia to Miss Pidgeon, while Adhemar, who grasped something of what was being said, began to wail:

'If the fellow is a convict, and he certainly looks it, he will maroon us all on some desert island. . . .'

'There are no desert islands in these parts, my poor friend,' Angélique reassured him.

And it was indeed an extraordinary thing to be so utterly alone between sea and sky, between rock and shore, and yet at the same time to see all about them a kaleidoscopic collection of sails, flotillas of canoes, wooden villages, a dockyard, the timber ribbing of cod-fishing vessels under construction, a distant convoy of big-bellied ships, and to see along the beaches groups of men gathered about a fire dressed in tawdry finery, busy melting down pitch, seal oil or whale oil in huge cauldrons, while others in woollen caps bustled around their outstretched nets and their oyster baskets, and to see others again, in black pointed hats and dark doublets, their wives dressed in blue or black with white coifs, searching among the rocks for shellfish or clustering around their soup pots, which were all that remained to them of their homes.

For over half a century the permanent inhabitants of the Casco Bay archipelago had consisted of a motley collection of Scots, Irishmen, Englishmen, and even French Huguenots, to which were added, in the cod and tunny season, fleets of fishermen from St. Malo, Dieppe or Boston, whalers from the Basque coast, and now, in these tragic, torrid late June days, refugees from along the coast.

In fact the entire bay was swarming with refugees from the Indian massacres. Everywhere lay ships loaded with pewter mugs and plates, Bibles and old muskets. From the lower Kennebec and Androscoggin the Abenaki torches had left a trail of fire, and—after Newehewanik —Brunswick, Freeport, Yarmouth, Falmouth, Portland, and, still farther south, Saco and Biddeford had gone up in flames. When, towards evening, the boat reached the mouth of the little Presúmpscot River, two miles from Portland, the stench of still smouldering fires and of rotting corpses came to them from the land on the fresh breeze, mingling with the tang of the pine woods. A small island rose up before them, decked in a variety of evergreen, a picture of harmonious colour and line. Apprehensively the occupants of the boat watched the spray-crowned rocks in the estuary growing ever closer, until they were pitching and tossing a few cables' lengths from the island, and the passengers cast anxious glances at Jack Merwin, who seemed totally unconcerned. This cold man sailed as the fancy took him.

During the course of the day he had often come in close to this island or that, almost to the point when it seemed he would run the vessel aground. Then he would scan the beaches as if looking for something or someone, and Angélique began to think that he must be searching for someone he knew among the refugees, which was proof in itself that he was not a Virginian. Occasionally he would hail another ship, and enquire about the advance of the Indians to the coast. . . .

CHAPTER 41

THERE, QUITE suddenly, close to the shore of the island, he took in sail and the boat began to roll aimlessly, being driven gradually in towards the shore by the swell. The little island looked like a crown of emeralds in the rays of the setting sun that made the brilliant, glossy pine needles shimmer with blue and green tints. In spite of the roaring of the surf and the wind, the celestial music of innumerable singing birds seemed to come to them from the island.

'That is Mackworth Island,' the pastor said in hushed tones, 'the Paradise of the Indians. Be careful,' he added, turning towards the owner of the boat. 'I would not be in the least surprised if the island was infested with savages at the moment. They come from inland via Lake Sebago and the Presumpscot River. This is their ancient paradise, or so they say, and they have tolerated the presence of Englishmen here. Last year, that damned Frenchman from Pentagoet, Baron Saint-Castine, seized the island with his savages. They joined forces with some other Terratines heading down from Sebago and massacred all old Mackworth's sons and those of Richard Vines and of Samuel Andrews as well; since then the island has been deserted. . . .'

No sooner had he uttered these words than the boat,

233

rounding a headland, came upon an inlet in which glistened a number of reddish-brown canoes lying empty in tight-packed rows on the beach. In the golden light of evening, these frail bark canoes caulked with balsam and resin, shone like the transparent wing-sheaths of giant cockchafers. At the same moment the sky suddenly grew dark as if a storm cloud had obscured it, and darkness literally fell on earth as thousands of birds suddenly rose up in flocks from the island trees, and swept across the sky in a dense twittering, and screeching cloud.

Dumb with horror in the sudden, shifting darkness they saw thousands of red ghosts rise up among the red pine-tree trunks—a great multitude of Indians with hideous, painted faces.

With one accord they clasped one another in terror, and later Angélique remembered that she had clutched to herself not only Sammy but Elias Kempton the pedlar from Connecticut. There lay the boat, tossed hither and thither by the waves which were gradually carrying it nearer and nearer to the bar that enclosed the beach.

Angélique cast a terrified glance at Jack Merwin, who like a man suddenly awakened from slumber, grasped his rudder, and, with alacrity that made up for his earlier rashness, hoisted the mainsail in a flash and whisked his boat out of the treacherous surf. But, having done this much, he still showed no haste to get away, and, after sailing for a short distance on one tack, he went about and headed once more for Mackworth Island, keeping just out of bow shot, but sailing so close to the shore that no detail of the Indians' trapping escaped them, and they saw the entire company of Redskins forming a terrifying, motionless tableau, against the background of the trees, the branches and the rocks of the island. The vast, circling cloud of birds over their heads still held them in a sinister, noisy twilight. Jack Merwin continued his inspection of the Indians, sailing up and down the beach. Was it defiance, curiosity, or provocation? He would have been a clever man indeed who could have read Merwin's thoughts from the expression on his face.

Then, still with a kind of nonchalance, he signalled to the boy to hoist the jib and set his course south-east, drawing away at last from Mackworth Island, the legendary Indian Paradise.

Little by little the sky grew brighter again, and soon only a few gulls remained to escort them on their way.

Angélique was trembling almost as much as the English people. She did not know whether it was an illusion or an obsession but she could have sworn that in the yawning darkness that had suddenly engulfed them she had seen among the trees the mocking face of Sagamore Piksarett.

'You're a reckless one, Jack Merwin,' the pedlar remarked sharply. 'It's three weeks now that I've been travelling with you and putting up with your macabre whims, and I can't stand much more. Every time we skim past some rock or you decide to sail just as a storm is breaking, I think my last hour has come. . . . And what about Mr Willoughby, the poor creature! Can't you see he's pining away with fright? His skin is hanging off him. He hardly stirs now, he can't even dance any more. . . .'

'Just as well if he doesn't stir again,' growled Merwin. 'What use do you expect us to have for a dancing bear on board this boat?'

And with supreme disdain, he spat into the waves.

Angélique could not help laughing, a natural reaction after the fright she had had. And it had to be admitted that they were a somewhat picturesque band on board that cockle-shell. The Negro boy, entwined in a red homespun cloak, looked rather like a round, black radish and his white eyes were almost starting out of his head.

And where was Adhemar? Had he fainted? No, he was being sick over the side of the boat. He had never been able to endure the sea.

'And while you were busy parading back and forth in front of that assembly of red snakes, Jack Merwin,' the pedlar continued soliloquizing, for he had a lot to get off his chest, 'did it ever occur to you that a flotilla of their canoes might suddenly have come paddling round that point and taken us from the rear?'

But the skipper seemed no more put out by the little

man's recriminations than he would have been by the prick of one of his needles.

In a sudden burst of curiosity Angélique took a closer look at the skipper. Beneath his faded red woollen cap he had long, very dark hair. His features were nondescript and not very clearly delineated, and he had a long face. His complexion was manly, neither swarthy nor ruddy by nature, the kind of complexion found in men of European extraction, maintained by good health and lightly tanned by the sea breezes.

He looked forty, give or take a year or two. His eyes were dark, rather like mercury, beneath heavy lids that often dulled their brilliance, giving him a vacant, unintelligent look.

He chewed continuously a quid of tobacco, but when he spat into the sea he did so with an air of casual distinction.

Under his open-necked coarse linen shirt and his waistcoat with its horn buttons, his shoulders looked narrow but powerful. He wore trousers of drugget—a tough, extremely hard-wearing woollen cloth made for sailors—and the legs were cut off below the knees. His calves were like cables of plaited rope, and he did everything with his calves and his feet.

Angélique thought to herself she did not care for this man Merwin, and considered that Colin had not made a good choice in stopping this particular boat. But he probably had had no option anyway. Colin. . . .

Gold Beard! She felt her heart tighten, a brief moment of shame, of fear. Their day at sea had been so full of varied impressions that her memory of Colin had begun to fade. Deep down, she felt a sense of relief that things had ended this way, but inasmuch as she now felt secure against her own weakness, the illogicality of her feminine nature caused her an occasional pang of regret, a vague sadness. Colin . . . the depth of those blue eyes intoxicated by her presence, the strength of his primitive embrace. Something she knew, something which belonged to her alone. Her secret place. Why could one not love according to the dictates of one's heart and one's body? Why should the quality and strength of one's love depend on so difficult a choice? As if the dispersal of feelings and the gift of oneself condemned one never to know them in their fullest intensity. Was it the truth, or was it a mere illusion, left over from her early teaching, that made faithfulness to her husband the foremost of all the obligations of honour for a woman. Was she not burdening herself with pointless constraints? If she had given in to Colin, what a delectable moment she would have enjoyed . . . and Joffrey would never have known anything about it.

She felt herself grow red at her own thoughts and felt humiliated by the mere fact that she had formed them within her.

Impatiently, she shook her head in the wind.

She must forget . . . forget at all costs.

Mackworth Island was fading into the distance and looked more than ever like a crown of brilliant jewels in the mint-green dusk.

'Look! Look! I can see the White Hat,' shouted little Sammy.

The Old Whitehead was an enormous granite dome that crowned little Cushing Island, rising fully one hundred and fifty feet above the sheltered entrance to Portland Harbour.

The fresh water from inland, endlessly churned up with the ocean brine at their point of contact, formed a soapy lather that was tossed into the wind by the everlasting ebb and flow of the tides and spattered in fringes of white foam across the grey granite brow of the rock, lending it, as they dried out, the appearance of a huge hat or the head of an old man with white locks, according to the prevailing light.

On drawing nearer, it was possible to differentiate between the snowy cover of foam and the equally thick deposits left by seabirds nesting or perching on every available rock face. And it was through a kind of white blizzard that they made their approach, discovering the island with its teeming life beneath this downy plumage.

Here one could truly say that in these last days of June—a June bright with intense, short-lived blooms—every beach was swarming with Puritans and with seals, while above them the birds wheeled, joyously, and that anyone attempting to disembark among the skuas, seagulls, terns, and seamews, anyone trying to set his foot down on a rock white with foam or feathers might equally well bump into a waddling seal or a grave Puritan dominie draped in a Genevese cape, both equally solemn, severe and indignant at finding themselves in such company, but equally determined to make the best of a bad job. Eggs were trampled on in their nests, piles of clams, scallops, lobsters, crabs, oysters and mussels, lying beside the fires on a carpet of seaweed were trodden underfoot, and to be heard one had to have a voice more shrill than those of the assembled birds of the sea.

'Don't come here! Don't come here,' cried the refugees as they saw the boat approaching the shore. 'We have no food and there are too many of us already. There will soon not be enough shellfish left for everyone and we have too few guns and too little ammunition!'

Merwin went about some distance from the shore, and little Sammy Stoughton cupped his hands round his mouth:

'There are no end of Indians over on Mackworth Island,' he cried in his thin childish voice that carried across the roar of the surf and the shrieking of the birds. 'Mind they don't come and kill you all. . . .'

'Where do you come from, laddie?'

'From Brunswick-Falls, on the frontier.'

'What has happened up there?'

'They are all dead,' the little boy called back in his thin voice, and the words floated away like the notes of a flute.

The tide was high and the boat was able to sail a considerable distance up the bay where landings were made, but Merwin, faced with a volley of protest from the first occupants of the island made no attempt to land. Once again he was content to examine everything about him curiously and attentively.

A fat woman with her skirts hitched up high, searching among crevices in the rock for lobsters, hailed him as he passed.

'Are you from the coast?'

'No, I come from New York.'

'And where are you making for?'

He pointed with his chin towards the north.

'Gouldsboro.'

'I know that place,' said someone, 'that's at the mouth of Frenchman Bay. You will get yourselves scalped by the French and their savages. . . .'

Jack Merwin grasped the tiller again and steered the ship towards the mouth of the little harbour, but as he rounded a rocky point, another woman rushed towards him gesticulating, dragging behind her a girl with a small bundle of possessions.

'Take her with you,' the woman shouted, 'she has no family left, but I know she has an uncle up there somewhere near Frenchman Bay, on Matinicus Island, or on Long Island this side of Mount Desert, I'm not sure which. Take her with you. . . .'

The woman gave the girl a shove and the bewildered child leapt into the boat just as a wave carried it out to sea.

'Old fool!' Merwin exclaimed, roused at last, 'what do you take me for, a custodian of orphans? I've better things to do than to worry about these Bible-bangers, the Devil take the lot of you!'

'You talk like a heathen,' retorted the woman from the end of her rock, 'and you have a Devonshire accent too. Belphegor gave you a doubly hard heart at the hour of your birth. . . . But take the child to safety, or your evil deeds will choke you, however far away you may be, that I wager.'

Merwin, whose anger had made him rise to his feet, seized the tiller again and only just managed to avoid a sharp rock projecting from the water.

'Old fool!' he growled again, 'if they have Hell on their side what are they waiting for to conquer the whole world?'

'The woman is right, your words . . .' began the Reverend Thomas, but the boat skipped a wave and interrupted the argument by soaking them all, whereupon Merwin set the boy to work bailing out.

The sea was growing rough and the vessel plunged deeper and deeper between the waves. Merwin had to concentrate so hard on handling it that it was out of the question to return to White Hat Island to put the orphan girl ashore. A pearl-grey and pink mist heralded the evening, one of those long-drawn-out June twilights that would hang over the sea. It was essential to find a haven for the night. Fortunately Merwin seemed to know the locality and sailed along the coasts of Peak Island, the next in the series, then Long Island, next to which came Chebeague Island. Half-way along the eastern coast of Long Island he turned his boat in towards a shingly beach, in an area that seemed less thickly populated. He sprang down into the water and made fast the boat in a rocky cleft, then made for dry land, leaving the ladies to get ashore as best they could. This they did without worrying about getting their feet wet, for, after long hours of sitting and standing still, it was delightful to paddle in the cold water and stroll along the sands. The girl from Cushing Island, whose name was Esther Holby, was telling her tale of woe to Miss Pidgeon, while Mr Willoughby, the bear, emerging from his shelter, made his way up the beach, pointing his nose towards the smell of the woodlands. Angélique saw that he was a huge, slow, gentle creature. He went off to forage among the tree roots, although Elias Kempton called him back from time to time to avoid alarming other people in the area.

As Angélique listened to young Esther she began to feel considerable respect for the poor child. Suddenly thrown into the midst of strangers among whom she had discovered a French Papist and . . . a bear, she had shown not the slightest dismay but had accepted her situation with considerable dignity. When disaster befalls the English they do not jabber about it as the French so often do. Rather it is as if a stone had been dropped into a deep well, whose surface is even stiller than before.

As Angélique listened to Esther telling how she had seen her father, her mother and her brothers scalped by the Indians and her little sister taken away into captivity, she felt like wringing her hands and weeping for the child.

Merwin came back carrying armfuls of branches and lit a fire. Then he filled a cast-iron pot with water, threw in a piece of salted pork and set it to boil. His movements were neat, those of a tidy man, accustomed to living alone. With astonishing rapidity the tide went out, uncovering an expanse of land brown with seaweed and glistening with innumerable tiny pools as far as the eye could see.

Little English children came out of the woods and began to look for sea-shells among the exposed rocks.

Dusk was falling behind the black trees and both sky and sea took on the hue of a ripe orange that grew gradually darker and darker until it had been transformed into a brilliant pink glow that seemed as if it would never fade. The children leapt from rock to rock humming a refrain then, pleased with their gatherings, they came over and held out their baskets to the new-comers. Merwin bought two pints of scallops and clams from them, and Angélique asked them to sing the refrain she had heard them humming before, which, as a little girl born on the island told her, was a song the shellfish liked. Then their fresh, rhythmical voices rose up, giving the lie to threatening misfortunes. Among them were many refugees from the coast, delighted by this escapade into the Bay, far from the toils of farm work or long hours spent in study at the meeting-house, and they were by no means backward in stressing and proclaiming with conviction:

'Clams is physic the whole year through, come eat my clams, bid the doctors adieu.'

To thank them for being so obliging, the pedlar called his bear and, to the great astonishment of the children, the animal stood up on its hind legs and made them a deep bow, then, on being asked to choose the prettiest little girls or the most impish, or the most pugnacious of the boys, he complied, appearing to think the matter over, to hesitate, and finally placed before the chosen person a cloth flower, a trinket, or a coin.

Soon quite a crowd had gathered around the strangers' fire, and Elias Kempton, seeing an athletic-looking man with muscular arms among the spectators, asked him if he would care to measure his strength against the bear. It was a good clean fight: the man was allowed to use his fists and Mr Willoughby undertook not to use his claws. With the skill of a born actor the bear pretended several times to stagger beneath the man's blows, then, just as the fellow was beginning to think the victory was his, the animal knocked him flying with a mere flick of his paw. . . .

After much laughter and applause, the pastor led them all in prayer and the gathering broke up.

CHAPTER 42

ANGÉLIQUE WAS unable to sleep, for the night was cold and she could not get warm, even by sitting close to the fire. The others had wrapped themselves up, some in coats, some in cloaks or blankets, and the pedlar and Mr Willoughby were snoring in unison clasped in one another's arms. Angélique envied the little man from Connecticut, who must have found his rustic friend's fur warm and cosy.

Henceforth she must resolve that wherever she was, she would never go to sleep without having three things to hand—her coat, her pistols and her shoes, and that her very first move, even before opening her eyes, would be to seize these indispensable objects; and only after this would she concern herself with what was going on about her, whether it was a pirate raid or anything else. Because she had not reacted quickly enough, the night had caught her with half-naked arms in her fine frieze bodice, and the cold chilled her to the marrow although the air was so dry it almost cracked.

She got up and began to stroll along the beach. The air was crystal-clear and vibrant, and the sleeping island breathed a harmonious plaint in deep, singing intakes of breath, a mingling of wind, murmuring voices, the sound of human breathing, the clamour of seals and the roaring of the surf. . . .

As she moved away from the camp where Jack Merwin's horn lantern cast a yellow glow that served as a landmark, Angélique made her way towards another glow she had glimpsed through the trees, that lighted a larger, neighbouring beach. She had been told that the island boasted a 'singing beach' which could be heard when the wind blew from a certain quarter when it sounded like a sweet melody or the footsteps of an army on the march. ... Was this what she heard, a hallucination of souls in torment, or the approach of Indian canoes pursuing their prey through the maze of islands? ...

The light she saw was not the fatal decoy she had imagined, but only the brilliance of the long June night, so slow to die, as it stretched out over the earth its green, phosphorescent awning. ...

A colony of sea-lions lay along the beach, and the big bulls, called the masters of the beaches, stood out here and there, dark monolithic creatures, gazing out towards the shimmering sea, watching heaven knows what, while the smaller and blacker glistening females lay coiled around them. ... They were a peaceful people, full of grave innocence, troubled by the comings and goings of human beings in these their private domains where they had ruled for so long, and she caught herself looking at them with a kind of tender pity. So as not to disturb them, Angélique made her way along the edge of the wood and the big bulls turned their thick, moustachioed heads towards her. During the previous century a traveller had described the seals with some surprise: 'Their heads are like those of dogs, but without any ears, and their coats are the colour of the brown homespun worn by mendicant hermits, like the habit of our Minim Friars.'

Angélique had read this when she was a child and had dreamed of sailing to America ... and now, here she was, on this god-forsaken American shore, a woman who had reached her middle years, no longer the dreamy, excitable child from the old château of Monteloup, and yet she felt as if little had changed within her. 'Our characters are formed in the cradle.' ... We can only change by disowning ourselves. ...'

What exactly was meant by disowning oneself? Now, Joffrey had never disowned himself. ...

She crossed her arms over her breast and rubbed her shoulders and forearms to warm herself up. Only last night she had been aboard Gold Beard's ship and Colin had taken her in his arms. She shivered even more at the memory of it. ... But all that had already become just a rather disturbing dream which she must endeavour to forget, to bury, to efface.

At the far end of the beach lay the skeleton of a whale that had been washed ashore, a giant, macabre frame of a translucid, snowy whiteness, in the luminous night—a forest of bones with a pearly sheen; and through its arching vaults, as if marked out in chalk against the night sky, she could see stars trembling on the horizon.

Angélique, startled, shuddered still more violently.

Then a woman appeared and came towards her, pale and white in the milky brightness.

'Thou art cold, sister,' she said in a gentle voice. 'Here, please, take my coat. Thou canst return it at sunrise.'

Unaccustomed to this seldom use of the familiar form of address which she had not had occasion to hear the English use except when addressing themselves to God, Angélique looked at the woman without being quite sure that she had before her a living person.

'But what about you, Madame, will you not suffer from the cold?'

'I shall share my husband's coat,' the woman replied with an almost celestial smile. Then, laying a hand on Angélique's brow, she added:

'God bless thee!'

When Angélique got back, she saw that Jack Merwin was seated on a rocky promontory as if keeping a lookout.

As she reached the encampment, more comfortable now under the charitable stranger's cloak, she stopped a few paces away to look at him.

The man intrigued her more and more. That morning, when she had seen him for the first time, she had taken him for a rough, common sailor, but here, considering him in meditative posture, it became apparent to her that he must be one of those exceptional natures, that often find refuge and concealment on distant seas. His immobility was so complete—he was not even chewing his everlasting quid of tobacco—that an almost disturbing quality of solitude emanated from him, and appeared to burn within him like a fierce, brilliant flame.

'He must be some erstwhile pirate,' she thought, 'possibly even a man of noble birth? A man weary of his crimes, who seeks to forget and be forgotten by dangerous companions of yore. . . . Is it for them he is on the watch, them he fears, them he seeks, pursued himself by remorse or fear? Or is he the youngest son of some great impoverished English family who thought that a life of adventure would make him a prince? And, weary of the company he found on ship board, gave everything up to return to the solitude of the sea. . . .'

He must also have been sadly crossed in love, for I sense that he loathes women. . . .

The curve of the man's shoulders seemed as if turned to stone. It was as if his soul had left his body like an empty envelope to wander abroad. What could he hear, what was he discovering in the secret moments of his absence? Was it the Indian canoes he saw coming towards him across the luminous sea?

It was a strange night, full of undefined dangers, tender, poetic spells, and possibly evil incantations too.

Angélique felt a desire to snatch the man from his strange lethargy which she found almost frightening.

'What a lovely night, is it not, Mr Merwin?' she said in a loud voice. 'A night that invites meditation, do you not find?'

Was he asleep? His eyes were wide open, but his pupils seemed blank and empty, and yet after a few seconds he turned his head towards her.

'The beauty of this land fascinates me,' Angélique went on, driven by an impulse of which she was no longer in control, in order to attempt to establish some sort of communication with him. 'One can breathe freely here. . . . I don't know how to explain it. . . . It is something unknown, gone for ever from Europe, to such an extent that the very idea seems alien, and one only discovers it on reaching these shores. . . . A mysterious and exciting thing that I can only call . . . the very essence of liberty. . . .'

She was thinking aloud, aware of the fact that the thoughts she was trying to put into words were complicated and obscure, and that as she tried to express them in her still hesitant English, it was highly likely that the sailor would not understand a thing. So she was almost surprised to see that on the contrary she had managed to draw him away from his dreams.

She saw his features quiver, his eyes flash, then his face relaxed and set in a sardonic, scornful smile, while his dark eyes threw her a piercing glance of detestation, almost of hatred. . . .

'How can you dare to utter such words, to make such judgments?' he asked in his drawling voice which he seemed to delight in making still more slurring and vulgar.

'How can you talk of liberty, you, a woman?'

And he gave a scornful laugh. And behind him she thought she could see the glow of a sneering, enemy face, the face of some superior being, who despised and rejected her. . . . A demon! That was what lay hidden beneath this strange exterior, a demon on the prowl amongst men. . . .

She stepped back, overcome by a chill sense of numbness, and began to walk away from him.

He called her back peremptorily.

'Wait a minute,' he cried. 'Where did you go just then?'

'I went for a short walk because I was cold.'

'Well, don't go off again for any more midnight revels in the forest, because I intend to leave at dawn and shall wait for no one.'

'What a coarse brute!' said Angélique to herself as she lay down beside the fire.

That's all he was, just a coarse beast. A coarse brute in an Anglo-Saxon mould. 'A land which has given birth to a race of swashbuckling ruffians. The most tiresome barbarians in the world. . . .'

She wrapped herself in the cloak lent to her by the woman with the glistening eyes. They are all a bit mad, these English!

'You speak of liberty! You, a woman! . . . You a woman!'

She could hear his contemptuous voice.

'You . . . a woman . . . you . . . a woman.'

And in spite of herself, in the weary hours of the night, she felt dreadfully alone, overwhelmed by forces that nothing could ever overcome. How foolish of her to think that she could attack them!

Fortunately there was one man on earth whose companion she was and who loved her. . . .

'Joffrey, my love,' she sighed.

Then she fell asleep.

CHAPTER 43

WHEN SHE awoke Angélique saw that a thick fog had enveloped everything and that it must already be fairly late, since the sun, which could just be made out through the mist, already seemed high in the sky.

Jack Merwin had once again become to all intents and purposes an ordinary, grumpy man and was busy stowing a number of kegs of drinking-water away on his boat. This was a good sign, for it showed that the skipper intended to make a long trip without intermediate calls and would probably resist the temptation to go on pottering about among the islands. He had also somehow managed to unearth half a large, circular cheese and some wheaten bread, so his passengers ran no risk of dying of starvation en route.

'The fog has delayed our departure,' Miss Pidgeon explained, 'so we let you sleep on, my dear!'

'I must find the kind woman who lent me her cloak,' Angélique replied.

But Jack Merwin suddenly urged them all aboard at once.

'How in the world do you expect to navigate in this pea-soup?' Kempton protested. 'It will be the death of us.'

'Death! You are crazy,' wailed Adhemar, who was beginning to understand more and more English. 'Oh! Madame, do stop him putting out to sea. Last night I had a terrible dream, and I feel sure that it is about to come true.'

Adhemar was a simple-minded man, and in France, in the provinces, it was commonly believed that the simple-minded have the gift of second sight.

'What was it you dreamt, my poor boy?'

'You were drowned, Madame, and I could see you right at the bottom of the sea where everything is green like a Venetian lamp, with your hair streaming out behind you like seaweed.'

'Oh! Stop it for goodness sake!' cried Angélique, 'you can never open your mouth without spreading alarm all round you. And in any case you ought to be pleased to see me drowned since you take me for a She-Devil.'

'Madame, don't say things like that,' Adhemar stammered, crossing himself several times.

The pastor gave him a sidelong glance and pinched his lips. He had had more than his fill of this papist company, to which had now been added the presence of Merwin, obviously a godless and irreligious man. He was half minded to remain on Long Island but Miss Pidgeon dissuaded him by saying that if he wished to be reunited with what was left of his flock from Brunswick-Falls he must go on to Gouldsboro.

'Come along now, get aboard,' Merwin growled, adding an expression in English unfamiliar to Angélique but which seemed to imply something half-way between 'you spineless lot', and 'you good-for-nothings'.

But in spite of all his urging no one seemed in a hurry.

'You have the cloak of a Quaker woman there!' the Reverend Patridge suddenly remarked, pointing to the garment Angélique was attempting to hand to him. 'You did not speak to a member of that infamous sect, did you? You wretched woman! That could put the salvation of your soul in great danger. You are right, Miss Pidgeon. It would not be right to remain in a place where there is a risk of meeting people of that ilk—although I thought that New England had been cleared of them all, but I suppose we shall have to hang a few more to deter the others.'

'But I don't see why people should be hanged whose only crime is to lend their cloaks to those who are feeling the cold,' Angélique protested.

'But the Quakers represent a serious threat to public order,' the pastor replied.

'Yes,' chimed in Miss Pidgeon, 'they refuse to raise their hats even to the King himself, and they call him brother,

248

and say "thou" and "thee" to him. They claim they are in direct communication with God.'

'Irreverence personified,' the pastor shouted.

'They refuse to pay tithes to the churches. . . .'

'There must be no tampering with doctrine,' the pastor went on, and he was about to embark on a long sermon when Jack Merwin exploded. First he swore roundly two or three times, calling them bloody fools, an effective phrase, for Miss Pidgeon and young Esther gave shrieks of horror and covered their ears.

'Blasphemer!' roared the pastor.

'Shut up, you contemptible dolt,' said Merwin with genuine hatred in the expression of his bitter mouth; you are incapable of opening your mouth without causing trouble and confusion.'

'And what about you, unhappy wretch? I realized from the start that you were a godless man, a son of Lucifer, of him who dares to look his God in the face and say: I am your equal!'

'It would be better if an ignorant fool like you did not take it upon himself to judge his fellow men; you're more than likely to make some sorry mistakes.'

The Reverend Thomas could not tolerate it that a common sailor, as like as not from some convict colony, should speak to him in such a tone of voice and employ such language in front of weak women whose conduct largely depended on the confidence they felt in their pastor. To tolerate being thrown in this humiliating fashion from his pedestal meant running the risk of plunging simple, faithful souls into doubt. Before devoting himself to the study of theology, Thomas Patridge had been an energetic young man and a keen boxer. He had kept his strength, and now that he had recovered from his wound he was still a formidable opponent. He grabbed Merwin by the collar of his shirt and would have crushed his face with a terrible punch had not the latter, also a nimble fighter, freed himself with a sharp blow with the edge of his hand across the wrist that held him. The pastor let out a roar and his face went purple.

Angélique threw herself between the two men.

'I beg you,' she said with all the authority at her command, 'I beg you, gentlemen; you are losing your wits.'

She held them back forcibly, with one hand on each of their muscular frames, and could feel their seething anger ready to explode like the rumblings of an active volcano, but her imperious glance prevailed over their feelings and she succeeded in holding them apart.

'Pastor! Pastor!' she begged, 'try to forgive a man who has not received the same spiritual benefits as yourself. Do not forget that you represent a God who condemns violence. . . .'

The pastor had become ashen with the effort he was making to control himself and as a result of his pain, for Jack Merwin's blow had almost broken his wrist.

Jack Merwin had also grown waxen, a vein at his temple throbbed violently and his eyes looked even more steely and inscrutable.

Beneath her fingers Angélique could feel Jack Merwin's heart thudding irregularly, and at that moment he once again seemed human and vulnerable.

'And you are not sensible either,' she said to him, as if scolding a child. 'It is not the act of a good Christian to insult someone invested with ecclesiastical authority. And furthermore, this minister is wounded; only a few days ago he was half scalped by the Indians.'

The sailor's eyes made it clear that he thought it would have been a good thing if they had finished the job.

It was the Reverend Thomas who gave in first.

'I defer to you because you so wish it, my lady, although you are a Frenchwoman and a member of a scandalous religion, Babylonian and fanatical. I bow to you because you have shown yourself to be our friend. But as for him. . . .'

'He too . . . he too has shown himself to be your friend. He has taken us all on board his boat and is taking us to Gouldsboro, where we shall be safe and out of danger at last.'

She maintained her hand on Jack Merwin's chest until she felt his heartbeat grow calmer and he stepped back, breaking away, once more master of himself.

Once the quarrel was over everyone took his place in the boat including Mr Willoughby. As they left the harbour the fog was lifting and they saw a great crowd of people on the beach waving them good-bye, including the Quakers in their round hats and big white coifs standing apart from the others as if plague-ridden, but no less cheerful and demonstrative.

As they sailed past them Angélique shouted a message about the cloak which she had left with a helpful woman on another beach.

Then they passed the tip of Clipp Island and then Jewell Island. The latter was the farthest out to sea in Casco Bay, and consequently farthest removed from any possible attack by the Indians, but the people were already at work organizing its defences with a speed that did credit to the local leader, Captain Joseph Donnel.

Settlers from Boston, Freeport and Portland whom he had fetched himself with his little fleet, were working night and day, men and women, on the fortifications, and after less than a week it was already a small fort with crenelated ramparts rising above the one point on the island where boats could land. Lime-kilns had been set up to make mortar from shells for packing the interstices between the planks and beams, while another group was busy sowing wheat and cultivating the soil against the possibility of a long siege. The children had been sorted out as they landed, all those old enough to handle a knife, whether boys or girls, being despatched to help with the heavy work of clearing land or fishing, while the little ones, under the supervision of a few of the women disported themselves, pink and naked, in the icy sea among the seals and porpoises.

This information was obtained by the occupants of Jack Merwin's boat along with a final basket of shell-fish before they headed for the open sea.

Then they were out on the ocean, all blue, white and speckled with gold, and nothing but the occasional sail glimpsed here and there.

Angélique rejoiced at the open horizon. The islands had disappeared. They continued to head east-north-east, every puff of wind in the sails carrying them farther from the imperilled coast and closer to Gouldsboro.

The day passed quickly, stories from the pedlar alternating with Bible readings by the pastor. During these

251

readings Angélique watched Merwin out of the corner of her eye, but the skipper of the *White Bird*—for such was the boat's name—had resumed his expression of disdain and chewed away nonchalantly at his plug of tobacco, contemptuously spitting out jets of brown saliva whose lengthy trajectory was greatly admired by Sammy and the little Negro boy, Timothy.

There was always something going on to amuse the passengers. For a long time a white dolphin followed the boat; it was as big as an ox and as lithe as a grass snake, and kept falling back then racing forward at top speed, greatly amused by the children's shouts and appearing to give them a mischievous glance each time from its piggy little eyes.

Towards the middle of the afternoon Monhegan Island hove into sight. This is an isolated island, a considerable distance out to sea, south of the Damariscotta archipelago and the coast of Pemaquid. It is also known as Sea Island because it stands alone, like a single precious stone, its pink and blue cliffs wearing like a diadem its forests with their countless varieties of wild flowers. It is also called Wolf Island, for at one time it had abounded in the animals, which also explains why it is called the Island of the Mohicans, for that is the name of a great Indian tribe that took the wolf as its emblem.

But, at the time with which we are concerned, there were no wolves left on the island, or Mohicans either, for that matter.

The island was now inhabited by a considerable number of Basques, Bretons and Normans, Swedes and Dutchmen, Spaniards and Portuguese, Englishmen and Scots, and flotillas of ships from the whole world over made their way into its narrow fiord, opposite the granite hump of Ramana Isle.

As the island came more clearly into sight the passengers noticed a huge black cloud hanging over it, a cloud that seemed even darker towards the west, and they fell silent, their hearts struck with fear.

The dark cloud seemed to be standing still, sometimes assuming the shape of a flat mushroom with pointed extremities, then suddenly reforming again.

'Is that smoke?' murmured Angélique.

Even Merwin for once seemed intrigued, but he said nothing. Young Esther, who had been brought up on the sea coast, was the first to explain the mystery. The cloud consisted of birds, she said, which had come together from every direction and were wheeling over Monhegan, no doubt attracted by some particular choice prey.

She was not wrong, for as they drew nearer, they began to hear the piercing cries of thousands of wheeling birds.

Later they learned that a Basque ship had harpooned a whale in the waters off Monhegan and towed it to the island where the crew was loading the oil into barrels.

CHAPTER 44

Skilfully Merwin steered the *White Bird* among the jagged tips of rocks just breaking the surface of the water, and guided her smoothly up a narrow passage that scarcely merited the name of creek but which ended in a tiny sandy beach that sloped up towards the forest.

He leapt waist deep into the water and pulled the boat in until he felt its keel brush the sand. Then he climbed onto the nearest rocks in order to make her fast, and, making haste himself, he signalled to his passengers to leave the boat.

'Look lively! Don't hang about here, get up into the forest,' he called to them.

He knew the dangers of lingering on the east coast of Monhegan Island. Obediently they made haste at the sound of his voice and ran up the beach, carrying their bags and the baskets containing the remains of their meal.

'Quicker! Quicker!' cried Merwin, although it was not clear why.

It was at that moment that the catastrophe occurred.

The ground swell that comes crashing up the steep cliffs of the Black Head and the White Head on the eastern shores of Monhegan Island is a devastating thing. It steals up on you treacherously and never from the expected direction, hurls itself upon you, then straight away draws back, clutching its prey.

It began with a tall, snowy spout of water that sprang up to the right almost in front of the group of women and children, like a geyser suddenly gushing from the ground to bar their way. The water showered down over them and as they were still looking to the right another wave crept up silently behind them, round-backed, huge and glistening, and engulfed them all. They fell to their knees pell-mell, were dragged down the beach with the ebb, then, suddenly released, most of them promptly got to their feet again, and clinging to the rocks, gathered their floating possessions together, and hastened once more up the beach. Some were even laughing at the unexpected soaking, but Angélique turned and glimpsed little Sammy's head bobbing up and down in the foaming waters at the mouth of the inlet. Without a moment's hesitation she ran along the promontory and plunged into the water just as the retreating tide brought the child towards her. She met him half-way and seized him.

Then the sea swept them away in a demented dance. Looking towards the coast Angélique could see at the far end of the rocky promontory—the point she had just left—the tall figure of Merwin, who had quickly made his way to exactly the right spot. In a frenzied gallop the sea hurled them back towards him.

'Catch him!' Angélique shouted, throwing the little English boy in Merwin's direction.

He caught the boy literally in mid-air. For her part, Angélique had tried to grasp a rock but the pull of the sea had been so swift and irresistible that once more she found herself carried out to sea in the frothy layer of intertwining trails of foam. The troughs of the waves sucked her down as if a hole had suddenly gaped beneath her, then all of a sudden she would find herself at the top of a foaming crest that was so high that she thought that she was going to be hurled like a cannon ball at a point half-way up the cliff side. Her skirt, now saturated with water, was beginning to weigh her down like lead and she found she could no longer move her legs to keep herself on the surface. Then once again, with a convulsive lurch from the depths of the abyss, the waves brought her back towards the land. Hurled towards the promontory where Jack Merwin was standing she saw him draw nearer at a fantastic speed. He was now alone at the extreme point of the peninsula, having placed the rescued child in a safe spot.

He was alone, gigantic and sombre in the wind that tossed his long black hair, sombre against the bright sky flecked with whisps of white foam, and his red woollen cap stood out like an approaching beacon. She held out her hand towards him, ready to grasp his, but, contrary to all her expectations, instead of moving, he remained motionless with crossed arms.

He did not offer her his hand. Angélique's fingers clutched at the empty air, scraped along the craggy rocks, too weak to get a grip on them, and as the monstrous suction of the waves drew her back once more, she gave a cry. It was the cry of a child, a cry of frustration and astonishment. . . . 'If only he had held out his hand to me that time, I could have made it. . . . *He did not hold out his hand to me.*'

Salt water filled her mouth and she began to choke. Summoning all her strength she fought to keep calm in order to remain afloat and let herself be carried by the current which sooner or later would bear her back to the shore. Her only hope lay in those swirling waters that plunged ceaselessly into the caves at the foot of the cliffs, whose walls thundered with the pounding and made the inlet echo with a sound like gunfire.

A black wave engulfed her, rolling her over and over in a furious torrent, and Jack Merwin's eyes suddenly appeared again, this time close beside her.

Then she understood.

He had not come there to save her, but to see her die.

For he wished her dead.

This resolution was written all over his inscrutable face with its two burning eyes fixed on a world beyond this, seeming to stare right through her, through that poor battered, bruised female body, that the sea sought to rend to pieces, and which was already nothing more to him than a mere piece of flotsam.

As she discovered him to be thus in one last crazy

flash, he seemed even more demoniacal than on the previous night, and a cry of agony rose from her tortured depths:

'Joffrey! Joffrey!'

Her cry was one of despair. Deep down inside her a voice called 'Joffrey! Help! Help! The demons are trying to kill me. . . . They are here! . . .'

Then in a flash of lucidity, she added:

'Dirty swine of an Englishman! . . . I should have been on my guard against him.' You a woman he had said, and here he was, delighting in watching her die, a woman!

She began to struggle violently as panic gained the upper hand, and only sank farther and farther. Suddenly she felt as if something had seized her from below and was dragging her down to the bottom. She gave a kick to reach the surface again, and realized with horror that her skirt was caught between two rocks, while the water rushed back and forth over her, tossing her this way and that, but still held fast in the trap. Her temples were drumming as if they would burst, and every time she struggled madly to escape from the grip of the rock she was brought up short, and could not reach the air. The legendary monster that lurked in caves by the sea now held her in its claws, kept her close to its den, held her prisoner as she spun round under the blue-green water, among the seaweed that bound her hand and foot.

She could hold on no longer. She was about to open her mouth to breathe, to breathe in death.

Then a sudden jerk freed her. Her skirt tore, and she could see the light of day once more. But she was exhausted and scarcely managed to take a breath before disappearing once more.

The bitter spittle of the waves rolled over her, pummelled her, devoured her, crushed and powerless.

'No! No! I don't want to die! . . .' she cried, despairingly within herself, 'I don't want to drown . . . it is too horrible. Joffrey, Joffrey, I must see you again . . . I don't want to remain alone, far from you, at the bottom of the sea. . . .'

Had not Adhemar seen her in a dream that night, tossing at the bottom of the sea, deep in the green gulf, with

her hair trailing behind her like seaweed . . . alone . . .
alone . . . gone to sleep for ever. . . .

Something struck her on the temple. It was like a nail
brutally hammered into her head. A rock she had struck,
whose blow had awakened her, thrust her for a brief
moment up to the surface again.

A dazzling vision in the sunshine, and still that same
motionless form standing erect over her—which suddenly came to life, stooped, and dived.

A mirage!

She was sinking, sinking, vanishing for ever.

CHAPTER 45

SOMEONE WAS dragging her up the beach by her hair.
Angélique felt her body gradually liberated from the
viscosity of the sea, become as heavy as lead and begin
to score a deep furrow through the pebbles of the beach.
She was covered in grazes, bleeding and inert, while
Jack Merwin, likewise exhausted, hauled her up the
beach as he would have hauled a boat or a dead animal.

He only came to a stop when he had passed the last
band of seaweed right up beside the trees, where the
sea could no longer reach them. Then he too fell to the
ground beside her, and in her half-conscious state she
could hear his breath wheezing like the bellows of a
forge.

It had been a terrible struggle, in which she had
clung convulsively to him, and he had had to strike her
in order to stun her, and in which the sea, twenty times
over, had borne them so far from the shore that it
seemed no more than a phantom shadow, unattainable.
They had finally come ashore some considerable distance
from their point of departure.

Angélique's lungs seemed to be on fire, and it was in
vain that she tried to breathe, for with every movement
she had the impression that her chest would burst.

She tried to raise herself on her hands and knees like
a dying animal making a last supreme effort to get to its
feet. Groping blindly, she clung to the man beside her,

as a wave of nausea swept over her and she began to vomit uncontrollably. The salty flood seemed to corrode her throat as it came up, and she collapsed on her side.

Jack Merwin stood up. For a moment he had been overcome with exhaustion, but now he was once more master of himself. He threw off his filthy waistcoat and cast it aside, then removed his shirt and wrung it out, before doing the same to his red cap, which he put back on his head, and hung the twisted shirt round his neck.

Then bending down towards Angélique, he grasped her upper arm with one hand, forcing her first to her knees, then to her feet.

'Go on! Walk! Go on!'

He hustled her along, now pushing her before him, now pulling her along, and his voice sounded different, full of contained anger but also a new note of emotional turmoil. She managed to take a few steps, but was unable to lift her feet from the ground without a superhuman effort. The world was spinning, giving way beneath her, and she fell back face downwards in the sand which stuck to her cheeks.

'Joffrey! Joffrey! . . . "They" are trying to kill me. "They" have always wanted to kill me.'

Merwin tried to get her on her feet again, but she kept falling down. She was crying and vomiting, and her throat and the back of her nose hurt so much that she thought she could feel them bleeding. She was shivering and her teeth were chattering, and she kept wiping her face unconsciously as she sobbed. 'Leave me alone. . . . Leave me to die. . . . I don't mind dying here . . . but not in the sea. . . . I didn't want to drown, it's too ghastly.'

Jack Merwin had walked on without waiting for her, then he turned round with a look of exasperation at seeing her once more lying on the ground, and retraced his steps. He seemed to resign himself to the situation and, reaching a decision, took hold of her once more; but this time he stretched out full length, face downwards, with arms extended and head turned to one side.

Then taking his knife from his belt he slit open her dress right down the back, and tore away the saturated cloth sticking to her ice-cold flesh, cloth that had already been torn to ribbons against the rocks. He laid her bare to the small of her back.

Then he placed his two hands at the base of her ribs and began to press down on them rhythmically, which immediately made her feel better. Her breathing, assisted by these regular movements, grew deeper and less disordered and she was able to take in some air.

Then he began to massage her back vigorously with the palm of his hand, and bit by bit the freezing blood in Angélique's veins began to circulate again. The twisting pains inside her began to ease, her nerves calmed, her teeth stopped chattering uncontrollably, and a gentle warmth flooded through her as her thoughts floated, vaguely wandering but calm.

'This man is as evil as sin . . . but his hands are good . . . yes his hands are good. . . . How good it feels! What a blessing! Oh what a blessing it is to be alive!'

The world had stopped spinning and grown solid and sweet beneath her outstretched body.

'He will have all the skin off my back if he goes on like this. . . . Has he noticed the fleur-de-lys branded on my shoulder? I am frightened . . . does it matter? He too may be a bandit, a gallows-bird . . . supposing he betrayed me. . . . No! He's an Englishman. He probably doesn't even know what the fleur-de-lys means. . . .'

She was feeling much better, and sat up unaided.

'Thank you,' she murmured. 'I am sorry!'

'Everything all right?' Merwin asked briefly.

'Yes, more or less!'

But she had over-estimated her strength for once again the black veil came down over her eyes, and she let her head fall on to Jack Merwin's shoulder. The shoulder was bone hard but had a gentle, reliable curve. A man's shoulder.

'How comfortable that feels,' she murmured in French.

Her mind was wandering; she became aware of her nakedness and in an instinctive gesture of modesty she tried to cover her bosom with the remaining shreds of her bodice.

Merwin put one arm round her shoulders and his other hand under her knees and picked her up effortlessly in his arms. Angélique thought she had become a child again. Nothing more could harm her, and the roar of the sea grew fainter as he went striding off with her down a track through the woods. He could not have walked for long, but she was unaware of anything, for she must have fallen asleep. She did not lose consciousness but rather sank into a brief, deep sleep from which she awoke feeling completely rested, only a few minutes later. She found herself sitting on the ground leaning against a tree trunk, with her head resting on her knees, while above her Jack Merwin's authoritative voice was instructing young Esther to take off one of her petticoats and her chemise for Angélique to wear. The girl ran off behind a bush and came back shortly afterwards to hand over the two items of clothing to Angélique, who, in her turn, went off into the woods to change.

The English girl's skirt and chemise still retained some of the warmth of her body and made Angélique feel better. She rinsed the sticky sea water and sand from her hair in a nearby spring that gushed up from the moss and then made her way back to her companions. The worthy Elias Kempton had lighted a small fire to warm Sammy who was swathed in the pastor's coat, and they all stared wide-eyed at her, for they had thought they would never see her again.

'Sit close to Mr Willoughby, Mistress de Peyrac,' the pedlar insisted. 'Yes! Yes! You will see, he will keep you warm.'

'We must be on our way,' Merwin cut in. 'We shall be able to get help on the other side of the island.'

So they set off one behind the other through the pine trees, which were like pillars in a cathedral. The night was warm and dry and crackling with electric sparks. But was it night? . . . A pale turquoise sky still shone through the trees.

'It's Midsummer night,' Adhemar said, 'the night when the sun never dies, and when the bracken blooms with a tiny rust-coloured magical flower that only lasts for a few hours. They do say that people who see this flower bloom never came back. . . . Let us hurry out of this wood. There is so much bracken here and night is falling . . . Midsummer night. . . .'

Angélique walked on like a sleep-walker. She was half-dead with sleepiness and the pit of her stomach still felt ice cold.

Merwin cast an occasional glance in her direction.

'How are you feeling?'

'Quite well,' she replied, 'but I think I would feel better if I could have a good swig of rum or something hot to drink.'

As they rounded a bend in the path, the village on the west side of the island came into view at last, caught in the light of the setting sun, and the clamour of the birds and the shouts of fishermen burst upon them, together with the stench of rotten fish and melting fat.

A farmhouse built of logs appeared on their left at the entry to the village.

Standing on the threshold, Jack Merwin called out to the occupants, but as no one replied, he and the others went inside without further ado. Taking for granted the sacrosanct laws of hospitality prevailing in these distant colonies of the New World, that authorized anyone lost or starving to treat any dwelling that Providence threw in his way in these deserted lands as his own, he went straight to the wooden dresser, took from it a blue and white china bowl and a pewter ladle, walked over to the hearth and lifted the lids of the various cooking-pots.

From one of these he served a brimming, piping hot portion of clams and scallops, and from another he took three boiled potatoes, then poured some milk over the mixture from another pot that stood warming among the ashes.

'Eat that,' he said to Angélique, placing the bowl before her on the table, 'eat it quickly.'

Then he went on deftly handing out soup plates to all and sundry as if he had spent his whole life dispensing soup to the poor.

CHAPTER 46

IN TIME to come Angélique was to make no secret of the fact, that she had never tasted anything more delectable, more delicious, more comforting, than that shellfish soup which she ate in the poor farmhouse of some settler on Monhegan Island, after she had narrowly missed being drowned.

Thus it was that she made her acquaintance with the national dish of the region between Cape Cod and the northernmost point of the gulf of Saint Lawrence, taking in the Bay of Fundy and Nova Scotia. The French, Canadians and Acadians, call it *chaudrée*, the English *chowder*, that heavenly, nourishing soup which is a blend of all that is most delightful along those shores— the potato, that grows wild in America, health-giving shellfish from the fertile, motherly sea, and milk, delectable, delightful product of the Old World, a reminder of distant, grassy lands, a luxury in this new country, so hard to tame, that is surprised to see a few exiled cows as they graze, somewhat out of place, on the verge of the Indian forest lands. . . .

All these things are to be found in that beautiful bowl with the delectable smell.

Add to this a juicy onion, a pinch of pepper or nutmeg, a few cubes of salt pork, and at the last minute, a knob of butter per portion. . . .

It should have been round a clam chowder in a silver tureen—or a gold one, why not?—that the treaties should have been drawn up that decided the fate of this part of the world. Everyone would have been the gainer.

They ate hungrily and not a sound could be heard save sighs of contentment and the smacking of tongues.

'Hello there! Make yourself at home, you English,' said a voice in French, and they saw a big peasant woman standing on the threshold.

'Ho there! Whatever is that, gentle Jesus?'

'It's but a bear,' murmured Kempton as he lapped up the last drops of his soup.

'I can see that, you great oaf! But do I have to have a bear right in my very house? Has my house become a kennel? Am I supposed to offer him some soup too in one of my beautiful plates that my good mother brought all the way from Limousin forty years back without breaking a single one?'

'Madame, are you French?' Angélique asked her in the same tongue. 'Is this an Acadian household by any chance?'

'Well, perhaps it is now, and perhaps it isn't. I couldn't tell you what we are exactly here in Monhegan. . . . I myself come from Port-Royal on the Acadian peninsula where I landed at the age of five with Monsieur Pierre d'Aulnay's party of recruits, but that was ages ago. When I was twenty I married our neighbour, a Scot called MacGregor, and we settled together on Monhegan and have been here nigh on thirty-five years.'

Jack Mervin questioned her in English, asking her whether the Indians had tried to launch any attacks on the island and whether there was any trouble in Penobscot Bay. She shook her head and replied in English which she regularly spoke, although with a strong French accent.

She told them that the Indians, Mohicans, Tarratines, Mic-Macs, and Etchemins from Penobscot and Dariscotta were still at peace. This time they had not unearthed the war hatchet, for the great French nobleman who ruled over Gouldsboro had managed to persuade all the white men in the Bay, and especially that little hothead Saint-Castine not to have anything to do with that wicked campaign. Only last week her man, old MacGregor, had gone off with his three sons to Popham Point to meet 'the great Lord of Gouldsboro' and together with all the white men from the area and the chief sagamores from the neighbouring lands they had made an alliance, exchanged promises, and smoked the peace-pipe together. The lord of Gouldsboro was strong and wealthy; he had his own fleet and money to burn. He had promised to protect anyone against their own governments who found himself in difficulties for having undertaken to keep the peace. And quite right too! People here had just about enough of being made to dance like a lot of puppets in accordance with the whims of the Kings of France or England, who took good care not to set foot in the colonies themselves.

Angélique had grown red with emotion at the mention of the name of her husband, Count Peyrac. She plied the good lady with questions, from which she learned

263

that after Joffrey left the mouth of the Kennebec he had made his way back towards Gouldsboro. So there was every likelihood that she would find him there, if they reached it tomorrow, which seemed likely since the sea remained calm in spite of the equinoctial tides.

When she discovered who it was she had welcomed into her humble cottage—the great Lord of Gouldsboro's very own wife—Mrs MacGregor clasped her hands together in rapture, dropped a deep curtsy as her mother had taught her to do to nobility, and danced attendance on them all, speaking now in French and now in English according to whom she was addressing.

Angélique told of her mishap, how she had almost been drowned as they had landed on the island, and the woman revealed that this was an almost daily occurrence. Every family had more members drowned than alive; that was how it was!

'I'll fetch you some good clothes, Madame,' she concluded in a voice devoid of emotion.

'You wouldn't have a pair of breeches for the man who rescued me, would you? He is still soaking wet.'

'A pair of breeches? No, there's nothing like that here, my poor lady! My menfolk wear nothing but their big plaid wraps, tartans they call them; a Scot would not feel right unless he went about with a bare behind, saving your presence. But the assistant from the shop, Mr Winslow, our neighbour, who comes from Plymouth, should be able to help these gentlemen find what they want.

And she sent the men off with the bear to her English neighbours, retaining only the women and children, among whom was the little black boy.

'A real little jack-in-the-box, popped straight up from Hell, is that kiddy there. But it's Midsummer night, isn't it? This is the night when all the brownies and hobgoblins come out. . . . Look! Look how light the sky is still. . . . At midnight the Basques will light their fires and dance.'

For people were gay on Monhegan, in spite of all the drownings. Furthermore the Basques from Bayonne had harpooned a whale two days previously.

After a desperate struggle during which the whale's tail had sent whole boats flying and one man had been killed, the catch had been brought in, under a screaming cloud of birds of prey. The whale, already cut into pink and white slices by the whalers' knives, still floated in the water between the anchored boat and a small, quiet sandy beach upon which three huge cauldrons had been set up. A fortune lay there bobbing up and down on the tide at Monhegan and it was pieces of gold that the sailors handled in their imaginations with the cubes of fat they threw into the cauldrons. Some of them were busy bringing up buckets full of spermaceti from huge cavities in the whale's head, a white oily substance used in the manufacture of the most expensive candles, while the whalebone would be used for the manufacture of clothes, feather tufts, plumes, bodies and fans. . . .

The tongue, the choicest morsel, would be salted and served on princes' tables, while the blubber would provide broth for the poor during Lent. The bones would be transformed into beams, joists and fencing posts.

The great harpooner Hernani d'Astiguarra, who was also captain of the little 150-ton ship, swaggered, proud as a peacock, around the harbour leaning on his harpoon as an Indian leans on his lance. As soon as the first star began to tremble in the firmament and the contours of the forest loomed dark against the green sky, they would stop work and light great bonfires along the beach, for it was Midsummer night and they had to dance and leap over the fires.

Meanwhile Angélique had been negotiating with Mrs. MacGregor the purchase of a sealskin coat, quite enchanted by the velvety softness of the fur.

'I have nothing with which to pay you just at the moment but as soon as I reach Gouldsboro I will send you a purse containing twenty crowns and a small gift, the choice of which I will leave to you.'

'Listen,' said the old lady, 'we have all we need here and there's no need to go to all that trouble. They say you have the power of healing, and if you could get my grandson Alistair on his feet again, that would be payment enough. It would be a blessing for the child too.'

So they went to see young Alistair. Mrs MacGregor had had twelve children, and her surviving sons and daughters, who had all married on the island, made up a family of considerable size. In order to avoid jealousy between the national saints of the two Franco-Scottish families, the children had been given French and Scots names alternately. Thus a Leonard preceded an Ogilvey and an Alistair was followed by a gentle Janeton.

A few days earlier a strange thing had happened to young Alistair; as he ran across the rocks to escape the high tide, he had tried to leap across a crevice. This was no occasion to miss his footing as there was a sixty-foot drop below. He just managed to save himself from falling on landing on the other side, and since then a terrible pain prevented his putting his feet to the ground.

Angélique immediately saw that as the boy had gripped the rock face with his toes he had torn the main tendons under his arches. Coaxing them back into position was a painful business but after an hour of massage the boy placed a timid and incredulous foot on the flag-stones again, delighted that it no longer hurt, then, going to the other extreme, said he thought he would be able to dance the crossed sword dance that very evening, which Angélique told him firmly he was not to do. He must rest, so that the ligaments could unite. She called for some good woodchuck grease, which was something all self-respecting housewives always kept a pot or two of in stock, and after a final massage left the boy leaning on a stick. At least he would be able to attend the festivities.

A considerable crowd, draped in tartan, hooded and wrapped around in red and green or green and black—for there were two clans, the MacGregors and the Mac-Duffs—wearing blue berets with pompons, had watched the miracle. And intermingled with these bright costumes were the dark coats of the English traders and settlers. Their families were descendants of the first inhabitants of Plymouth in Cape Cod Bay—the Pilgrim Fathers—and, like old Joshua whom Angélique had met at Houssnock, they all had, in spite of their strict ways, a certain sprightliness about them which was not at all to the liking of the Reverend Patridge. There were also two families of Irish fishermen, and one of French origin, called Dumaret, who claimed to hold the record for drownings. But then, in this land where, as soon as a child can stand, it dashes into the waves astride a plank of wood, how could it be otherwise? These people constantly sail from island to island, in a region where the sea is even more treacherous than elsewhere, and one day, especially around the age of fourteen or fifteen—an age which knows no fear but still lacks experience—these indefatigable vagabonds of the straits get drowned.

In the Dumaret family the old granny always had a premonition of disaster. Whether by day or by night, she would be seen to rise and begin to fold and put away the clothes of a boy who was at sea. 'He has just been drowned,' she would say.

Angélique heard all kinds of tales as she was taken round the hamlet and the various farms. Her visit did great honour to the island and the healing of young Alistair completed the legend. Some sailors from Dieppe who had landed with two boats to replenish their stocks of drinking water mingled that evening with the population, and the whole place buzzed with a strange lingua franca, consisting of a mixture of Indian dialects, a bit of French from Saint-Malo and a smattering of English. Some peaceful Mic-Macs, who were related to some of the inhabitants of the island, began to make their way out of the forest, placing furs and game at the doors of the houses, then squatting on the heights, anxious to participate in the Paleface festivities. Most of these Indians were very tall, almost giants, with square, copper-coloured faces.

Towards ten o'clock in the evening Angélique decided that she had made sufficient sacrifice to the vanities of this world and that she must snatch a little sleep before the fun began.

She had managed to get a good hot bath at Mrs MacGregor's and the sweltering night air had dried her thick hair, but she was overcome with weariness.

So she wrapped herself up in her beautiful sealskin coat and sat down away from the others, leaning against the roots of a great oak.

Tomorrow she would be in Gouldsboro. Would to God the sea remained calm.

Below her things were growing more and more lively

round the houses and along the beach, where firewood was being piled up.

Casks and tankards were brought out, and bowls laid on trestle tables. The night was getting on but the big midsummer fires were not to be lighted until the last moment, at midnight.

Some children rushed by holding hands, sweeping Timothy the little Negro boy, Abbial the ship's boy and Samuel Corwin along with them.

Monhegan, the eternal, Monhegan the mother of all sea-going peoples, was living through another magical night and its heart could be heard beating in the dull thud of the swell pounding the cliffs and the first beats of the drums rehearsing a dance at the Basque encampment.

Into this narrow fiord, driven by the mist, towards the year 1000, ships with dragons on their prows had once glided, discovering then as now the granite cliffs covered with flowers. And since that time, on the grey stone, mysterious markings kept fresh the memory of the Vikings' visit, those Normans with golden beards and hair. After them had come John Cabot, Verrazano the Florentine sailing for France, the Spaniard Gomez, the Englishman Rut, a French priest called André Theot, Sir Humphrey Gilbert, Gosnold, Champlain and George Weymouth and John Smith who, in 1614, had been sent on a mission 'to explore North America for gold and whales'.

The island's history was long, crowded and multicoloured. The isle of the Mohicans breathed its stirring saga in the varied cries that rose through the night air in the Gaelic lilt of Irish and Scots voices, in the earthy smells, in the oaths in every imaginable language, and in the laughter of men, women and children, and the costumes from all parts of the globe—Scots tartans, red basque berets, black Calvinist hats and the satin neckerchiefs of the handful of buccaneers from Barbados, and the multi-coloured woollen caps of sailors from every port in the world.

The crickets, hidden in the grass, played their endless, high-pitched saraband, and along the saffron-coloured horizon, where night was at least beginning to fall like a dark froth from the green firmament, sails, still more sails passed by.

And then suddenly there was nothing left: the sea was deserted, the coast was empty. Angélique was alone gazing out at the sea and the abandoned beach. Why are there so many ports along this coast whose names suggest desertion, abandonment? The names sound like the tolling of a death knell. All is empty, all has faded and gone—the whales gone, and the shoals of cod and sardines, those great silver shields on the surface of the sea, the vast clouds of birds along with the seals in their Minim's robes, the white porpoises, the blue sperm-whales, the fierce grampus and the gentle dolphin. . . .

But it is not only that which is so sad. . . . A sense of discouragement grips one's heart, an infinite nostalgia seizes the soul . . . a dull feeling of despair in the deserted creeks. . . .

Too many memories, too many battles, too many massacres, too many drownings, too much greed, too many passions, too many souls wandering in hate and desolation, forgotten, gathered together weeping and lamenting in the mists, in the wind, in the spray of the waves, borne hither and thither by the gigantic, terrible tides that are swallowed up in the bowels of the earth, whistling and wailing as they go.

So many deserted shores. . . .

Shimmering, fine mists that rain down heavily on the cedar forests, on the green pine needles, on the glistening foliage of maple and copper beech, falling on fields of wild lupin and rhododendrons, on lilac trees beside a ruined house, and on roses growing in a forgotten garden.

Land of ghosts—French, English, Dutch, Swedish, Finnish, Spanish, Breton, Norman, Scots, Irish; pirates, peasants, fishermen, whalers, trappers; Puritans, Papists, Jesuits and Recollects; Indians, Etchemins, Tarratines, Mic-Macs, Malacites, where are you all? Where are you, ghosts of Acadia, land of a hundred names, kingdom of creeks and peninsulas, of leafy haunts with a sail passing by?

The smell of the woods and the smell of the seaweed, the smell of the Indians, the smell of scalps, a smell of burning, a smell of the seashore, a smell that wafts off the sea, and off the land, that surrounds you with incense, that makes you numb, and over it all a relentless, cold gaze watching you die. . . .

A wailing broke the silence, a peculiar, shrill wail that startled Angélique out of her sleep and out of the nightmare she was having and made her straighten up once more with beating heart at the foot of the tree where she had drowsed off.

'What's that? Are they killing a pig?'

No, it was only the Scottish bagpipes beginning to play down on the beach.

A few paces away Angélique noticed that Jeck Merwin was sitting looking towards the shore where the big bonfire had just been lighted, while the Scotsmen danced over crossed swords or wrestled with the black bear.

'I had a dream,' Angélique said, almost to herself, 'people fought so much amongst themselves that these lands became deserted and forgotten.'

Then she noticed that she had spoken in French.

Jack Merwin's back remained as motionless as the rock. He sat with his forearms resting on his knees and his hands hanging limp, and she noticed for the first time that in spite of their calluses they were long, aristocratic hands.

The uneasy feeling she had often had when she looked at him came back to her still more forcibly, with the memory of his extraordinary behaviour in refusing to hold out a hand to her as he watched her in the throes of death with his cold, relentless eyes.

Whatever had possessed him to allow her to sink and go through that terrible struggle and then to dive in when it was almost too late and save her life at the very last moment, at the cost of a superhuman effort? He was a very strange man. Perhaps he was mad, after all!

'Give me your hand, Jack Merwin,' she said suddenly, 'and let me read your fortune.'

But he threw her a furious glance and clasped his hands tight together as a clear indication that he intended to keep them to himself.

Then Angélique gave a sudden laugh. She really must

be still half asleep to have dared to show even that degree of coquetry and provocativeness to a hostile misogynist like him. Her own heart was like a ship with billowing sails, ready to speed towards the horizon, and she was delighted by all the hurly-burly including even the wailing bagpipes.

'It is so wonderful to be alive, Merwin I am so happy. . . . You saved my life.'

Merwin scowled, his hands still clasped firmly together. In any case, listening to her talking to herself like this, he considered she must be mad.

Then she laughed again, intoxicated by this June night, spellbound by its endless strident sounds.

Louder even than the bagpipes, came the rhythmic call of the fifes and drums.

Angélique leapt to her feet.

'Miss Pidgeon, Mrs MacGregor, Mrs Winslow and you, Dorothy and Janeton, come, come. . . . Let us go and dance the farandole with the Basques.'

And she seized them by the hand drawing them along with her as she ran down the slope.

CHAPTER 47

THE BASQUES advanced one behind the other, barefooted and on tip-toe, capering and whirling as they went; they were prodigious dancers, full of grace and vigour, and the glow of the fires shone on their poppy-red berets.

A tall supple fellow spun round and round in front of them, holding aloft a tambourine with copper jingles which he tapped with his nimble fingers.

When Angélique and her companions entered the ring of firelight the men gave them a noisy welcome and made room for them at their sides.

'By Saint Patrick,' cried the Irishman Parsons, 'that divvil of a lass is getting our womenfolk to join in the dancing!'

'I have heard tell things about her,' the Englishman Winslow replied. 'They do say that she is a She-Devil.'

'A She-Devil!' old MacGregor roared with mirth. 'Hold your whist, you know nothing about it. She's a fairy! I used to meet them on the moors in Scotland when I was a child, and I recognized her straight away. Let it go, neighbour, let it go. Tonight is the mad night. The very sound of those Basque flutes makes my feet itch. Come and dance too, neighbour. Tonight is the mad night.'

The farandole went on weaving its sinuous way among the bonfires, the houses, the rocks and the trees.

Every woman, old or young, grandmother, mother, girl or child must join in the dancing on Midsummer night. The tall harpooner, Captain Hernani d'Astiguarra, held out his hand to Angélique and drew her into the dance, his eyes never leaving her face. He soon discovered that she knew most of the traditional steps of the Basque farandole and, once back on the beach, he swept her into the centre of the circle. There, yielding to the spell of the exciting music she danced with him a multitude of complex, dashing yet graceful figures traditional in the Basque country.

At Toulouse, in Aquitaine, Angélique had danced the majority of these figures, for in the château they were preferred to the excessively stiff and formal Court dances. Joffrey de Peyrac had often taken his young wife to the Basque country, in the Pyrenees, to attend the big popular festivals, where in her capacity as Suzeraine, she had happily joined in the merrymaking of her vassals.

One by one these memories came back to her as the frenzied music continued.

Young Esther's short skirt made it easy for Angélique to kick her legs high in the lively measures, and she laughed gaily as the irresistible Basque captain swept her along, treading so lightly she scarcely touched the ground, her golden hair at one moment streaming out behind her like a banner, then striking against her cheek and swathing her face in a silky net.

He spoke to her sometimes in Basque and sometimes in French whenever the figures of the dance brought them together and his steely arm encircled her more and more possessively with each encounter.

'A fairy rose up out of the sea for Midsummer night,' he said. 'Monhegan is a happy island. It is all so much magic, Madame; how can you possibly know our dances?'

'Because I am the Countess de Peyrac de Morens d'Irristru.'

'Irristru? . . . That's a name from our part of the world.'

'Yes indeed.'

'Are you from Aquitaine, then?'

'Yes, by marriage.'

'And what is your husband doing leaving you to wander about alone at the ends of the earth?'

'He is not very far away, so take care, sir.'

'Madame,' he went on in Basque, 'you have the loveliest figure, and the trimmest waist that I have ever held in my hands and your eyes are intoxicating. . . . Do you know the wine-harvest jig?' he went on in French.

'I think so.'

'Then come along.'

He drew her wildly into the dance and spun her round until she was giddy; the deep blue sky swung across the red flames of the bonfires, and joyous faces bounced up and down like so many balls before her eyes.

'I've had enough,' she cried, 'my head is spinning.'

He came to a halt but not before he had lifted her off the ground and whirled her several times round.

Everyone clapped and Angélique laughed as they passed her the goatskin flask from which one was expected to pour the wine straight to the back of one's throat without touching the flask with the lips. A further burst of applause greeted this new exploit.

Farther up the hillside, the Reverend Patridge who disapproved of such goings-on, and the sailor Jack Merwin, who was in no mood to participate, sat leaning against a tree-trunk contemplating the scene with the same sombre, reproving stare.

Angélique caught sight of them and burst into peals of irrepressible mirth; the two of them were just too comical for words.

Her gay laughter encouraged the others to yet more mirth, and everyone began to dance again, the adults in pairs and the children in a ring, with the bagpipes supporting the drums, the *bourrée* of Limoges intermingled with the Scottish jig and the Cornish brawl, while the less agile or exhausted members of the party kept time by clapping to the music.

Occasionally one or other of the dancers would collapse beside the trestle tables to quaff a mug of beer or take a long swig of wine. All the ships in the harbour had brought out the supplies they held for special occasions —Spanish wines from the Caribbean, French wines and a rough wine with a strong bouquet from the wild vines on Matinicus Island. The drinkers switched from one to another and the sunshine of so many continents, mingling in their glasses, gave them a glorious feeling of warmth in the pits of their stomachs and put lightning into their calves, although later they would be left perilously weak.

Sitting at the tables were two old ladies from the island—one of them being granny Dumaret, who had the visions of those about to be drowned—tirelessly opening clams and oysters with their busy knives.

Monsieur d'Astiguarra reminded Angélique of the correct way to eat 'loubinkas', a favourite dish of the Béarn and the Basque countries.

He had taken good care when leaving Bayonne to stock his ship abundantly with strings of these highly spiced little sausages, which were eaten fried, each one being swallowed burning hot, and followed up immediately with a raw oyster—the height of gastronomic bliss —a burning sausage and a cool oyster. Then a few moments dancing followed by a draught of Jurançon wine. Then another of those diabolical sausages, so highly flavoured they made your eyes water, and a green, icecold oyster, swimming in its salty juices, drunk straight from its iridescent shell. The dancing, the laughter, the rhythmic clapping of hands, the amber-coloured wine with a flavour as strong and vibrant as the piping of the fifes. . . .

Some of the revellers sat down, some fell to the ground . . . some began to giggle uncontrollably, some did not feel very well and looked rather pale, but no one paid much attention.

Up above them, beside the houses on the edge of the wood, sat the Mic-Mac and Mohican Indians, looking almost as serious as the Reverend Patridge, as they watched the Paleface revels. There seemed to them to be little point in drinking wine, which did not make you really drunk, and they thought that fire-water alone had divine and magical properties. When they had accumulated sufficient brandy from the ships in exchange for their furs, then they would organize a great carousel somewhere deep in the forest; then they would go mad and be reunited with the Spirit of Dreams. They would not be content with just laughing and dancing stupidly like the Palefaces . . . and eating nothing but a few shellfish. . . .

On the stroke of midnight, the first man to leap the fire shot out of the flames like a black devil.

Then one by one the other Basques, with legs like steel springs, leapt over the flames, feet spread wide, arms raised, every jump being greeted with a cry of fright and admiration from the spectators.

'The Devil is powerless for a whole year against anyone who leaps over the midsummer fire,' said Hernani d'Astiguarra.

'In that case I shall jump too,' cried Angélique.

'But women can't do that,' one of the Basques protested, shocked at this break with tradition.

'So you'd abandon women to the devil, would you?' Angélique retaliated, pulling the man's beret down till it touched his nose.

She was a little foolish and a trifle tipsy, but what of it? This was an opportunity that might never come her way again and was something she had always dreamed of.

'It's all right for *her, she* can!' Hernani said with considerable force, his eyes full of smouldering passion as he gazed at her. 'But your hair, Madame . . . you must take care of your hair,' he added, laying a caressing hand on Angélique's head—a gesture she was scarcely aware of in the fever and intoxication of the moment.

'Have no fear! I was born under Sagittarius, the sign of Fire, whose children are the cohort of the Violent and the legion of the Salamanders and can pass with impunity through flames. I MUST jump! Monsieur d'Astiguarra, your hand!'

He led her to within a few paces of the crackling fire, and everyone fell silent.

Angélique kicked off the shoes she had borrowed from Mrs MacGregor. Beneath her bare feet the sand felt cool, and the roaring flame rose up before her, tall and golden.

Angélique, who had also partaken of the scalding 'loubinkas', of fiery wine and the salty tang of the sea, felt as if she herself had become a flame about to crackle and leap into action.

Hernani handed her a small flat flask, which she sniffed, recognizing the smell.

'That is Armagnac from the Piquepoul vines! . . . A thousand thanks, sir!'

And she took a long draught of the brandy.

Everyone was watching her. No one remembered her name very clearly but the things that had been said about her floated hazily in their befuddled minds.

As she stood there barefoot and ready to leap forward, she looked to them like the incarnation of some goddess, not altogether of their world, and yet dominating them by the quiet independence of a creature who was sure of herself.

They could see that her slender waist showed no sign of fragility, that her graceful shoulders, in spite of their elegance, bore witness to a life rich in experience and struggle, and they sensed, by the glint in her eyes, that in challenging the flames she wished, so to speak, to set a seal on so many other infernos through which she had passed.

But Angélique herself had no such thoughts for her mind was entirely bent on this difficult and fascinating ordeal.

At first it had been a kind of yearning of her body, overwrought by the heat of the night, to leap into the air—the living body which that very day had almost died, and now among the writhing flames she seemed to see a resplendent, fearsome face calling to her, the mythical spirit of Midsummer night, a dazzling succubus whose hair was now dusky blue now purple, the She-Devil!

The tambourine began to beat. Hernani d'Astiguarra grasped Angélique by the hand and launched her forward, faster and faster. . . .

The golden wall rose up before her.

Gripping her tight, Hernani lifted Angélique up into the air, and as she leapt forward, she felt the hot breath of the fire, passed through its shifting, incandescent drapery, felt the fleeting nip, the glowing red whirlwind that sought to wrap itself around her and hold her fast, then she made her escape, landing on the other side in the coolness of the night, where another of the Basques was waiting to pull her to safety still farther away, out of all danger.

Two others rushed forward and beat out the smouldering edge of her skirt with their palms.

There was a slight smell of singed hair, and Angélique shook her locks.

'It's nothing! I got through, thanks be to God!'

'You make me ill!' cried Adhemar bursting into tears. 'What would have happened to us all if you had fallen in? Wasn't the water enough for you to die in without having the fire as well?'

He was dead drunk.

The music began again, in a somewhat confused and jerky manner, and the tall Hernani ran his harpooner's arm round Angélique's waist and drew her to one side.

His black eyes shone like two carbuncles, and he spoke to her in Basque with a note of urgency in his voice.

'Meeting you is an unforgettable experience, Madame. You have ravished my soul. We shall finish the night together, shall we not?'

Angélique shook herself free in order to see him better, and her astonishment was due less to the over-bold proposition he had just put to her, than to the fact that he had spoken in Basque, which should have been completely unintelligible to her.

'What an extraordinary thing,' she exclaimed, 'but.... I appear to understand Basque! Me, Basque! That incomprehensible gibberish that no one seems able to learn unless born on the banks of the Soule! ... Did your Armagnac contain some magic potion, Monsieur d'Astiguarra?'

'No ... but ... is it not a fact that you, Madame, speak some of the Acadian Indian dialects?'

'I am in fact familiar with the Abenaki tongue as spoken in the Kennebec region.'

'That explains the mystery. Our tongue and that of the Indians are related. I presume that, both starting out from Asia, our races went round the world in opposite directions, the Indians ending up here and we in Bayonne. When my forefathers hunted whales in these regions, they had no difficulty at all in understanding the savages and often, entirely without study, we were able to act as interpreters between them and the missionaries.'

Once again he made to draw her towards him.

'And so, if you understood my bold proposal, Madame, what is your reply? . . .'

She placed two fingers over his lips.

'Hush, sir! On Midsummer's night people say many foolish things, but they should not do them. It is a time of fairy enchantment, not a time of realities.'

The time seemed to have come for all respectable ladies to retire, and Angélique with Miss Pidgeon clinging to one arm, and Mrs MacGregor in tow on the other, the latter herself supporting one of her daughters to whom her little girl and a whole bevy of children were clinging, not without difficulty climbed the hillside towards what looked vaguely like a group of houses at the top.

Their slipping and sliding set them laughing till the tears ran down their faces and their sides ached with laughter.

A dour figure of righteousness, the Reverend Patridge, loomed up before them, and thundered:

'Miss Elizabeth Pidgeon, I heartily condemn your present behaviour. You, so pious. . . .'

'Oh leave the poor creature alone,' Angélique cut in, in a voice that struck her as a little hoarse. 'After all, she has had her fill of horror and suffering over the past two weeks! She has every right to enjoy herself a bit now that we are out of danger!'

She swung the giggling Miss Pidgeon round her in a circle, and began to dance once more.

'I shall take you to Gouldsboro, darling, and there you will be safe. . . . Mistress MacGregor, may we rest beneath your roof?'

'Yes, my dears,' sang Mrs MacGregor, who was three sheets in the wind; 'my house is at your disposal.'

They lay down to sleep on kelp-filled mattresses laid out on the living-room floor. No sooner had they found a comfortable position to sleep than a group of sailors banged at the shutters, shouting for women.

Old MacGregor leapt to his feet and took up station in the doorway, his shirt tails flapping and musket in hand, shouting that he would shoot full of holes anyone who dared disturb the ladies' rest.

After this all was calm, and then came the dawn.

Thus ended the crazy Midsummer night on Monhegan Island, the shortest night of the year, the pagan celebration of the summer solstice, with fires lighted along the hills and the beaches, the night in which the bracken bursts into flower in the undergrowth, when old Shapleigh goes off into the forest of the New World to pick wild vervain . . . Juno's tears, Mercury's blood, the joy of simples. . . .

CHAPTER 48

THE THIRD day of their journey dawned. The morning after the night before. . . . A mist that might at any moment turn to rain hung over the island, heavy with the smell of burnt-out fires and dead fish. Only the seagulls, the cormorants and the shrikes had resumed their chattering calls. 'It's our turn now!' they seemed to say somewhat spitefully.

As Angélique made her way down towards the landing-stage with Adhemar and young Samuel, Mrs MacGregor's daughter ran after her, with two little girls aged eight and twelve following behind her.

'Take them with you, would you,' she said, puffing and blowing, 'take them to Gouldsboro. I understand there is a school there, where they can be taught to speak good French like my grandmother's and learn their prayers. It is three years now since we had a pastor here. . . . And as for knowing their letters, the poor creatures! They are more likely to learn how to blaspheme here!'

279

With Dorothy and Janeton in tow Angélique felt a certain embarrassment as she presented herself at the landing-stage.

'I shall pay these children's passage when we reach Gouldsboro,' she said to Jack Merwin, who merely looked away with the distasteful look of a man whose boat was being treated as a kind of rubbish dump.

Yawning and somewhat unsteady on their feet, the other passengers on the *White Bird* took their customary places, then at the last moment Captain Hernani loomed out of the fog, every bit as lively as the previous day, and placed something heavy on Angélique's knees.

'That is for your friends in Gouldsboro,' he said. 'I know they are from Charentes, and will know how to appreciate it. . . .'

It was a white oak keg full of the very best Armagnac, a priceless treasure!

Merwin was already pushing his boat out, and Angélique scarcely had time to thank the friendly captain.

'Come and see us in Gouldsboro,' she cried out.

And they watched him standing there, blowing kisses to her, until the bright red of his big beret had faded into the mists.

Accustomed to the whims of the English captain, Merwin's passengers had embarked as soon as he had given the order to do so. But they soon realized that it had been sheer madness to put to sea in a 'pea-souper' like this.

Fortunately none of them was in much of a state to reflect on the matter. Lack of sleep had made them all drowsy, and Angélique, for her part, was delighted at their hasty departure. That night they would be in Gouldsboro, and nothing was going to spoil her mood of happiness, neither the wretched weather, nor the dark sea, nor the even more louring looks cast by the Reverend Patridge, who was sulking with Miss Pidgeon, while she gazed at him with a repentant expression, nor even Jack Merwin's expression, which was even colder and more hostile than usual.

She found the two little Scots girls adorable with their little round, roguish faces peeping out from the voluminous red-and-green-checked plaids in which they were swathed from head to toe. They both clung tenaciously to their little bundles consisting of large kerchiefs tied round a few possessions, and the younger girls clasped a simple Indian doll made from corn husks with cheeks dyed red with raspberry juice and dried grass for hair.

Angélique thought of Honorine and of the bright grace of childhood.

The fog was growing thicker, and Merwin had set the ship's boy the task of sounding the fog horn. As the lad puffed and blew into the enormous shell, the shape of a large fishing sloop loomed up, drifting towards them. There seemed to be no one on board, but as the vessel approached, a terrifying cry rent the air, a Redskin war cry. And as they all sat petrified, the barrel of a long pistol appeared over the side of the sloop and an unseen man called to them in French:

'By the Blessed Sacrament, are you Englishmen?'

'We are French! We are French!' Angélique and Adhemar replied hastily.

The sloop came alongside the *White Bird*, and threw on boat hooks which brought the vessel to a halt. It was an Acadian boat from the mainland in search of some English capture.

A youthful, beardless, sunburnt face, framed in long black tresses, beneath a felt hat adorned with eagle feathers, suddenly appeared from nowhere and two dark magnificent eyes swiftly scanned the passengers in the sloop.

'Ho! ho! I believe I see a fair number of Englishmen among you!'

He revealed himself in full. A silver crucifix and several medallions jingled on his soft leather jerkin, which was fringed in the Indian style. On his belt he wore a cutlass and a hatchet, while in his hand he held a riding pistol with a mother-of-pearl butt. Behind him appeared a row of hang-dog faces, looking very much like those of a lot of wreckers, with three or four Mic-Macs among them wearing pointed black bonnets decorated with pearls.

Their young leader looked suspiciously at Angélique, and his eyes narrowed.

'Are you quite sure you are French and not English?'

'And you,' she retaliated, 'are you quite sure you are French and not Indian?'

'I,' he exclaimed indignantly, 'am Hubert d'Arpentigny, from Cape Sable. Everyone in Acadia and in Frenchman Bay knows me!'

'And I, young man, am the Countess of Peyrac and I think that everyone in Acadia and in Frenchman Bay knows my husband!'

Quite unabashed, Hubert d'Arpentigny sprang down into Jack Merwin's ship.

While, on his mother's side, he had a grandfather who had been a great sagamore of the forests, his paternal grandfather had been one of King Louis XIII's equerries and had taught him the manners of the French Court, and he kissed Angélique's hand very elegantly.

'Madame, I recognize you by your reputation—beautiful and daring! Nothing could be farther from my mind than to cause you any harm. But it seems to me that you have among your companions here a handful of Englishmen—just what I want to put up for sale as hostages.'

'These people belong to me and it is my task to take them back to my husband, Count Peyrac.'

Young d'Arpentigny heaved a deep sigh.

'And . . . have you no supplies, no wares on board this sloop? The winter has been a hard one in our hands and we are still waiting for one of our company's ships to bring us supplies from Bordeaux. If it turns out to have been wrecked or seized by pirates we shall find ourselves completely destitute.'

'So you indulge in a bit of piracy from others,' Angélique replied, doing her best to hide the keg of Armagnac that Hernani d'Astiguarra had given her. 'I am terribly sorry, but you will find nothing here. We are as poor as Job.'

'Indeed! . . . You there, English captain, move aside and let me have a look in the well-deck.'

With a peremptory gesture with the barrel of his pistol he signalled to Merwin to move out of the way, while his companions continued to hold their ship close up against the sloop, exchanged a few jokes in Indian language, made eyes at young Esther, and furtively scrutinized Angélique while laughing outrageously at the heretic pastor.

Angélique was beginning to wonder how it was all going to end when she saw young d'Arpentigny leap back on board his own ship and sweep off his hat respectfully and repeatedly to her, with a grin that stretched from ear to ear.

'Off you go, Madame; you and your hostages are free. God speed!'

'A thousand thanks, Monsieur. If you are in difficulty before the harvest time, come to Gouldsboro.'

'I shall most certainly do that. Monsieur de Peyrac has always been generous to us. And you, you are every bit as lovely as they say in Frenchman Bay. My day has not been wasted. . . .'

'What a young lunatic!' said Angélique with a shrug of her shoulders.

Then they found themselves alone once more, tossing up and down in the fog.

Jack Merwin, grumbling, hoisted his sails once more, and tried to get his bearings. The pedlar wiped his brow. If the Acadians had rifled his stock, he would have been ruined.

'Milady, thank you. Had it not been for you . . .'

'Please do not thank me; it was not my doing.'

She did in fact have the impression that the young pirate lord's sudden change of heart had not been due solely to her presence. Was it the discovery of Mr Willoughby in the well-deck that had driven him away? No, certainly not, for a man like Hubert d'Arpentigny would never have allowed himself to be intimidated by a bear, tame or not!

She found herself looking about her, and even up into the air. These French Acadians who spent as much of their lives on the water as in the forests might have sensed some impending storm, seen some indication as yet invisible to other eyes, that enjoined them to make for shelter as soon as possible.

She already thought the sea was getting rougher, and Jack Merwin had apparently reduced speed, no doubt reluctant to sound the fog horn any more for fear of attracting further pirates. So he put himself athwart the wind, tacking back and forth through the mist, concentrating all his attention on avoiding obstacles.

Angélique looked at him anxiously.

'Shall we reach Gouldsboro tonight?' she asked him.

He appeared not to have heard her.

Fortunately the fog was beginning to brighten. It became translucent like porcelain, disintegrating into long gauze-like strips, then suddenly the horizon appeared, glittering like enamel and sparkling with colour. The sun was still high in the sky, the sea still furrowed with huge waves, blue-black and tipped with white, but the coastline was already in sight, and there was something about its green outline that reminded her irresistibly of the country around Gouldsboro.

Angélique's heart gave a leap.

She could think of nothing now but of their swiftly approaching reunion, and sat gazing out into the distance, heedless of her companions' expressions of satisfaction, as they too foresaw the end of the journey.

'Joffrey, my dear love!'

An interminable time had passed since they had been so unexpectedly separated.

Over and above all the difficulties that had since arisen along her way, she feared that some immaterial obstacle might still appear, something that could not be fought against, like ill fortune. She would not feel completely reassured until she was with him once more, able to touch him and hear his voice. Then everything else would be effaced. How well she knew his way of looking at her, that look in which she could read that she was beautiful, and in his eyes, unique, alone, that look that enclosed her in the enchanted circle of his love. He possessed in the highest degree the gift of isolation and separation that is the prerogative of men when their hearts are full of the gladness of love. This clear-cut aspect of the male character had sometimes shocked Angélique, for she was a woman and in her everything mingled together, feelings, passions, anxieties and desire, like the deep waters that swirl where a river joins the sea.

Such is the nature of woman, forever seething with an excess of different sensations. She did not always follow him, but she needs must follow him and he had the gift of forcing her to do so, for at such moments it seemed as if he had nothing else to do than to love her and to prove it to her. So successful was he in persuading her that all doubts, fears and dangers stopped short on the threshold of any room in which they were to make love, so skilled was he in drawing her with him into a world in which they were alone, their hearts and bodies filled with joy and wonderment.

She also knew that she would make no mention of Colin to him at first. No! Later. . . . Afterwards. . . . When she had won her way back into his heart again, when they had discovered one another again in the intoxication of abandon, when she had been refreshed in the freedom of her body offered without restraint to the sweetness of his caresses, when she had savoured the intoxicating delights of lying naked and defenceless in the warmth of his arms.

Angélique's eyes met Jack Merwin's gazing at her.

How long had he been watching her? How many of her thoughts had he been able to read on her face as she sat day-dreaming?

Then almost immediately he looked away, and she saw him spit a great jet of tobacco juice out into the sea. Still calm and meticulous, he took the quid of tobacco from his mouth, slipped it into his woollen hat as was the sailors' custom, and put the hat back on his head. There was an air of finality about these familiar and homely gestures which she was to understand only later. Then he seemed to sniff the wind.

As if he had come to some decision, he stretched out his gnarled leg with its big toe as prehensible as a crab's pinchers and seized the mainsail sheet with greater strength than if he had been using his fist. Coping alone with the rudder and the other topping-lifts, he brought the heavy boat about, laying it almost flat upon the water, and caught the wind on the quarter, sailing close enough to keep the ship steadily under way, but avoiding by a hair's breadth taking the wind head on.

Angélique gave a cry.

It was not this brilliant manœuvre which, had it been carried out by a less skilful man might have had them all in the water, that had caused her exclamation, but the fact that she had just seen how close they were to the shore. They could make out the lines of trees passing by and hear the surf breaking at the foot of the cliffs.

On the other hand the two pink hills familiarly known as the Mount-Desert Bulbs, behind which lay Gouldsboro, were beginning to vanish into the distance towards the east.

'But you are not going in the right direction,' Angélique cried. 'Gouldsboro is over there. You are sailing away from it.'

Without replying the Englishman continued on his way, and very soon the Bulbs disappeared.

The *White Bird* veered north-west and made its way into a large bay crowded with islands. Young Esther, who had once visited her uncle on Matinicus Island, recognized the bay as the one at the mouth of the Penobscot.

Angélique glanced at the sun to judge the time. It was still high in the sky. With luck, and provided that Jack Merwin did not hang about too long, they might still, thanks to the long June evenings, reach port before nightfall.

'And now where are you taking us?' she asked him.

She might as well have been speaking to a block of wood.

They sailed up the estuary for about an hour, and when the boat then headed off to the left up a narrow, shady river Angélique could not help exchanging a glance of exasperation with Elias Kempton. Both of them felt a murderous desire to hurl themselves on the skipper, Jack Merwin, overcome him once and for all, and seize the tiller.

In the shelter of the trees the wind dropped, and became a mere warm, light breeze, that pushed the boat slowly upstream. Merwin furled the sail, took hold of the oars, and soon after guided the boat towards a willow and alder-shaded beach. Beyond, pines, oaks, maples and beech trees mingled in luxuriant disorder from which rose the warm scent of the summer undergrowth. The smell of the sea did not reach this far inland, and there was the buzz of wild bees.

Merwin jumped into the water, that came half-way

up his thighs, and hauled his boat up towards the shore where he made her fast.

'You may disembark,' he said in unruffled tones. 'We have arrived.'

'But we should have been at Gouldsboro tonight,' Angélique shouted, beside herself. 'Oh! This damned Englishman infuriates me! . . . He drives me mad. . . . You are a . . .'

She was looking for an adequate way to express her feelings about this block-headed individual and could not find the words . . . especially in English.

'You are utterly unreasonable, Jack Merwin,' she went on, forcing herself to remain calm. 'You must be aware of the fact that a terrible Frenchman lives hereabouts, who is much given to cropping English hair, Baron Saint-Castine by name, and that if he and his Etchemins come upon us I am not at all sure I shall have time to make myself known to him and them before we are all killed.'

'Do you hear what she says?' the pedlar added, 'you damned fool. The place stinks of Frenchmen and Indians, and we are defenceless. Do you want us all to be massacred?'

'Just come ashore,' Merwin repeated, utterly indifferent.

Mr Willoughby the bear had followed him willingly, for he loved the smell of the land. There must have been wild honey in the offing for he stood up on his hind legs and began to claw at the trunk of a pine tree, making excited little grunts.

Sighing, the other passengers did as they were told. The place spelt no good to them, and they felt heavy-hearted.

Intrigued, they watched Merwin's goings on. After getting his bearings, he kneeled down at the foot of a tree and began to dig with his hands through a thick layer of leaf mould between the tree roots.

'What's he doing?'

'Has he got some treasure buried there?'

'He might well have. Many pirates hide their loot along these shores.'

'Hi there, Merwin, you damned scoundrel,' the pedlar

exclaimed, 'how's your fortune made up, Spanish doubloons, Portuguese moidores or silver pesos?'

The sailor made no reply but continued digging.
Under the layer of leaf-mould he came upon a screen of
interwoven branches which he removed, followed by
some moss and stones. Then at last from the depths of
the hole he drew out a largish parcel wrapped in old
skins and oilcloth. Another smaller packet followed and
the Englishman stood up, satisfied.

'Good! Wait here for me,' he said, 'I shan't be long;
while I am away, get something to eat. There's still some
cheese on board and some bread and a flagon of wine
Mrs MacGregor gave me.'

So pleased was he to have found his parcels in their
hiding place that he had become almost amiable.

He repeated:

'Wait just a minute!'

And he went off into the willow thicket. Angélique began to discuss matters with her companions then, exhort-
ing herself to be patient, went back to the boat to fetch
the provisions. They might as well eat. The place seemed
completely deserted and a long way from anywhere.
If they did not stay too long they had a chance of getting
away before the savages of the region sensed their presence.

It was no use getting angry. They simply had to put
up with the captain's caprices and his sudden changes of
mood. Given his impossible character, the dangers of the
war, and bearing in mind that three days before they had
all been prisoners of Gold Beard in Maquoit Bay, it had
to be admitted that the voyage had been particularly
swift and had gone as well as could have been hoped.

She returned to her companions and with Sammy's
help began to set out portions for each person on a big
flat rock. They began to eat in silence. Then, towards the
end of the meal, as Angélique looked up to ask someone
to pass her the wine, she saw all the English sitting
deathly pale, open-mouthed, wide-eyed with fear, staring
fixedly at something behind her. It cost a tremendous
effort to bring herself to turn round and face the new
danger.

From among the willows, whose long, greenish-gold

leaves trembled in the wind, a Jesuit in a black soutane had just made his appearance.

CHAPTER 49

ANGÉLIQUE'S FIRST reaction was to jump up and position herself between the terrified Englishmen and the newcomer. Her second reflex sent her eyes to the priest's crucifix -to see if it bore the ruby by which Father d'Orgeval's was distinguished. But she could not see it, so this priest could not be he.

The priest in his black robe, standing motionless in the shadows just a few paces from them, was a very tall, thin man, clean-shaven, and his dark hair hung loose over his shoulders. His high black turn-down collar with its white bands encircled a long, muscular neck, under a head whose features were both noble and distinguished. One of his arms hung stiffly at his side, but his other hand, resting on his chest, had two fingers clasped round the end of his crucifix, which hung from his neck by a black silk ribbon, as if he were introducing it to them.

Two dark fearless eyes stared at the petrified group of men and women as if trying to rivet them to the ground like so many hypnotized animals.

Finally he moved and came out from under the shade of the trees into the full glare of the sunlight on the little beach. Then Angélique noticed that, beneath the hem of his soutane, which was crumpled and creased, the Jesuit's feet and ankles were bare. And those bare feet seemed somehow familiar to her.

'Hello, all of you, how do you do?' came Jack Merwin's voice. 'Don't you recognize me?'

Transformed into pillars of salt, Angélique and the English people uttered not a word in answer to this greeting, which, by some piece of witchcraft or some hallucination, had seemed to issue from the Jesuit's mouth.

He continued to advance towards them while they backed away from him until they found themselves standing at the very edge of the water.

Seeing their terror, he stopped again.

'This,' he said in English with the ghost of a smile, 'is the treasure I removed from its hiding place a few moments ago—only my poor soutane, which I left here when I set out, and which I am at last able to put on again after eight months' absence.'

Then, turning to Angélique, he went on in French:

'Are you so astonished, Madame, at my transformation? I had the impression you had begun to suspect me.'

'Merwin,' she murmured, 'you are Jack Merwin?'

'The very same. And I am also Father Louis-Paul Maraicher de Vernon, of the Society of Jesus. So you see it can happen that a damned Englishman can change into a cursed Frenchman, even a shocking Papist.'

A hint of humour brightened his transformed face. He went on to explain:

'Last autumn my superior entrusted me with a secret mission in New England. My sailor's disguise was only one of many I was forced to assume down there in order to fulfil my mission without running the risk of being recognized. Thanks be to God I am now back safe and sound in the territory of French Acadia.'

He spoke polished French but it still bore a trace of an English accent, out of sheer habit, since for many a long month he had spoken nothing but that language.

'But . . . are you French too?' Angélique stammered, quite unable to overcome her astonishment.

'Indeed I am. My parents came from the Auge region, but I have spoken English since I was a child, as a pageboy to the English royal family during its exile in France. Later I went to London to perfect my knowledge of the language.'

In spite of these urban explanations Angélique still found it hard to take in the fact that it was Jack Merwin, the skipper of their boat, who stood before her. She stood transfixed, and as he saw her half-open mouth and her uncomprehending eyes, he could not help laughing.

'Come, Madame, do not be so astonished! Some of your remarks made me quite anxious, but I see now that I had nothing to fear. You never guessed my true identity.'

It was the first time any of them had seen Jack Merwin

laugh. Yet paradoxically it was by that token that they finally recognized him. Yes, it really was the skipper of the boat that had brought them who stood before them now in his black robe, so reviled and so feared, the same man who but shortly before had nonchalantly chewed his quid of tobacco while his muscular foot struggled with the billowing sail, as he pottered from island to island, curious, taciturn and solitary. . . .

In a flash, Angélique saw into the depths of Jack Merwin's personality which had so intrigued her.

But, of course! Of course he was a Jesuit!

How was it she had not noticed the fact sooner? She had been brought up in Catholic convents, so masterfully governed by the members of the most lofty and powerful religious order of the time—every week all the pupils had to make their confessions to one of the reverend fathers, hiding nothing of the shadows on their consciences—how could she ever have allowed herself to be taken in?

How was it that with so many clues, not even a shadow of suspicion had crossed her mind?

That night, sitting on the rocks on Long Island, so 'far away' that he had quite frightened her, *he had been praying* as only the sons of Saint Ignatius know how, and what she had interpreted in him as abstraction or lethargy had been rapture, mystical rapture!

And when he had handed out their food on Monhegan how was it that she had failed to recognize that quick deftness that characterizes all members of whatever religious order, irrespective of their rank, who, ever since the days of their noviciate, have been accustomed to serve the poor their daily ration of soup?

And that very day, had not the sudden change of manner in the young Acadian nobleman, Hubert d'Arpentigny, been due to the fact that he had penetrated the English seaman's disguise and recognized him as perhaps the very missionary who had prepared him for his first communion in days gone by. The priest must somehow have indicated to him that he should say nothing.

Mr Willoughby went up to the Jesuit and sniffed at him then, recognizing the familiar smell of the skipper of the *White Bird*, rubbed himself against his soutane, and the Jesuit father's hand stroked the bear's big soft head.

'Actually, we are already acquainted, Mr Willoughby,' he murmured.

For many a long day since they left New York they had shared the same shelter of weather-beaten planks on the treacherous seas. Mr Willoughby's friendliness finally convinced the most incredulous among them, and their morale collapsed. They were plunged in gloom, realizing that their fate had been decided, and that they had lost. Angélique was incapable of uttering a single word. Never had she felt so mortified; and, reflecting on the consequences that this impersonation would have for her and her companions, she no longer had the heart even to laugh at herself for being so utterly and completely taken in. She wondered whether it had been pure chance that had brought the craft of the alleged Jack Merwin alongside Colin's ship or whether, yet again, she had fallen into a trap.

She hung her head, defeated, and a bitter furrow creased the corner of her lips.

The Jesuit turned towards the Englishmen.

'You have nothing to fear,' he said in English. 'Here you are under my protection.'

He walked to the edge of the water, lifted his eyes towards the trees, then cupping his hands round his mouth, gave an Indian call which he repeated several times like a signal.

The leaves began to stir and shortly afterwards a horde of noisy savages appeared, some crossing the river in the shallows while others came down the hill. They fell to their knees before the Jesuit, asking for his blessing and showing every sign of friendliness towards him. And of course the great sagamore Piksarett appeared, proud and boastful.

'You thought you had escaped me,' he said to Angélique. 'But I always knew where you were; I followed what was happening to you and Black Robe has brought you back to me. You are my captive.'

Some of the savages laughed as they ran their hands over Elias Kempton's scant remaining hair, while he seemed more dead than alive with fear, and his tame bear growled threateningly.

On seeing the bear some of the Indians drew back and pointed their spears at it, while others seized their bows. But the Jesuit calmed their agitation with a word. Seeing him lay his hand on the bear's head, the Indians looked at him with reverence, but nothing a Black Robe ever did astonished them.

'Fort Pentagouet, under the command of Baron Saint-Castine, is not far from here,' Father de Vernon told Angélique. 'Would you be good enough to follow me, Madame, and we shall make our way there.'

'Ah, good,' Adhemar's voice suddenly exclaimed as they began to climb the hill, 'are you, Father, by any chance a brother of Jack Merwin's? You don't half look like him. Where's he got to, by the way? It's about time we set sail again! 'Bout time we got away from here, because, here, you know, with all these savages . . . I. . . .'

CHAPTER 50

'JUST LOOK, Father,' said Baron Saint-Castine, pointing emphatically at a wall covered with English scalps, 'am I not a loyal officer in the service of God and His Majesty? I have campaigned with my Etchemins and my Mic-Macs against the English heretics more than enough to win myself a place in Heaven. Could *I* ever be reproached for being lukewarm in matters of religion, I who brought about the conversion of the great Mateconando chieftain and his children, I who even stood godfather to them since there was no one else on this godforsaken coast to perform this Christian duty at the time they were baptized.

'And yet now Father d'Orgeval, your superior, writes to me reproaching me acrimoniously with what he calls my evasion of duty, or even betrayal, over this matter of the new holy war into which he has just launched the Abenakis. In the first place, I would like to say that I consider that this campaign has been started prematurely. The Indians are still busy trading and planting their crops, which are vital matters for them.'

'A crusade can suddenly become a matter of urgency,' replied Father de Vernon, 'if it is carried through with the help of every available staunch heart. It may be that your . . . evasion of duty . . . will result in the campaign lasting longer than it should, thus preventing the Indians from doing their bartering and sowing their crops before the winter season.'

'Well anyhow my Indians will be spared that,' Saint-Castine replied sullenly.

'Do you not consider that it was their DUTY to fight for the God in whose name they have been baptized?'

It was the day after their arrival at Pentagouet. The three of them were sitting in the main hall of the Pentagouet outpost finishing the midday meal that had brought them together.

Angélique sat at the end of the big wooden table, Father Maraicher de Vernon in the middle, while Saint-Castine was pacing up and down in some agitation, all the feathers of his Indian headdress a-quiver.

A thick mist that had come up with the dawn had enclosed them all in a grey, opaque world, pierced only by the heart-rending cry of invisible seagulls, like the wailing of lost souls.

The French outpost was a modest building.

Saint-Castine had placed at Angélique's disposition a small room which must have been his own, but she had spent part of the night in a lean-to shed where the Englishmen had been shut up, doing her best to cheer them, for they were plunged in gloom.

Now that they had fallen once more into the hands of the French they would doubtless be taken off to Quebec and sold to those terrible Canadian Papists. Unless of course Baron Saint-Castine managed to negotiate with Boston to buy them back. The Reverend Patridge could rest assured that his co-religionists, for the most part notables and magistrates, would not abandon him, even if it meant clapping on a tax to raise the sum necessary to buy him back, but Miss Pidgeon, who had no family, would find herself doomed to lifelong captivity, the most painful aspect of which would be the necessity daily to resist all solicitations to abjure her faith and be baptized a Catholic.

Being all worn out, they did finally get some sleep, after partaking of a little maize and fish, and Angélique sat thinking for a long time how she could get a message to her husband.

In the end everything began to go round and round in her head. By what piece of ill-fortune had Colin stopped, that morning, the very ship carrying the disguised Jesuit back to Acadia, after completing his period of espionage. Had Colin known the identity of the English captain who chewed his quid of tobacco and spat so expertly into the sea? . . . Was that why he had murmured: 'Take care, they wish you ill?'

Piksarett's darting shadow seemed to hover ubiquitously over all her peregrinations. He had been at Maquoit the day before Gold Beard's ship cast anchor; she had thought she caught sight of him on Mackworth Island and now here he was waiting for her on the banks of the Penobscot.

Having made up her mind that she must speak to Saint-Castine, she did not have to seek him out, for the very next day he himself came to invite her to join him and the Jesuit in a meal.

The priest had been very busy ever since their arrival the preceding day. Informed of his coming by their drums, the Indians poured in from all sides, for they considered it better to be baptized by Black Robe than by the modest, worthy Recollect monks.

High Mass had been sung, and the prisoners had heard the distant sound of plain chant.

During the meal, Baron Saint-Castine kept winking encouragingly at Angélique. 'Everything will be all right, have no fear' he was trying to tell her. Nevertheless, he kept a close guard over his tongue in front of the Jesuit, who, after saying grace, ate frugally and unhurriedly, his eyes downcast. Then the debate began. Castine claimed that he had never refused his help to the Reverend Fathers in their heavy, uninspiring task of converting the Indians and bringing Catholicism to North America. By way of proof he showed him his monstrous collection of red, brown and blond scalps which, hanging from wooden pegs, covered the whole of one wall of the room with a stale-smelling, repulsive layer of human hair. They had been mounted on little wicker rings, to which they had been sewn with pieces of gut like beaver skins, and hung up to dry beside the cabin doors of the Etchemin, Tarratine and Mic-Mac braves. Then, when they were ready, they had been brought to Fort Pentagouet and handed over to Saint-Castine, who had thanked the Indians in the name of the King of France and given them small gifts in return.

'When I think how many of these heretics' scalps I took myself!' said Saint-Castine, with the pained expression of one whose devotion to duty has passed unnoticed. 'My score was always double that of any of my braves.

'And, what is more, Father, this year we have been at peace. It was clearly understood, when you met Father d'Orgeval and Jean Rousse before you left for New England, that no move was to be made against the heretics until you got back, since the point of your mission was to discover some pretext to break our treaties. And then Father d'Orgeval goes unearthing the war hatchet, as we Indians say, more than ten days before your return!'

'No doubt he had found better grounds for doing so than any I might have brought him,' Father de Vernon retorted without emotion. 'He is guided by God and I have rarely seen him embark on any course without weighing all the consequences.'

'I think I can tell you why he began this war without waiting for you,' Angélique interrupted.

Father de Vernon, who throughout the entire conversation had addressed his remarks entirely to Saint-Castine or had sat deep in thought looking down at the remains of his frugal repast, slowly turned upon her the cheerless, enigmatic glance that she knew from her experience of him as Jack Merwin.

'Yes,' Angélique went on, 'I am certain that Father d'Orgeval saw an opportunity to have me taken prisoner by the Canadians when I went alone to the English village of Brunswick-Falls to the west of the Kennebec, and he immediately declared war, knowing that a few days later I would have reached the safety of Gouldsboro and and that any such action would no longer be possible.'

To her astonishment the Jesuit nodded in agreement.
'Yes, that is indeed what must have happened. What
were you doing in that English village, Madame?'

Angélique gave him a defiant glance.

'I was taking a little girl, whom we had bought from
the Abenakis, back to her family.'

'So you, a Frenchwoman and a Catholic, considered it
right and proper to take an innocent child back to that
nest of obscurantist heretics, when fate, nay, Providence
I should say, had decreed that she should have the opportunity of discovering the true light of Christ in
Canada?'

At first Angélique made no reply, for she could not
get used to hearing Jack Merwin speaking in this manner, but eventually she retorted with a half smile.

'The nest, yes! Children are like birds. However poor
their nest, that is where they like to be.'

'So you opposed God's will for the child,' he broke in
severely. 'And . . . how is it that after this . . . ambush,
you were not taken off to Quebec?'

'I fought,' she replied angrily. 'I fought for my life and
my freedom.'

Then remembering the disdainful look he had given
her in the moonlight on the beach at Long Island she
repeated: 'my freedom!'

'So you fired on the soldiers of Christ?' he went on.

'All I did was fire on savages who were trying to scalp
me.'

'But . . .'

'And I was lucky enough to be able to come to an
agreement with Sagamore Piksarett, your notable con-
vert.'

The Jesuit frowned. This seemed to him the more incredible part of her story.

'And why, in your estimation, Madame, should Father
d'Orgeval wish to take you prisoner and have you sent
to Canada?'

'You know that as well as I do. . . .'

'I am sorry, Madame, but I don't. I left these parts
several months ago, during which time it has been extremely difficult for me to keep in touch with my superi-
or. My life among the English was dangerous, for had

297

they discovered that I was spying for Christ and the King of France they would undoubtedly have given me a hard time of it. At the time I set out you had only just landed at Gouldsboro.'

'But you already regarded us as thorns in your flesh, if not as actual enemies, settling as we did at Gouldsboro with much greater means at our disposal than most settlers have. What a wonderful opportunity to discredit my husband's name and hold him up to the fanatical execration of the people of New France by the revelation that his wife was the incarnation of the She-Devil,' Angélique retorted bitterly.

'That you must know about, I feel sure. . . . The visionary nun described a settlement by the shore, which could have been any one, but which ill-intentioned people insisted could only be Gouldsboro. . . . Did she not see the horses we brought with us in the symbol of a unicorn, the mythical animal the She-Devil was riding when she first appeared? And when I rode into the back country, the similarity between the two scenes was obvious and the Canadians fell to their knees in terror. And yet all this was pure chance. . . .'

'Yes,' the Jesuit father replied thoughtfully, 'when diabolical processes are set in motion, it often happens that chance seems to favour those through whom Evil is being perpetrated.'

'But who is perpetrating Evil in all this?' cried Angélique, 'and why must it be I who has to be your She-Devil? After all there are other women in Acadia onto whom you could have pinned the name as well as me. Was it not you, Saint-Castine, who mentioned a woman somewhere in the depths of Frenchman Bay renowned for the debauched life she leads and nicknamed Marcelline-la-Belle?'

The Baron burst out laughing.

'Oh no, not her. That would be too funny. She is just about capable of bearing children to every ship's captain that comes ashore, and she can open clams faster than any other woman in the Bay. They say she can get her knife between the two halves of the shell and spilt it open before the preceding shell has reached the ground. . . . She's a juggler, I grant you that.'

'And might not this skill also be considered magical?' Angélique asked with a laugh. 'What do you say, Father!'

But Jack Merwin remained icy, refusing to be drawn into light-hearted discussion of so serious a matter. He seemed to be considering the suggestion, then shook his head.

'Marcelline Raymondeau? No, she is not intelligent enough.'

'So a She-Devil has to be intelligent, does she?'

'Indeed she does! If you think about it. Who, next to God, is more intelligent than Lucifer, the Lord of all Demons?

'It is a well-known fact which has often been observed that succubi, that is to say She-Devils, when incarnate in a female body, have great difficulty in hiding their brilliant intelligence during their sojourn on earth. It has even proved possible sometimes to unmask them by the predominance of this particular quality—which is so rare in women.

'Let us not forget that the most important of all the infernal spirits, Behemot, the Beast, Mammon, Cupidity, and Abadon, the Exterminating Angel, are capable of possessing succubi.'

'I've got it,' cried Saint-Castine as if suddenly inspired. 'The woman we are after must be Madamoiselle Radegonde de Ferjac, who is governess to the children of Monsieur de la Roche-Posay at Port-Royal on the Peninsula. She is as ill-natured as a weasel, as miserly as your Mammon, and as ugly as the seven deadly sins.'

But once again the Jesuit shook his head.

'No, you are on the wrong track. What you suggest is out of the question because you are talking about an ugly woman. It may be that the femininity of these succubi cannot manifest itself in any other way, but it is a fact that they have never been known to inhabit the body of an ugly woman.'

'And what about witches?'

'There's more to it than that. Witches are only human beings who have dealings with the Devil, whereas the infernal spirit that enters the body of a woman or becomes incarnate in her at her birth is truly a demon, one of the fallen angels that followed Lucifer in his fall from Heaven at the beginning of Time.'

'But you cannot think that of me, it's impossible,' cried Angélique, wringing her hands. 'I have done nothing, nothing to deserve so horrible a reputation.'

'And yet the prediction is quite specific. It speaks of a woman who is very beautiful and seductive. . . .'

'Am I so beautiful, then?'

Her disturbance was such that it removed all coquettishness from her question, and young Saint-Castine gave her a broad smile of admiration.

'Yes, Madame, you are. But I shall not accuse you for that. . . .'

'And seductive? . . .' Angélique went on, turning towards the Jesuit. 'Come, Father, I spent more than three days in your company. . . .'

He looked down at her with his mercurial gaze, sometimes sombre, sometimes sparkling, and sometimes expressionless, a gaze in which one could read nothing, and thoughtfully stroked his chin.

'Seductive? . . . I don't know . . . but captivating, yes. . . . On Midsummer's night at Monhegan. . . .'

Angélique, fearing that the blushes she felt covering her cheeks might reach her forehead, interrupted him.

'Yes indeed! Midsummer night . . . since you mention it. . . . What could anyone possibly reproach me for? I laughed, I drank, I danced, granted. But since you were present, you can bear witness that I did nothing dishonourable. Is the Catholic Church going to prove as strict as the Reformed Church in matters of merrymaking? I grant that had I known who you were and what you did. . . .'

It was his turn to interrupt her smartly:

'Really? Were you really not in any way suspicious, Madame? I was occasionally anxious about your shrewd eyes.'

'Oh no, not at all! Have no illusions about that. At the very outside I thought you might be the erstwhile captain of some pirate ship, or the youngest son of some noble family seeking his fortune. . . . So you can see for yourself that, alas! I am no sorceress in spite of the powers with which I am credited. Had I known, as I said, who you were, a Jesuit, I should certainly have been less . . . exuberant, more careful. But beyond saying this, I have no regrets. . . .' For a moment her mind went back to that wonderful night.

'How can I explain the delight I felt on that lovely June night, after all the danger we had been through. . . . Had not death itself laid its hand on me that very day? You know that better than anyone, you who rescued me from the sea. . . .'

Then she broke off, as she realized that it had been in fact that very same priest sitting there now with one hand on his crucifix who had dragged her by her hair up the beach, had brought her back to life, and had carried her in his arms back to the fire.

Never had Angélique felt so embarrassed in all her life as she tried to find words that would not land her from the frying pan into the fire, when she noticed a tremor in Father de Vernon's lips, a fleeting sparkle cross his eyes and a shadow of a smile on his stony features, and she guessed that he was trying not to burst out laughing.

In fact since the beginning of his conversation with her he had been laughing. He had been laughing inwardly, enjoying her embarrassment and confusion, as he made her say all kinds of silly things.

'And you are making fun of me again,' she exclaimed. 'Well! I must say. . . .'

And he began to laugh openly. Then he looked at her ironically, but with a certain warmth as well, and for the first time she discovered the spark of humanity hidden behind those severe eyes, and thought she glimpsed a look of friendly complicity.

Could she hope then that during those three days she had spent on Jack Merwin's boat between the bear and the little black boy, he had really got to know her? He did not think that she was a She-Devil. She could read that in his eyes.

'Let me go free, Merwin,' she murmured warmly, reaching out impulsively towards him.

The priest immediately looked away, his heavy eyelids drooped forthwith and he resumed his haughty expression.

'But . . . you may go, Madame, who is stopping you? You are not my prisoner, as far as I know. . . . You are only Piksarett's. . . .'

CHAPTER 51

SEEN IN the evening light, Gouldsboro was already a small town.

Thus did Angélique discover it the next evening, as she glimpsed in the distance, through a veil of light drizzle, the winking lights of the houses grouped about the port, spread out along the shore and climbing up to the very top of the cliffs.

The boat danced up and down on the black sea, in which the lights, yellow and white from lanterns and candles, and red from the huge bonfires that served as beacons to mark the dangerous reefs, shone back in a thousand glistening reflections.

The Acadian conducting them said he would put in towards the west side of Gouldsboro and that he wanted to set off again immediately for Pentagouet. Father de Vernon had offered them the use of his boat for the final stage of their journey home, and once Angélique, her English protégés, the little Negro boy and the bear, had been set ashore at some point along the Gouldsboro peninsula, the man was to make his way back immediately.

Angélique delighted in the smell of the land, and of the village borne to them on the wind.

'I shall see you again in Gouldsboro,' Piksarett had promised her, just before she set out from Pentagouet. 'Don't forget that you are my prisoner and that I have to claim your ransom from your husband.'

But apart from this reminder of their relationship, he had shown himself very liberal, for reasons known only to himself, and had allowed her to set off, after giving her his solemn blessing, literally as well as metaphorically, for this great Sagamore invested with supra-terrestrial powers enjoyed pontificating and was only too happy to distribute, after the manner of the Black Robes, his protection in the form of a large sign of the Cross.

The fog cleared towards the beginning of the afternoon, thus enabling them to set sail. Father de Vernon and Baron Saint-Castine accompanied them down to the Pentagouet shore. The Jesuit retained the golden-haired lad who had served as his ship's boy; the boy's name was Abbial Neals, an orphan Merwin had picked up on the quayside in New York. No one knew whether he was of Irish, English or Swedish extraction, but be that as it might, he was to be baptized.

At the last moment someone came down with a large trunk, into which Baron Saint-Castine had hastily piled part of his collection of English scalps.

'Monsieur de Peyrac has told me of his plans to go to Quebec,' he explained to Angélique, 'and I thought I would ask him to be so good as to take this present from me to the Governor with him. I hope that it will create a good impression, and that those in high places will stop accusing me of not being sufficiently keen to fight the English.'

They also found room for the barrel of Armagnac; then the helmsman, an Acadian farmer, took the tiller, while Sammy, who had served his apprenticeship in seafaring during the past few days, helped him with the sail.

Very soon, the pearly curtain of rain masked the shapes of the trees, and hid from their view, standing on the shore of a lost river, in the heart of the American forest land, the tall figure of a man in a black soutane, a man whose name had been Jack Merwin.

CHAPTER 52

How MANY times since the previous evening had Joffery de Peyrac turned over in his mind the terrible tidings he had received?

The night had passed without his moving; he had remained sitting at the table, his head resting on one hand and his eyes closed.

How many times during the course of that night had

he heard the echo within him of the rough, mocking voice of the Swiss mercenary?

'Her name? . . . I don't know. But when he was making love to her he called her Angélique! . . . Angélique! . . .'

And every time the same spasm of pain gripped him.

And then there had been Yann's words, which had thrown a little more light on the situation—if one could talk of light amongst the gloom of these intrigues which had suddenly drawn a hideous mask over his beloved's face:

'They were kissing one another like long-separated lovers . . .'

Was this the key to the mystery, the explanation of her shocking betrayal? A former lover? A man from her past, from that part of her life which she no doubt missed— when she had been free, her life easier, when she had been free to satisfy the desires of her delightful body as she wished, without fear of the anger of a jealous husband.

He could see now how it all must have happened . . . the stranger, a man from the past, hearing the name Angélique and learning that she was in the neighbourhood, had sent a message to her at Houssnock, and she, under the pretext of a journey to the English village, had taken advantage of Peyrac's absence and set off to meet her lover. Then an accomplice had met Peyrac on the Kennebec and given him false information to keep him away from her more effectively, and for longer. . . .

No . . . it did not tie up. There was something else. . . . And Angélique appeared to him as she had been that last night at Wapassou, when she had raised her head to listen to the wolves howling, and the last glimmers of the aurora borealis had lighted her face, so that her complexion exactly matched the pale pink of the sky. The lustre of her dreamy eyes, inscrutable and wondering, had sent a tide of adoration coursing through him, for in those eyes he had read the certainty that she was a unique woman, unlike any other—his, and his alone.

How naïve and presumptuous he had been! What an arch fool! How had he failed to see that she was a mere wanton, with a life rich in experience, magnificently endowed with all the witchcraft of her sex, a woman who played upon the things that made her so different from the rest in order to permit herself, whenever desire or pleasure urged, to be just like the rest—unfaithful, weak-minded, without honour or memories. . . . Nothing is sacred to such creatures . . . nothing but the pleasure of the moment, and the hope that afterwards a smile or a glance will serve to obliterate the wounds they have inflicted. . . . It is so easy to win back an infatuated man, so tempting for that man to believe what a pretty mouth tells him—that she loves him . . . that she has always loved him and none but him! Yes, in spite of everything, in spite of her betrayal. . . .

From time to time he would be filled with a mad hope. It was all just a bad dream, Angélique was about to arrive, she would appear, and in a few words would explain everything . . . and he would find her again, entire, pure, his friend, his lover, giving herself to him alone, caressing and passionate, as she had been in the solitude of the woods, during the winter, snug in their big bed, or in the springtime, when they had walked together among the wild hyacinths, feeling free and intoxicated by the renewal of this wild landscape over which they reigned, triumphant sovereigns, and he would look at her with rapture, and kiss her over and over again, until he could bear it no longer, then sure that they were alone . . .

Angélique's eyes upturned towards the trees reflected the fresh green of the new leaves, and she would say with a laugh: 'You are crazy, my dear lord . . .'

Then she was his. His alone, and had pleasure through him alone. . . .

This was how it would be when he found her again. . . . It could not be otherwise. But then his thoughts stumbled like a blind man against the indisputable reality of the facts:

'When he was making love to her, he called her Angélique! Angélique!'

A blow, a muffled cry. Every time the memory of these words shook him, made him double up as if he had been pierced by a razor-sharp blade.

He could not stop his mind returning constantly to the

305

same point: she had been seen, naked and languid with pleasure in Gold Beard's arms!

The idea of doubting poor Kurt Ritz's story had never so much as crossed his mind. The straightforwardness with which the fellow had told his tale was the direct consequence of the fact that he had no idea it concerned his master's private life. And the wine he had been given to drink on an empty stomach, had for a brief moment dulled his perceptions, making him all the more frank. Had he been sober, he might have noticed the general embarrassment, grown wary, and cut his story short, for he was by nature a cautious man.

No, there was no doubt about it. Kurt Ritz had been an eye-witness of the scene as he made his escape. One night, when separated from her husband, Angélique had abandoned herself to the caresses of a strange man. She had been caught unawares, she, the wife of Count Peyrac, his wife, in the arms of the pirate Gold Beard, and there was no way round that. . . .

In Joffrey de Peyrac's eyes, the other woman, the Adorable one, was fading away. . . . Only the Stranger remained—the woman he had once suspected her to be, the proud, sensual woman, who had lived a full, free life, the play-actor, the more skilled for being only half conscious of her own wiles, finding them natural and necessary.

Life had left its mark on her and in facing its difficulties she had blunted her capacity for affection. Nothing mattered to her but the gratification of the moment. The dominance Angélique had over all men, did it not come precisely from her intimate understanding of them? She knew men too well, she was too close to them. . . . With a smile, with a word, she had them at her beck and call, be they lords or rustics. Her skill was no doubt due to her having been for too long and from too tender an age the victim of men. But now it was too late, the harm was done, the terrifying truth was there. Now she stronger than any man, feared nothing from them, and took those she desired. . . . She liked all men, any kind of man, such was the secret of her charm and her unfailing hold over them—except possibly those who made themselves ridiculous by their infatuation with themselves and their military superiority, like that fellow Pont-Briand. She had not deserved much credit for repulsing him—she did not like him. But what about Loménie-Chambord? Peyrac had noticed the warmth between the two of them, and he began to wonder whether the virtuous gentleman had not deceived him beneath his own roof? For was she not capable of dragging a saint down to hell?

Angélique! Angélique!

The red mist of vengeance clouded Peyrac's eyes.

To set sail, come up with Gold Beard's ship one night ... climb aboard, surprise the two of them, kill them. ...

It cost him a superhuman effort to take a hold on himself again.

Day was breaking over Gouldsboro. The mist transformed the countryside into a cold, deserted waste echoing with the mournful call of conch shells across the bay.

Only a few miles away Angélique was waking up at Fort Pentagouet. In a few hours' time she would embark, joyous and impatient to see her husband again, and by night she would be there to stand before him.

Utterly exhausted, Peyrac saw in the depths of his heart a shattered image. He was so weary that he no longer sought excuses for the truth which he must face in all its bitterness; and he at last accepted that he must see her as she was, cheap and deceitful ... like the rest ... a woman just like them all!

CHAPTER 53

DAY HAD dawned with all its heavy tasks upon which human lives depended.

Count Peyrac set off towards the port. Alone in the white, muffled world, in which he would henceforth have to walk alone, with this astonishing sense of bereavement, this unexpected wound, the depths of whose pain he had not yet fully plumbed ... Angélique! ...

As he made his way down to the beach he began to feel a burning impatience to do battle. It was this that gave him strength to stand upright, and it occurred to him the fog was a blessing, for he well knew that not one of his ships was ready to put to sea that day and give chase to the pirate. The fog would protect him from acting with ill-considered haste and would enable him to lay his plans with care. Tomorrow or the day after he could begin his hunt to the death, and then nothing would stop him until he had come up with Gold Beard and killed him with his own hands.

The fitting out of the *Gouldsboro*, the chebec and two other luggers anchored in the harbour was immediately put in hand.

Obsessed with his ideas of vengeance, he received at first with indifference, then with irritation, the news brought by some Indians that two English ships were in distress off Shoodic Point. Let them go to the devil, English, French or whoever they were.

Then he pulled himself together.

Let it never be said that a woman had made him forget his duties and responsibilities, that a woman had so unmanned him as to render him indifferent to the lives of human beings which he alone had the power to save.

Gouldsboro, which he had created, was the beacon of Frenchman Bay. Everyone looked to it to provide aid, life, and counsel. Oh! how little it all mattered to him, suddenly. But he must not flinch, not for a single moment. The slightest sign of wavering on his part would bring the entire structure down.

And those who knew already, what were they expecting of him? Had he lived so long, and triumphed over so many pitfalls, in order to doom and destroy it all in a few hours for the sake of a disastrous love affair?

The long habit of strict inner discipline, an innate sense of responsibility which had always, throughout his already long career, marked him out as a leader, a man apart from the common herd, came into operation within him and helped him to bear up.

Bear up! . . .

Promptly he went on board his ship, mustered his crew, set off for the disaster area, and was successful in rescuing the little fleet which the State of Massachusetts had despatched to Frenchman Bay to avenge the Abenaki massacres fomented by the French. One of the ships was commanded by the Bostonian Phipps, the other by the English admiral Bartholomew Sheringham himself.

Back in the shelter of Gouldsboro Bay the English admiral was only too pleased to accept Count Peyrac's generous hospitality. Very elegant, in a powdered wig, and his sword at his side, he made no secret of the fact that he had little appetite for this expedition deep into Frenchman Bay in pursuit of an invisible adversary, constantly liable to vanish up some creek. But these damned French had to be taught a lesson. An undertaking must be obtained from the Quebec Government to restrain their hordes of dedicated savages. It happened that they had heard that Monsieur de Ville d'Avray, the Governor of Acadia, was touring up the Saint John river, visiting his best friend, Monsieur de Grand-Bois. If he could be penned up and taken prisoner, it would be an excellent thing for the English Government.

Peyrac had little difficulty in convincing Admiral Sheringham that the expedition could have no other outcome than a declaration of war between the French and the English, since any pretext to extend the conflict would be welcome in Quebec, and that he would do better to join Peyrac in hunting down the pirates that infested Frenchman Bay and hampered the activities of the English as well as Portuguese and French codfishers during the annual season.

But Phipps, the Bostonian, quite a number of whose relatives had been scalped by the Canadians and their Abenakis, refused to give up the chase, and set sail again as soon as the fog had lifted. All the same, since he was acting on his own, and no longer in the company of the British admiral, the diplomatic implications of his action would be less serious and the battle in the Saint John river less bloody. Peyrac, after considering all possible means of defusing the bomb, summoned the local Etchemin chieftains and their principal Mohicans.

He agreed with them that messengers bearing two wampum necklaces should be sent to the Malecites and the Souriquois in the east: let them, if they had to, help the French to whom they were bound by ties of friendship and family, but without killing any Englishmen, if possible. If the war hatchet were disinterred in Frenchman Bay, it would be of little advantage to the local tribesmen, who had already suffered heavy losses during the cruel winter famine, and who would be left to protect them from bands of raiding Iroquois, a constant threat in the summer months?

Having sent out these words of wisdom, he entrusted Cromley with the task of warning the few scattered Englishmen clinging to their plots of land at the mouths of the St. Croix and Machias rivers.

Old Salprice would no doubt refuse to leave his little fort, but the Strington family at Merchnaisby would find it in their interest to take refuge in Gouldsboro for the month of July.

Each and every one of these measures had at first cost Joffrey de Peyrac a superhuman effort, then little by little he had come to carry them out automatically; and the performance of these essential and inescapable tasks acted as a temporary balm to his open wound, conferring a kind of oblivion.

And yet, in spite of the bustle and activity of that day, no other in his life had ever seemed so long, so dreary and so cruel.

Meanwhile, he was supervising the preparation of the ships for the expedition that was to set out the following day against Gold Beard.

He must not weaken.

His revenge too must be carried out in a level-headed manner, without losing sight of the general interest. He had no right to do otherwise.

And yet, what did the others matter, what did his work matter, what did life matter . . . *without* her? . . .

That evening he again convened the same people as the day before, in order to continue the council meeting which had been so dramatically interrupted by the arrival of Kurt Ritz, and he asked the admiral to join them.

With the exception of the latter, who was unaware of the painful and embarrassing nature of the situation, they all entered the room with downcast eyes and circumspect tread.

Peyrac sat waiting for them behind the carved table, on which had been placed, his ink stand, his pens, a sandbox, his measuring instruments and, as on the previous day, his maps spread out to view.

He begged them cordially to come in and take their places.

At the sound of his voice, so calm, with that slight hoarseness to which they had grown accustomed, they looked up, and in spite of his normal appearance, gave a shudder.

He was wearing a magnificent costume of ivory satin slashed with scarlet moiré, and with tiny diamond-shaped pleats each held in position by a pearl stitch. Every movement revealed a gleam of red. It was a costume that had been brought from London on the *Gouldsboro*, together with his tight-fitting red knee-boots and his gauntlets. Peyrac preferred the English style of dress, which, favouring as it did the doublet and hose and soft leather boots, suited his roving life better than the French-style jerkin and vests and boots with very wide turn-down tops. On the other hand, the pearl-studded lace of his cravat and cuffs was in the French fashion.

His thick black hair, framing his weather-beaten, scarred face gave him the air of a pirate and contrasted disconcertingly with the refinement and elegance of his dress, while the lighter patches of hair at his temples gave an unexpected softness to the dark skin of his sun-and-wind-tanned face. Was there a touch of pallor lurking beneath that brown skin, a trace of emotion under those impassive features, or of suffering behind that bold, penetrating gaze that came to rest upon them and did not turn away? No one could have guessed it! It was they who looked down and seemed to suffer acute embarrassment.

'A lesson,' the filibuster Gilles Vanereick was often to repeat later, 'a lesson, that's what that fellow Peyrac gave us that night! A lesson to all us men, who seem destined by nature and from the moment of birth to be cuckolded one day . . . I tell you, that never did a cuckold face the world with such superb dignity!'

'Gentlemen,' Peyrac said to them, 'you know that I must needs go to war and I do not know what fate Heaven has reserved for my arms. Now at every point on the horizon a storm is brewing. The least I can do is

311

to leave you with the full knowledge of a situation which your courage, your good sense, and your skill will help you to face. And, I would add, your desire for peace. We have no enemies. In this can reside your strength.

'I am speaking particularly to you, gentlemen from La Rochelle, for it is into your hands that I shall shortly commit the fate of this establishment and its land defences. Monsieur d'Urville is to accompany me, as will Monsieur Vanereick, and our English ally Sir Bartholomew Sheringham, in pursuit of the pirate who has already caused us all a great deal of trouble. He must be got rid of once and for all. So we must concert our plans for defence, pursuit and attack. And first we must take stock of and allocate the ammunition we have at our disposal.'

Absorbed in their calculations and plans, they did not see that the night had fallen. A Spaniard entered to light the candles in the candle-sticks and in the wrought-iron chandelier that hung from the ceiling.

Little by little, they became caught up once more in the routine of life and forgot the incident of the previous evening. Consequently, they thought at first that it was only the return of a bad dream when the same sentry as the night before poked his head round the door with the same alarmed expression and called to Peyrac:

'My Lord! Someone to see you!'

But this time it was not Kurt Ritz, haggard after his escape from the pirate.

This time it was She.

As they turned round, they saw a dazzling apparition; framed against the dark backcloth of the night, they saw HER! . . .

CHAPTER 54

DAZZLING IN her beauty, she stood looking at them with a radiant smile on her lips. And swiftly her eyes sought out, at the far end of the room, the tall figure of Count Peyrac. Joffrey! Wearing a costume she had not seen him in before. He was there. . . .

Everyone present, petrified, looked at her in utter silence.

The golden, velvety sheen of the big sealskin cloak she wore draped about her heightened the warm tones of her flesh and, standing out against the night, her hair shone so golden that it looked like a halo.

It was little Laurier Berne who had escorted Angélique to the door of the main hall of the fort where he knew his father and the other notables, in company with the filibuster captain and the English admiral, were holding council with Count Peyrac.

She just did not know the place, so much had Gouldsboro changed. That almost deserted shore of the previous year was teeming with life, so full of activity continued into the dusk that she might well have thought she was in some other settlement, had she not very soon encountered her friends Abigail and Séverine Berne.

Her impatience to join her husband as soon as possible and to make sure that he was in Gouldsboro prevented her from noticing the embarrassment and coolness of the two women's welcome. It was only later that she remembered and understood why. But young Laurier had appeared with a basket of shellfish on his shoulder, and had thrown his arms around her neck with all the irrepressibility of his ten years. 'Dame Angélique! Oh! Dame Angélique! How marvellous!'

At her request he had guided her through the winding streets of the new Gouldsboro. As they reached the fort they passed a man carrying a halberd.

'That's the Swiss mercenary,' Laurier had whispered. 'He arrived here yesterday evening. . . .'

'Hi, you there! Haven't I seen you somewhere before?' Angélique called, struck with uneasiness on perceiving the grim look the man gave her as he went by.

'Yes indeed, Madame!' he replied. 'You have seen me before.'

There was a note of contempt in his Teutonic voice.

But Laurier had already led her up the wooden steps and the council chamber door stood open before her.

In complete silence—a crushing silence which immediately struck her as unusual—she walked into the room. There were faces she knew, faces turned to stone. . . .

'Monsieur Manigault, how do you do . . . Oh! Master Berne, how pleased I am to see you again. . . . My dear Pastor, how are you? . . .'

All these Protestants in their black jerkins, all these motley strangers, a French filibuster, an English officer, then a Recollect father in grey homespun. . . .

Not one of them, not a single one, made any reply. No one . . . no one. . . . Their eyes followed her. And all these people . . . they just stood there like so many wooden figures, Joffrey like all the rest of them, motionless, watching as she made her way down the room.

Now she was standing before him and her eyes sought his in vain. And yet he was looking at her with a fixed gaze that was both strange and sombre. A nightmare! Joffrey bent down over the hand she held out to him but she did not feel his lips on her skin, it was merely a show of politeness.

She heard herself ask in a far-away voice that seemed to tremble as she spoke:

'What has happened? Has some disaster befallen Gouldsboro?'

Then everyone came to life, and one by one they bowed and left the room. No one thought to smile. In the same atmosphere of catastrophe as the previous day, the same ceremonial began all over again.

Once outside, Gilles Vanereick said, gasping for breath:

'Was that her?'

'Well, who do you think it was?', Manigault growled.

'But she's . . . she's wonderful! She is marvellous! . . . That changes everything. . . . Gentlemen, how do you expect so beautiful a woman to help making conquests wherever she goes, how could she help succumbing occasionally to the love she stirs up in people? . . . It would be immoral . . . I myself feel. . . . Oh! my God, what will happen now? It's terrible! I hope he doesn't. . . . No, she is too lovely for him to kill her. . . . My legs are giving way beneath me. . . . I am a very sensitive man, you know . . .' and he was obliged to sit down on the sand.

CHAPTER 55

'WHAT IS going on?' Angélique repeated, turning towards her husband. 'Has someone died?'

'Possibly! Where have you come from?'

Looking up at Peyrac's clouded brow and icy expression, she tried to understand.

'What do you mean? Where have I come from? . . . Did Yann not get here? Did he not tell you that. . . .'

'Yes he did! He told me . . . he told me you were taken prisoner by Gold Beard . . . He told me a lot more too . . . and so did Kurt Ritz.'

'Kurt Ritz?'

'The Swiss mercenary who has been working for me, and who was also taken prisoner by Gold Beard last month. Ritz managed to make his escape three days ago. Before doing so he saw you on board Gold Beard's ship. He got away one night by climbing down the poop. . . . The window was open. . . . He saw you . . . on board the ship . . . in the chartroom . . . with him . . . WITH HIM. . . .'

Joffrey de Peyrac spoke in broken phrases, his voice muffled and terrible, and with every word the truth began to dawn in Angélique's mind.

Paralysed by this overwhelming sense of surprise and terror, she could see the truth advancing towards her like a monstrous but real beast, ready to pounce and baring its claws to rend her to pieces. . . . The man! . . . The man whom she had seen making his escape that night in Casco Bay. . . . That had been the Swiss mercenary, one of Peyrac's men . . . and he had seen her . . . he had seen Colin enter her room and take her in his arms. . . .

'The window was open,' the strangled voice went on as if far away. . . . 'He saw you, Madame! You were naked . . . naked in Gold Beard's arms and responding to his kisses . . . to his caresses . . . to him! . . . To him! . . .'

What had he expected to hear by way of reply? An exclamation of indignation, vehement denials, possibly a laugh? But no! . . . silence!

Nothing but silence! The most terrible thing to suffer after such words.

And in the silence that fell drop by drop, every second adding its leaden weight to the one before, Joffrey de Peyrac thought he would die of distress.

Time was passing. The moment had passed . . . to retrieve herself. Every second had fallen like molten lead, setting its seal on the inevitable. Confirming her guilt, which was still manifest in her sudden livid pallor and the hunted look in her wide, startled eyes.

Angélique's brain was quite incapable of gathering two thoughts together at once. Everything jangled together in a dreadful fog.

Colin! Colin! . . . She must tell him that it was Colin. . . . No! That would make matters worse. . . . He had already hated him before all this.

If she had wanted to, she would have been quite incapable of offering the least explanation, of uttering a single word. Her throat would not let a single sound through, and she was trembling from head to foot. She began to feel faint and had to lean against the wall and close her eyes. And seeing her lower her eyelids with that tender, pained and secret expression that always moved him to the depths and occasionally irritated him, the Count's anger was unleashed.

'Don't lower your eyes!' he shrieked at her, almost breaking the table beneath his fist, 'Look at me!'

He grabbed her by the hair, and forced her head brutally backwards.

She thought that he had broken her neck. Leaning over her, his burning eyes scanned the face which he could no longer read, a stranger's face. He may have been speaking, she did not hear him. 'So it was true! You! . . . You! You whom I had put on so high a pedestal!'

He shook her furiously in his mad desire to smash the false image she was holding out to him and find the other woman, his beloved.

Then suddenly he struck her with the full force of his raised arm, so violently that Angélique's head was knocked sideways and struck the wooden wall. A red mist came down over her eyes. He let go of her and pushed her away from him. She did not know how she managed to remain standing.

Joffrey de Peyrac walked over to the window, and looked out through the panes at the damp night, breathing heavily in an attempt to regain control of himself.

When he turned back towards her again, his wife was standing there motionless with closed eyes. A thin trickle of blood had began to run down from one side of her delicate nose.

'Get out! Get out!' he said in an icy voice. 'I loathe the sight of you. Get out, I say! I don't want to see you ever again! I don't want to kill you. . . .'

CHAPTER 56

SHE LURCHED and staggered on, bumping into corners and unfamiliar pieces of furniture in the semi-darkness of a room fitfully lit by the pale light of the moon as it came out between clouds. Her desire to hide, to vanish for ever had sent Angélique deep into the heart of the wooden fortress, and rather than face the gusty wind outside and the busy life of the village, or the terrible solitude of the open country where she would find no refuge from hostile creatures, the instinct of a wounded beast that seeks out its burrow in order to die there had borne her through corridors and stairways to the door of this huge, private room, and without recognizing it, she knew that this was 'their room', the one in which they had made love the previous year, the one in which she had dreamed of finding herself alone with him again.

She groped around, stumbling against sharp corners, and finally came to a halt in the middle of the room, where, in the midst of the infernal chaos that had crushed her, she became aware of the first sound perceptible to her—the intermingled sound of two people breathing, a sound that encompassed her and which, she only realized after a moment of fear, was none other than the echo of her own convulsive breathing and the sound of the surf outside, beating upon the rocky spur below the fort.

317

She was alone.

The fear which for an instant had swamped all other sensations, now left her only to be replaced by the crushing certainty of an irreparable catastrophe. One half of her head felt enormous, having acquired a shapeless excrescence like the lumps one sees on pumpkins, which seemed to radiate pain down one side as if the swelling were made of red-hot iron. She raised one hand gingerly to it and encountered an area of flesh devoid of all sensation. There was in fact no swelling but the mere touch of her fingers sent a terrible stab of pain through her. In the same flash everything came back to her with merciless clarity. Colin! . . . His arms about her, his hands exploring her body, his lips taking possession of hers in a kiss that went on and on. . . .

The man, hiding outside, had seen all this by the light of the candle. . . . And now Joffrey knew . . . and was accusing her of the worst. How could she make him understand, how could she explain things to him, how could she get him to accept that? . . .

Were she so much as to mention the name of Colin, he would kill her. He had almost killed her once already that evening. She had felt this in the depths of her petrified flesh and had been incapable of reaction, unable to make the slightest move to defend herself. He had the power to annihilate her, to reduce her to nothingness. Because for HER, HE was everything.

She remained thus in the dark, scarce breathing now, for fear that she might awake not only the terrible physical pain, but shreds of the terrible vision she had had—Joffrey! Joffrey! His terrible face, and the glint of his doublet in which, whenever he moved, one caught a glimpse through the ivory satin pleats of that scarlet lining, as if she had caught sight of an endless stream of drops of blood, the shedding of tears of blood. Blood was flowing now, down her face. Her fingers were smeared with it and when she ran her tongue over her numbed lips they tasted salty. She tasted the blood with a kind of incredulous stupor. He had struck her! . . .

He had struck her and she deserved it! A bottomless chasm had yawned beneath their feet. . . .

She remained there with straining senses in the blackness and trembled in every limb as she thought of this gaping crevasse, then once again fear rose up within her and a thousand demons seemed to surge up out of the abyss and creep towards her with glistening eyes, sniggering. . . .

It had all happened too soon, just when she had really come to believe that their time spent at Wapassou had permanently renewed the bonds between them, and that their love was unassailable and indestructible.

It had come like a hurricane, like an earthquake, yet it had come stealthily and treacherously.

A beast spawned by hell, whose cruel eyes she had not noticed in time, had slithered towards them and had launched its attack.

She had been caught in a trap—they both had—a trap whose exact nature and functioning she did not understand, but whose jaws she now felt begin to crush her inexorably. So artful had been its approach that she and Joffrey had been struck to the heart at the very first blow.

'Joffrey! Joffrey! Please come! . . . Don't leave me alone! I'm frightened!'

The room was teeming with dangerous shadows, as she began to measure the insurmountable barriers that had risen up between her and him, her beloved husband whom she had mortally offended.

A hand was clutching at her throat, half choking her, suffocating her. In order to prevent herself fainting she pressed her two hands to her swollen mouth, both to stifle the cries that sought to burst forth and to awaken, through the pangs of intolerable suffering, her fast sinking consciousness, until the combined effect of pain and a shattering vision of all that she had lost, her grief at both broke out into childlike sobs of despair. . . . 'If he doesn't love me any more. . . . If he doesn't love me any more . . . what will become of me?'

CHAPTER 57

THE MOMENT he had just lived through seemed to him to have been the most terrible of all his life.

Two men within him, frenzied and beyond control, had divided his being. Had he not driven her away, would he have been able to resist for much longer his overwhelming desire—as strong as his desire to kill her— to take her in his arms? Two separate beings within him, had, throughout those terrible minutes, shared his body, his blood, his soul, so that he was torn in two— into a being bent on revenge, and one thirsting for adoration and sensual delight.

His veins were filled simultaneously with hatred and love.

And when he had seized her by the hair, had his hand not felt its fine silkiness, its soft warmth, and when he had bent over her, over that upturned face, over that forehead as broad and smooth as a beach of silvery sand had his lips, as they spat out their cruel words, not longed to lay themselves on hers in a passionate kiss? . . . And had not the thought flashed through his mind:

'What a lovely forehead she has! . . .'

And so, rent by these cross-currents of desire and anger, he had stood humiliated, trembling with rage against the woman to whom he owed this revelation of another side to his own character, who had forced him to see himself capable of blind violence, of irresistible lust, and of a degree of craven indulgence capable of abandoning itself to the prompting of the senses and to feelings contrary to all reason. . . .

So superb a creature for love! . . . That was what he thought. That was what they had all thought, when she had appeared to them on the threshold of night, and the obviousness of her beauty and her femininity had struck them like a blow, to such an extent that in a single moment all rancour, indignation, scorn and suspicion had vanished leaving these men surprised and subjugated and with thoughts only for the indescribable enchantment of her presence.

So superb a creature for love! . . . Oh! you male idolaters, sensual idiots that you are! Ever ready to kneel before the goddess!

An unreflecting impulse brought Joffrey de Peyrac outside into the silence of the night.

Clouds scudded across the dull silver of the moon, against which stood out the black outlines of masts bobbing up and down in the harbour. The light of a few fires danced in the wind, and this, with the slow movement of an occasional sentry was the only sign of life.

The world was dead.

Where was she? 'Angélique! Angélique! . . . my love!'

He went back into the fort and sprang silently up the wooden staircase. He could hear her through the door, sobbing. And he stood there, consumed anew by a wild flame, his body tensed until it ached with the torment of temptation. He wanted to push open the door, to go in, to find himself alone with her, to bend over her, to grasp her, to clutch her to his heart, and to forget, to forget in the joy of their movements, their caresses, the murmur of their voices, of their intermingled breaths, of their kisses, and passionate whispered words 'My love! My love! It doesn't matter! I love you!' To forget, to forget it all. . . .

He came to himself again in the downstairs room, where the wax in the torches had burned right down, leaning his forehead against the window through which the pale light of dawn was beginning to shine.

No, Angélique would not be the cause of his downfall, he would not become the thrall of an unworthy woman.

No, never!

Why was she crying so loudly up there? Had she not known what she was doing when she let another man, the stranger, make love to her? She, whom he had thought of so highly! Had she not known what she was destroying? . . . No she had not. She had not known! . . . She was a woman, an irresponsible woman, just like the rest!

They want to have everything, and they destroy everything!

'I should never have forgiven her before. . . . They are all the same! . . . All the same! . . .'

At high tide he would set off out to sea with his ships, he would find Gold Beard, even if he had to chase him right down to the Caribbean . . . and before he killed him with his own hands he would snatch from that unknown and hated face the veil of the past. He wanted to know what kind of a man it was to whom Angélique had shown the face of a mistress.

'Oh! If only I could pluck her from my heart! I shall do so if I have to.'

Such a superb creature! . . .

The *Gouldsboro* had brought her dresses from France!

He walked over to a chest at the end of the room and opened the lid. He picked up watered sliks and the daintiest of lace, while his fingers ran mechanically over the dress, smoothing the heavy folds of skirt and bodice into the shape they would have assumed when inhabited by a woman's body.

'How lovely she would have looked in this! That silver cloth with the pinkish tinge draped about her regal shoulders! I would have taken her to Quebec with me . . . and she would have won the hearts of all! . . .'

His fists clenched on this shadow of womanhood that seemed to fade and collapse expiring beneath his grasp.

In an uncontrolled gesture he lifted the crumpled stuff to his face and stood there for a long time, as if lost and far away, nostalgically breathing in the delicate fragrance of flowers and femininity that came from the sumptuous finery.

Through the morning mist, figures came running towards him.

'My lord! God is with us. The ship of that cursed Gold Beard is not far off. . . . He has just been sighted in the archipelago.'

PART FIVE
Gold Beard's Downfall

CHAPTER 58

THERE WERE a large number of children in Gouldsboro always running about barefoot in a merry band, the little girls' hair streaming out from under their round bonnets or white coifs, the boys' heads uncovered, skirts or breeches tucked up so that they could paddle more easily in the pools, climb into boats, leap about on the beach, chase seals; as they gulped down shellfish and gulls' eggs, or sucked at a flower—a whole troop of them in company with a crowd of little naked Indians, popping up here then there, constantly on the wing.

They glued their little faces curiously to the weather-boarding of the shed in an attempt to catch a glimpse of the captured pirates through the cracks, then ran off to the harbour to admire the beautiful painting that rose and fell on the stern of the *Heart of Mary*, the ship captured that morning, then they rushed off to fetch spring water from the forest and knelt down to give the wounded a drink.

The sun was going down in Gouldsboro on the defeat of Gold Beard the pirate.

That morning Angélique had been awakened by the distant rumble of gunfire.

Her soul and her body were aching with pain and she did not know where she was; it was quite a time before she realized she was in Gouldsboro. Then she took a look at her swollen face in the mirror. All down one side it was black and blue, and one corner of her mouth was swollen. She could only turn her head with difficulty. She had looked round the room and discovered some clothes in several linen chests, which she herself had folded away in the autumn before they left the fort. She dressed and did her hair, her mind still numb. She

325

must find some pommade, some balm, anything to disguise her disfigurement.

Pushing back the shutters, she had caught sight of a number of ships sailing under the lee, near the edge of a rain-washed sky, against whose grey background, from time to time, a red flash could be seen. Then the dull thunder of the explosion reached her. A naval battle was taking place off Gouldsboro, apparently involving three or four ships attacking a single adversary which, after skilfully disengaging, fled under full sail, pursued by the others, and was soon outside Angélique's field of vision.

Soon afterwards a woman's voice called to her from somewhere inside the house.

'Dame Angélique! Dame Angélique! Where are you! Ah! Here you are! God be praised! Come! Come quickly, dear lady! There are wounded men, and blood everywhere!'

Angélique recognized the little woman as Madame Carrère from La Rochelle who had emigrated to the New World the year before with her ten children and her husband, a barrister.

'What is happening? Why are there wounded men?'

'They've just been settling up with that damned Gold Beard.'

'Who are "they"?'

'Monsieur le Comte, the filibuster Vanereick, the English admiral, all of them, in fact, who swore to make that scoundrel beg for mercy! They heard this morning that he was on the prowl among the islands, and Monsieur le Comte immediately set sail and gave chase. They cornered him and forced him to give battle, and Monsieur d'Urville has just brought news of victory.

'But it seems that when they came to board her, it was sheer slaughter. . . . The ships are coming back to harbour with their prize and all the wounded. Monsieur de Peyrac has sent word to us that you were here and that you must be warned to get ready to care for the unfortunate victims.'

'Are you sure that it was my husband who asked you to tell me this?'

'Of course! What could we do without you? Apparently the surgeon on board the *Fearless* has been wounded too and is unable to perform his duties. As for our doctor, Parry, you know him. He isn't much help when faced with slaughter like this. . . . Good Lord! Whatever has happened to you, you poor creature! . . . You are in a mess!'

'Oh, it's nothing!'

Angélique raised her hand to her cheek. 'I . . . I was shipwrecked off Monhegan Island and was hurled against a rock. . . . Wait for me, I'm coming. I only have to pick up my bag and put a few essential instruments in it. Have you any spare lint? . . .'

Methodically, she gathered together everything she thought she might need, moving like an automaton, while her mind buzzed with agonizing thoughts.

Colin. . . . Colin had died by Joffrey de Peyrac's hand. . . . If only she had said something yesterday evening . . . if only she had had the courage to speak. . . . But no, that had been impossible! She had been unable to say anything, to explain anything. And now Joffrey de Peyrac had killed Gold Beard . . . and he had sent for her to tend the wounded. . . . So he did at least remember her existence. But why? Was he planning some further revenge? What if he threw Colin's body in her path. She could never bear that. She would never be able to help falling to her knees and taking Colin's big bearded head between her hands and weeping.

'Oh God!' she begged, 'let Joffrey not do anything so terrible. Oh! God, how has it come about that he and I should so suddenly be such utter enemies?'

She tumbled down the stairs behind Madame Carrère and ran towards the place where the villagers were laying out seaweed-filled mattresses, leather buckets of fresh water, and blankets. The first of the wounded were being unloaded from the longboats and laid on the ground, moaning or swearing colourful oaths.

The remainder of the morning was a nightmare during which Angélique could think of nothing but cutting into flesh, sewing up or cleaning out wounds, dressing them, running from one man to another, calling for assistance, organizing a field hospital, sending children off in all directions to fetch herbs, bandages, water, rum, oil, thread, needles and scissors.

With her sleeves rolled up and blood-stained to the elbows, for hours on end she did nothing but perform emergency operations, taking upon herself the responsibility of diagnosing the gravity of wounds, and indicating what kind of treatment should be given and what remedies prepared. Very soon she found the old order forming itself about her once more. She recognized the women who spontaneously placed themselves at her disposal: Abigail, diligent and efficient in spite of her pregnancy; Madame Carrère, active, the young women prompt and docile, courageous in the face of death and suffering, just like their elders. Suddenly she found Aunt Anna beside her, passing her her surgical instruments, precise and attentive, and old Rebecca comforting a dying man.

A young lad followed her everywhere carrying a large copper basin which he kept filled with fresh water for her to wash her hands and soak bandages in. It was only after a while that she recognized him as Martial, Maître Berne's eldest son.

All at once, she had resumed her place among them. But while she busied herself about her tasks with her customary diligence, her feelings, as raw as an open wound, noticed certain tiny details in their behaviour towards her. A faint suggestion of contempt in their voices, a sudden tightening of the lips, a hostile glance. . . . It was perhaps only an impression. . . . No! The people of Gouldsboro knew . . . everyone knew.

And yet Madame Carrère had been straightforward and cordial with her. But Madame Carrère had never been a scandal-monger. The rumour she had heard in Gouldsboro that Countess Peyrac had deceived her husband with the pirate was one she refused to pay heed to. The furtive eyes that followed Angélique that morning as she worked away indefatigably, were busy calculating the extent or the possibility of calumny. . . . But the most terrible thing about it all was that there was no question of calumny, but of truth . . . or rather of half-truth. She had lain in Gold Beard's arms, she had responded to his caresses. She would have liked to have shouted out for all the world to hear that she had not been guilty. She would have liked to have persuaded herself of the fact, to have become once more as she had been before. She bent over the men's wounds with infinite gentleness and infinite compassion for she felt within herself too, an open wound, every moment more painful, and she would so have welcomed a compassionate hand laid upon it. But no one would do that for her.

'Ah! Madame, save me,' implored the seriously wounded.

But as for her, to whom could she beseech—'save me'?

Her pain was of the kind that merits no compassion. And at times it shot through her so cruelly that it left her almost paralysed.

'Joffrey does not love me any more. . . . How could I have done this to him, when he is so kind, so wonderful? How could I have humiliated him thus in the eyes of the world? . . . He will never forgive me. He has asked me to care for the wounded . . . why? But of course, because he needed me. His men come first, his resentment next. . . . That is typical of him. But afterwards, he will drive me away, he will repudiate me. He will never want to see me again. He shouted: "I never want to see you again."

But in spite of everything, she felt as if having to work for him like this, as it were at his side, was in a way like a truce between them. The thought that he had sent for her was like a gleam of hope.

He had sent for her. He had remembered her. So she did still count for something. She resumed her task with renewed vigour.

The poor unfortunates who moaned in pain as she bent over them, reassuring, encouraging, thought they were seeing an angel from Heaven come down to them, and as soon as she laid her hands upon them, they grew quiet.

'Is that Count Peyrac's lady?' asked all those who did not know her.

'Yes,' the others called out. 'You'll see, she'll make you better.'

And all this confidence around her stirred Angélique's courage, gradually dulled her inner torment, helped her to lift her head once more, to hold fast, although she was aware of her own swollen face, now covered with sweat.

She listened carefully, in the hope of overhearing some snatches of conversation about the course of the battle.

But no one mentioned Gold Beard's death.

Only the horrible, bloody combat between the crews of the various ships which had taken place after the *Heart of Mary* had been boarded. 'And Monsieur de Peyrac was the first to jump.'

Towards the middle of the morning the ships entered the harbour, encircling their prey.

Listing heavily, bereft of her masts, with a pall of smoke hanging about her like an ill-boding cloud, Gold Beard's ship came to rest against an island in the middle of the bay.

Then it was the turn of the prisoners to be brought ashore in long boats and they began to file up the beach, escorted by sailors from the *Gouldsboro* and soldiers from the garrison.

Monsieur d'Urville had them taken to the barn where maize was stored, a rough-and-ready building but fairly large and with only one door, which would make it easier to mount guard.

One of the captive pirates was yelling like a man possessed as they dragged him up the beach.

'Let me go, you dolts, you murderers. I'm wounded, I tell you, seriously wounded at that! You'll kill me!'

Angélique pricked up her ears at the sound of this shrill voice, and recognized it as that of the unspeakable Slit-Belly, the man she had operated on in Casco Bay.

She made her way towards the men and said:

'This good-for-nothing is telling the truth. You mustn't make him walk! Lay him down there.'

'Ah there you are at last, and not too soon either!' Beaumarchand moaned. 'Where did you get to, Madame? You shouldn't have left me like that, with this seam across my belly.'

'Be quiet, you loathsome creature! You could have gone to the devil a hundred times as far as I care, after the foul trick you played on me.'

She nevertheless examined the man and noted with satisfaction that Aristide Beaumarchand's monstrous scar looked healthy enough and seemed to be mending. A miracle indeed since his companions on board the *Heart*

330

of Mary seemed to have paid precious little attention to him since they had taken him back on board.

'How I missed you, Madame! I certainly did miss you!' he repeated. 'They left me to die in a hole full of rats, like so much rubbish!'

She changed his dressing, bound him up with strips of linen like a newborn babe, and left him for the time being on the sand.

A little later she knelt down beside Monsieur de Barssempuy to attend to his shoulder, which had been slashed with a cutlass. He was the gentlemen, second in command to Gold Beard, who had taken her prisoner at Maquoit. Today his face was black with gunpowder and he looked weary.

'What about your captain?' she whispered to him, 'Gold Beard, where is he? What happened to him? Was he wounded or killed?'

He threw her a bitter glance and turned his head away.

Her nagging fears continued, and she felt paralysed with anxiety.

The sun had reached its zenith, and the heat added to her distress and fatigue.

At that moment someone came to fetch Madame de Peyrac, asking her to be so good as to come on board the pirate ship to see whether . . . among the more seriously wounded, there were any whom they could risk moving to dry land and which among the rest it would be best to allow to die where they were.

She went on board a longboat, accompanied by Martial, who carried her emergency bag, a small barrel of fresh water and the copper bowl. At the gangway she was met by a man in a black doublet full of holes and singed with gunpowder, wearing a moth-eaten wig in an oddly lopsided fashion, who led her limping to the battery-deck.

'I am Mister Vanereick's surgeon, Nessens. A cannon-ball fell on the store-room where I was operating. . . . As for my colleague on board the *Heart of Mary*, they found him stone dead beneath a pile of bodies. So you see the wounded would have been in a nasty fix had you not happened to be in Gouldsboro, Madame. As soon as it was known that you were there, the wounded cheered up, and I gave orders to evacuate as many as possible so that they could be placed in your charge since I was hampered in the performance of my work. Such is your reputation that people have begun to hear about you overseas. As for me, I have had to content myself with clearing up three ships today. But there are a few unfortunates here about whom I find I cannot reach a decision. . . .'

It was difficult to move about the ship, for the deck was tilted at an alarming angle. Some barrels of cider had been pierced and the place was awash with sour-smelling liquid mingled with blood. They floundered and slithered through the noisome mixture and had to cling to anything available in order to make any progress.

But orders had been given to prevent the damaged ship from sinking and they could hear the gangs of men at work calling to one another.

'This was the ship that was most heavily damaged,' Nessens explained. 'Four of us came alongside her: Monsieur de Peyrac's chebec, the *Gouldsboro*, the *Fearless* and the English ship. Shortly after this the little yacht *Rochelais* arrived too. It was a good policing operation we carried out, half those bandits are out of action.'

The surgeon was a man in his thirties. When, back in France, he realized that, although a qualified surgeon, he had no right to practise because he was a Protestant, he found that the only possibility open to him was to become an exile and take up the dangerous profession of surgeon on privateers. After he and Angélique had examined the dying men, she suggested that she might dress his wounds for him. Furthermore, noticing that his limp came not from a wound but from a dislocation of the hip he had suffered in a fall during the bombardment, she reduced the dislocation and massaged it firmly to help the bruised, stretched sinews back into place again, and when he left her he was almost his active self again.

As she crossed the deck to re-embark, not without difficulty, a feeble voice called to her:

'Madame! Señora!'

The man who had called her was lying, half crushed against the ship's rails, hidden by coils of rope that had fallen across him. He must have been overlooked until then in the disorder and confusion after the battle. She freed him and dragged him a little higher up the deck, propping him up against the base of the mizzen mast. Looking at his waxen face and his huge black staring eyes she thought he seemed familiar.

'I am Lopez,' he breathed.

'Lopez . . . Lopez?'

She searched her memory. Then he helped her, with a ghost of a smile on his grey lips:

'You remember . . . Lopez! . . . Over yonder . . . the bees.'

She remembered. So he was one of the filibusters she had sought to defend herself against by hurling a hive full of bees at their heads. Now, after being picked up by Gold Beard's ship, his last hour had come.

'It's my stomach,' he murmured. 'You'll do for me like you did for Beaumarchand, won't you, eh? You sewed him up again, I saw you. And now he's running about as lively as a rabbit . . . I . . . I don't want to die, milady, if you please. . . .'

He was still young, this bit of a boy from Portugal. A miserable wretch from the Lisbon quayside, brought up to the age of twelve on dust, sunshine and a handful of figs. And after that, life at sea. And that was all.

As a pure matter of form Angélique slit open his breeches which had already become distended by the crushed and putrifying flesh, filthy with blood, pus, cider, and sea water. Already the hollows round the man's eyes had told her the worst. Even if he had received attention in time, he could not have been saved.

'You'll do something for me, won't you?' he repeated.

She gave him a reassuring smile.

'Yes, my lad. First I'm going to give you something to ease the pain. Swallow this.'

And between his lips she slipped one of her last remaining pills, made of mandrake and Indian poppy seed.

He was unable to swallow the pill but kept it on his tongue and it began to make him slightly drowsy.

'Are you a good Christian, my lad?' she asked again.

'Yes, Señora, I am.'

333

'Then pray to the Good Lord and the Blessed Virgin while I make you better.'

She took his hands and crossed them over his chest and held them there, transmitting her life and warmth to him in this final contact with the world he was leaving, so that he would not feel alone as he crossed the last threshold.

His leaden eyelids opened again.

'Mamma! Mamma!' he breathed, staring hard at her.

She released his hands, now chill and lifeless, closed his eyes, and covered his face with the scarf she had hastily tied that morning about her shoulders. She had never managed to remain indifferent to violent death in battle, to the sudden metamorphosis of one who had lived, laughed and moved about in the sunshine only a few hours earlier, whom a single blow could change into an amorphous mass, vanished for ever from the earth and soon from the hearts of those about him. Although she herself had on occasion killed with her own hands, the senselessness of death and its irreparable cruelty still continued to cause deep pain to her feminine sensibility. And although she knew how worthless a creature this poor man was who had just completed his sojourn on earth, in spite of herself she found her eyes filling with tears.

CHAPTER 59

As SHE stood up she found herself face to face with Count Peyrac, who had been standing for several moments, watching his wife bending over the dying man.

Gilles Vanereick, who was accompanying him on his final tour of inspection, had been the first to notice her blonde hair, like a vision of sweetness after the rough hours of battle; he had laid a hand on the Count's arm and both of them, interrupting their inspection, had stood there watching her as she bent over the cavernous face of the dying man and they had overheard her compassionate voice murmuring: 'Say your prayers, my lad. . . . I will make you better. . . .'

Then they had seen her cross herself and take off her scarf to cover the poor boy's face, while tears glistened on her eyelashes.

When she caught sight of Joffrey de Peyrac she was so disconcerted that Vanereick felt sorry for her. Painfully, she turned away under the pretext of rinsing her hands in the basin young Martial held out towards her.

'Have all the wounded fit to leave the ship been sorted out by you, Madame?' Count Peyrac asked her, without any particular inflection in his voice beyond a note of distant calm.

'This one is dead,' she replied, pointing towards the outstretched body.

'Yes, I can see that,' he replied dryly.

She obstinately refused to let him see her face with its blue bruise which had embarrassed her the whole day long. It was the first time she had seen him since the terrible scene of the previous day, and she felt a sensation of icy cold as if she were suddenly faced with a stranger. . . . A wall had sprung up between them.

The Flemish gentleman accompanying Peyrac seemed a gay, light-hearted fellow. His yellow jerkin, adorned with knots of ribbon that streamed out in the wind, his red ostrich feathers, and his lace revers and cravat were in the gaudy taste of the Caribbean filibusters. On the other hand, his jolly face was marked with streaks of blood which obliged him to half-close one eye.

In order to give herself a countenance Angélique turned towards him.

'Can I do anything for you, Monsieur?'

Gilles Vanereick, delighted at the prospect of getting to know her better, eagerly acquiesced.

She sat him down on an upturned barrel, and as Joffrey de Peyrac began to walk away, she gently cleaned his wounds for him, asking herself meanwhile with what kind of weapon they could possibly have been made.

He pulled a wry face and yelped like a puppy.

'You do make a fuss for a gentleman of fortune,' she told him. 'Any one as faint-hearted as you shouldn't get involved in battles.'

'I am the captain of the *Fearless*.'

'One wouldn't have guessed it.'

335

'But you see, I was never wounded in my life before, dear lady! Ask anyone, they will all tell you that Gilles Vanereick always gets off without a scratch.'

'Not this time, anyway.'

'But yes, this time too. The wound you are dressing with your dainty fingers is no war wound, far from it. I owe that to Ines's fury last night.'

'Ines?'

'My mistress! She is as jealous as a tigress, and she has the sharp claws of one too, and took umbrage because I kept going on about how dazzlingly beautiful you were.'

'But I do not know you, sir.'

'Oh yes you do . . . I was in the council chamber yesterday when you made your appearance. But I shall forgive you for not having noticed my humble person, for I know you only had eyes for Monsieur de Peyrac, your husband, who is also my dear and much revered friend from the Caribbean.'

Angélique, who was winding a bandage round his forehead restrained her desire to pull his hair by way of vengeance for his irony. Vanereick's dark eyes were peeping up at her from under the bandage, full of admiration, but quick enough to have noticed the blue marks across one side of her lovely face, which he had not seen there the day before.

Apparently, or so he assumed, there had been a violent domestic scene, and the couple were still sulking with one another, but this woman was too beautiful for things to fail to sort themselves out. A little jealousy adds spice to a passionate love affair. He had seen worse with his Ines. And, like Peyrac, he did not like sharing either. But this was the kind of accident one had to risk when one got involved with such beauties, endowed with nature's every gift to delight the heart of man, including the gift of arousing other men's lust.

This woman too, this crazy, footloose Countess of Peyrac, she possessed this gift and knew how to make the most of it, and it was just too bad for Peyrac!

With trembling nostrils, as she delicately sponged his scratches, Vanereick revelled in her fragrance, so close to him, delicate and elusive, a fragrance like fresh-mown

336

hay—the delicious fragrance of woman, a true blonde, which made him long to explore more fully the mysteries of her golden skin.

Taking advantage of his status as a combatant in an enfeebled condition, he had managed, as he sat down, to slip one hand around Angélique's hips. She had a magnificent figure, but he could only brush it, for she immediately moved away.

He told himself that naked, she must reveal the most opulent curves, and yet, her gracefulness and the suppleness of her movements made her seem slimmer than she really was with her splendid body hidden beneath her clothes. The practised eye of the merry corsair envisaged the perfect shape of a body which, from the nape of the neck to the small of the back, must express a perfect harmony of line. A cross between Venus and the huntress Diana. And certainly very strong! This he realized when she brought his reverie to an abrupt end with a simple pressure of her wrist, bringing him sharply back to his feet, as she might have done to a bit of a boy whom she judged a trifle spineless.

'There you are now, quite recovered from the spite of the lady Ines, my friend. Tomorrow there won't be a trace left!'

With his swollen eye he gave her a knowing wink.

'I trust that the same can be said of you, lovely lady! I see that the planets Venus and Mars collided yesterday in the heavens and that we were both victims of this squabble between the gods. . . .'

Angélique suppressed a grimace, as she felt a stab of pain down the left side of her face. She had done so much since the morning that her despair had begun to fade. Through a natural reaction of her irrepressible nature, her optimism was beginning to get the upper hand, and Vanereick's remarks about a squabble between the gods of love and of war had almost made her laugh.

Seeing her less distant in her bearing, he went on:

'Listen,' he whispered, 'I understand about love, and I am not a man to be hard on any lapses a pretty woman might make even if I am not the one to benefit. Would you like me to give you news of Gold Beard?'

Angélique's face froze and she threw him a glance of

337

anger, humiliated to find him ranking her with casual indulgence among women of easy virtue, and humiliated also on Count Peyrac's behalf. Now she was sure that Kurt Ritz's confidences had not been kept secret and that everyone was gossiping about her escapade and his humiliation.

And yet, tormented at the thought of what might have become of Colin, she could not refrain from murmuring:

'Yes! What did happen to Gold Beard?'

'Well, to tell the truth, no one knows. He has disappeared!'

'Disappeared?'

'Yes! An extraordinary coincidence! You see, he was not on board when we attacked his ship and it was his second-in-command who organized the defence. Some say he left the ship during the course of the night in a little dinghy, without saying where he was going, nor when he would be back. He instructed his lieutenant Barssempuy to remain within sight of Gouldsboro but to keep hidden in the archipelago, until he himself returned with further orders. Whether he went off to reconnoitre, to see how best to attack Gouldsboro this time. . . . But we stole a march on him. As soon as dawn broke Monsieur de Peyrac's chebec surprised the *Heart of Mary* lying at anchor. First we pursued her, then we boarded her, then it was hand-to-hand fighting. And now our Gouldsboro men have won! As for Gold Beard, wherever he might be, his reign over sea and ocean is finished for a long time, I imagine!'

'I see. Thank you, Monsieur.'

Angélique returned to the harbour. The sun seemed as if it would never fall below the horizon. The clouds of dust and smoke had softened to gold and sulphurous yellow, while the heat, which had been overpowering in spite of the incessant wind, began to grow less intense at last.

Attracted by the noise of gunfire, the Indians had come out of the forest, bringing furs to trade with the ships, and game which was more than welcome in view of the considerable number of extra mouths to be fed. The English and French sailors and filibusters, even the wounded who were still mobile, rushed off to engage in

338

barter with the Indians, so powerful was the attraction of fur trading along these shores and the lure of the money that could be made. They bartered anything they had, their caps, their tobacco, brandy, ear-rings, even the wooden or pewter spoons, which, along with their knives, were the most precious items of equipment in a sailor's life.

Through the weather-boarding of their lock-up even the prisoners shouted to the Indians to come closer, and passed them various baubles to barter.

It was on this occasion that Angélique discovered among the captives another acquaintance from Maquoit Point.

After a battle in which so many worthy men had died, of course a man like Hyacinthus Boulanger had had to survive. He had been making a thorough nuisance of himself and he had already had to be knocked out twice in order to keep him quiet.

'He's a buccaneer, so let him do some buccaneering,' Angélique decreed. 'At least if he does that, he won't be a nuisance, and might even make himself useful.'

She scolded him roundly:

'And don't let anyone regret having left you alive, you wretch! If you would rather have your wrists and ankles fettered than make yourself useful, that's up to you, but I would like to make it clear that you had better do as I say since the only alternative to behaving yourself will be to find yourself hanged like the dangerous good-for-nothing that you are.'

'Do as she says, Hyacinthus!' Aristide called across from where he lay. 'You know it's no use arguing with her, and in any case don't forget that she did sew up your blood-brother's belly!'

Subdued, the hideous butcher indicated that he had understood and went off swinging his ape-like arms to collect some green wood with which to prepare fires for smoking the meat. Angélique found two or three others who were buccaneers by trade among the crew, and sent them off with Hyacinthus Boulanger to a small beach apart from the others, under custody of an armed guard, with instructions to skin and joint the stags and does which the Indians had brought, and then to roast some of the meat and to smoke the rest.

The tasty smell of roasting meat that soon began to permeate the golden evening air reminded her that she had eaten nothing all day, nor since the previous day and even then. . . . Goodness, yes! Her last meal had been the one at Pentagouet on Penobscot Bay, which she had eaten with Baron Saint-Castine and Father Maraicher de Vernon, alias Jack Merwin, the Jesuit. Ages ago! . . . It all seemed very remote and she sensed that she had still not reached the end of her troubles.

Then suddenly she felt hungry.

Her encounter with Vanereick had made her feel a little more cheerful. Now that she knew that Colin was not among the casualties, she felt better. Vanereick was probably right after all. Was it necessary to make such a fuss, to destroy two lives, even several lives, for such a trifle! Joffrey was no easy husband to face, but she would have to tackle him and overcome her fear. . . . 'I shall say to him. . . . Well! I shall tell him the truth . . . that I have not betrayed him to the extent that he believes . . . that Gold Beard is Colin. . . . He will understand . . . I shall find the words to make him understand. Things are already better than they were yesterday. We are working together at the same tasks again. Life has forced him to remember me, to remember all that unites us. Haven't we been through other battles, other periods of separation . . . other . . . betrayals? . . . And we got over them, have managed to love one another in spite of them, even more than before.'

After all they were no longer children with all the intransigence and inexperience of youth. Life had ridden rough-shod over them, and had taught them to appreciate the value of true feelings, to know what one should accept or sacrifice in order to preserve the best and most priceless things.

And there were too many people depending on them. She must tell him that too. They had no right to weaken, no right to let these people down. She thought of her children, especially Cantor, who might well put in an appearance at any minute now.

Someone had told her that her youngest son had gone

back to Casco Bay to look for her, and she had felt relieved that he was not present. But soon afterwards it had been announced that the *Rochelais* had returned just in time to take part in the naval combat that morning, and was still patrolling among the islands.

For Cantor's sake too, she must explain things to Joffrey and be promptly reconciled, before all kinds of rumours and tales reached the ears of the sensitive lad. That very evening she would endeavour to catch Joffrey on his own.

But the day was not yet done, and she still had a thousand things to do. Close to Madame Carrère's inn she fortified herself with a head of corn on the cob which she hastily grilled over some glowing embers and nibbled equally quickly while supervising the preparation of some herbal tea. She had neither hemlock nor mandrake root with which to make her sedative pills, but failing these ingredients, rosemary, cloves and oriental poppies would do. She went round more or less all the houses, and rummaged through the supplies in the fort until someone told her that there was an 'herb man' on board the *Fearless*, as was the case with many ships, one of those sailors who kept a pinch of this and a trifle of that tucked away in a pocket or in the corner of a sea chest, gleaned from the four corners of the earth. She would be able to recognize the man by the black patch he wore over one eye and by the fact that he was followed wherever he went by his slave, a fellow from the Caribbean with olive-coloured skin and wearing a magical green stone round his neck on a string of cotton. The black patch would not have been sufficient on its own to identify him for there were many one-eyed men among these battling seafarers.

Some of the crew had been landed at the far western end of the main beach where they were bivouacking. 'They'll be drunk tonight,' said Madam Carrère with a knowing look. She had never stopped pouring out beer, wine, rum and brandy to the able-bodied. . . . Admittedly, they sometimes paid her in pearls or even in gold ducats.

The booty was brought ashore in open boats from the *Heart of Mary*, landed, numbered, laid out in rows, in barrels, casks, coffers and sacks, under the delighted gaze of sailors of every nationality who would each receive a bounty for their part in the action.

Gold Beard's vessel had the reputation of being extremely well stocked. The ship's clerks bustled around the supplies, calling out figures and affixing seals. There was tobacco from Brazil, molasses, soft brown sugar, white sugar, rice, rum, and more wine, as well as all the run-of-the-mill stores of a merchant vessel—barrels of peas, of beans, of salt pork, of biscuits plus a few delicacies: seven barrels of pigs' ears, seven pots of legs of goose, hams, cheeses, dried fruits, flakes of vinegar, oil, fruit preserved in grape juice, and finally a small studded chest, which was extremely heavy and said to contain precious jewels and the famous Caracas emeralds which Gold Beard had conquered. . . . Two guards were posted over this box until it could be transported to Count Peyrac's fort.

Picking up the hem of her skirt, Angélique pushed her way through the noisy crowd. Attracted by so many different sights the English Puritans from Camp Champlain as well as the Huguenots from La Rochelle were enjoying themselves hanging around the throngs on the beach, and round the fires could be heard the sound of English and French voices telling the children fantastic tales of piracy in the blue Caribbean with its endless glittering string of long white beaches fringed with palm trees where one drinks rum mixed with the cool milk of big hairy coconuts.

A child in a red dress threw her arms round Angélique's neck and, unaccustomed to such spontaneity, she almost failed to recognize her.

'Rose-Anne, my darling, how delighted I am to see you again!'

The little English girl seemed to be having a wonderful time, as were Dorothy and Janeton from Monhegan. Their Bible and reading lessons would certainly not be starting today.

At last Angélique found the herb man, with his half-naked Caribbean in tow, and bought a few items from him.

As evening fell, the gilding of the picture of the Virgin

on the poop of the *Heart of Mary* glittered in the light of the declining sun. Tilting at an angle on account of the list of the ship, the reflection of its colours trembled in the harbour waters, and as the shadows grew darker, so did the faces of the Virgin and the Angels begin to look more and more like sweet, nostalgic apparitions watching over the motley crowd gathered on the shore. The whole bay smelt strongly of black iodine-steeped seaweed, for the tide had been out all day. The tangy breath of the sea borne on the wind mingled with the smell of wood smoke and tar. A woman suddenly began to dance wildly to the sound of castanets. Her full, flame-coloured embroidered skirt wavered about her like a red and gold mist and her glance was keen and povocative beneath her heavily-blackened eyelashes. Her eyes followed Angélique for a long time as she went by.

'That's Ines,' someone told her, 'Mr. Vanereick's mistress. Apparently she is as handy with a sword as with the castanets.'

Angélique halted for a moment to watch the 'tigress' leaping into the air with feline grace.

There was laughter and singing and shouting that night in Gouldsboro as well as the moans of the wounded, the dying and the vanquished.

In all this feverish agitation, this tumult born of victory and defeat that muddles and confuses men's mind as much as the noisy seething of waves and wind, the Devil with his cloven hooves found many an opportunity to dance, intrigue, sow seeds of unhappiness and discord, lead his infernal ballet escorted by every invisible spirit of Evil. . . .

CHAPTER 60

THE MAN appeared to Angélique, towards the end of the day, in the guise of a pale creature who, crossing the bay at low tide, and leaping from rock to rock, seemed to have come on foot from the remoteness of the sea. At the time Angélique was standing at the door of Madame Carrère's inn and for the umpteenth time washing her hands in a basin beside a rain-water butt, surreptitiously trying to rub a bit of balm into the bruise on her temple. She had been unable to attend to herself during the day, and she was now utterly exhausted.

'Monsieur de Peyrac wishes to see you,' said the man, 'on that island over there; you must go immediately.'

'Are there more wounded, then?' Angélique asked, glancing down at the open bag at her feet which had never left her side.

'Possibly . . . I don't know.'

For a fraction of a second Angélique hesitated. Madame Carrère had just told her that she had warmed up a bowl of pickled pork and cabbage, to 'set her up' and as a change from those everlasting shellfish. And then there was something else too which she found hard to put a name to at that moment, something that made her hesitate to follow this man.

'Where is your boat?' she asked him.

'No need to take a boat. You can reach it on foot. The tide is right out.'

She followed him, and together they crossed the broad stretch of sand between the shore and the island that the man had pointed out. Slimy pieces of seaweed burst beneath their feet with a sharp crack and a hiss.

The reflection of the setting sun in the many pools of water dazzled Angélique and made her eyes ache.

The tiny island rose up before them at a distance of about a mile, the first of a chain of reefs, topped with the usual crown of black pines, growing straight as lances, parasol firs, green bushes and birch trees. An old-rose-coloured beach sloped gently up towards the shade of the little wood.

'Over there,' said the man, pointing to the edge of the trees.

'I can see no one. . . .'

'There's a clearing a bit farther along. Monsieur de Peyrac is waiting for you there with some other people.'

His voice was monotonous and listless. Angélique looked at him. She was surprised how sickly he looked and wondered whose crew he could possibly belong to.

Slowly she made her way up the beach, her feet

sinking into the damp sand, reached some grass which was short at first then grew thicker.

There was indeed a clearing among the trees, in the centre of which lay the wreck of an old vessel. The ghostly shape of the ship rose up at an angle in the green shadows, sticking up out of the tangle of grass, bushes and creeper. It was a small argosy of the previous century, little more than a hundred and twenty tons. She could make out the curving balusters, and the approximate shape of the figure-head on the prow, which was half rotted away but must once have represented the muscular torso and long-haired head of some sea god. The poop had been half buried by a fall of rock, and the masts broken off, but the mizzen, covered in red canker and black fungus, was still standing, its tip lost among the leaves.

Some tempest, some giant wave, some equinoctial tide, higher and more terrible than the rest, must have carried the wreck into this leafy haunt then retreated, abandoning it there for ever.

A bird began to sing, a pure, joyous sound, which only made the silence more apparent. The place was deserted.

At the same moment Angélique at last remembered what it was that had caused her to hesitate about following the pale man. Had she not, just a few moments before, caught sight of Count Peyrac putting in to the beach and heading for the shed where the prisoners were kept? He could not be in two places at the same time.

She turned to shout to the stranger who had brought her, but he had vanished.

Perplexed and overwhelmed by a sense of danger that made her flesh creep, she looked back towards the old ship. The only sound was of tiny waves splashing among the rocks, and the sensuous trilling of the bird that rang out at regular intervals, like a call . . . like a warning.

Angélique's hand moved to her belt but she knew she would find no weapon there.

Her breast was heavy with oppression and she dared not call out, for fear of breaking that torrid silence and provoking she knew not what horrible discovery.

Just as she had finally decided to attempt a cautious

retreat she heard the sound of footsteps coming from behind the ship.

It was a heavy tread, the sound deadened by the grass and moss, but it seemed to her to shake the earth to its foundations.

Angélique leaned against the rotten keel of the ship, and her heart stood still.

Coming as it did at the end of a difficult, exhausting day which for her had followed hard upon a terrible night of pain and tears, the approach of that inexorable tread advancing towards her as slow and heavy as Destiny itself—neither her husband's, nor a sailor's, nor an Indian's tread, since both sailors and Indians preferred to walk barefoot, nor even—who knew!—that of a human being—caught her in a completely demoralized state and awoke within her all the superstitious terrors of childhood.

And when a powerful shadow appeared at the corner of the ship, standing out somewhat hazily against the bluish-green darkness of the undergrowth, she really believed it must be that of an ogre or a giant.

CHAPTER 61

FILTERING THROUGH the branches, a ray of light glittered on a head of golden hair and a thick blond beard—Gold Beard!

'Is that you?' he asked.

As she made no reply, he continued to move warily towards her.

His heavy boots, whose turn-down tops exposed his big brown knees, crushed the grass dotted with dainty flowers. He was wearing short breeches, a white open-neck shirt and a sleeveless leather jerkin with a broad cross-belt slung from one shoulder. But the belt did not contain the customary four pistols, nor did his boarding sword hang from it. He too was unarmed.

He came to a halt a few paces from Angélique.

'Why did you send for me?' he asked her. 'What do you want of me?'

Angélique shook her head vehemently.

'I didn't send for you,' she finally managed to say.

Gold Beard's blue eyes scrutinized her keenly. The magic he could not resist, as soon as he found himself in her presence, was already acting upon him and he began to look less like a hunted lion as his heart softened.

'How pale you are, my lamb!' he said softly, 'and what have you done to your face? . . . Were you wounded?'

He raised his hand and ran the tips of his fingers over the bruise on her temple.

Angélique shuddered from head to foot, not only on account of the pain caused by even this light touch but at the terrifying thought that had just occurred to her. She was alone on this little island with Colin! Supposing Joffrey were to find them. . . .

'It's nothing,' she stammered, in a frenzy of despair. 'But go away, Colin, quickly, get away . . . I must not stay here.'

And she began to run down the grassy slope towards the beach, heading for the exposed stretch of the sea bed by which she had crossed the bay.

But on reaching the shore she came to a sudden halt, horror-stricken.

The transparent sheen of the sea now spread nonchalantly over the rocks which but a short while before had lain uncovered, and an arrogant wave ran bubbling and foaming up the beach.

Angélique began to run as if demented along the beach, flinging herself first onto one still unsubmerged rock, then another. A wave swirled around her feet, then a second almost threw her off balance.

A firm hand grasped her and pulled her back.

'What are you doing?' said Colin Paturel. 'Can't you see it's high tide?'

Angélique looked up at him in dismay.

'We are cut off on this island,' she murmured.

'It looks like it.'

'But I must get away!'

'There's no boat,' Colin replied.

'But that's impossible! You must have a boat. How did you get here?'

347

'I don't know how I got here,' he replied somewhat mysteriously.

'And what about the man who brought me here, where is he? Didn't you see him? He had a face like wax.'

All of a sudden Angélique felt faint and clutched at the lapels of Colin's jerkin.

'Colin, that was the Devil, I feel sure!'

'Calm down,' he said, taking her in his arms. 'The tide will be out again at dawn. . . .'

She tore herself from his arms with a heart-rending cry.

'No! It's impossible! . . . I can't spend the whole night here . . . with you. . . . Especially not with you! . . .'

And once again she rushed down to the water's edge and began to undo the fastenings on her dress. A moment later Colin was with her once more.

'What are you trying to do? Are you mad?'

'I shall swim if I have to. I don't care! I shall reach Gouldsboro naked but I shall not stay here. Let me go!'

'You must be mad!' he repeated. 'The current is very treacherous and you'll be drowned in the channels.'

'I don't care! I'd rather be drowned. . . . Let go of me, I say.'

'No, I will not let you go.'

She began to shout and struggle with him, but in vain. Colin hurt her horribly with his vice-like grip about her arms, but he would not let her go and she felt utterly powerless against his herculean strength. Then suddenly he whisked her off the ground like a wisp of straw and carried her up to the top of the beach where he continued to held her without yieding an inch until, with frayed nerves and exhausted body she collapsed sobbing on his chest.

'This is the end of me! . . . This is the end of me. . . . He will never forgive me.'

'Was it he who struck you?'

'No! No! It wasn't he! . . . Oh! Colin, it's terrible! . . . He found out! . . . He found out! . . . And now he doesn't love me any more! . . . Oh! Colin! . . . What will become of me? . . . This time he will kill me!'

'Now calm yourself.'

He rocked her gently back and forth, clasping her very

tightly to him in an attempt to arrest her uncontrollable trembling. When she began to grow a little calmer, Colin Paturel looked up at the first star to appear in the emerald-coloured sky.

An evening mist had come down, veiling the lights of Gouldsboro. They were really alone. Colin's eyes returned to the golden head buried in his shoulder.

'It's not as terrible as all that,' he said in his deep voice. 'For the moment we can do nothing but wait for daybreak. The tide is the tide! . . . After that we shall see. Now calm yourself, Madame de Peyrac.'

His solemn entreaty and sudden formality acted on Angélique like a jet of cold water. She grew quiet, still trembling like an animal at bay, but suddenly mindful of her dignity as a woman and as wife of Count Peyrac.

'Do you feel better now?' he asked.

'Yes, but . . . let go of me.'

'I shall let go of you when you have promised me that you will not rush down into the water, and that you will wait quietly until it is safe to cross. What do you say?'

He leant forward laying bare her face and looking at her with tender irony as if she were an unreasonable child that had to be persuaded.

'Is that a promise?'

Angélique nodded her assent.

He released her and she took a few hesitant steps before dropping down on the sand.

She was aching all over, in her arms, in the back of her neck and in her head. She felt as if her whole body was bruised and beaten. Yes, she would long remember this day and her homecoming to Gouldsboro! . . . A sudden spasm of cramp gripped her stomach.

'And I'm hungry as well!' she exclaimed angrily. 'That really is the limit!'

Without saying a word Colin went off and soon returned with an armful of dead wood, kindled a fire between three stones, and went off once again. A little later he reappeared holding a large lobster, which was waving its enormous claws indignantly.

'This customer will help to pass the time,' he announced.

Deftly he turned the lobster over and over on the red
349

embers until it went a handsome bright red. Then he broke open the burning-hot shell and proffered the best part to Angélique. The white, firm, delicately flavoured meat comforted her, and she began to take a less tragic view of the situation.

Colin watched her eat, fascinated by her movement, which he knew so well and which had always delighted him by their inimitable grace. How naïve he must have been when he had first met her not to have recognized immediately just by watching her eat, that she was a great lady! . . . The deft way she held the food, the easy grace with which she bit into it without any trace of vulgarity, were unmistakable pointers to the elegance which is learnt only at the table of kings. . . .

Angélique fed eagerly but her mind was so pre-occupied that she was unaware of Colin's gaze resting on her.

At Wapassou she had often imagined what a delightful moment it would be, once she got back to Gouldsboro, and had the children and her woman friends about her, to roast a lobster or a crayfish in the hollow of a rock. Never would she have imagined that it would be like this in the darkness of a diabolical nightmare. Wapassou had disappeared and seemed very remote. So did Father de Vernon, alias Jack Merwin, in whose inscrutable eyes she had suddenly seen a flash of warm feeling for her, and yet that was only yesterday! . . . It was only yesterday that the dreamy voice of the Jesuit had murmured: 'When the Devil's work is afoot, things go very fast. . . . Time stands still. . . . Everything occurs outside of time. . . .'

Three nights ago she was enjoying herself and dancing at Monhegan, and her conscience was at peace. Today she realized that she was in danger of losing for ever Joffrey's love, and perhaps her life.

'I'm afraid,' she said half aloud. 'These parts are full of evil spirits. I sense them prowling about, dogging our every footstep and planning our ruin.'

Sprawled on the other side of the fire, leaning on his elbow, Colin never took his eyes off her. She struck him as so pale in the firelight that he said not a word.

She got up to rinse her fingers at the water's edge, and

the gesture reminded her of the day's exhausting tasks from which she had just emerged into the silence of the evening, stunned and still weary in every limb.

The wanton, languid movement of the waves made her feel giddy, and she came back, shaking her skirt out about her.

'My clothes smell of blood, of gunpowder, of the sweat of those unfortunate men, of death. . . . How many a soul has left this earth today! . . . I can stand no more!'

She sat down again and realized that, without intending to, she had come closer to him.

'Tell me,' said Colin, 'what happened at Gouldsboro and in the bay? Something decidedly unpleasant, I'll wager. It was my ship they were after, wasn't it?'

'Yes indeed! And they got her. She is lying in the harbour now, half-filled with water. Half your men have been killed, and the others wounded or taken prisoner. . . . It's the end for you, Gold Beard! You won't be troubling honest men any more. . . . Where were you while it was all going on?'

She was astonished to hear her own words sounding so full of peevishness and violence, and to find herself longing to strike him in her turn.

Sitting there, all on edge, with her arms around her knees, she stared out towards Gouldsboro, so keen was her desire to be back there again.

The mist was not so thick as to cut out the glimmer of the fires that had been lighted on the outermost points of land and on the most prominent rocks. Pieces of resin would be kept burning all night in those carefully sheltered bonfires to warn ships of the location of dangerous reefs.

Occasionally, when the roaring of the surf died down a little, Angélique thought she could just make out a confused murmur of sound from the port, and several times she seemed to catch a gleam of light from houses or the lanterns of ships lying at anchor, thinner and fainter than the light of the beacons.

'What was happening over there? Had anyone noticed her disappearance? Were they searching for her? No matter what,' she told herself . . . 'I'm finished . . . finished!'

Colin remained silent, as if crushed by fate and the news she had just given him so abruptly.

Behind them the moon was rising, huge, shapeless and golden, the mist forming a halo around it. Its brilliance began to spread out, whitening the languid waves, the sand on the beach, and vying with the dying glow of the fire. An owl hooted. Then Angélique gave a start of mingled fear and hope, as she thought she glimpsed human shapes moving about among the rocks, and swimming in the swell. But it was only a small band of seals, which splashed about for a bit then disappeared out to sea again, no doubt scared to discover humans on the beach where they had chosen to rest. Their short, sharp yapping cries faded into the distance and died away nostalgically.

No one would come out to the Old Ship Island that night. Angélique would have to spend with Colin one more of those lonely nights remote from the world, which only fugitives, outcast lovers, the condemned and the hunted know, nights such as they had once shared in the desert. Nights full of sweetness, or fear, or the sense of a hostile surrounding world, that draws together fearsome hearts and trembling bodies.

Colin Paturel stirred.

'And so I've lost everything,' he said, as if speaking to himself. 'This is the second time . . . no, the third . . . possibly even the fourth. That's what life consists of for a gentleman of fortune and a poor sailor. Off you go . . . off you go across the blue seas. Far away, over there. You win once, twice. And then because you happen to pass a certain ship, or the wind changes direction, the whole of your life is wrecked, and you have to begin again. . . . Twelve years of captivity on the Barbary coast. . . . You escape, you make a new start, you rebuild your fortune. . . . Then once again there's nothing left . . . nothing but death to hope for . . . or what other kind of life? A beach to be alone on and that's all.'

Angélique, her heart moved by some obscure remorse listened to his monologue.

'And I have lost you too,' he went on, looking up at her with his keen blue eyes, which, in spite of herself, never failed to move her. 'Before, I always had you as a presence, a dream, a woman's face, a precious possession . . . but now all that has vanished.'

'Colin! Colin!' she cried, 'my dear friend, you are torturing me. Have I hurt you that much, I who loved you so? . . . Why these regrets? I am not worth it. You have idealized some memory or other which you now use to torment your heart quite pointlessly. I am only a woman like other women, who happens to have crossed your path as many other women cross a sailor's path . . . and I wonder what was so seductive about that miserable creature with the sunburned skin that I was then, with my dusty feet and emaciated body, dragging myself along over the stones, holding you back, encumbering you with my weakness. . . .'

'Don't try to destroy or to explain,' said Colin softly . . . 'your poor bleeding feet, your cracked lips, your tears that left trails of salt on your cheeks, your body, growing thinner and thinner every day, more and more fragile beneath its burnous, those are the things of which I have made a secret paradise. . . . And in any case, you cannot be expected to understand what kind of "charm" a woman like you can have in the eyes of a simple man without means of defending himself. All that your eyes and your smile promise, your body can fulfil only too well. That is what one will never get over. Because there isn't one woman in a thousand who . . . One might wander all over the face of the earth without ever finding her, without ever finding her again. After that, other women just don't count. After that, other women are hell!'

He spoke the last words with bitterness and was surprised to hear her laugh.

'That I just don't believe,' she said.

'What?' he exclaimed, straightening up, half angry.

'When you say that other women are hell, you are just dramatizing things in order to touch my heart but I don't believe you! You men are far too sensual not to take advantage of any agreeable opportunity even if you do carry an eternal love in your heart.'

'Oh! Do you think so?'

'You must understand that when we were together in the desert I regarded you as the master. You were the boss and . . . I was terrified of you. Later on you became the man who carried me, protected me, and made me happy . . .' her voice dropped a murmur—'very happy! Colin Paturel, you are to beg my pardon for what you said just now. Now is the time to fall on your knees.'

He had listened to her, fascinated. Then slowly he lifted his massive body from the ground, and knelt down before her.

'Forgive me,' he said, 'forgive me, Madame.'

He saw a maternal, indulgent smile on Angélique's lovely lips.

'You are foolish, Colin.'

Her tender woman's hand brushed his rugged forehead, while her slender fingers ran through his thick boyish hair. He caught the delicate hand in full flight and kissed the palm.

'How you do dominate me!' he whispered. 'I suppose it is because you are a great lady while I am nothing but a poor bumpkin.'

'No, you are a king, Colin.'

'No, I am a bumpkin.'

'All right then, you are the king of bumpkins, there!'

The two of them began to laugh gaily, and a moonbeam flashed on Angélique's teeth. They were so close together, linked by such a tender complicity, that the slightest movement would have brought their lips together.

Angélique knew that Colin's head was beginning to swim. And she withdrew her hand from his as if she had been burned, a gesture that stirred him to the very marrow.

This recoil of hers was a homage to him, for with it she had given him back a strength he had doubted for so many years.

Then he stood up and walked a few paces away. So he really did have the power, he, Colin, to stir that haughty, magnificent, regal body, and the happiness he had given her was not a tissue of lies. Of course, in Meknès he had shown a lack of prudence and discernment, in spite of the fact that his captive subjects willingly conceded that he 'had an eye for these things'. In spite of the Moorish veils that enveloped her when she was a prisoner in the harem, he should immediately have guessed from her bearing, from her slender wrists and ankles, her beautifully inflected voice, her well-chosen phrases with their occasional touches of boldness, from her delicacy, her patience . . . and her moments of impatience, the way she had of always striking exactly the right note with everyone, and from her courage too— the hereditary courage of noble families—he should have known he was dealing with a great lady and not with a country wench.

He had paid dear for his mistake.

What a terrible awakening, afterwards, in Ceuta! What a blow!

'Now, my good man, away with you! This woman appears to be none other than the Marquise du Plessis-Bellière! One of the most illustrious names in the Kingdom, my good man . . . widow of the Marshal of France . . . a very great lady . . . and, so it is whispered, she was . . . not long since, the favorite of His Majesty. . . . The King himself has sent for her. Leave her now. . . . Let us take her to the Governor's apartments. . . .'

And 'they' had snatched her from his arms . . . and 'they' had taken her away, inert, taken her from him— his own heart! His dear love! His beautiful creature, his desert sister, his adored child . . . and he had remained there, covered with sores, sweat and sand, motionless, stupefied, for hours, just as if 'they' had torn his heart from his living breast, torn his guts from his belly, leaving great, bleeding holes where they had once been. . . .

What a ghost to carry with him across the world, the ghost of such a woman!

Then he had found her again. She had not changed. She was still lovelier, still more of a woman. She still possessed that patrician grace that hid such courage and . . . such spirit.

Yesterday she had been Madame du Plessis-Bellière. Now she was the Countess Peyrac. Still on the move, still inaccessible. Away with you, my good man. And he remembered with an inexpressible rending of his heart how good she could be and how tender. And how gay . . . and how merry and caressing she was when he made love to her. She was the most natural woman in the

355

world, the most straightforward, closer to him than anyone he had ever held in his arms. . . .

But if it was true that she did not despise him, he
could find it in him to eclipse himself, to go away, still
possessor of the past, his treasure, and he would leave
her to the other man. Had she not begged him to help
her to keep her sacred oaths?

CHAPTER 62

'COLIN, HOW is it that you come to be on this island?
Who brought you here? And why were you not on board
your ship at the time of the battle?'

The sound of Angélique's voice drew him from his
reverie. Her voice was vibrant with emotion and he
worshipped the fact that she was trying to create a
diversion in order to ward off temptation.

He came and sat down beside her and filled in the
picture of the suspicious events that had happened to
him during the day. He was forced to admit that some
evil forces seemed to have conspired to confound them
and lure them into this trap.

That morning at dawn, while lying at anchor in one of
the little inlets of the isthmus of Schoodic, where he had
been hiding for some days with the intention, he freely
admitted, of mounting a new attack upon Gouldsboro, a
small boat had appeared with three sailors in it. They
claimed to bear a message from Madame de Peyrac who
had allegedly sent them across from Gouldsboro to ask
Captain Gold Beard to meet her, as she needed his help
in some matter. The whole thing was to remain a close
secret and he was not to take any of his men with him.

'Did these strangers not give you a written message—
or an alleged message—from me, or some object as a
token?' Angélique asked him in astonishment.

'No, actually they didn't. And it never occurred to me
to ask them for one. I admit that where you are concerned I forget my customary caution. I knew you were
close, in Gouldsboro and . . . I was longing to see you
again. So I left the ship in charge of my lieutenant, and

jumped down into their boat without any further explanation. The fog was so thick that I don't think I should ever recognize the island they took me to, where they claimed you had arranged to meet me. We began to wait and went on doing so for a long time. I thought that the fog must have delayed your arrival. Then, when towards the middle of the morning I heard the sound of gunfire, I began to get worried. I had a feeling that it was my ship that was under attack. I asked the men to take me back to it. They beat about the bush and delayed things until eventually I lost my temper. There was a fight. I am not at all sure that one of the men hasn't seen the last of this world, but I myself was dealt a blow that knocked me cold, and the back of my neck is still aching from it. When I came to I found myself on this island, stripped of my cutlass, my sword and my pistols. Night was falling. Then a little later, when I began to feel better, I began to explore the island and . . . came across you near the old wrecked ship.'

Colin had stood up and was pacing up and down as he talked. Finally Angélique got up too and joined him, and they walked slowly side by side up and down the little beach that shone like a bright jewel in the setting of the night-dark trees. Their two shadows stretched out across the sand, fantastically drawn out and black as ink.

'What did they look like, these men who came to fetch you?'

He gave a shrug.

'Just sailors, such as one might encounter here or in the Caribbean. More or less any nationality, and speaking more or less any language . . . and yet no, I don't think they were foreigners. They were almost certainly French.'

Angélique had been full of anguish as she listened to him. She found it hard to resist an oppressive feeling of certainty that they had been the victims of evil spirits, which were making sport of them in order to destroy them. Events had been so precipitated and had become embroiled with such malicious cunning, that she no longer knew which thread she should seize to begin to disentangle the skein.

'Colin, did you know who the man was you handed me

over to in Casco Bay? The English skipper of that boat?'

'The Jesuit?'

Angélique stared at him, stupefied.

'So you knew?' she exclaimed.

Colin halted and stared thoughtfully at the dark horizon.

'He appeared that morning,' he said. 'He moored his boat to the bollard and climbed on board. He spoke English so I took him for the skipper of some ship. He asked to speak to me and when we were in my cabin he revealed his true identity. He said he belonged to the Society of Jesus and had been sent on a secret mission; he asked me to hand over Madame de Peyrac to him. I had no reason to doubt him; he had an abrupt way of talking and looked at me with those penetrating, black eyes of his that could not possibly have been lying.

'Then I realized that this was my chance to enable you to leave, a helping hand God was holding out to me, and it was precisely because he was a Jesuit that I thought that it must be God's way of sending me a sign. Had it not been for him, had it not been for that Jesuit turning up like that, I . . . I think I would not have let you go. I had kept on saying to myself since the day before that I would have to give you up, but I could not. . . . It was worse than in Ceuta . . . almost worse. Had you remained on board, I think I should have tried to win you back again . . . and I would have been the cause of your undoing . . . so this way out seemed best. I said: "All right, I understand. Let it be as you wish." Then he told me not to tell you who he was, but to let you think that he was the skipper of the boat, and an Englishman. I felt somewhat uneasy about this, but I have always bowed to the will of priests. I reckon they are fighting on the side of Good and that they know what they are doing. But I felt uneasy about it. I could not help feeling that someone was seeking to harm you. . . .

'Did he do you any harm?'

She shook her head.

"No!' she murmured.

Now she understood what had gone on in the mind

of Jack Merwin, the Jesuit, as he stood on that rock watching her die.

At Maquoit Point, he had captured her in order to conduct her back to other people who wanted to see her cut off, isolated, brought into question, utterly destroyed. And then at Monhegan the cruel sea seemed to have taken upon itself the task of getting rid of her. Everything had been simplified. He must have thought 'This is God's will!' and he had folded his arms across his chest and refused to offer her a helping hand.

But it was one thing to say of a fellow human being: 'This person must die' and quite another to watch him as he struggles with death.

He had just not had the heart to watch her death agony to its bitter end and to see her disappear beneath the waves never to appear again.

He had dived.

'My backers in Paris and Caen belong to the Company of the Blessed Sacrament,' observed Colin. 'I have undertaken to serve the missionaries in the new countries where I was going to establish myself. But I did not think that it would be such a difficult matter. I had been assured that the Gouldsboro region was clear of English settlements.'

'We are not an English settlement,' said Angélique. 'This territory belongs to my husband by virtue of his being the first occupier and of having promoted its prosperity.'

'Why did you marry this lord of Gouldsboro?'

Angélique hardly had the heart to give him an answer. It was too long a story, and besides everything relating to the intimacy of her life with Joffrey was an extremely delicate topic for her. She was reluctant to put into words things that concerned them alone, Joffrey de Peyrac and Angélique de Sancé—their dreams, the drama of their early relations, their ordeals, their struggles and weakness, their final happiness, and all that established between them this intangible bond: their life in common, their own private ship which was ceaselessly imperilled and storm-tossed and on which for so long they had been interwined with one another in a way that made it impossible for anyone ever to separate them. No one, no, no one, she thought, gazing passionately up at the sky with its night clouds fringed with gold by the moon. And for the first time since the previous evening she suffered atrociously as if the blow she had received in her face had at last reached her heart, after a long period of wandering in the unconscious regions of hope. Joffrey! It was all over. . . . He despised her, he detested her, he no longer believed in her.

'Why did you marry him?' insisted Colin. 'What kind of a man must he be for a woman like you to want to link her existence to his and be willing to follow him even to these remote lands?'

'What does it matter?' she said dejectedly. 'He is my husband and he is more than anything in the world to me in spite of my latent weakness which sometimes betrays me.'

For a long time neither of them spoke.

'You know exactly the line to take with me,' said Colin Paturel at last with bitter irony. 'Respect for sacred vows! . . . That was what you hit upon and it was the one thing which could stop me. I have remained true to it in spite of my own weaknesses. . . . One does not shed one's blood for twelve years in order to remain faithful to one's God, without finally becoming more attached to Him than to anything that one might find admirable on this earth. Let Him make but a sign . . . "Stay, Colin! Thy Master has spoken."'

And he added almost below his breath, and with profound faith:

'And I know how to recognize Him when he makes a sign.'

Angélique, who was less simple than Colin and who had wandered on more diverse paths, was less willing to admit this intrusion of the divine into the logic—or the illogic—of her actions.

'Are we so strongly attached to the teachings of our childhood that we continue to let ourselves be governed in spite of ourselves, precisely, in fact, because it is in spite of ourselves?' she asked. 'Is it possible that we are merely frightened of things that we have learnt?'

'No,' said Colin, 'it is not only things that we have learnt which govern us. Fortunately! But there are times when man finds himself, whether he wishes it or not, in the fairway of truth. It would be as difficult to prevent him from following it as to prevent a star from passing across the sky.'

Noting an abstracted expression on Angélique's face, 'Are you listening?' he asked gently.

'Yes, I am listening to you, Colin Paturel. You are such an eloquent talker. How many things you have taught me which have remained engraved upon my heart. . . .'

'I am happy to hear it, Madame, but the words which I have said are, if I remember rightly, those I learned too from the Grand Eunuch, Osman Faraji, the tall dark fellow who guarded you in the harems of Mulai Ismail. Often at Meknès, the king would summon me and make me sit in my squalid rags on his gold-trimmed cushions. And together we listened to Osman Faraji. What a sage that Negro was! What a splendid fellow! He influenced my soul more strongly than any other being in the world. He was a seer.'

'How I liked him! How fond of him I was!' Angélique exclaimed, moved by a poignant nostalgia. 'He was a greater friend than any other.'

She broke off, moved to the depths of her heart, for from the limbo of memory came back to her the fact that it was Colin's hand that, in order to save her, had killed the noble eunuch with a stab in the back.

'Enough of all this,' said Colin softly, 'enough of all these hurtful memories. You are tired and we are now far, very far from those places and farther still on the road of our lives. If at least I could say that I had made progress, that I had advanced towards something in the course of the years which followed upon Ceuta. . . . It is not merely that I have fallen back, but rather that I have spoilt all that I had garnered up in the prison hulk of God.'

'One always progresses when one suffers and yet does not give in, does not succumb, does not turn one's back decisively on good,' and Angélique fervently.

Thinking of the long tunnel full of stumbles and recoveries that she herself had passed through when she was far from Joffrey's side, she felt she had earned the right to encourage Colin.

361

'You are not as sick as you were making out a moment ago, Colin, my dear, dear friend. I know it. I feel it. From moment to moment it seems to me that the old Colin is going to reappear before me, in his grandeur, laying aside the cheap frippery of Gold Beard, and I see him greater even than before, stronger, readier to fulfil the task that awaits him. . . .'

'What task? . . . unless it be have myself hanged high and dry like a common pirate.'

'No, not you, Colin! That will not be. Fear nothing, fear no more. I do not know how it is to be done, but I do know that God will be faithful to you, you will see. He cannot abandon you, you who were so cruelly crucified for Him. . . .'

'But he has abandoned me for so long.'

'No, no do not doubt any more, Colin, you who were such a firm believer—that is the very essence of your being. . . . It is not for nothing that He has placed in you so many invaluable qualities. You will see. . . . For my part I do not doubt you.'

'Oh you are adorable,' said he in muffled tones, and he took her in his arms.

Angélique trembled from the roots of her hair to the soles of her feet.

In her infinite longing to carry Colin, as a wave might have done, towards the shore on which he would at last rediscover himself, she had spoken with fire, lifting up towards him her face radiant with that wonderful look in which he could read the sentiment more precious to man than all the hazards of the Universe—the trust of a woman. A trust in him, in his strength, in his grandeur, in his power, in his transcendental destiny.

And now pressed up against him, in the magic circle of his embrace, she felt this wave of tenderness changing into a wild voluptuous current which she recognized with deep dismay. For Colin's arm in the hollow of her back, that steely arm too often unaware of its own strength, was welding her to him with irresistible passion, and from this contact there surged up once again a strong attraction to him, which was like a ground wave, a torrential, sweet and delicious longing.

Standing pressed close to him from head to foot, she

threw back her face in the moonlight, her eyes closed as if she were going to die. . . .

'Do not be afraid, my love' he said in his deep low voice, with a note of teasing in it which appealed so strongly to her heart and emotions, 'do not be afraid of me any more. This is the last time . . . I promise you, it is the last time that I will hold you thus pressed close to my heart. But I would still like an answer . . . did you cry, tell me . . . did you cry, Madame du Plessis-Bellière, when I parted from you at Ceuta, when I turned my back on you to leave you for ever?'

'Yes, you know very well that I did,' she breathed. 'You know it very well. You saw. . . .'

'I was not sure . . . for years I have wondered . . . those tears, those tears that I saw shining in the eyes of that great lady, were they real? . . . Were they for me? . . . Thank you, thank you, my love. . . .'

He pressed her closely to him then released her and pushed her gently away. He refused to see her half-open lips trembling, offered to him. He straightened up and stood to his full herculean height under the moonlit sky.

'Now I know what I wanted to know. I have received all the answers. And from your mouth! From your mouth! . . . I seem to be able to breathe more freely. Thank you, my dear one. You have restored to me what I had lost. Now go, go and rest. You are exhausted.'

And as she hesitated, he took her by the shoulders, pressing her against him with infinite tenderness and led her back to the fire that he had lit earlier on. She dropped rather than sat down on the sand. He stirred the flames a little, then went off to the other end of the beach, where he lay down, visible in the shadow of the trees, in order to rest a little at a distance from her.

Shortly before when she had been walking along the beach, a higher wave than the rest had lapped her ankles. Her shoes were damp. She kicked them off, drew her feet in under her skirt, and resumed her former somewhat chilly posture, her arms folded around her knees. The nearby fire did not warm her and she was still trembling. 'How weak my body is, when it comes to love!' she said to herself bitterly and ashamedly. 'I have been wrong to neglect prayer for so long. It gives the grace to resist such impulses.'

She was very angry with herself and despised herself somewhat. For one whole part of the night she had felt very reasonable, capable of holding at bay the temptation roused by the revival of her memories and the proximity of Colin, and then quite suddenly had come this hot, greedy wave! . . .

When things had reached that point, even if one stepped aside in time, there was an element of betrayal. A burning blush swept over her face and she hid it against her knees. How long the night was! 'Forgive me, Joffrey, forgive me, it is not my fault. It is because you are far away. . . . I am weak. You have cured me and revived me only too well, my wizard. Ah! how far off those days are when I could not suffer a man to even touch me without having convulsions. . . . It is your fault too. You have given me back my taste for kisses, for . . . everything. . . . Today I am weak!'

She was talking to him in a low voice, in order to banish fear. And it was to the lover, to the adorable and adored husband that she spoke, to the man who had pressed her tight to his heart in the great bed at Wapassou, through all the length of the winter, and she held this image before her in order to forget the terrifying man who the evening before had seized her by the hair and struck her so harshly.

'If he finds out . . . if he finds out about this senseless meeting, on this island all night long . . . all night long with this pirate who for him is nothing more than Gold Beard, he will kill me. I shall never escape . . . that is certain. He will kill me before I have had time to open my mouth. . . . And that I would be incapable of ever doing, just as I was last night. . . . Oh God! How helpless and frightened one is when one loves too much. . . . Help me, God, help me . . . help us. I am frightened and I do not understand any more what is happening. I do not know what to do any more. . . .'

In spite of her present distress she was unable to regret entirely the chance which had brought Colin and her together again that night, alone on the little island of the old ship. Since she had seen him stand up as he said

364

'Thank you, my dear one, you have restored to me what I had lost,' she had felt a sensation of relief, a lightening of her conscience, she was going through a period when it is a duty to rid onself of the burdens of the past. Thanks to God if, before one finally forgets, one is given the chance to make good the omissions of the past.

In the fullness of the gifts which had made her a woman, she was reaching that extraordinary age at which for each and every woman, life, while continuing its headlong course, seems to grow lighter, to grow purer, and to be renewed in the apotheosis of a liberty of mind and soul, which has been hard won but is all the more precious for that, when the weight of the mistakes which were often no more than the apprenticeship to the harsh trade of living, becomes less irksome. It is permissible to leave behind along the way the burdens of the past, to forget what can be forgotten, to remember only the richness of that imperfect and difficult adventure of the full time of life.

She realized that she had for a long time borne within her unconscious remorse about Colin, her desert lover.

Now he was safe.

The one thing which he would never know was that she had carried a child of his in her womb. The too intimate bonds between them must be dissolved. How difficult it was for human beings to help one another!

A spark of humour flashed in her numbed mind—she knew well the ways of that droll bird, ever ready to take flight within her in her darkest hours—and the idea occurred to her that she would like to be an old lady. Old age enables one to help one's neighbour, one's friends, without complicating their life or one's own.

It makes it possible to follow the impulses of one's heart in all their sincerity, and to give unselfish and effective help to one's fellows. It gives one the right to live frankly, in the company of one's own heart, such as it is, without becoming involved in the perpetual conflict of caution, retreat, advance and retreat, which the seductions of the flesh impose upon emotional life.

'How good it will be to be old one day!' Angélique told herself, and began to smile, then to laugh to herself. She was shivering, and her feet were frozen and her forehead hot. The sound of approaching footsteps, crushing the sand and breaking the gentle silky rustling of the waves, put her on the alert. Colin was returning.

'You must sleep, my little one,' he said softly stooping over her. 'There is no sense in staying curled up like that, mulling over your thoughts. Lie down and you'll feel better. It will soon be day. . . .'

She did as he bade her, putting herself in his hands as she used to do, experiencing once again the firm patience of his hands as he tucked her up carefully in her cloak and placed his own buffalo-hide jerkin over her feet.

She closed her eyes. To her aching body, the passionate adoration that emanated from Colin was like a balm, something to appease her heart, worn down with anxiety and grief, and which now, as it began to emerge from its state of shock, was becoming increasingly aware of its own pain.

'Go to sleep now,' Colin whispered, 'come now, you must sleep.'

And as she let herself slip into the black water of sleep, she thought she heard a voice murmuring through the solitude of those nights in the Magreb. . . .

'Go to sleep, my lamb, go to sleep. Tomorrow we have a long way to go, both of us, across the desert.'

Perhaps he really was murmuring those words.

CHAPTER 63

AND COLIN was there once again, silhouetted against the brilliant dawn sky as he shook her gently.

'The tide is going out.'

Angélique raised herself on one elbow, brushing back her hair from her face.

'There is still a thick mist,' said Colin. 'If you hurry you can get across the bay without being seen.'

Angélique was on her feet in a flash, shaking the sand from her clothes.

It was indeed a favourable moment to cross. The haze hung over the bay some distance from the shore, one of those light mists full of brightness, that nevertheless formed a protective screen between the island and Gouldsboro. The wind had not yet begun to blow; it was the hour of calm in which the cooing of the turtle doves mingled so sweetly with the silence that it seemed to make it even more profound and overwhelming. The seagulls, tiny alabaster figures poised on the brown tips of exposed rocks, were of the general immobility of dawn, and when they did move it was only to glide slowly and silently, flashes of white through the pink and gold mist.

A strong smell of kelp filled the warm morning air, an indication of the vast stretches of mud and seaweed uncovered by the outgoing tide.

Angélique began to hope that she might manage to reach Gouldsboro without attracting attention and that by some miraculous set of circumstances her absence might have gone unnoticed. For, in fact, who would be concerned whether she had spent the night in her room or not? Apart from her husband . . . who, in view of their cool relations since the previous day, had probably not bothered to enquire. With a bit of luck, her chance escapade might well have gone unnoticed.

She hastened down to the beach, with Colin close behind, watching her as she tested the first stones of the ford with her foot.

'And what about you? What is to become of you?' she asked suddenly.

'Oh, me! . . .'

He pointed in a vague general direction.

'I shall try to find the men who stole my knives and pistols, and then I shall try . . . to get away. . . .'

'But what then?' she cried. 'Colin, you are all alone! You have nothing left!'

'Don't worry about me,' he said sarcastically. 'I am no babe in arms. I am Gold Beard . . . don't forget that.'

She remained undecided, one foot poised, unable to make up her mind to leave him.

She sensed the terrible state of abandonment in which Colin found himself. He no longer even had any weapons. She could see him standing on the shore of some desert isle, a giant with empty hands, and, once the fog

367

was dispersed, nothing better than a hunted animal, a ready target for the sharp eyes of his enemies, who would hunt him down among the islands.

'Go on, go on!' he said impatiently. 'Go on.'

She thought: 'I must go and find Joffrey . . . I must tell him everything . . . so that at least he will give Colin a chance to escape, to get away from Frenchman Bay. . . .'

Then one last time she turned towards him so that she could carry away in her mind's eye a picture of him with his Viking's head and his two eyes as blue as small pieces of sky.

It was the sudden horror he saw in Angélique's eyes that warned him of the approaching danger.

He swung round, turning to face it in a single leap, his hands powerfully out-thrust, ready to grasp, to strangle, to strike, to kill.

A man in black armour leapt upon him, then four more, six, ten. They seemed to come from everywhere, as they leapt from the cover of the little wood behind the rocks.

Angélique recognized Joffrey de Peyrac's Spaniards as if in a nightmare, as if they had been devils hiding their ferocious features beneath a familiar face.

They had moved forward and crept up on him without disturbing the silence by a single sound, by the slightest crunch on the sand.

Even at the moment when she had seen them bearing down upon Colin, she had not understood. It had been like a crazy vision, a figment of her frightened imagination.

She had forgotten that these men, chosen by Peyrac, had once fought in the Peruvian jungle, had been trained to act with all the cunning of serpents, to move like cats, to be as cruel as the Indians, and that Moorish blood ran in their veins.

Pedro, Juan, Francisco, Luis . . . she knew them all but at that moment she could not recognize them. They had become the incarnation of an evil, wild force, in hot pursuit of Colin, while in their efforts to overcome him their teeth gnashed and glistened, ridiculously white in their tanned faces.

Colin fought like a lion attacked by a pack of black Salúkis. He fought them bare-handed, cutting himself on the crest of a steel helmet, and wrenched himself away from them so furiously that on several occasions he managed to drag along and hurl to the ground the men who were clinging to his clothes.

His knees finally gave way beneath their weight. His shoulders were seized from behind and he was tipped over backwards. Someone raised a pike over him.

Angélique cried: 'Do not kill him!'

'Do not fear, Señora,' came the voice of Don Alvarez. 'We only want to stun him. Our orders are to take him alive.'

The dark eyes of Don Juan Alvarez, haughty and heavy with solemn reprobation, fixed upon Angélique. His long ascetic face, still a little yellow, was framed as usual by a ruff, quilled in the old-fashioned way.

'Would you be so good as to take a seat, Señora,' said he in formal but commanding tones.

She realized that if she refused, he would not hesitate to use force. He was responsible to Count de Peyrac, and, having lived several months in the compulsory intimacy of Fort Wapassou with them, she knew that for Don Juan and his men the orders of the Count were sacred.

A nameless terror opened a dark hole within her and as yet it was only fear realizing the precise meaning of what had happened.

In the eyes of Don Juan Alvarez, she read her condemnation. To him, this woman that he had honoured as the wife of the Count de Peyrac had been found in the arms of a lover. It was the collapse of everything that mattered. There was sorrow written on the proud features of the old Spaniard.

Angélique glanced towards the woods from which they had emerged, as dark as night in their black steel breast-plates, their lances pointed towards Colin's back, and she was quite prepared to see him appear, 'him,' the master, the man who had given orders for Gold Beard to be seized and for her to be brought back as a captive, an accomplice of the pirate, a contemptible woman. But the sinister masses of leaves remained closed, stirred only by the breath of the wind.

Then she clutched at the hope that 'he' did not yet know, that it was mere chance which had brought the Spanish guards to the island. Was it not the case that the archipelago had been combed since the previous day in order to find Gold Beard? . . .

'You must follow me, Señora,' repeated the commander of the guards.

He laid his hand on her arm.

She shook herself free and passed in front of him. It would be useless to attempt to justify herself in the eyes of a man like Alvarez. As far as he was concerned she was guilty and she would remain. And she fully deserved the penalty of death.

Wapassou was far away—the place which had bound them together in calm friendship, when they were all in the cold grip of winter.

A succession of uncontrollable and fiendish events seemed to have cast them into an eddy in which self-respect, mutual respect and gladness had all gone under.

There was blood flowing from Colin's forehead.

He had drawn himself erect and, closely surrounded by his guard, he was saying nothing and making no further attempt to defend himself. His wrists and his forearms had been drawn behind him and were tightly bound, and his ankles had been put in shackles. A short length of cord between them allowed him to hobble along slowly.

Turning their backs on the distant prospect of Gouldsboro, whose wooden houses and pink cliffs were beginning to emerge in the light of the morning, the small company escorting Angélique and the prisoner passed across the island close by the hulk of the stranded ship. On the other side the rocks were steeper. Two small boats were waiting in a small cove. Low tide had left a channel giving access to the open sea.

Inviting Angélique to take her place in one of the boats, Don Alvarez held out his gloved hand to assist her. She disdained to take it.

He sat down beside her. She noticed that he was even more yellow than usual and that his spasmodic tic, the ferocious expression which made him suddenly bare his teeth, one of his permanent features since his torture by Atakap Indians, was troubling him particularly. It was the first time that she had noticed grey threads in his old-style Spanish beard. The truth was that during the last two days Don Juan Alvarez had aged ten years. Angélique's gaze met his in passing and what she saw moved her deeply.

Divided in mind between his loyalty to Count Peyrac and the loyalty which in his own despite the noble Countess had inspired in him in memory of the harsh winter which she had so heroically shared with them, the noble Spaniard was suffering the torments of the damned.

He took up his stance before her as a solemn guardian and custodian of the law. Sailors and mercenaries who were waiting on the beach took their places on board and pushed the boat out into the current. Another craft took on board the rest of the detachment.

Angélique found herself thinking, 'I'm going to die; when he finds out he will kill me.'

It was perhaps a childish notion but she could not shake her mind free from this persuasion. It was as if her brain were paralysed. The fatigues of a trying day caring for the wounded and a too short night had destroyed her defences and made her incapable of resisting anxiety. She felt ill and in actual fact she was ill.

She was pale to the lips and shivering in spite of the rising warmth of a summer day, but she tried to put on a good countenance. The hostility of those about her was tangible, like a kind of leaden cloak weighing down upon her.

'But I use to carry round warming drinks to all these men,' she thought somewhat resentfully.

But now she was a woman who had dishonoured her husband, and in the eyes of these males, fanatically attached to a punctilious code of jealousy, she deserved death. It was a senseless act but in this harsh, savage, virgin land everything appeared possible and as if dictated by the intransigence of nature herself. Anger, fury, jealousy, hate and the gestures of death were woven into the very fabric, sensitive and subtle as it was, of this splendid summer morning, and glowed like burning coals of fire in human hearts.

In the rising wind of the open sea blowing into her face, she felt the same breath fanning the passions of the human creature forced back on his own strength. With a kind of painful intuition she sensed their solitude as men and women, without nation and without laws, set down in the midst of an untamed nature and the way in which, in spite of themselves, as day after slow day passed by, the wildness of this continent penetrated to the depths of their being. In such circumstances a single man, a leader meant everything. And on him and on his actions and his feelings depended life and death. Such is the law which has governed tribes and peoples since man has wandered over the face of the earth. What she had felt of Joffrey's secret strength, even in his gentleness and tenderness, was today leaving her almost without hope, in proportion as they drew nearer to the goal, more and more profoundly shocked and terrified.

But where were they going? The boats had veered towards the east, hugging the coast. The point of a peninsula was at a few cables' distance, and then they had rounded the cape and come almost immediately upon a rock-sheltered beach at the nearest point of which could be seen a number of armed men. It was a hidden place, remote from Gouldsboro and from any houses.

As they drew nearer to the group, she made out Joffrey de Peyrac's tall form with his wide cloak billowing in the wind.

'He will kill me,' she kept on telling herself, petrified but in a way resigned. 'Without even giving me time to open my mouth. He could never have loved me, after all, since he cannot understand. Oh, how pleased I would be to be killed. . . . If he does not love me what is the point of living?'

The lassitude which possessed her was largely responsible for the disjointed thoughts which flashed through her mind.

'And what about Cantor? What will Cantor say? My son should not be involved in all this!'

The boats reached the shore. The surf was fairly violent and this time Angélique was obliged to accept the helping hand which Don Juan Alvarez held out to her in order to get ashore. In any case she would have been glad to accept it for her legs were scarcely capable of supporting her. She found herself at Colin's side, both of them closely surrounded by Spanish soldiers, while the sailors were busy making the boats fast.

Stepping out from the distant group Count Peyrac came towards them. Angélique would never have believed that the sight of her husband could cause her so much apprehensiveness, especially after those long months of love and comradeship which they had spent together in Fort Wapassou—still so close in time. . . . But . . . but all that was gone with the wind of the shores and it was no longer the man that she loved who was advancing towards her. It was the master of Gouldsboro, of Katarunk, of Wapassou and sundry other places, a leader and at the same time a husband that his wife had flouted in the sight of his men and one might even say of his people.

'Is it he?' said Colin in a muffled voice.

'Yes,' murmured Angélique with a dry throat.

Count Peyrac was in no hurry. He was advancing with an off-handed haughtiness which in the circumstances was an insult and underlined the contempt but also the threat in his bearing. It would have been better if he had come forward mad with rage, as he had been on that recent evening. Angélique would have preferred such a paroxysm to this horrible waiting, this approach like that of a wild beast gathering itself to spring.

She was overcome once again by a panic which emptied her mind of all thoughts as she came face to face with him, just as it had done over and over again since Colin's fate had been at stake. It was partly a sense of guilt towards her husband, partly a desire not to lose him and partly loyalty towards Colin, but it paralysed her and deprived her through excessive fear of her best capacities—including the gift of speech, and of movement. Instead of running towards him, she remained rooted to the ground, struck dumb. Nevertheless, her eyes took in almost unconsciously every detail of Peyrac's dress, which was clearly a ridiculous thing to do in such a moment, and could be of no assistance to her in resolving the inextricable dilemma in which they all found themselves.

It was a green velvet costume. She had seen him wearing it on board the *Gouldsboro* the year before; it was one of those dark, sumptuous colours he liked to wear, whose subtle shades were heightened by a trifle of Flanders lace at the collar and revers, the points of which, embroidered with silver thread, covered his shoulders. The same lace picked out in silver formed the cuffs of the jacket, and adorned the tops of his knee-boots of fine English leather. A short-haired black beaverskin hat with a cluster of white feathers tossing in the wind, covered his thick hair. He was not carrying weapons in his belt that day, but had slipped his two silver-handled pistols into slots on his silver-embroidered cross-belt which ran across his doublet from shoulder to hip and held his sword. He came to a halt a few paces from them.

Angélique made a slight movement, she knew not to what end. Colin growled:

'No, don't get in front of me, I won't have it.'

The Spaniards clung to him, restraining him with considerable difficulty.

Motionless, Count Peyrac continued to scrutinize him from a distance with great concentration.

With his head held slightly on one side, the lord of Gouldsboro stared intently at the Norman filibuster, and Angélique, unable to take her eyes off her husband, saw his eyes grow dim. Then a sardonic smile twisted his scarred cheek on which the old gashes seemed even more prominent that morning, as if Peyrac's inner tension had made them whiter.

With his left hand he doffed his hat and advanced towards the prisoner. On reaching him, Joffrey de Peyrac raised his hand to his brow then to his heart in an oriental greeting.

'Salaam aleikom,' he said.

'Aleikom salaam,' Colin replied automatically.

'Greetings to you, Colin Paturel, King of the Slaves of Meknès,' Joffrey de Peyrac went on in Arabic.

Colin, taken aback, scanned his face closely.

'I recognize you too,' he said finally in the same tongue.

'You are Rescator, Mulai Ismail's friend. I often used to see you sitting at his side on embroidered cushions.'

'And I often saw you chained to the gallows in the market square, with vultures for company. . . .'

'And I am still in chains,' Colin said simply.

'And in all likelihood soon to be hanged from some gallows,' the Count replied with the same icy smile that made Angélique tremble.

She still remembered her Arabic and had been able to follow the gist of this extraordinary conversation.

Almost as tall as Colin, Joffrey nevertheless seemed, from the lordly way he bore his slender body, to dominate his massive adversary. They were two utterly different types, from two entirely different backgrounds. Finding themselves face to face like this was nothing short of terrifying. And a long, heavy silence ensued as the Count appeared to think.

He had shown no sign of violence, even restrained violence, and his eyes had not even flashed menacingly. But Angélique felt that she no longer existed for him. Or, if she did exist, it was a mere object, a nuisance whose presence he wanted at all costs to ignore. Whether it was detachment or scorn, she knew not, and she found the situation inconceivable, unbearable. She would have preferred him to kill her, to strike her. But this was worse. By this attitude he was forcing her, in spite of herself, into the position of the woman she did not want to appear to be, the woman *she was not*, an adulteress, a dishonoured wife, cast out from her husband's heart as she stood beside her 'guilty lover' awaiting a verdict. But even that was gradually becoming a matter of indifference to her. She felt indifferent to those who surrounded them, indifferent to the background in her desperation for a single glance from him, some sign from him, no matter what it was.

Now that he knew who Gold Beard was, would he understand a little . . . her weakness? . . . She wished she had the courage to open her mouth and say: 'Let us have it out. . . .' But the presence of the soldiers and sailors cast a chill upon her, as did that of all the gentlemen gathered around them in a silent circle, concealing their curiosity beneath a mask of indifference, and stiff formality—Gilles Vanereick, the Flemish corsair, Roland d'Urville, another Frenchman whom she did not know, and even the English admiral, very finely turned out, and his second-in-command, still more beribboned.

Why had Joffrey brought them all here to this tragic encounter, in which his honour as a husband risked being so sorely tried?

But above all she felt fear. Fear inspired by this stranger who was yet so close, Joffrey de Peyrac, the Magician, the Man of Mystery, her husband! . . . People are afraid when they love too much. They lose their self-confidence.

She felt sure that he would not throw a single glance.

So distressed was she that she did not see that there was someone who looked at her—Colin. Glancing surreptitiously at her, he noticed her expression of anguish, the pallor of that beautiful face disfigured by the great blue bruise, and what he read in Angélique's eyes—her feelings for the man who had struck her—made him bow his head, heartbroken.

He had glimpsed the truth of the situation.

It was that man standing there, and he alone, that she loved. That man Rescator he had seen at Meknès, as he entered the city accompanied by his splendid escort. Another renegade whose presence was an insult to the wretchedness of the slaves. Gold and silver gave him unequalled prestige and Mulai Ismail had loaded him with honours.

And now he was the man Angélique loved. It was he who possessed her heart. It was that dark nobleman, as slender and vigorous as a Moor or a Spaniard who possessed her, that ugly man with the alarming features marked by the sabre slashes of duels, yet handsome with the radiance of his spirit shining from his sparkling eyes. It was this great nobleman with the full weight of his heritage and grandeur behind him who possessed her.

And he did possess her . . . to the marrow of her bones, to the innermost corner of her being . . . to her very heart. It was obvious. He only had to look at her . . . to see that devouring expression, that childish confusion he had never seen in her before, courageous creature that she was. . . . But when a woman's heart has been reached, she has neither shame nor pride, nor anything else left. She becomes a child again. He understood.

He, Colin—Colin the Norman, Colin the captive—he was nothing to her, in spite of the womanly weakness she had once shown towards him. He need not deceive himself about that.

Face to face with that man there, in her eyes he was nothing. And what did it matter anyway? He was going to die. This deserted place, this lost corner of the American continent, this would be the end of his journey!

And his generous heart longed to do something more for her, for Angélique, his sister in captivity, who had been the only light—warm, heavenly, dazzling—in all his hard existence.

This at least he owed to her. And he would do it since this was the only thing which mattered to her.

'My lord,' he said, raising his head proudly and looking straight into Peyrac's impenetrable eyes, 'my lord, today I find myself in your hands, and after all, it is according to the fortunes of war. I am Gold Beard, and I had chosen this place for my raid. I had my reasons and you had yours for stopping me. Let the most skilful and the swiftest man win, I say. I lost! . . . I defer to you—you must do with me as you will. . . . But before you begin the process of trial and conviction, I want everything to be made clear, so that if you hang me it should only be because I am a pirate and one of your enemies, a bandit on the high seas to your way of thinking, a filibuster whose trade is an obstacle to yours, a man who has lost this particular game, but . . . NOT FOR ANYTHING ELSE, my lord! There is nothing else, that I swear.

'Just memories, nothing more. You must know this, since you recognize me. People remain friends when they have shared captivity on the Barbary Coast . . . and when they have made their way together back to Christian lands. Those are things that can never be forgotten . . . between those whom the hazards of life have brought together again. You must understand this. But each man has his destiny. And I can swear to you under oath, my lord, that it was neither my doing nor hers,' he nodded towards Angélique—'that the unfortunate occurrence of last night happened. The tide is not to be

377

treated lightly in these parts, as you know as well as I; and if you are surrounded on an island, there is nothing for it but to be patient and wait.

'But once again I give you my word as a seafaring man, before your men here and before these gentlemen who are listening to me, that nothing happened during the course of this night which could possibly damage the reputation of your wife, Countess Peyrac, nothing which could stain your honour as a husband.'

'I know that,' Peyrac replied in his hoarse monotone, 'I know that. I was on the island.'

CHAPTER 64

THIS TIME Angélique was seized with rage, that shook her like a tempest, and there were moments when she told herself that she hated Joffrey de Peyrac with all her heart and soul.

The blow had struck her full in the heart, dragging her out of her anguished stupor as, with an ironical grimace, he had murmured: 'I know, I was on the island!'

Then turning away, he had given the signal for all to set off back to Gouldsboro.

He had refused to see the expression of horror on Angélique's face, an expression she had been unable altogether to repress on hearing his revelation, and as they all moved off in a heavy silence, along the rough track at the edge of the sea, he strode on, his head held high in his customary manner, his full cape flapping in the wind, with never a glance back at the prisoner who was being pushed along by the Spanish soldiers, nor at the young woman who walked alone, wrapped in her own thoughts, and occasionally stumbling, without noticing it, on the rough ground.

Had he looked into her green eyes, he would have seen nothing but a woman's exasperated rage. It dominated all else, this rage that sprang from her burning humiliation, from a sense of shame whose origin she had not analysed.

In her agitation, she did not realize that above all she

was wounded in the privacy of her feelings. Her friendship for Colin, her tenderness for Colin, these he had seen. He had seen her lay her hands on Colin's forehead, and laugh at him, and to that he had no right. That was hers alone, it was her secret garden. A husband, however dear he may be, has no right to see everything, to know everything. Besides, he was no longer a beloved husband to her, but an enemy.

In her sudden introspective state she rediscovered the age-old image—man, the essential enemy of woman—more profoundly hated still because deceptive and disappointing.

Then a surge of anger and bitterness helped her to regain her footing and to go forward with her head held high.

That he should have insulted her, that he should have struck her, she could accept, and she bowed before the violence of righteous anger. But the horror of this Machiavelian deceit discredited him in her eyes, in proportion to the utter confidence and boundless esteem in which she had held him. Everything was ruined! Everything! He had played with his wife's heart, with her senses whose fragility he well knew, and he had driven her into the arms of another man . . . in order to see! . . . In order to see! . . . To amuse himself! Unless it was that in his jealous fury and his wounded pride he had sought, in launching her into a new temptation, a pretext for killing her . . . KILLING HER! . . . Her! His wife! Who had believed she had a privileged position in his life and in his heart! . . . Bitter sobs welled up in Angélique's throat. With a superhuman effort she succeeded in shaking them back and in controlling the flood of tears which was rising to her eyes. She tilted her chin defiantly.

Such was her inner turmoil that she did not wonder what was going to happen. Would he lock her up, have her guarded in the fort? Would he drive her away! Would he exile her? In any case she would not allow herself to be bullied and would know how to plead her case this time. On the other hand, Colin's fate appeared to her inevitably tragic, and when, as they reached the outskirts of the establishment, a babel of shouts and cries went up from the woods like the blast of a gale, her own feelings faded into the background leaving only a sense of acute fear for Colin's life. She summoned up her strength, ready to defend him by word and deed against all and without concern for herself; for this could not be, she would never tolerate this shocking thing, to see Colin hanged, butchered, to see Colin Paturel's life destroyed because of her.

She would throw herself down on his body, she would defend him like one of her children. Had he not carried her on his back in the desert? . . .

The shouting from the woods was that of a mob ready to kill.

Warned by the invisible messenger which is said to pass on the wings of the wind in savage climes, the entire population of Gouldsboro, swollen by foreign sailors, Acadians in transit, and Indians who had come to barter, was racing to meet them, tumbling down the slopes, crossing the spaces laid bare by the retreating tide, and the white bonnets of the women mingled like a flock of seagulls with the dark, motley, surging mass of the men. The people of La Rochelle and the sailors from the ships had been joined by English refugees, and by Indians, always in search of excitement and diversion and quick to take up the cudels on behalf of their friends.

'Gold Beard! Captured! . . .'

And 'she' was with him. That too was already known. She had spent the night with him, on Old Ship Island. 'They' were being brought back in chains.

Cries, howls and insults created an immense uproar which came to meet them as they advanced, and when the crowd, wildly excited, emerged from the forest and the beaches, the Spanish soldiers were obliged to form a barrier, with levelled pikes, in order to prevent the prisoner being overwhelmed and falling a victim to the frenzy of the mob.

'Kill him! Kill him!' they howled. 'There you are, Gold Beard! Bandit! Pagan! . . . You wanted our property, now you are in chains! Where are your emeralds? And your ship? . . . It's our turn now! Ha! Ha! Your golden beard will not save you. It will serve to hang you as a punishment for all your plundering raids!'

In the swirling mass of seamen and settlers, all seething with anger and united in a common execration of the enemy who had come within an ace of ruining them when he had laid siege to the little community, just emerging from the rigors of the winter. This man was today nothing more than a colossus finally vanquished, after the violent skirmish of the previous day, which had resulted in the death of several of their people. In their cries of hate, their need to heap insults upon his head, there was a blend of triumph, relief, and a kind of regret. Their victory was too dearly bought. Their wild hearts were somehow touched.

At Gold Beard's side was the Lady of Gouldsboro, the Lady of the Silver Lake, the Fairy with the healing hands. So it was true what they said about her and the pirate! How dreadful it was to find that the allegations were confirmed!

This low-born plunderer had destroyed what had been for them a precious source of strength in their grim exile—the respect which they had come to pay, in spite of themselves, to two superior beings—the Count and the Countess of Peyrac.

In the tumult of execration and hostility surrounding them, Angélique missed the only look which Joffrey had deigned to cast upon her that morning.

If she had seen it, perhaps the pain which was tormenting her would have been somewhat eased. For the glance was to make sure that she was protected by the Spanish lances.

'Ungodly man! Woman-stealer! Gallows-bird!'

The boos and sarcastic cries kept bursting out in volleys. Colin, his hands bound, shoved, pushed and battered, kept on advancing as well as he could in the midst of the soldiers.

The wind ruffled his long hair and his tangled beard. With his clouded brown and his bristling eyebrows and his eyes fixed in the distance above the bobbing heads of the mob, he was like Prometheus, son of the Titan, bound powerlessly to his rock and abandoned to the vultures.

On entering the village the group was obliged to halt once more by the thrust of the crowd which neither d'Urville's injunctions nor Vanereick's threats nor the forbidding aspect of the Spanish guard could control.

A stone whistled through the air and struck Colin on the temple. Another rolled at Angélique's feet and from somewhere another cry went up: 'She-Devil!'

The anathema hung in the clear morning air. And suddenly, as if terrified by its own violence, the mob fell silent.

They were then able to hear the Count's voice, whose calm manner and hand raised as a sign of peace did not fail to act upon their over-excited nerves.

'Order!' came his voice, which was hoarse but calm, solemn and firm. 'Your enemy, Gold Beard, has been captured! Leave him now, leave him to my justice!'

With bowed and submissive heads the crowd withdrew. The fort was near. Angélique heard orders being given for the captive to be taken to the guard-room and locked up under double vigilance.

Before the palisade gate there opened for her the refuge of the apartment in the keep. But the stopped and suddenly turned round to face the close-packed, scowling crowd, which was watching her. In the front ranks there were the Protestants from La Rochelle.

Angélique realized that, if she adopted the attitude of a guilty woman and buried her fears in the apartment in the fort, she would never be able to come out again without risk of being stoned by the mob. She knew the uncompromising character of the people of La Rochelle, the superstitious impulsiveness of the seamen, which was exceeded only by that of the English. Once she and her husband became the butts of malicious gossip, each of these groups of people, in accordance with its own particular beliefs, would arm itself with holy water or muskets as the case might be, just as the people of La Rochelle had done during the mutiny which had taken place on board ship during the crossing from Europe. The only way to quell these over-sensitive consciences was to assert oneself, to discourage gossip by showing that one's own conscience was clear, and since there was no hiding away this face of a woman taken in adultery with which she was credited, to have the boldness to display it to all and sundry with its pallor, the rings around the eyes, and the ignominious marks of the blows she had suffered during her conflict with her husband.

She shook off the hand—perhaps that of Don Alvarez —seeking to guide her in the direction of the interior of the building. She would not passively accept being put on trial or being held a prisoner and, if that was what they wanted, force would have to be used and it would be clearly seen whether Joffrey was prepared to add this new indignity to all those he had already inflicted upon her.

Adulterous woman! So be it! Well then, how should an adulterous woman behave in order to avert the flood of calumnies and preserve her own dignity and that of her husband, to save what could be saved? Surely by facing the music, by acting as if nothing had happened, as if nothing were known, 'just like before'.

'I would like to examine the men wounded yesterday,' she said in a loud voice and as calmly as usual, to the woman standing close to her. 'Where were the men from the *Fearless* put?'

The woman turned away roughly, but Angélique marched boldly on through Gouldsboro, as one might walk on water, her mind firmly made up to show what she was and what she intended to remain in the eyes of all.

On a sign from the Count, two of the Spanish guards fell into step behind her. To that too she was indifferent. She would assert herself, and gossip would die away at her approach for lack of fuel to maintain it. Angélique was determined that the youthful mind and heart of her Cantor should not be disturbed either.

All these things were going round in her head, which felt strangely empty as a result of hunger and fatigue, but she would not rest until she had regained control of Gouldsboro, and she went tirelessly from one wounded man to another. The majority of the complement of the *Fearless* had gone back on board their ship, which was anchored in the roadstead, but the most seriouly wounded and the sailors from the *Gouldsboro* were being nursed in private houses. Angélique went into the houses, called for water, cloths, salves and assistance, and the people of La Rochelle, both men and women, found themselves assisting her in spite of their feelings.

The wounded greeted her with impatience and hope and she felt calmer as she handled the dressings wet with blood and pus. These gaping wounds in the healing of which she saw the reflection of her own power gave her back her sense of dignity.

All this unshaven and sick humanity was in fact less receptive to the rumours circulating at the expense of the beautiful noble lady, whom they had met in the wild antipodes of the Americas on a day of battle, than they were to the relief they felt at her coming and because of her presence.

'Madame, will you be able to save my eye?' . . . 'Madame, I couldn't sleep all night because of the gnats and mosquitoes. . . .'

The wounded pirates from the *Heart of Mary* had been put with the able-bodied prisoners in the corn barn, surrounded by a cordon of heavily armed sentries. Furthermore, the building was covered by the guns of the corner bastions of the fort; and these precautions were by no means superfluous, for the sentries told Angélique that their prisoners had been in a state of high excitement since they had heard of Gold Beard's capture, and that it would be risky to go among them.

Two sailors proposed to escort her inside, with levelled muskets and lighted matches, but she refused their services.

'I know these people, and I am not concerned!'

She ordered the two Spanish guards to stand outside with such an imperious expression that they did not dare disobey her. Divided as they were between the authority of the Count de Peyrac, which was sacred to them, and that of this fascinating woman, poor Luis and Pedro had never been so distressed as on this harsh day.

Angélique was not afraid of being alone with the pirates from the *Heart of Mary*. On the contrary, she felt herself more at ease, for today they were very much like her—unhappy and in peril.

The wounded were in dire need of care and the comfort of a hand which they knew to be skilled and soothing. As for the able-bodied prisoners, they concealed their anxiety about their unenviable fate, which was rapidly drawing nearer. Was this the last morning that they would see? The conqueror, the master of Gouldsboro, had come to inspect them on the previous day, fixing his eagle eye on their hang-dog faces.

'Monsieur,' the Chevalier de Barssempuy had ventured to ask, 'what fate have you in store for us?'

'A rope for the lot of you,' replied Peyrac roughly, 'there is not shortage of yardarms on the masts of our ships.'

'Just our luck!' the pirates grimaced. 'We've fallen into the hands of an even more bloodthirsty fellow than Morgan!'

Being men of blood themselves for the greater part, and having to their account many tortures, severed hands, poor victims hanged or roasted alive in the islands—for the Caribbean sun sets the taste for evil ablaze in the heart of man—they expected no mercy for themselves. The better elements among them no longer congratulated themselves on having wished 'to settle down and turn over a new leaf'.

'And we wanted to become settlers and family men! This last campaign has been our undoing.'

·In their black despair or grey resignation, which they felt alternately, Angélique's appearance was a ray of light. It is a hard world, particularly for gentlemen of fortune. No crack in the rough shell of a life spent cutlass in hand, a thirst for gold in one's heart, and a thirst for rum in one's throat. Suddenly a woman was filling a void in their hearts, passing among them, a woman who was neither booty nor a whore, and there was not time to wonder what she really was before she took you in hand and you found yourself once again under her sway, with no alternative but to respect her and obey her humbly.

For all of them it was a relief to see her coming in once more, when Gold Beard had been captured, into the barn, her bag of lint and medicines in her hand, and kneeling down at once at the bedside of these sick and wounded men and beginning to dress their wounds and nurse them without further delay. A few put forward the suggestion that she should be seized and held as a hostage in order to save their skins; they would negotiate on that basis with the Gouldsboro swine and, according to the results achieved, they would send a finger, an eye, a breast of the lovely lady to her husband, the 'bloodthirsty rogue' who wanted to kill them all, and it would be highly surprising if they did not succeed in getting out as a result of this manoeuvre. What about it? In such an extremity was it not the right thing to do, as indeed they had already done in the past more than once? But the plan got no farther than that. Glittering eyes followed Angélique's fair hair as she came and went in the stench of the half darkness, but no one said a word or made the slightest move. Only young Barssempuy dared to break his silence to ask her a question:

'Is it true, Madame, that Gold Beard has been taken?'

Angélique nodded without speaking.

'What will happen to him?' went on the lieutenant in an anxious voice. 'He can't be executed, Madame. . . . He is such an extraordinary man! We are devoted to our leader, Madame.'

'His fate depends on the decision of Monsieur de Peyrac,' replied Angélique dryly. 'He is the master.'

'Yes, but you are the mistress,' piped Aristide Beaumarchand in his reedy voice. 'From what they say. . . .'

Immediately, under Angélique's withering gaze, he curled up, his arms folded across his belly which he constantly nursed as a pregnant woman who fears to be beaten protects her precious burden.

'You would do better to hold your peace,' she said coldly, 'I'll cut your throat for you one of these days.'

The others chuckled with a sudden sense of relief. Having finished her work she left them. She felt in no mood to laugh and chat with these ruffians. But when she had closed the door behind her, she no longer felt any sense of resentment towards them.

Try as she might, she always ended up by allowing her heart to be touched by the wounded and the vanquished. Bandits or soldiers, highwaymen or sailors, as soon as she had nursed them she could not help loving them. This irresistible attachment was the result of the knowledge she acquired of them as she attended to their sufferings.

A sick man is so vulnerable. At such times he lowers his defences and reveals his inner character, and, if he resists, it is easy to circumvent him. Through the armour of an embittered, cruel and inflexible character, which in its state of weakness, had lowered its defences, Angélique always succeeded in reaching in the end the simple and childish heart. When they were up and about again, she kept them under her spell. They felt, sometimes with dismay, that henceforth she knew them better than they knew themselves. Outside, she gave orders for gaming boards, playing-cards and tobacco to be taken to the prisoners to help them pass the time of their captivity.

CHAPTER 65

STANDING UP to the ladies of Gouldsboro was quite a different kettle of fish! No quarter and no faltering to be expected there, she well knew. Their virtue exuded a sense of self-righteousness and condemnation of others and seemed possessed of an infinite capacity for virulence.

But it was up to her to shut them up too before the wave of bitterness engulfed them all and ruled out the possibility of ever making a new start.

Before pushing open the door of the Inn-Beneath-the-Fort, where she expected them all to be foregathered, Angélique paused briefly and instinctively prayed to Heaven. Naturally there they all were, in their dark skirts and white bonnets. Madame Manigault, looking more imposing than ever, was presiding. Madame Carrère was bustling about. Abigail Berne was standing on the far side of the chimney place, pale and dignified, a resolute expression on her beautiful face, which reminded one of a Flemish madonna. Angélique's entry seemed to have interrupted an argument, in which Abigail must have incurred the displeasure of her companions because of the moderation of her opinions.

'Madame Carrère,' said Angélique, addressing the proprietor of the establishment, 'would you be so good as to have dinner brought to me in the apartment in the keep? And I should also be grateful if you would heat me a basin of water so that I can wash.'

'All the waters of all the rivers on the earth cannot wash clean a guilty soul neither can any earthly food nourish those who are dying for having offended the Lord,' Madame Manigault declared in a loud aside.

Angélique received this Parthian shot, but she had been expecting it.

Over and above her exasperation, and the irritation she felt towards these gossips, she knew that these women, whom she could not help considering as friends, were torn between two opposing views.

Behind the uncompromising attitude of these Gouldsboro ladies towards Angélique's presumed scandalous conduct, lay a feeling of indignation at the betrayal of a man for whom more or less all of them felt a profound admiration, even a trace of something warmer. It was a repressed, disguised sentiment but a sentiment all the same, for the hearts of these Huguenot ladies were susceptible beneath the layer of frigidity imposed by their early upbringing.

Madame Manigault's 'I always said as much' came into its own now, spreading out like the bands of calico hung across the streets on the Papist feast day of Corpus-Christi! Had she not always considered Angélique, Master Berne's servant, a dangerous trouble-maker!

To which Abigail retorted that Madame de Peyrac's present conduct just went to show that she had a clear conscience.

'That's only pride!' Madame Manigault replied, 'I always said as much!'

'And in any case, what did anyone know about what had actually happened?' rejoined those who remained faithful to Angélique. . . . Gossip, allusions, hints. . . . The Swiss had been drunk when he said those outrageous things about her, as Master Manigault and Master Berne would bear witness. . . .

And now Angélique herself had appeared holding her head high among them, and had replied to Madame Manigault's aspersions with a slightly disdainful smile.

She was close to them, and very different from them,

just as she had been when she had shared persecution with them in La Rochelle.

And they remembered how Angélique had run with them over the moors to escape from the King's Dragoons, how she had rushed them away in order to save their lives. . . .

'That is a fine pretext, an impressive piece of truth,' said Angélique, eyeing the august lady calmly, 'and I think it was intended for me to meditate on, wasn't it, dear Madame Manigault? Thank you for the thought, but just for the moment, my soul, guilty or not, is less in need of food than my body. It is two days now since I reached your settlement in Gouldsboro, ladies, and I would just like to point out that the only thing that has passed my lips from its well-stocked larders has been one cob of Indian corn, which would not be saying much for your hospitality were I not aware of all the worries and tasks you have been overwhelmed with since yesterday, what with the battle and the wounded men to care for. When I asked for water and food I was only expressing an extremely natural need which you too, ladies, seem also to feel.'

It happened that some of the worthy ladies from La Rochelle were in fact sitting down to a tasty looking stew accompanied by goblets of wine. Having divided their time since the previous day between the care of their houses, their children, their farms and the men wounded in battle, they too were feeling exhausted and had taken advantage of a lull to obtain some sustenance from Madame Carrère's cheerfully welcoming inn. Caught in the act of regaling themselves, they sat abashed and confused, their spoons in mid-air.

'Please, I beg you,' Angélique insisted condescendingly, 'do not put yourselves out on my account. Please continue. I am in no way casting stones at you. You are quite right to take some refreshment, my dear friends. But pray allow the Countess of Peyrac to do likewise. So please send me something as soon as possible, Madame Carrère. . . .

'Abigail, my dear, could you come with me for a moment? There is something I would like to say to you in private.'

With one foot on the first step of the stairs that led to her room, Angélique looked up at Master Berne's wife, her gaze frank and free of all deceit.

'Abigail, do you doubt me?'

The bold front she had put on was breaking up, her exhaustion was beginning to tell. Abigail felt an impulse of affection for her.

'Madame, nothing can ever change my feelings of friendship towards you, as long as you do not find them offensive.'

'You have got things the wrong way round, my gentle Abigail. It is I who has always found your friendship a precious thing. Do you think I shall ever forget how kind you were to me when I came to La Rochelle with my child in my arms? You never despised the poor servant girl I was then. So please don't be so reverential towards me—it is quite unfitting between the two of us. And thank you for what you have just said. You have given me back my courage. I cannot yet explain to you what is going on but none of it is as serious as some nasty-minded people would have you understand.'

'I know in my heart of hearts that this is true,' Abigail agreed.

How charming Abigail was, the pure, chaste girl from La Rochelle, in the radiance of her approaching maternity! Happiness had ennobled her still further. Her blue eyes pledged her affection. Angélique weakened, and, feeling she could not bear it any longer, let her forehead fall on Abigail's shoulder.

'Abigail, I am frightened, I feel as if I were caught up in some infernal whirlpool . . . as if I were hedged about by threats. . . . If he doesn't love me any more, what is to become of me? . . . I am not guilty . . . not as guilty as people say . . . but everything seems to have conspired to condemn me.'

'I know what an honourable heart you have,' said Abigail, running a soothing hand over Angélique's brow. 'I am on your side and I am very fond of you.'

Hearing the sound of footsteps Angélique straightened up abruptly. No one but Abigail must see her weaken. But Abigail's kindness to her had renewed her strength.

She gave her friend a meaningful wink.

'They would like to see the last of me, wouldn't they?' she said. 'They have already had enough of having to put up with the presence of a sinner like me in Gouldsboro! But don't worry, Abigail. I have come here to help you at the birth of your baby and I shall stay with you as long as you need me, even if they make life hell for me.'

Alas, nothing had turned out as she had forseen it. She had dreamed of sitting in her friends' houses, exchanging news with them. Then they would have gone a tour of the recently established facilities of the township. They would have checked accounts and organized celebrations to which they would have invited the crews of all ships docked in the harbour. There was always something to celebrate during the summer months. Quickly, oh how quickly the mild season went by! They had to live their lives at double or treble speed, to gather in, store up, exchange, while hordes of people rushed down to the sea and there was feverish activity everywhere. Quick! Quick! Winter would soon come close in upon them again.

But nothing was as she had dreamed it. Far from being a period of celebration, these summer days ran on like a muddy torrent, carrying with them passions, griefs, despair, swelling hourly with a new flood of obscure dangers.

CHAPTER 66

WHAT WAS Joffrey thinking? What decision had he reached about her, and about Colin?

This silence, this absence were becoming intolerable to her.

Throughout every moment of the day which seemed to last for centuries she feared and hoped alternately that he would send for her. She would be brought to justice before him, admittedly, but anything was preferable to the uncertainty in which he had left her. Had she been able to cry, to storm, to implore, to beg, or to accuse him in turn, this would have given her a new lease of life.

Her fury, her pride, and her instinct of self-preservation which had kept her going that morning, were beginning to weaken as the hours passed. By driving her away, by ignoring her, he was torturing her in a way that so completely sapped her inner strength that she could scarcely swallow a few mouthfuls of the meal she had ordered Madame Carrère to send her.

That afternoon, she went in search of Cantor whom she found busy down by the harbour.

'Pay no attention to any of the gossip you may hear about me,' she told him earnestly. 'You know how superstitious all these people are. I have already been called a She-Devil in Quebec, haven't I? A woman only has to be taken prisoner by a pirate for a whole web of calumny to be spun about her. Gold Beard behaved chivalrously towards me and one day I'll explain to you who he is and why he happens to be a friend of mine.'

'In any case I shan't be here to see him hanged,' declared Cantor, who seemed not to want to dwell any longer on these matters. 'I am off today at high tide on the *Rochelais*. Father has just told me I must go.'

He straightened up, sufficiently proud of his responsibilities as a fifteen-year-old skipper not to show overmuch concern for the underlying tensions dividing the little colony. He was pleased that he had got back in time to take part in the naval battle, and still more delighted to be setting sail again, in command of his own ship, across the sea to lead the kind of busy existence with which he was familiar. He stuck out his chest and added, full of self-importance:

'I have to take some goods as far as Houssnock which will then be taken on as far as Wapassou by Kurt Ritz and six recruits whom I am taking on board with me.'

'What!' Angélique exclaimed. 'There's an expedition leaving for Wapassou in a few hours and no one has even told me? . . . Laurier! Laurier!' she called to the little boy who was going by, 'Quick, come and help me collect some shells for Honorine.'

392

She only just had time to scribble a note to the Jonases and the Malaprades.

'Hurry, hurry, the tide won't wait,' Cantor enjoined.

Kurt Ritz was standing on the harbour breakwater, halberd in hand, inspecting the bundles of goods being loaded into the sloop, and his men who, like himself, were of German or Swiss origin, wore their full dress regalia—a survival of the sixteenth-century German infantry costume with the short, tight-fitting doublet with huge full sleeves slashed open to reveal the shirt, and full, buttercup yellow cloth breeches, tucked in at the knees and sewn with perpendicular bands of scarlet ribbon that hung slack, giving them the appearance of petticoat-breeches, and, in accordance with the improper and boastful fashion of the previous century, a cod-piece shaped like a cocoon of golden-yellow satin.

One thing only was different: soft bands had replaced the goffered ruff.

They wore great broad hats, a cross between the ancient toque and the broad-brimmed modern felt, decorated with short, red ostrich feathers. A gilded steel helmet hung from each belt, and with their pikes, they made an impressive display.

Kurt Ritz fulfilled all the conditions of the manual which requires a sergeant to be 'a man at once learned, valiant, wise, courteous, who has had many encounters with the enemy, and where possible, is tall and good looking'.

He also carried a sword, a sign of the noble rank he had been given in the service of the King of France, in Austria, against the Turks.

Angélique had not seen him since that night when she had surprised him clinging to the poop of the Heart of Mary, apart from their brief encounter in the dark on the evening of her return, and she glanced round for him for a moment, not recognizing him.

Someone pointed him out, and she handed him her message for the Jonases, taking no notice of his haughty, disdainful look. Of course, he would always despise her, after what he had seen of her on board ship. But would he mention it at Wapassou? She could not stoop to ask him to keep quiet, but as she spoke to him in a steady

393

voice, adding, as she suddenly thought of them, several important instructions—for instance, that she hoped they had not forgotten to pick the fir-tree buds to make herbal tea for chest infections!—her intuition told her that this stranger was a sound man. He might be rough and cold, with that lordly look characteristic of mountain folk, but he was not a petty man. Never again would this man mention the secret he had stumbled on by the light of a candle, that night when he had made his escape from the pirate ship.

Catching sight of Count Peyrac walking down towards the harbour with Roland d'Urville and Gilles Vanereick, she hastened away.

Why had she run away? From him? From her husband?

She wandered amongst the new houses of Gouldsboro, deserted by their owners who had also gone down to the harbour to see the yacht set sail. . . .

She had lacked the courage this time to hold her ground, only a few paces from him, mingling with this crowd that was busy watching them. She should have been there, she told herself. She should have been waving her scarf while the little ship, under the command of that valiant young man, Cantor de Peyrac, spread its sails . . . but she had been incapable of it. It was her first moment of serious weakness since that morning.

He would triumph over her. But how would the battle end?

As long as she remained uncertain about Colin's fate, Joffrey would be a threat to her, his arm raised to strike, and in her heart of hearts, he would be the enemy she could not overcome.

How many a time in the past had Count Peyrac stated his implacable resolution to kill anyone who tried to steal his wife from him?

And she, sick at heart, could think of nothing but those words he had spoken to Pont-Briand and to Loménie.

Colin was condemned, less for being a plundering pirate than for Joffrey's rival. But this was impossible! Not for so little! Not just because of her! Oh! God! Do not allow this to happen!

CHAPTER 67

THAT EVENING, back at the fort, to which, after once more going the rounds of all the wounded, she had returned as night fell, worn out with fatigue and care, she nevertheless noticed two chests in her room that had not been there before.

One contained dresses, clothes, lace, underclothing, gloves and shoes, while the other held various luxury items to make day-to-day life more agreeable.

The clothes and other things smelt of Europe. Joffrey de Peyrac must have ordered them from Erikson before setting off in the autumn, and the *Gouldsboro* had just arrived with them. They represented all the refinement, the prettiness and beauty of a lost world.

Angélique scarcely touched them, just turned them over almost indifferently as if they were the last remains of a love that had died.

Why they had been brought to her room that evening was a mystery to her, and in the state of mind she was in, they were more of a source of anxiety than anything else, for she feared a trap.

She turned her back on these sumptuous presents as if they were a mockery of her present misery, and tried to sleep a little.

She trembled at the thought of what might happen while she was unconscious; would she, when she awoke, catch sight of Colin's body dangling from the arm of some gibbet in the dawn light?

With the coming of twilight, her courage had returned, and she had done her best to find her husband. But she had been unable to find him anywhere. Some said he had set off for the interior, while others informed her that he had taken the chebec out to meet some ship or other. In sheer desperation she had decided that she must try to get some rest.

But her anxiety remained, and after a brief, heavy sleep, she awoke in the depths of the night, and unable to sleep again, began to toss and turn, tormented by gloomy thoughts.

The rest had re-awakened her anger towards her husband. Yes, she was deeply hurt by the way he had behaved like an intolerant and suspicious master.

Had not Joffrey abandoned her to her fate for a period of years, yet now he wanted everything, even her faithfulness in the past? Had he been so scrupulous when he was away from her about taking his pleasure with other women? . . . But that didn't stop him tearing roughly aside the veil covering secrets which were hers and hers alone. And he was demanding from her an account of herself, attributing considerably more to her of these activities, incidentally, than she had in fact indulged in during the grass-widowhood which haunted his jealousy.

For her part, when she thought over the memories of the fifteen years she had spent apart from him, what she saw above all was a long succession of lonely, chilly nights during which her youth, beauty and femininity had been consumed in weeping for him, calling up his image and missing him . . . and in sleeping too, fortunately, alone and soundly. She had always slept as soundly as a child and it was this gift which had been her saving. When she had been running the Inn of the Red Mask in Paris, she had gone back night after night to a narrow bed, weary to the bone, and dawn had found her ready to face a day's work in which there would be hardly any place for love, unless one was prepared to count throwing out an over-cheeky musketeer; and at the time when she had kept the chocolate shop Ninon de Lenclos had teased her for being something of a prude.

Like luminous points of light, flickering and rapidly extinguished, there had been here and there a night of love, in the arms of a Parisian poet hunted by the police, and even in those of the man who was hunting him, Desgrez. Both of them had been too preoccupied with their cruel little game to bother about her overlong.

At Court, in spite of the erotic atmosphere prevailing there, could her amorous life be considered more sensual? Hardly, and perhaps in fact rather less so. The King's passion had isolated her. And her personal ambition, combined with her persistent longing for a beloved ghost to whom she never ceased to hold out her arms, had kept her away from light adventures and trivial affairs which would very quickly have become unbearable to her. What then had remained of all these things?

A few nights with Rakoczy, the persecuted prince. A fleeting embrace one evening after the hunt with the Duke of Lauzun—a mistake which had very nearly cost her extremely dear. And with Philippe, her second husband? Twice, perhaps three times. Scarcely more. And then Colin, and the comfort that had come to her in the desert. . . .

All in all, she thought, she had made love less frequently in fifteen years than any prudish middle-class wife of a lawful husband in three months, or than she herself had done in Joffrey's arms in a much shorter time. Was that an adequate reason to hold her up to public obloquy, to put her in the pillory, to credit her with the amorous temperament of a shameless Messalina? . . . It would be useless for her to try to bring these realities home to Joffrey, even if she were to reconstruct for him an account in detail which would enable a man of science like him to understand the logical scope of such matters. Alas! She sensed that even in the case of a scholar and scientist like Peyrac, one could hardly expect to count upon his detachment in matters of the heart, and he was liable to react like all other men when their proprietary instincts are at stake. In such cases men lose control of themselves and even the most intelligent refuse to understand.

But why such a lot of fuss about a kiss?

What is a kiss after all? Lips that meet and merge. And hearts that are touched.

Two lost creatures intertwined within a divine sense of security, warming one another with their breath, recognizing one another in the darkness of a night where for too long they have walked alone. Man! Woman! Nothing else, that is all.

And what is an embrace but the prolongation and a fulfilment of that supraterrestrial state so rarely enjoyed by the human creature? . . . In some cases never enjoyed!

Well, if that was what a kiss was, Joffrey would be

right to begrudge the one which she had exchanged with Colin, Gold Beard, or was that really so?

Life was a work of art, a difficult artistic task. The most difficult point for Angélique was to face the fact in her pride that ostracism, contempt and the anger of other people, the force of whose attacks she felt to the depths of her consciousness, were justified by her own conduct, which at times she herself knew very well was inexcusable.

In order to re-establish her balance, she would have needed to give this blunder, this accident, its just place, and she was incapable of doing so entirely on her own. Alternately she condemned herself utterly or saw in her brief abandonment nothing more than a pleasant intermission that a pretty woman has every right to steal from life from time to time.

The coming of a damp misty dawn released her from this eternal round of thoughts. She emerged weary and aching from her tossing on her cold deserted bed. Uncertainty about Colin's fate tormented her.

The restless, pinkish-grey dawn brought the tireless singing of the turtle doves in full, swelling, insinuating notes. The sickly-sweet, cloying sound of this cooing would be intolerable to Angélique for the rest of her life. Henceforth it would always remind her of this short, distressing season spent at Gouldsboro, which in her memory she would call the accursed summer.

It was a season of subdued horror and foreboding in which every warm morning, every tragic dawn was punctuated by the monotonous cooing of that bird.

Behind the mists, the sounds of the fort and the waking village were echoed and amplified. There was a sound of hammering! Was a scaffold being erected?

There came the lilt of a seaman's voice singing the lament of King Renaud:

'And in the middle of the night
The soul of Renaud took to flight.
Ah! tell me, tell me mother dear
What is that hammering I hear?
The carpenter, 'tis nothing more,
A' hammering on the old barn door.'

Angélique shuddered. A scaffold, or perhaps a coffin.
. . . She must rush out to act. But the day passed, and
the wind blew unceasingly, and nothing happened.

And now it was evening again, and the darkness was
already profound and without a trace of light, for the
sky, swollen with rain, hung low over the sea and merged
with the tops of the trees.

Clinging to the wooden framework of a window,
Angélique watched two men facing one another. A
moment before she had crossed the courtyard and headed
for the council chamber intending to have it out with
Joffrey face to face:

'Let us have it out. . . What are your intentions?'

Then, from outside, she had caught sight of them—
Joffrey and Colin standing face to face in the council
chamber. They were alone and did not know that they
were observed.

Colin had his hands behind his back, doubtless because his wrists were bound. Joffrey de Peyrac was standing beside the table on which were laid out scrolls of
parchment and maps. He was unrolling these documents
one by one, slowly and methodically, and reading them
attentively. From time to time he would take out of a
coffer standing open before him a precious stone and examine it in the candlelight with the eye of an expert. The
green sparkle of an emerald twinkled elusively at his
finger tips.

When she saw his lips moving, Angélique guessed that
he was questioning the prisoner and that the latter was
answering briefly. At one moment Colin moved and his
finger pointed out a place on the map. So he was not
in bonds after all. . . .

She began to be afraid for Joffrey's sake. If Colin were
suddenly to seize him impulsively by the throat. . . .
Was Joffrey not aware of the tremendous physical power
of this Gold Beard standing so close to him? But no. He
was pretending to be quite impervious and indifferent to
such considerations. How imprudent! This constant challenge of his to events, to the elements and to men, this
constant resolve to go further, to press on beyond the
extreme limits of experience, to see. . . . One day death

would pronounce upon him like a swooping eagle. 'Joffrey! Joffrey! Take care!'

She trembled as she clung to the window frame, powerless, feeling instinctively that she had no right to intervene between these two men. She must leave fate to decide, and let these two powerful wills confront one another in a combat in which she could have wished to see neither victor nor vanquished. Her eyes passed from one to the other anxiously, and fastened greedily as if drawn by a magnet on the tall, powerful, angular figure of her husband. Separated from him by the wall of silence of the window panes as she was, it was like catching him unawares and watching him as he slept. . . . This she had never been able to do without feeling a mixture of excitement and fear, tinged sometimes with a sense of acute jealousy, because at such times he had as he slept an expression on his face which seemed to symbolize his enigma to her as a man, a mystery into which she could not penetrate.

There was a touch of silver at the edges of his brown temples, which had a suggestion of gentleness about it, but that was a mere illusion. He remained distant, hard and unattainable. And yet every subtlest detail of his person was familiar to her, his wife, and tugged spontaneously at her heart strings as she contemplated him. Detail by detail she reconstructed in her mind all that she knew of him—his caution and his dash; his skill and self-control, his intellect, his knowledge, overlaid by so much human simplicity, and if the meditative expression on his face hinted at his genius as a thinker, Angélique nevertheless remembered as she followed the movement of his muscles under his dark velvet clothes, his energy, his vigour and an extraordinary amorous health which he had always shown and which pulsed through his tough indomitable frame.

Then her eyes went back to Colin. Rising up out of the mists of the distant years, it was the image of the King of the Prisoners of Meknès that stood there in the narrow room. The motley costume he had worn in his role as Gold Beard seemed now no more than a disguise. This particular evening his eye had its sovereign shade of blue, the great Colin's blue eye, accustomed to gaze into the distance of the desert and to read in the depths of human hearts.

In spite of herself, because she was a woman, and as such belonged to a race which for many thousands of years had been downtrodden and humiliated, Angélique could not help being on the side of the weaker of the adversaries in this silent duel—Colin. Knowing them both, she knew that Joffrey was much stronger than the Norman. Learned as he was in the great philosophies and sciences of the world, and concerned with the subtle and infinite passions of the intellect, he could endure anything, or almost anything, without flinching—even the wounds of the heart. Colin, on the other hand, was an uncultivated man in spite of his native intelligence, a man who did not even know how to write, and he was helpless before unforeseen blows.

And it was she who had inflicted them upon him. She fetl remorseful, and her heart was torn seeing him there helpless and conquered in advance, in spite of his undeniable physical strength.

Suddenly her heart quailed. She saw Joffrey push the heap of parchments aside and advance upon Colin. Her dread was as great as if she had seen him pointing his pistol at Colin and firing straight into his heart. It took her a moment to persuade herself that the Count's hands were bare. Nevertheless, her fear remained. On the other side of the window a decisive moment had come. She felt it in the trembling of her flesh, in the tension of her mind, and in the straining of her senses, trying to catch what was said, trying to understand. Something decisive was going on. But it was happening in silence. It was happening in words that she could not hear, and that sprang from the lips of the two men like the blows of sharpened daggers. . . .

Joffrey was speaking, standing very close to the prisoner, his flashing eyes fixed on Colin's hard, attentive face. Little by little a sombre fury and profound indignation marked the Norman's face; and Angélique saw his fists opening and closing, rising even, and trembling with powerless rage. Several times, he shook his head, meeting Joffrey de Peyrac's word with the pride of an indomitable lion.

Then Peyrac left him. He began to walk up and down, like a caged animal, and to circle round and round Colin, darting quick, penetrating glances at him, like a hunter trying to decide the best point at which to strike. Then going up to him again he seized the big man by the collar of his jacket and drew him close to him as if to speak confidentially to him, and this time he spoke in a low voice. There was now a kind of dangerous gentleness on Joffrey de Peyrac's face, and a subtle ambiguous fold at the corner of his lips, and Angélique could almost sense the insinuating charm of his tone. He was wearing his most charming expression, but there was a little flame dancing in his pupils that frightened her. What she was afraid of was occurring—Colin was succumbing to Jeffrey de Peyrac's ascendancy.

Little by little the rugged determination faded from his face, and was replaced by an expression of confusion and despair, and even a fleeting panic. Suddenly, he let his head fall forward in a movement of weariness or avowal.

What had Count Joffrey de Peyrac succeeded in saying thus to vanquish Colin Paturel, who had never bent his back before Mulai Ismail and all his tortures?

Joffrey de Peyrac stopped speaking, but he continued to hold Colin and to watch him closely. At length, the heavy blond head was raised. Colin gazed straight ahead, fixedly. Angélique was afraid that he had glimpsed her through the window. But Colin saw nothing outside, his gaze was turned in upon himself. And suddenly she saw in him too the kind of naïve innocence which he had in his sleep, an expression of face which was like that of Adam as he must have been in the first days of creation. His blue eyes, with something drowsy in them, turned towards Peyrac once more, and the two men stared at one another for a long time without speaking. Then Colin bowed his head again and repeated the gesture several times. This time it was a mark of agreement, of acquiescence.

Count de Peyrac went back to his place behind the table. Shadows moved in the back of the room. Several Spanish guards came in and stationed themselves behind the prisoner. Angélique had not heard them summoned. They went out, taking Colin with them.

Joffrey de Peyrac remained in the room. He sat down.

Angélique drew back, fearing that he might suspect her presence. But she stayed there, fascinated. Just as he had spied on her the other night, in the shadows of the island, without her knowing it, she also wished to discover him naked and unaware of the fact that he was being observed. What feelings would he betray? What mask might he let fall which could reveal him to her and which might enable her to guess at his thoughts and his decisions?

She saw him stretch out his arm towards the coffer of emeralds, the famous Caracas emeralds, plundered from the Spanish by Gold Beard. He picked up an exceptionally large one between two fingers, and holding it up to the light of the torch he became absorbed in contemplating it. And he was *smiling* as if watching in the transparency of the precious stone some pleasurable spectacle.

CHAPTER 68

THE FOLLOWING day was a Sunday. There was a wailing call of a conch in the distance, and the sprightly tinkling of a bell in the little wooden belfry, calling the Protestants to divine service. Not to be outdone, the chaplains and Father Bauce, joined by another Recollect father, recently back from the woods, decided to hold a solemn Catholic service on the cliff-top, with monstrance, procession and all.

Through the mist the rival hymn singing went on all morning, but the religious ceremonies were completed without incident.

When divine worship and Mass were both over, the people strolled down to the harbour, where new arrivals were being announced. Soon, mingling with the foghorn came the sound of more literal bellowing. A small cutter from Port Royal on the peninsula was bringing in two cows and a bull, long promised in exchange for a gift of fresh food and ironmongery that had saved the lives of a French colony abandoned by the remote administration in Quebec. The unfortunate animals were unloaded by suspending them from a system of ropes and pulleys, and they were landed without undue difficulty amidst the acclamations of the population.

The arrival of the cattle created almost as much interest as the imminent hanging of Gold Beard. Would it be today?

Amidst all this hustle and bustle the arrival of a small ship bringing John Knox Mather, a doctor of theology from Boston, with his chief curates, went unnoticed. The jovial, noisy Acadians, followed by their red Mic-Macs, giants with square, copper-coloured faces, rubbed shoulders with the honourable Puritan gentleman without even noticing him.

He wore a ruff and a full, long, dark Genevese cape that reached to his heels, which he wrapped about him right up to the eyes to protect himself from the wind, while the crown of his hat, with its severe silver buckle, seemed higher than the others.

'I wanted to meet you,' he said to Peyrac who came down to greet him. 'Our Governor reminded us, at a recent synod, that after all Maine belongs to England, and he asked me to enquire from you whether the situation still remained the same. . . .'

He had been casting anxious looks about him.

'The place reeks of saturnalia to me . . . I say, it is rumoured that you are living with an enchantress. . . .'

'Absolutely right,' Peyrac replied. 'Come . . . let me introduce you to her.'

John Knox Mather went pale and began to tremble like the surface of a pond at the approach of a storm. He grew uneasy, and he had good cause. The Protestants had got rid of the Virgin Mary and the saints, as well-disposed intercessors in the Other World, and they were left with nothing but demons. So any intrusion of an evil spirit left them disarmed and helpless. They could count only on their own spiritual strength. Fortunately the worthy Mather possessed plenty of this; he stiffened and prepared to face the ordeal of meeting the enchantress.

404

Angélique, on learning that Count Peyrac had urgently requested her presence, left a man whose wound she was dressing and set off with beating heart to the encounter, only to find herself face to face with a sombre monolithic monument, called a doctor of theology from Boston, who examined her with a stony gaze. Actually he was as astonished as she was; this she realized, bade him welcome and dropped him a brief curtsy. She gathered from his conversation with Count Peyrac that he would be staying in Gouldsboro for several days, and that on this Lord's day they intended to hold a feast to thank Him for His blessings.

The arrival of all these people at Gouldsboro put off the settlement of the bitter matters that hung over the townspeople, tormenting their hearts and their consciences, and she did not know whether to be glad or whether the suspense would be just too much for her. She wanted to have done with the anxiety, to finish the game they were all playing. She wanted to cry out, to beg them: 'Let us put an end to it, let us know! . . .'

But Joffrey de Peyrac's inflexible hand kept them all in suspense and expectant, awaiting his good pleasure, forcing them to play their part to the point of exhaustion. Since her husband had introduced her to the guests, she would have to preside at the festivities.

She went back to the fort to select a dress from the chests that had arrived from Europe.

Soon afterwards there was a sharp shower of rain and the sky cleared. The delicious smell of the preparations for the feast down at the inn began to permeate the air and dominate the powerful tang of the sea.

Voices took on a resonant lilt, and several blasts of trumpets rang out. Gouldsboro already had its own well-established traditions. Angélique did not know that these trumpet blasts were intended to call the population together on the esplanade before the fort, but, intrigued by the sound, she went outside.

There, everything was glistening as if varnished by the recent storm, while thin trickles of mud poured down the cliff side, hollowing out little channels down to the shore. The women-folk lifted their skirts to leap over them.

The people gathered, like the torrents, at first in thin, isolated streams issuing from the ships, the houses and the woods, emerging from all sides and converging on a single point to form a compact mass, a heterogeneous gathering of sailors, settlers, Huguenots, Indians, Englishmen, soldiers and noblemen, finally united by the temporary but unforgettable feeling of all belonging to the same remote African shore and looking forward to witnessing a rare spectacle.

Those who had come on horseback from Camp Champlain along the lupin-lined road, and those who had come down from the tiny hamlets up the coast along the anemone track, carried muskets or blunderbusses and formed a tight guard round their women and children. Everyone was under strict orders never to go more than half a league beyond the range of the cannons in the fort without being armed. With the summer months upon them, the season of Iroquois raids had begun, and in addition no one was immune from the possibility of a sudden Abenaki attack upon any Whites against whom their suspicions might have been aroused.

The open space in front of the fort was black with people.

Children rushed hither and thither and Angélique heard them calling:

'They say they're going to hang Gold Beard!'

'And before that, they're going to torture him. . . .'

Her blood ran cold. The moment she had never ceased to dread since Colin's capture had come.

'No! No! I shall not let them hang you,' she told herself. 'I shall scream, I shall cause an uproar, but I shall not let them hang you! Joffrey can think whatever he likes!'

She came forward in all her finery as far as the square, and heedless of the eyes that followed her, made her way to the front of the crowd. By now she felt completely unconcerned about what people might think of her and heedless of any remarks her presence might occasion. Inwardly she was trembling but managed to show a pride that both intrigued and disconcerted.

She had selected, almost without thinking, a dress that was both severe and sumptous. It was an unusual black

406

velvet dress covered with spidery lace and studded with tiny pearls, and she had thought to herself: 'A dress to wear at a king's funeral.' But she had made up her mind that she would not be attending Colin's funeral, for she intended to save his life!

At the last moment with a hasty finger, for there was no time for meticulous care, she had rubbed a little alkanet rouge on her pale cheeks.

She looked ghastly, but never mind!

If anyone noticed her feverish pallor, no one said anything. Her flashing green eyes froze any unkind words on people's lips.

'Look at her,' Vanereick whispered to Lord Sheringham in English. 'She is fascinating. What nobleness of bearing, how superbly proud she is! Very English, old chap. She is as good as Peyrac any day. She is holding her head high in spite of all glances, hostility and reprobation, and she could scarcely have shown greater arrogance had she been wearing the letter A embroidered in scarlet in her bosom, a penalty imposed—as you undoubtedly know, sir—by your Puritans in Massachusetts on adulterous women.'

The Englishman—an Anglican—gave a disabused smile.

'Puritans have no sense of the *nuances* in these matters.'

He gave a sidelong glance at Knox Mather, who was busy discussing with his curates the theological implications of hanging a man on the Lord's Day. Was it a breach of the Sabbath to haul on a hangman's rope? Or, on the other hand, might not the choice of this day allow the Lord greater leisure to receive this new soul He had to judge?

'We men of the world,' the English lord went on, 'must admit that we find it easy to forgive so lovely a woman for having sinned a little.'

'How much do you wager that she will defend her lover with as much fire and passion as Lady Macbeth?'

'I'll stake you twenty pounds. . . . Shakespeare would have liked this country which is English not only by right, but also in spirit. . . .'

Lord Sheringham raised to his eyes his beribboned

spectacles—all the rage that season in London—which were suspended from his brocade coat.

'And what about you, Vanereick, how much will you wager that, in spite of her slender appearance, that lady is full of delightful curves when she slips out of all that finery, like Venus rising from the waves?'

'Let us not wager, sir, for I am already aware of that particular state of affairs, for I have had my arms about her. You English lords are indeed men of good taste. You guessed right, my lord. When you actually get your hands on that sylph, she is as well padded as a feather-bed.'

'For goodness' sake hold your tongues, you lewd rakes!' burst out Gabriel Berne, the Huguenot from La Rochelle, who, overhearing their ribald conversation was unable to contain his indignation.

There followed an exchange of insults in English, and Lord Sheringham spoke of a duel. But his lieutenant pointed out that one could hardly fight with common men like these, whereupon all the settlers from La Rochelle rose like a single man to this insult and began to close in upon the beribboned admiral with clenched fists.

The guards and militia-men who stood around the platform were on the verge of intervening, but fortunately the amiable d'Urville appeared and managed to calm everybody down. But he could not entirely still the storm that was brewing among the Rochelais, who, their attention diverted from their English guests, turned upon Angélique, 'the apple of discord' whom they considered far too conspicuous and shameless on such a day. People began to dart furious glances at her, the murmurs grew louder, and comments could be heard all round her until finally they reached her ears through the mists of her distracted mind.

She glanced at the sombre crowd moving towards her, in which she saw the flash of accusing eyes.

'It's your fault too,' Madame Manigault shouted at her, seeing that at last she had come down to earth. 'How dare you show your face among honest folk?'

Monsieur Manigault stepped solemnly towards her.

'Yes indeed, Madame,' he continued, striking a further blow, 'your presence here at such a time is an insult to all laws of honourable behaviour. As head of the Protestant community of Gouldsboro I must ask you to leave.'

She stared at him with eyes that seemed suddenly to have grown pale, and they might well have thought that she had not heard them.

'And what do you have to fear from me, Monsieur Manigault?' she enquired softly, at last breaking the breathless silence.

'You must not side with that bandit,' cried Madame Manigault, unable to keep out of it any longer, 'And don't try to wriggle out of things or put on airs of innocence. We all know there's something between the two of you. It's a most disagreeable and deplorable business for us all, and you should be ashamed. Not to mention the fact that we owe it to ourselves to get rid of this scoundrel who caused us so much trouble last month and would have killed the lot of us had we not fought to the death. And here you are, ready to intercede for him and ask for his pardon. We know you.'

'Yes indeed,' Angélique conceded, 'I think you have good cause to know me.'

It was not the first time she had had to face the wrath of Calvinists. In the long run she had ceased to be impressed by these jousting matches between them. She drew herself up to her full height and looked at them.

'A year ago, on this very spot, it was your lives I begged for, begged for on my knees . . . and for crimes which, according to the law of the sea, merited hanging even more than those which Gold Beard has committed. . . .'

In spite of herself her lips began to tremble and kind-hearted Vanereick thought she was going to burst into tears, which he could not have borne.

'I knelt . . .' she repeated . . . 'I did that for you . . . for you who cannot even kneel before God himself. For you who no longer even know your Gospel.'

Then she abruptly turned her back on them.

A superstitious silence hung over the crowd.

CHAPTER 69

THE PRISONER came out, hands behind his back, onto the balcony of the fort overlooking the esplanade.

He was closely surrounded by the Spanish guards in their gleaming cuirasses and red-plumed morions.

Colin Paturel was bareheaded. He wore a chestnut-brown cloth doublet with gold-braided revers, fetched for him from his wardrobe on board the *Heart of Mary*.

This simple costume, worn with short-clipped beard and hair, made a considerable impression, for the terrible, flamboyant Gold Beard was not recognizable in this dark-clad giant prepared for death. They had not thought him so tall!

Joffrey de Peyrac appeared almost immediately behind him, dressed in saffron-yellow satin in the French fashion, with an open jerkin over a long embroidered jacket which was a marvel.

A cry of astonishment and admiration went up from the crowd and a wave seemed to travel across the sea of faces. Even the Huguenots were affected by this further sensation produced by the noble man from Aquitaine, who was a personality outside their normal range of experience and quite beyond their comprehension, but who had been thrown by a stroke of fate into their hitherto reasonable lives, and who now held them all under his spell.

His presence checked the jeers and dangerous excitement that lay close to the surface and were about to burst forth as the other prisoners, the pirate crew of the *Heart of Mary*, were led forth, in chains or with rope bonds. Closely encircled by a ring of muskets, they were pushed forward in a troop to the foot of the platform.

Some of them pulled faces and gnashed their teeth villainously, but most seemed resigned like men who, having gambled and lost, know that they have reached their journey's end and that the hour of reckoning has come.

Count Peyrac did not need to lift a little finger to impose silence.

Impatient for the verdict which was about to be announced, the crowd held its breath. And all fell silent. Not a sound could be heard save the lapping of the sea. The Count advanced to the edge of the balcony, leaned over, and directly addressing the group of Protestants from La Rochelle who stood at the front of the crowd, forming the compact nucleus, sombre, incorruptible and indefectible, of his settlement.

'Gentlemen,' he said, pointing to Colin Paturel who stood there between his guards, 'gentlemen, I present to you *the new governor of Gouldsboro.*'

CHAPTER 70

IN THE thunderstruck, incredulous silence that followed this announcement, Joffrey de Peyrac took time to turn up his delicate lace cuffs.

Then, quite unperturbed, he went on:

'Monsieur d'Urville, who for a long time has discharged this most difficult responsibility, is to become admiral of our fleet. The number and size of our ships, both merchantmen and men-of-war, continues to increase and multiply, and the time has come to appoint a professional naval man to take charge of them. Similarly, the way in which Gouldsboro has developed over the past months, thanks largely to your activity and industry, gentlemen of La Rochelle, makes it imperative for me to choose as a governor someone who has had experience both of the sea and of governing a wide variety of peoples and nations, since, as our port is gradually coming to occupy a more and more important place, a unique place, in the area we have chosen to live in, we shall find that henceforth we shall have the whole world on our doorstep. Now, I would like to make it clear to you that I know of no one more capable of dealing with the many tricky problems that such a position will entail for all of us than the man whom I have designated to you today, the man into whose hands I place with the utmost confidence the fate of Gouldsboro, its repute, its prosperity and its future greatness.'

411

He broke off, but not a single voice echoed his words. The crowd before him was as if turned to stone.

Among them Angélique was by no means the least dumbfounded. Joffrey's words entered her ears as a string of disconnected sounds and their meaning did not penetrate her mind. Or rather, she tried in vain to see a meaning in them, some other meaning that would signify that Colin was to be hanged.

Before the sea of open mouths and staring eyes, Joffrey de Peyrac gave a sardonic smile, then he went on:

'This is a man whom you have known under the name of Gold Beard, a Caribbean corsair. But allow me to inform you that before that he spent twelve years as King of the Christian slaves in Meknès, in the kingdom of Morocco on the Barbary coast, the sultan of which dealt harshly with the Christians, and that in this capacity this gentleman, Colin Paturel, ruled for twelve years over a nation of thousands of souls. These people, from every corner of the globe, speaking every language, practising many different religions, abandoned to their wretched fate as slaves in a strange, hostile, Moslem land, slaves with no possibility of escape or relief from the burdens that oppressed them and the evil that seared their souls, for twelve years these people found in him a sure and indomitable guide. He knit them into a powerful, dignified, united people, who together fought against the temptation to despair and abjure their baptismal faith.'

Then Angélique began to realize the truth—Colin would not be hanged. He would live. He would rule again.

It was of him that Joffrey was talking when he said: 'He will guide you with his wisdom. . . .'

Then peace came back to her, accompanied by an underlying pain. But first and foremost she felt peace, and she literally drank in the words that fell from her husband's lips, seized by an emotion that quite overcame her and at last brought tears to her eyes. Was it this he had been asking of Colin so insistently that previous evening in the council chamber, this that Colin had so passionately refused? Then he had bowed his heavy head and had assented.

'Although we are not slaves here like the Christians in Meknès,' Joffrey went on, 'we do nevertheless have to face similar strains—a sense of abandonment, doubt, mutual animosity, and the constant peril of death. He in his wisdom will be able to help you to face these things, just as he will know how to guide you in your dealings with neighbouring peoples, for he speaks English, Dutch, Spanish, Portuguese, Arabic and even Basque, which the Indians understand. He originates from Normandy and is a Catholic, and will prove equally valuable to you in your relations with the Acadian French. Monsieur d'Urville, would you be so kind as to repeat through your megaphone the salient points of what I have just said so that each man may hear it and think it over at his leisure?'

While d'Urville did as he was bade, the Protestants at last began to emerge from their stupor—which, it must be admitted, was not without cause.

They began to grow restless and mutter amongst themselves.

As soon as Peyrac's announcement had been repeated, Gabriel Berne stepped forward.

'Monsieur de Peyrac, you have already asked us to stomach many an affront, but this one, I warn you here and now, will never be accepted. Whence do you have such detailed information about this dangerous man? You have let yourself be taken in by a lot of chit-chat from a vagabond with the gift of the gab, as they all are, these pirates who live on the property of others.'

'I myself saw the work of this man when I was in the Mediterranean,' Peyrac replied. 'I saw him tied to the whipping post, taking upon himself the punishment of his brothers who had made so bold as to attend Mass one Christmas night. On another occasion he was crucified by his hands on one of the city gates. I realize that Monsieur Paturel is not anxious for me to bring up all these details of the past, but I am telling you of them, gentlemen, so that you may rest assured as regards your faith. I am putting at your head a proud Christian who has already shown that he can shed his blood for his beliefs.'

The protests of the men of La Rochelle grew louder.

Martyrdom endured for the Catholic faith had no value in their eyes and this was no way to win them over. On the contrary, they saw in it the obstinacy of narrow-mindedness, clinging to superstitions and diabolical beliefs.

A confused murmur broke out and began to swell:

'Hang him! Hang him! Treachery! We cannot accept this. . . . Hang Gold Beard!'

Colin who, until then, had stood impassively aside from the debate, keeping his place between the Spanish mercenaries, stepped forward and posted himself beside Joffrey de Peyrac.

With his hands on his hips, he looked down at the seething crowd with his penetrating blue eyes.

It was as if they all recoiled before his massive presence, and the calls to hang him slowly died down, finally fading away in a stupefied silence.

Berne reacted with his customary impetuosity. He rushed forward.

'This is madness,' he cried, one hand reaching to the sky as if calling it to witness to the folly that possessed them all. 'You should hang him twenty times over, Monsieur de Peyrac, if only for the harm he has caused Gouldsboro. And you yourself, Count, have you forgotten that he has dishonoured you, that he has . . .'

With an imperious gesture, Peyrac cut short the accusing sentence that would have dragged Angélique's name into the mud.

'If he did deserve to be hanged, it would not be for me to lead him to the scaffold,' he declared in a quiet voice that nevertheless brooked no reply. 'The debt of gratitude I owe him would make that impossible.'

'Gratitude? . . . *Your* gratitude? Yours?'

'Yes indeed, my gratitude,' the Count insisted. 'Allow me to tell you why I feel like this. Among the exploits that Monsieur Paturel has to his credit, not least is that of his escape—attempted in company with several other slaves, that brought them face to face with the most terrible dangers, in order to get away from Morocco—an escape which proved successful.

'Now it happened that among those whom he helped in this way to reach Christian territory there was a woman, a prisoner of the Berbers, whom in this way

414

he managed to save from the terrible fate reserved for unfortunate Christian women who find themselves in Moslem hands. This was at a time when my own exile and my wretched fate kept me ignorant of what had happened to my own family and made it impossible for me to come to their assistance when they too were in danger and abandonment by everyone. That woman was the Countess of Peyrac, my wife here. Monsieur Paturel's devotion saved the life I valued above all else. How could I ever forget that?'

A thin smile creased one corner of his scarred lip.

'And that is why, gentlemen, forgetting our present misunderstandings, we, the Countess of Peyrac and I, can consider this man, the object of your hatred, only as a friend, a worthy recipient of our complete confidence and esteem.'

Among these last words, to which she had listened in a kind of trance, one phrase had struck Angélique, rousing her like the crack of a whip, had almost stung her like an urgent appeal from that hoarse and apparently serene voice, enjoining her, ordering her to submit to his decision in this entire matter.

'The Countess of Peyrac and myself.'

In this way he encompassed her in his plan, making it impossible for her to escape, and his hidden intentions became clear to her, namely to wipe out the insult. To wipe out the insult that his wife and Colin had inflicted *publicly* upon him. What had there been between them? Nothing more than memories of friendship and gratitude which he deluded himself that he shared with them. Thus he managed to confuse everyone about the nature of the passions that were rending the three of them, presenting them with a travesty of the truth.

Had she not, instinctively, in her own pride, adopted the same attitude?

Would the Protestants be taken in?

They had to be! Let everyone behave as if they were. Joffrey de Peyrac had decided that Colin Paturel was worthy of a place at his side in governing his people, and that the only feelings he could entertain towards him were those of gratitude and friendship.

415

The crowd would simply have to submit to this image he was imposing on them.

Who could ever resist the unbending will of a Peyrac?

Never had Angélique felt so conscious of his steely hold over all of them, that literally grasped them and moulded them according to the laws of his personal authority.

She felt a sense of awed admiration, which had nothing to do with warmth of affection, and her suffering grew all the more intense, all the more penetrating.

He had just given an order to the 'Countess of Peyrac', but he had never even glanced at her throughout the course of his long explanation, and at no time had his voice registered those tender inflexions which once he had been unable to restrain whenever he spoke of her, even to a stranger.

Everyone looked from her to the two men standing there side by side on the platform, and Angélique's trembling looks, the astonishment which in spite of herself could be clearly seen in her eyes, disconcerted and dismayed the bystanders....

Colin went on staring impassively into the distance, over the heads of the agitated crowd, his arms folded on his chest. Such was the imperiousness of his countenance, such its extraordinary nobility, that he was no longer recognizable as the same man.

They began to look elsewhere for Gold Beard, the coarse pirate, hung about with weapons and stained with bloody misdeeds. Standing there beside him, as if protecting him and sheltering him beneath his own power, Count Peyrac, disdainful but half-smiling, contemplated curiously the effects of his sensational announcement.

'Look at the three of them,' cried Berne, panting for breath, pointing first to the two men then to Angélique. 'Look at them! They are making fools of us, they are deceiving us, they are making fun of us....'

He kept on spinning round on his own heels, like a man demented, half-crazed, beside himself. He tore off his hat and threw it as far as he could.

'Just look at them, the three hypocrites! What are they planning now? ... How much longer are we to be gulled

416

by people like them? Have you forgotten that Papists are without shame! That they will go to any lengths in order to carry out the intrigues of their tortuous, idolatrous minds. It's unthinkable! Brothers, are you going to acquiesce in these iniquitous decisions, this ridiculous trial? . . . Are you going to agree to be placed at the mercy of the most vile individual we have ever had to deal with up to now? Are you going to agree to admit within our walls a criminal, debauched mob which he intends to foist upon us as settlers? . . .

'What about your crimes, Gold Beard?' he shrieked, turning upon Colin full of hatred. 'And those of the ruffians in your crew?'

'And what about yours, Huguenot!' Colin replied, leaning down over the balustrade so that his steely blue eyes looked straight into those of Master Berne.

'My hands are not tainted with the blood of my fellow man,' the Protestant replied emphatically.

'Oh no? . . . No man here can claim to have hands untainted by the blood of his fellows. Think carefully, Huguenot, and you will remember those you have sacrificed, killed, or strangled, men whose throats you cut with your own hands. However far off, however deep you have buried this memory, search well, Huguenot. You will see them floating back to the surface of your conscience, those crimes of yours, with their dead eyes and stiff limbs.'

Berne stared at him in silence. Then he staggered as if struck by lightning and backed away. Colin Paturel's deep voice had cast in his face the memory of that subterranean struggle that had been going on among the Protestants in La Rochelle for over a century. Once again he smelt the acrid scent of the darkness, the stink of decaying corpses down those wells that led into the sea where they used to tip the dead bodies of *agents provocateurs* or Jesuits.

'Oh yes,' Colin went on, narrowing his eyes to a slit through which he observed them, 'I know. I know, it was self-defence! But it is ALWAYS self-defence when people kill one another. To defend oneself, one's family, one's life, one's aims, one's dreams. He is a rare man indeed who kills out of sheer evil impulse. But as far as indulgence for the sinner goes, God alone can share that, for He alone can read into our hearts. Wherever a man goes, he will always find a brother who says to him: "You are a murderer, and I am not!" There is not a man alive in this day and age who has not killed. In these days, a man worthy of the name always has blood on his hands. I might even go so far as to say that killing is a mission and an inalienable right we receive at our birth, we males, for our age is still the time of wolves prowling on the face of the earth, although Christ has come. So give up saying of your neighbour: "You are a criminal, I am not." But since you are obliged to bring about the death of men, at least work on behalf of life. . . . You Huguenots from La Rochelle have saved your skins and escaped from your tormentors; are you going to refuse to others, to condemned men like yourselves, the same opportunities that you have had, even if you consider yourselves the Elect of the Lord and believe that you alone deserve to survive. . . .'

The La Rochelle folk, who had been somewhat intimidated by Colin's attack, regained possession of themselves on looking at the crew of the *Heart of Mary*. On this point, their consciences would not be led astray. Monsieur Manigault advanced to the foot of the balcony:

'Let us leave aside your assertions about alleged crimes we all are said to have on our hands. God absolves his Chosen Ones. But do you mean, *Monsieur*,' he said, ostentatiously stressing the word, 'that you intend to impose on us here at Gouldsboro, with the agreement of Monsieur de Peyrac, the company of these dangerous ruffians who formerly made up your crew?'

'You're badly mistaken about the nature of my crew,' explained Colin. 'The majority are sterling fellows who had engaged to serve under me on this campaign precisely in the hope of becoming colonists and finally settling down in a favourable place where they were promised good earth and women to take to wives. Even the right of ownership of the place where you have settled has been paid for by me on their behalf in hard cash, and contracts have been exchanged. Unfortunately it is obvious that things have not worked out as expected and I realize that I have been deceived by my backers

418

in Paris, who expressly indicated Gouldsboro to me as a place which was unencumbered and belonging to the French. On parchment we have no more right to it than you refugee Protestants, and Monsieur de Peyrac has recognized this, but the pompous ignoramuses in France seem to have forgotten that the Treaty of Breda left the region under English jurisdiction. This I recognize and accept on my side too. One can do what one likes with documents; land is another thing. Enough good men have been sacrificed for the sake of a fool's plunder —or it might be more exact to put it down to ill-will— by which we have been duped.

'Of all these matters Monsieur de Peyrac is ready to supply evidence, and to discuss them with you in private. But with regard to the decisions which we have both taken and the contracts with one another into which we have entered, all that is fixed and settled and there is no going back upon them. All that remains to be settled is what all of us are going to make of these matters for good or for ill. . . .'

His voice, which was both inflexible and persuasive, was taking effect and checking the protests which rose to the lips of his listeners; and at the same time his gaze held their attention.

'He's done it,' thought Angélique, an irresistible tremor running through her whole body, 'He's got them, he's got them in the palm of his hand. . . .'

Colin Paturel's powerful eloquence, his grip on the mob, had always been his strongest weapons. He had brought them to bear with masterly dash.

Leaning towards them, and speaking confidentially, but in a voice which carried to those standing at the back of the crowd, he resumed:

'There is one thing that I want to tell, that I learnt when I was a slave among the Saracens. It is how much the Sons of Christ, the Christians, hate one another. So much more than the Moslems and Pagans! . . . I'll tell you what I realized—that the whole lot of you—Christians, schismatics, heretics or Papists—are all alike: sharp-toothed jackals ready to devour one another for a mere comma in your dogmas. And what I want to state to you is that Christ, whom you claim to serve, did not want that, and that He is not happy about it. . . . Now, I am warning you, from this day on, Protestants and Papists alike, I'm going to keep my eye on you Gouldsboro people, and I'm going to see that you live together in peace, and on good terms with one another, just as I established peace among the slaves of Meknès for a period of twelve years.

'If there are genuine thugs among you, I shall find them out. But I don't think there are many of them, except in my most recent cargo, two or three characters that I tried to get rid of but who continue to stick to my legs like Malacca leeches. They had better keep quiet or it'll be their turn to dangle at the end of a rope for good and all.'

He shot a glance that was far from reassuring in the direction of Beaumarchand, who had dragged himself to the front row supported by his 'brother' Hyacinth.

'And now,' Colin went on, 'I am going to establish three institutions to function from this day forth, the first day of my governorship at Gouldsboro. The first is that I am going to provide the port and settlement of Gouldsboro with night-watchmen, one to every thirty households, the expense to be borne by my salary as Governor. We all, I think, have happy memories of that aspect of life in our French towns and villages—being able to go to sleep with the knowledge that the night-watchman is going his rounds in the streets keeping an eye on things. Here we have an even greater need for such a watch, for if fire breaks out in the wilderness it spells the end—ruin, winter, and death. And in a port where there is a constant through-traffic of disorderly and drunken people, an alert guard is required to keep an eye out for the mischief such people may get up to. Finally, there is the ever-present danger of an attack by Indians or anybody else who might take it into his head to dispossess us.

'The night-watchmen will be appointed by the Governor and their maintenance and equipment will be paid for by him. This is a gift to mark my assumption of power at Gouldsboro.'

He was about to go on when a woman's voice rose up in the heavy silence.

'Thank you, Governor,' said the weak, thin but energetic voice. It was Abigail's.

There was a commotion in the crowd, and a babble of voices in which timid expressions of thanks mingled with the protests of the majority of the men. So they were giving in! . . . They wanted to make it clear that they had still not given their approval to Colin's establishment in power and that they were not to be bribed with night-watchmen.

Abigail looked Master Berne straight in the eye. Colin Paturel gave the young woman a slight smile and went on, holding out his hand to demand silence:

'The second institution is particularly appropriate after this amiable lady's remark. We hope to hold a meeting every three months of women, or rather mothers, although a woman old enough to be in charge of a family but who has no children would be allowed to attend. Monsieur Peyrac suggested the idea to me and I thought it a good one. Women always have a great many relevant things to say with regard to the good management of a city. But they don't say them because they are afraid of their husbands' sticks.'

The remark was greeted by laughter.

'There are to be no sticks or husbandly interference in this matter,' Colin went on. 'The women will discuss matters among themselves and then send on their views to me. Monsieur de Peyrac has been telling me that the Iroquois govern themselves in this way, and that no war is entered upon unless the Mothers' Council considers it necessary for their nation.

'Let us see if we can show ourselves at least as wise as the redskins.

'The third measure I propose to take was suggested to me by the colonists of New Holland. I believe that we should never hesitate to borrow ideas from our foreign neighbours to make our life more enjoyable. It is their custom to make a present to every young man getting married of a "pipe", that's to say 125 gallons, of Madeira. One third is to celebrate his marriage, another to celebrate the birth of his first child, and the third is to console his friends on the day of his funeral. Do you like the idea and do you agree to its adoption here at Goulds-boro?'

There was a temporary shock, a pause of supreme hesitancy, and then a unanimous clamour arose, consisting of mingled applause, approval and laughter. Angélique realized that Colin had won through.

There he stood with his hands on his hips, calm and dominating, while the ovations rained down upon him, just as he had stood when they had booed him. Colin Paturel, King of the Slaves, the outcasts, and the persecuted, was showing himself to be the strongest man present, and was standing out before them with his strong figure erect under the cloudy sky, as invincible as a rampart in his essential honesty, the straightforwardness of his simple heart, and the incredible toughness of his resourceful mind.

They had recognized from the very outset that he would be their permanent protector, their just and unbending Governor, and that they could rely on him utterly and completely.

The man, the sovereign that he was capable of being, had been raised up before their eyes by Joffrey de Peyrac. In this calloused hand Joffrey had set the sceptre which it was intended to bear. And all was well, Gold Beard no longer existed.

'Long live the Governor!' shouted the young people and children of Gouldsboro dancing and jumping up and down. The young people were the most enthusiastic, then the women, then the seamen of all nations, and last the transients, whether English or Acadian, who thought very highly of the decisions which had been announced, but were resolved to turn them to their own utmost advantage as neighbours.

The Indians, always of a cheerful disposition, added their own peculiar ebullience to this merry tumult, and the sour faces of the notables of La Rochelle disappeared from view, overwhelmed by the tide of general approbation.

'Hurrah! Hurrah! Bravo for our Governor,' bawled the prisoners from the *Heart of Mary* waving their arms exultantly and setting up a great clanking and clattering of chains.

Joffrey called to the Spaniards to unbind them.

'Do you know I'm tempted to settle here!' said Gilles Vanereick to the English admiral. 'The intentions of the new Governor strike me as highly entertaining. Did you notice, my lord, how he handled those sourpusses of Huguenots? And how cleverly he got himself unanimously acclaimed as Governor? Too late for them to back out of it now. . . . And as for Count Peyrac, what a delight to see the inscrutable expression on his face . . . like Mephistopheles getting the souls to dance at a Witches' Sabbath. . . . He's a juggler with sharp knives, a man who never hesitates to juggle with his own fate, with his own heart, in order to achieve his ends. But he has always been like that. I knew him well in the Caribbean. . . . Although, if that superb wife of his were my property, I would never have had his cheek . . . to place my wife's lover on my right hand, on the same throne! . . .'

With a lump in her throat, Angélique now realized why she was so distressed in spite of the happy outcome of the dilemma. Count Peyrac, because he was a man and Head of State, had had the power to save Colin's life, where she had not. He had made full use of it. And yet it was not just this subtle form of jealousy that rent her heart; she would have despised herself for it. It was rather the fact that he had excluded her from his discussions that proved that she no longer meant anything to him, and that it was not on her behalf that he had acted as he had. No! He had done it for Colin . . . and for Gouldsboro!

The solution he had devised was admirable. It solved all their problems. But as for her, he did not love her any more.

'My dear Abigail,' said Joffrey de Peyrac, stepping down from the stage and bowing to Gabriel Berne's wife, 'would you allow me to escort you to the banqueting hall? And you, my lord Governor, will you take Madame de Peyrac's arm? Let us form a procession, shall we? . . .'

The blood rushed to Angélique's cheeks on hearing her husband's suggestion.

As if through a haze she saw Colin's tall figure advance towards her, bow, and offer her his arm, on which she laid her hand, and together they walked off behind Joffrey de Peyrac and Abigail while the rest of the procession formed up behind them. Madame Manigault, furious at being ousted by Abigail from her position beside their lord and master, joined Master Berne, who was utterly dejected.

Monsieur Manigault somehow found himself with the lovely Ines on his arm, while the English admiral had a pretty Acadian girl as his partner. The Reverend John Knox Mather, whom the atmosphere was making more and more relaxed, was simultaneously favoured by the ravishing Bertille Mercelot and the charming Sarah Manigault.

Flanked by these two pretty girls, the respectable doctor of theology strode proudly along the sandy track leading from the fort to the inn.

Miss Pidgeon, full of blushes, walked arm-in-arm with the Reverend Patridge.

Bystanders lined the way, acclaiming and applauding the notables as they passed.

'So this is what that diabolical man has thought up to make us all play his little game,' Angélique muttered between her teeth.

'It was quite a feat, wasn't it,' Colin replied. 'I still haven't got over it myself. His strength of character quite overwhelms me.'

'How could you have agreed to his terms?'

'I didn't want to, but he availed himself of an argument that forced me to agree to his plans.'

'What did he say?'

'I can't tell you yet,' Colin replied meditatively. 'Maybe I shall one day. . . .'

'Oh, indeed! I am no doubt considered too stupid to share the grandeur of the visions and projects that you gentlemen have thought up!'

She clenched her fingers on Colin's sleeve.

'It is obvious that you two have become as thick as thieves; I should have guessed as much. How stupid I was to have worried so much on your account, Colin Paturel! Men always come to an understanding at women's expense! . . .'

CHAPTER 71

TRUMPETS WERE sounding and banners flying in the wind. The hall adjoining the inn, which was already so popular that it had come to be known by the name destined to be famous for a hundred leagues on all sides—'the Inn below the Fort'.

Outside, along the beach, around the port and the bay, game hung roasting on spits, and barrels were being broached for the seamen, the common people and the Indians.

As the guests began to take their places around the huge banqueting table, Angélique slipped away to the kitchens.

She must have a drink, or she would never get through the evening. She did not know whether she wanted to laugh or to cry, and she had never felt so close to breaking down completely. Joffrey had gone beyond all bounds and was making a fool of her.

'Give me a pint of that wine,' she said to David Carrère, after sniffing the contents of the barrels in the store.

'A pint!' the boy exclaimed, wide-eyed. 'For you! That's white Bordeaux, you know, Madame, as powerful as the sun.'

'It's exactly what I need!'

With her pint mug in her hands, Angélique went back to the kitchen where the spits were turning over the fire, and cast a scathing glance at the ladies of Gouldsboro who were busy titivating.

Madame Manigault, Madame Mercelot and all the others had come back into the kitchen under the pretext of lending a hand, but more particularly to check that their coifs were straight.

'Well,' Angélique asked them, 'what do you think of your new Governor?'

And she threw back her head and burst into peals of laughter.

'I can see what's upset you, my good ladies! After all that gossip about me, this was not at all what you ex-

425

pected to hear! There's the answer to all the talk about no smoke without fire. Gold Beard turns out to be a friend of mine who saved my life once on the Barbary coast. Is one to disown a man who has saved one's life— . . . Was I not within my rights to embrace him when by pure chance I found myself face to face with him again? But that was enough to stir up gossip and calumny, to turn a friendly meeting into a vile betrayal, an apple of discord. . . . And you were all too keen to see evil where it did not exist. . . .'

The Countess of Peyrac's sardonic laughter humiliated them all.

Although she knew that what she said was only half true, Angélique almost believed it. She went on taunting them. Kurt Ritz was far away, the poor man! No one would ever ask him to bear witness in public to what he had really seen—or thought he had seen—by the light of that smoky candle, on the night of his escape.

'So you see, my dear friends, gossip will be the ruin of the New World just as it has been of the Old,' Angélique concluded drinking down the last drop of her white wine.

Someone put a head round the door.

'Madame la Comtesse, your presence is requested in the banqueting hall.'

'I am coming immediately.'

'Now it is my turn to offer everyone here a gift to mark this joyous inauguration,' said Angélique as she took her seat at the banquet table.

Then, having aroused their curiosity, she went on:

'A cask of pure Armagnac which was given to me last week by a gallant Basque captain.'

Her announcement called forth a further ovation.

'Please fetch Adhemar,' Angélique bade one of the men serving the meal.

When the soldier arrived, still as bewildered-looking as ever, she instructed him to go to camp Champlain to fetch the things she had left there since the evening of her arrival. After Adhemar's departure, the appearance of this curious soldier of the King of France having caused considerable comment, Angélique related the history and exploits of the good fellow, thus starting off a round of gay conversation accompanied by innumerable anecdotes.

Dish after dish was passed round, abundant and tasty. A pig had been slaughtered, for these early settlers regarded oysters, lobster, turkey, salmon and game as food for the poor, because they were their daily fare.

Angélique found herself sitting on Colin's right hand, while he presided at one end of the table, and Joffrey at the other, with the gorgeous Ines on his right and Abigail on his left. Madame Manigault was sitting opposite her. A little farther along sat Gilles Vanereick, his fiery black eyes in his round, Flemish face never leaving Angélique. There was a generally fair balance of the sexes among the guests gathered round the table, French and English, people in dazzling livery or wearing dark, sober clothes with white bands, to whom were added as isolated figures, a Recollect friar, Father Baure, the Breton almoner of the *Fearless*, the Abbé Lochmer, a somewhat rough and ready man but jovial with it, and in no way concerned to have as his neighbours Pastor Baucaire and Pastor Patridge; an Acadian gentleman, Monsieur de Randon, who had disembarked that very morning from Port-Royal, talking with his blood-brother, an important Mic-Mac chieftain, who, in spite of the fact that he wiped his mouth with his hair, nevertheless seemed to dominate the entire gathering by reason of his regal stature.

While his presence among them astonished and even scandalized the Anglo-Saxons, they accepted it as one of the consequences of the French eccentricity that often makes them bristle but seems nevertheless to exist in order to enable foreigners to taste the joys of licence, of extravagance and even of sin, without forcing them to take the initiative themselves. At that moment the strict John Knox Mather had no sense of offending against the virtue of temperance while gaily emptying his pewter tankard, *for the wines were French ones.*

Their host was French, and likewise their hostess, which authorized her to be beautiful, dazzling and sumptuously dressed to delight the eyes of men, and never mind if so much dangerous provocation inevitably led her to sin against the Sixth Commandment, for even in God's own eyes, a French sin is a half-forgiven sin; and if the Spanish lady exuded the scent of jasmine, a perfume as sultry as the look that follows from those two velvety eyes half-hidden behind her black lace fan, all the fear and horror such an association might have called forth elsewhere was attenuated by the fact that they were sitting at a French table on French land.

Does not the genius of this giddy, thoughtless race lie precisely in the fact that they are able to impart to all situations a touch of their own levity?

Is it not true that the very daring of the astonishing mixtures which the French produce in their colonies, instead of leading to a blood bath as might be expected, produce no more than a mild euphoria that enables one to dream for the space of an hour that men are brothers and that damnation has been abolished? . . .

The English admiral declared:

'Gouldsboro will soon have become the most luxurious establishment along the whole of the American coastline. I am not even sure that the Spaniards in their fortified cities in Florida lead such a merry life as you do here. It is only fair to say that you gentlemen filibusters don't give them much chance,' he said to Vanereick.

'But they hit back pretty hard. That is, incidentally, why I am here. I share your opinion that it is a better place to live than anywhere else.'

'By what genius do you manage, Monsieur de Peyrac, to bring out of a situation apparently irremediably evil, something that is good and acceptable? For it is not enough just to will the good; the good must—how shall I put it?—be capable of materialization,' said Knox Mather, whose numerous libations were inclining him naturally in the direction of his governing interests, which were intellectual and theological.

'I do not think it is a matter of genius,' Peyrac replied, 'but rather of giving one's preference to life. Occasionally it is necessary to inflict death—one is obliged to by the imperfections of the world—but I consider that the only good is to be found in life.'

Mather frowned.

'Hum! You would not be by way of being a follower of that man Baruch Spinoza the philosophers speak of,

428

the Jew from Amsterdam, so strangely out of line both with Judaism and Christian Doctrine? . . .'

'I know that he said: "Whatever favours the persistence of the individual in Being, that is to say Life, is called Good, and whatever impedes it is called Evil . . ." '

'What is your opinion of the vague, disturbing sayings that seem to me to deny God his position of sovereignty?'

'I think the world is changing! But it is a slow and painful gestation. It is the common lot of all idolaters, to whom all of us here belong by our origins, to be unable to change their graven images. You gentlemen of the Reformed Church have already made an effort in that direction by destroying the statues in churches, and you English gentlemen have taken a step towards the liberation of mankind by beheading your kings, but take care, a step forward is often paid for by two steps backwards.'

'Gentlemen, gentlemen,' Father Baure exclaimed, in considerable agitation, 'what are you saying? I should not be sitting at your table. Your remarks have a smell of brimstone about them. . . . Beheading kings! Destroying statues! . . . Come, come! Have you forgotten that we are God's creatures and as such have an obligation to obey His laws, and to bow before the authorities. He Himself has set up on earth, such as the dogmas of the Holy Church first and foremost, and the decisions of rulers who govern us by divine right. Cut off their heads! What are you thinking of? . . . Hell awaits you. Things are being said here that make me shudder! . . .'

'An excellent wine is being drunk here, too,' Vanereick cut in. 'Drink up, my dear Father. The most shocking remarks are forgotten at the bottom of a glass.'

'Yes, drink up,' Angélique insisted, smiling at the priest to help him regain his composure. 'Wine is also one of God's gifts and there is nothing more likely to help the French and English to unite and forget their differences.'

Adhemar poked his head round the door:

'I've got your keg, Madame la Comtesse; and the Baron's box of English scalps, what am I to do with that?'

CHAPTER 72

ANGÉLIQUE BROKE into peals of hilarious laughter.

Her pint mug of white wine and the spicy warmth of the food had made her very animated. Adhemar asking what he should do with Baron Saint-Castine's coffer full of English scalps was the last straw.

By some miracle the simple-minded soldier's question had passed unnoticed in the uproar of conversation, and Angélique's light, airy laughter diverted the attention of the guests from Adhemar and concentrated it on this sudden outburst of delightful gaiety, so charming and so welcome.

Seeing that she had become the object of all eyes, Angélique led her guests on through a regular hail of jokes, witticisms and puns by which she tried to justify her excessive hilarity.

'Are we not plunged into the depths of licence, profligacy and dangerous depravity, brothers?' John Knox Mather asked his fellow Puritans, his eyes shining ecstatically like those of a martyr surrounded by the flames of the stake.

'It is by skirting such precipices without falling into them that the strength which the Lord gives his elect can be recognized,' the Reverend Patridge replied, his cavernous voice booming out over the peals of laughter.

Never had they been so happy to draw so close to the shores of licentiousness, and so satisfied with their own ability to resist temptation.

Angélique began to laugh more and more, and sometimes, in her effort to restrain herself, she was almost weeping. Borne along by the liberal supply of drinks, most of the guests found no difficulty in keeping pace with the general merriment.

It was too bad if her gaiety seemed inopportune and misplaced. The master of Gouldsboro had forced her to play this role, before them all, without a thought for her bleeding heart and her distress. He had decreed that she had to be the Countess of Peyrac. Without a crack

430

in her armour. The drama between the two of them must be buried, must be denied. No doubt this mattered less to him than to her. She no longer knew what he thought. She would almost have preferred the violent outburst of the other night to his apparent indifference, the kind of detachment that made her nothing more than a pawn to move about his chess-board, that carefully contrived set-up which he manipulated for his own personal ends. And he had carried his Machiavellism to the point of seating her on Colin's right hand.

If Colin had been less noble he would have disturbed her less. He would have kindled less warmth in her heart. Now, her nerves on edge, she felt a perverse desire to destroy the understanding that existed between him and Joffrey, to reach out towards him again, once again to try out her power over him. Her shining eyes sought his out, and she was furious to see, when he turned towards her, nothing but serene impassiveness, deliberate but unassailable. Joffrey had cut her off from him too. He had taken everything from her, seized everything she possessed and cast her out with nothing.

Thus did her heart and her distracted mind torment themselves, while she offered her guests a vision of exquisite vivacity, like an apparition of light and luxury at that rustic table at which a group of exiles, attempted to reproduce in spite of their poverty the sumptuous display of the Old World.

Alone among them all, Joffrey de Peyrac sensed the tension and slightly forced note of over-excitement in Angélique's laughter.

Like his guests he had caught from Adhemar's rambling remarks some vague story about 'English scalps', which had provoked Angélique's mirth, but also like them, inasmuch as Adhemar's words had been drowned by the general babble of conversation, he had preferred not to enquire more closely into the matter. There was time to look into that later. This was not the moment for dubious enquiries.

She was laughing, but she was also suffering. Inwardly moved by her brilliant beauty, roused by her boldness, the provocation of her slender chin proudly raised, of her lovely eyes turned towards Colin, and being, in

431

spite of himself, filled with admiration at the promptness with which she had taken up his challenge, and faced up to the humiliations that he had inflicted upon her, he could not succeed in guessing the source of the suffering that he felt vibrant within her.

As a result of his having turned her roughly away and cast her into the darkness, her woman's heart was becoming impenetrable to him again. He had lost that special gift of reading openly in it. The capacity to see and understand one another exactly as they were had been lost.

He did not dare to think that she was suffering precisely on his account. The bruise marking her lovely face, which she could only imperfectly disguise under her makeup, made him cautious in his approach. Angélique had pride, the pride of all high-born women, a mixture of self-confidence, of consciousness of value and rank, which, even if throughout their childhood they have eaten wild chestnuts and run about barefoot, makes them so difficult to handle and to tame. It is a sense of their lofty descent, and it is in their very flesh. Could Angélique ever forget the way he had treated her? A sense of anxiety which he was unprepared to recognize for what it was had been tormenting him since he had discovered the state of her face the morning after that terrible evening. He had been overwhelmed with dismay: 'I did not think that I had struck her so hard' he had murmured in his distress. He realized that no woman had ever been capable of making him lose control of himself so completely. 'I might have killed her!'

Being furious with himself he resented her all the more, and, paradoxical as it might seem, she attracted him all the more. . . .

When he set eyes on her, he felt a great tide welling up within him, both sentimental and sensual, which bore him irresistibly towards her with the desire to take her in his arms. For too long his arms had been empty of her. Gilles Vanereick might well have been right when, passing off his quite considerable philosophy as a good-humoured joke, he had advised him to take an indulgent

432

line: 'Believe me, Monsieur Peyrac, your wife is one of those women who are "worth while" forgiving. . . .'

He could not help reflecting that in spite of her apparent misery, she had not failed to fulfil her role as the Countess de Peyrac, which circumstance demanded of her, and had shown herself to be his worthy companion in every undertaking during those three painful, decisive days. And for this he would always be secretly grateful to her.

As he contemplated her surreptitiously, he could not help noticing all the qualities that made it 'worth while' to forgive her. Not only her beauty and the perfection of her body—an appalling temptation, to which he would have been loathe to succumb—but the things that constituted her very essence, the things he regarded as a priceless treasure.

Just when he thought he hated her, he found himself caught in the trap of those secret, unique qualities Angélique possessed.

On the morning of the terrible fight on board the *Heart of Mary*, he had made a pause, breathless from so much fighting, finally certain of victory, but seeing just how bloody the battle had been, and he had found himself thinking spontaneously: 'Fortunately *she* is in Gouldsboro! . . .'

As soon as they had learned that *she* was in Gouldsboro, the unfortunates who had been wounded took heart, even those who only knew her from hearsay. 'The Lady of the Silver Lake! The Frenchwoman with the power of healing! The Lovely Lady! The woman who knows all the secrets of the herbs . . . their healing virtues. . . . There is witchcraft in her hands, so they say. . . . She is on the beach, so they say. . . . She will come . . . she will save us. . . .'

All the men adored her. There was nothing to do about it.

At that moment her throaty laugh inflamed and tormented him alternately and subjected him, as it did all the other men present, to a charm that inclined him towards indulgence and abject surrender.

As he chatted with his guests at the banquet table, the faces of two women came and went, mingling in his mind's eye. Angélique's weaknesses could not detract from those human qualities which had finally won him over—he realized this in the light of the test to which they had been put—a feeling that was so intimately bound up with his pleasure in her, that he was unable any more to dissociate it from that other aspect of her female nature, treacherous and changeable, which aroused his wrath. He wanted to hate this woman for the weakness of her flesh and her contemptible fickleness, while passionately desiring the presence of the other woman, his friend, his companion, his confidante, his sensual, blissful haven of refuge.

His arms had missed her for too long. His body cried out for her with insistence that left him with a sense of abandonment.

Their sudden quarrel had wounded him, and through this wound he felt some of his essential strength ebbing away. He had slept badly during these impatient, troubled nights. Where are you, my smooth, gentle, white-skinned, soft-fleshed wife?

Where is your bare shoulder on which I love to lay my brow? Where are your delicate fingers, your magical fingers which used occasionally to dare to take my face between two hands and draw it down towards you to kiss my lips, in a movement full of the irresistible desire of a lover, but also of that warm, possessive tenderness that dwells in mothers' hearts, and which always occupies a unique place in men's memories! You were just beginning to feel less nervous of me, and then everything was destroyed.

Count Peyrac suppressed a sigh.

What was she thinking there at the other end of the table? He no longer knew.

During the past few days, he had found himself hesitating about what decisions to take, he had experienced self-doubt.

The only thing he had never hesitated about was what to do with Colin Paturel. Colin, the King of the Slaves, was the very man he had been waiting for so long. And as soon as he had recognized him, he had ceased to see him as a rival, and had decided that no 'woman trouble' was going to prevent his close association with so influential a man, such an obviously born leader of men.

And yet his was the rugged brow with the leonine mane, which, with his own eyes, he had seen Angélique stroke with her delicate hand.

On that island, what a torment it had been to him to think that the moment of betrayal had come. And yet, from where he stood hidden among the trees, as soon as his eyes had fallen upon the figure of the pirate, he had recognized him as the King of the Slaves of Meknès. This explained everything, and this made everything more serious, more tragic. He had always known that Angélique had loved this man, in a way that could not fail to make him intensely jealous.

For Colin deserved to be loved by such a woman.

This memory sent the subtle poison filtering back once more again into his heart. The plot he had hatched and set in motion against all of them now seemed to have become too big for him to manage.

Now her lovely eyes were fixed on Colin, seeking a glance of understanding from his as he sat there, rigid, through loyalty to Peyrac, pretending not to understand the provocativeness of her dazzling smile. He could hear her fascinating voice, a trifle mocking.

'My lord Governor, I seem to recollect that when we were in Barbary you used to call me Angélique. Should we not keep up the fraternal customs of the Christian slaves here?'

The little trollop! Not only was she turning a bold face to her shame, but here she was fighting back devastatingly.

How foolish he was to feel sorry for her. If she was unhappy, well let her be unhappy! She deserved to be taught a lesson.

He turned his attention once more to his neighbour on his left, Ines y Perdito Tenares, the voluptuous product of Caribbean, Spanish and Portuguese blood, whose black eyes were keeping a jealous watch on her Gilles, whom she considered to be far too fascinated by the charms of their laughing hostess.

Peyrac laid one finger on the chin of the pretty half-caste, to turn her head away from the distressing sight and to make her look at him.

435

'Let us console one another, Señorita,' he said to her softly in Spanish.

CHAPTER 73

'COLIN, HE doesn't love me any more! He is flirting with that woman Ines. He's tired of me.'

In the dark corridor Angélique staggered against Colin's shoulder. The feast was drawing to an end. A golden sunset sky with clouds scudding across it cast its tormented light on the noisy groups along the beach, dancing and laughing for joy. Some still sat in the banqueting hall, glued to their stools. A great deal of mutual support would be needed to get everyone back to their ships or their houses.

In the darkness of the corridor, Angélique staggered against Colin's shoulder.

'He doesn't love me any more . . . I shall die . . . I could never bear him to love another woman!'

'Calm yourself. You are drunk,' said Colin indulgently.

And he, fairly tipsy himself in spite of his resistance to alcohol, found it hard not to view the world through a slight mist and not to succumb to the temptation of taking her in his arms. He had left the banqueting hall to go and inspect his crew, saying that he must keep an eye on 'the lads'.

But Angélique had followed him. And now she clung to him, obviously very much under the influence of her repeated samplings of the cask of Armagnac, but also overcome by unhappiness.

'He is well disposed to you who led me into temptation, whereas he rejects and despises me. . . . It's not fair! . . . It's a shame!'

She was hiccuping slightly and stressing every word.

'Listen, my child!' said Colin. 'Go and take a walk in the fresh air. It will make you feel better.'

'That's right! You men are always hand in glove when it's a question of humiliating a woman, of mock . . . mocking her! You have betrayed me too!'

436

'Oh stop it! . . . Everything's all right now. Don't get in a state. There!'

She felt that Colin had become the true Colin once more, capable of being as intransigent as Joffrey and, like him, if he so decided, of controlling the most violent physical desire.

He pushed her firmly away from him, looking at her, and his expression grew a trifle melancholic.

'You love him too much,' he murmured nodding his head. 'It is quite obvious that his hold over you is complete. He dominates you. That is what hurts. That's what's got under your skin. Come on now, go and take a turn outside, my dear . . . my pretty one.'

He accompanied her down to the beach, where he left her and she headed off in the direction of the promontories to the east of Gouldsboro.

Colin was right.

The brisk evening air dispelled her giddiness and she began to walk with a firmer tread towards the rocks, hoping that she would not meet anyone.

Her mind was in a ferment like a wine-press at vintage time, full of noxious fumes.

Joffrey was flaunting his aversion for her.

That she could not stand! Never would she tolerate seeing Joffrey take another woman in his arms, seeking his pleasure in her, and, who knows, worst of all . . . forming an attachment to her and confiding in her. If that was how he wanted to punish her, he would succeed only too well. She would die for it . . . or she would kill the other woman!

She felt outraged that he found it easier to forgive Colin for having attempted to seduce her than her for having allowed him to.

The complicity between the two of them in their male sensuality exasperated her. It was useless to attempt to reach an understanding with men. They always managed to deceive you or to confound you with some argument or other. She had had enough of men and their demands.

Tending those wounded in their wars, feeding and bringing up the children that resulted from their pleasure, polishing their weapons, and, year in and year out, wiping their footsteps off the floors of their houses, cooking the game from their hunting parties, gutting the fish that they had caught. Their work had dignity and status, whereas women's was mere drudgery!

A week ago she had been dancing on Monhegan Island, leaping over the Basque's fire, raised aloft by the joy of living and big Hernani's strong wrists.

Although separated from Joffrey at that time, she had felt closer to him than she did now. For three days they had not spoken, and seemed to have ceased to exist for one another.

In a matter of a few days, less than a week, a chasm had opened at their feet, a wall had sprung up between them, an impregnable rampart. Everything had conspired to produce a situation in which their love for one another would be destroyed, had possibly already been destroyed.

A voice seemed to whisper to her through the wind:

'He will separate you . . . you'll see! You'll see! . . .'

She gave a shudder and halted at the end of the promontory. She thought again of the combination of circumstances that had led to the public humiliation of the man she adored. There was something diabolical in it all. An interweaving of pure chance and bad luck which seemed explicable only if one attributed it all to the ill-will of evil spirits bent on their destruction.

She was gripped with fear, the same fear she had felt the evening the stranger with the white face had led her off to the island. She was beginning to believe in the Devil . . . like everyone else in this god-forsaken land.

She turned towards Gouldsboro. 'There are places where the spirit blows. . . .'

Was Gouldsboro one such? Had it really been pre-destined, as the nun visionary in Quebec claimed, to be the setting of a suppra-terrestrial drama?

'But I am not the She-Devil,' Angélique told herself, almost aloud. 'So what then?'

In spite of herself she recalled the nun's prediction which had caused so much agitation among the Canadian population.

'I was standing on the seashore. There were trees growing right down to the edge of the sand. . . . The beach had a pink sheen. On my left stood an outpost built of wood, with a high palisade, and a turret with a flag on it. . . . The bay was crowded with islands like sleeping monsters. . . . At the top of the beach, below the cliffs, stood a number of houses built of light wood . . . and in the bay two ships lay at anchor. . . . At the far end of the beach, some distance away, perhaps a mile or two, there was another hamlet of small huts surrounded by roses. I could hear the screeching of seagulls and cormorants. . . .'

The wind tore at Angélique's hair which twined around her like some crazed being, leaving her at one moment, binding her fast the next, whispering words of terror in her ear.

Standing rigid and motionless on the point of a rock, Angélique gazed back towards Gouldsboro.

The beach was tinged with pink and there were the sleeping emerald-coloured monsters, the islands, and the 'wooden outpost with its turret and a flag on it,' and the hamlet of camp Champlain where the roses were coming into bloom.

'Then suddenly an extremely beautiful woman rose up out of the sea and I knew she was a She-Devil. She remained there, suspended above the water, in which her naked body was reflected. . . . Then a unicorn loomed up over the horizon, its long pointed horn glittering like crystal in the light of the setting sun. The She-Devil leapt astride the animal and bounded off through the air. I knew she was going to destroy Acadia, that beloved land we have taken under our protection. . . .'

Angélique stared desperately at the scene before her. It was as if some secret lay behind those sybilline words. Now she was sure of it. The irrational element in human nature that makes us sensitive to the meaning of symbols sounded the alarm and held her in a state of suspense as she gazed at the panorama before her eyes.

Yes, there were ships lying at anchor in the bay, there were seagulls and cormorants, and light-coloured wooden houses under the cliff.

She gave a sudden cry as a memory came back to her.

When she had disembarked here, a year before, THERE HAD BEEN NO LIGHT-COLOURED WOODEN HOUSES under the cliff. Those houses had been built by the Huguenots from La Rochelle during the course of the winter and spring.

She began to pace up and down in agitation, her mind confused by the wind and the wine she had drunk, while her thoughts jostled one another feverishly. She muttered:

'I'll tell them . . . I'll tell them all . . . I'll tell them in Quebec that I am not their She-Devil. .*. . You see, there were no light-coloured wooden houses when I arrived . . . and now there are. . . . So now is the time that the She-Devil should appear!'

She stopped short, as if an icy hand had clutched her throat, an impulsive terror. The words she herself had just uttered struck her as insensate, and yet inescapably true.

Apart from the number of ships—of which there were many that day and not just two—the whole scene described in the prophecy lay there before her very eyes.

She must be raving! Had she been able to run to Joffrey, he would have shared or dispelled her fears, he would have laughed at them. . . .

But henceforth she was on her own, and to her alone, behind the cloak of appearances, had been revealed the threat of the succubus, the She-Devil, that dazzling creature who was to rise up out of the sea, astride a unicorn, to bound off into the air over the land of Acadia, to ravage and destroy everything in her path . . . even to the depths of men's hearts!

I had had too much to drink! . . . And I'm so weary! Am I going mad? I must sleep, and not think any more.

Such were Angélique's thoughts on the evening of that proud day in the annals of Gouldsboro when the colony had celebrated the accession of its first governor.

As night fell, Colin had spoken once more from the platform and had ended his speech by throwing a hundred pounds worth of gold pieces into the crowd.

Everyone seemed happy. Only Angélique felt the threat behind the appearances. Ever since the 'revelation' she had had down by the sea, to her misery at being separated from Joffrey was added her fear that they might all be the victim of some evil spell.

440

On all sides she saw tangible signs of her foreboding, and the laughter, the singing, the dancing, and the general hilarity all shocked her, seemed insultingly misplaced in face of the misfortune that she thought she saw advancing upon them—that might already be amongst them! Like a worm in the fruit. A succubus on the prowl amongst them, gibbering and sniggering. The screech of a nightjar sounded like the She-Devil's laughter to her ears. To whom could she turn in her anxiety?

'I had too much to drink! I'll feel better tomorrow. . . . Tomorrow I shall go and see Joffrey. He will have to agree to see me. He will have to tell me what he intends to do with me, whether he intends to send me away, or to forgive me. But things cannot go on like this . . . because this way we are weak, and the She-Devil will get to us. . . . But no, I'm raving. There is nothing, truly, nothing coming towards us over the water! That terrible thing! We shall prove stronger than her . . . but we must not be separated . . . I think I am feverish. I have had just about my fill for today. Goodbye gentlemen, I leave you to your grandiose projects.'

She went from one group to another, finding that they were still singing around the fires lighted along the beach in the night, and they all gave her a cheer as she went by. She then made her way to where Joffrey de Peyrac and Colin Paturel were standing side by side below the fort, receiving the respects and congratulations of the assembled company. In silence she dropped them a curtsy and retired.

Her step was unsteady as she made her way along the path to the fort, unaware of the fact that the two men, in spite of themselves, followed her with their eyes.

Beneath her windows in the central courtyard of the fort, some sailors were talking together as they drank one last tankard.

'Meanwhile, we've been done,' said one of the men from the *Heart of Mary*. 'It's all very well being a settler in a pleasant spot, but all I can see here by way of women are either Huguenots or squaws. Working hard for your living in America is all right, but not on your own. We thought we'd have our dinner waiting for us when we got home and a white Christian woman waiting for us in bed, that was what was agreed! THAT's the part of the contract I liked.'

Lieutenant Barssempuy gave the man a dig in the ribs with his elbow.

'Don't be too greedy, my boy. You've seen another sun go down, although this was the day you were supposed to die. Tonight the loveliest woman you'll hold in your arms is Life. The other kind will soon come up over the horizon, you may be sure of that!'

'That doesn't alter the fact that there's no sign of them for the time being.'

'Pray, brothers,' Father Baure interrupted, 'pray, and God will provide.'

'Avast there, monk,' one of them said. 'Without wishing to contradict you, can you see how God could possibly make twenty or thirty marriageable girls spring up out of the sand between now and tomorrow, fit to be married to gallant gentlemen of fortune like us?'

'No, I cannot see how,' the Recollect father replied quietly, 'but God is great! And anything can happen by His hand. So say a prayer, my sons, and He will grant you these women.

'God is great. God is all-powerful, let it be remembered.'

And this is how these converted filibusters from the *Heart of Mary* were granted wives the very next day after all these strange events.

CHAPTER 74

A MAN came running along the path leading from Blue Creek to Gouldsboro. Gusts of wind and rain tore at his cloak, but he hurried along, puffing and blowing. It was the paper-maker Mercelot, whose mill stood at some distance from the village.

He reached the fort and called to the sentries:

'Quick! Make haste! A ship has gone aground at Blue Creek.'

Angélique, who had slept like a log, was awakened by lights in the courtyard of the fort. It was scarcely dawn and she thought at first that the festivities were still continuing, then all the stir and bustle made her realize that there was something strange going on. She dressed quickly and ran down to find out what it was.

By the light of lanterns, Mercelot was pointing at a map held by the Count.

'They must have struck the reefs of Bleak Monk at the mouth of Anemone Bay and then been driven inshore in Blue Creek.'

'But whatever were they doing in those waters?' exclaimed the Count.

'The storm. . . .'

'*But . . . there is no storm.*'

It was indeed surprising.

The wind was in fact blowing hard and the sea was rough, but for once the sky was clear and ships at sea must have had a perfectly clear view of the coast with its guide beacons.

'Is it a cod-fisher?'

'How can one tell? . . . It's still too dark to see, but they are crying for help fit to make your hair stand on end. My wife and daughter are already down on the beach with our servant-girl and our neighbour.'

Thus it was that the inhabitants of Gouldsboro, scarcely recovered from a day of festivities, found themselves, still half-asleep and tormented by anxiety, standing in the wind-swept dawn, on the beach of Blue Creek, listening to distant cries of terror that came tragically to them through the grey murk through which from time to time they glimpsed, just above the surface of the waves, the masts of a half-submerged ship.

Angélique was there with most of the other Gouldsboro ladies.

The wreck was submerged up to its rails. Strangely enough, it still did not sink, and the currents at the mouth of the bay were battering it back and forth between the two promontories of land lying at the entrance. Every time this occurred they expected to see the vessel crash against the rocks and explode like a heavy, overfilled barrel; but then off it would go again, its three masts swaying aimlessly, its sails flapping and its shrouds hanging uselessly.

If only they could hold on until the chebec and the cutter from Gouldsboro arrived with Joffrey de Peyrac and Colin Paturel, who were at that moment rounding Point Yvernec to get to them by the sea route.

Borne on the wind came heart-rending shrieks and cries for help, all the more distressing because over the crests of the waves no one could be seen on board the wreck.

The gang of sailors and fishermen who had come by the overland route from Gouldsboro were armed with boat-hooks, gaffs, anchors, ropes and life-lines.

Under the instructions of Hervé Le Gall, three of them got into the Mercelot's fishing smack and pulled out as hard as they could row.

The others spread out along the rocks ready to help out of the water any of the shipwrecked people who might try to swim for it.

'I shall go and get blankets, soup and hot drinks ready,' said Madame Mercelot. 'Come on, Bertille.'

Angélique had brought ointments and lint to dress any injuries there might well be, and a flagon of rum. She was just about to follow Madame Mercelot when, only a few cables' length from the shore, a kind of raft made of wooden planks and barrels hastily lashed together came surging up before their eyes from the hollow of a wave, with a group of dishevelled creatures clinging screaming to it.

'Women!' Angélique exclaimed. 'Oh! Lord! The breakers are driving them onto the rocks. They will be smashed to pieces!'

No sooner had she spoken than the raft, as if driven by some inner malice, canted up on one end and crashed against a particularly jagged rock, where it ripped apart, bursting and scrattering into hundreds of tiny splinters and shamelessly tipping its entire cargo into the sea. Fortunately the beach was near, and Angélique and her companions dashed into the water up to their waists to rescue the drowning women.

Angélique seized a head of long hair just as its owner disappeared beneath the surface of the water down into a deep bed of seaweed.

She managed to keep the half-drowned woman's head

above the surface and to tow her back to the shore.

It so happened that she was an enormous woman who must have weighed at least sixteen stone, and as long as Angélique was pulling her through the water, she did not notice how heavy she was, but as soon as they reached the sand she suddenly found herself dragging a weight like a sack of stones and was quite incapable of shifting the inert mass a single inch.

'Come and give me a hand!' she called out to the bystanders.

A sailor sprang forward, then a second, then a third and a fourth.

'In Heaven's name whatever was a woman like this thinking of to put to sea?' they complained. 'Such hefty creatures should never go near a ship, they should remain on land like cannons in a fortress.'

Meanwhile Madame Mercelot, her daughter, their maid and their manservant had helped the six other women ashore. Some of them were shivering dreadfully, their teeth chattering uncontrollably, while other were crying. One of the girls fell on her knees and made the sign of the cross.

'Thank you, Blessed Virgin, for saving our lives,' she said fervently.

They were all French but to judge by their accent they were not Canadian.

'There's Delphine still caught out there!' one of them cried, pointing to a young woman who had succeeded in clambering onto a rock. No doubt she was exhausted, for she lay there half-conscious, and at any moment another wave might have swept her away.

Angélique ran round the edge of the promontory to where the girl was and helped her back onto firm ground again.

'Put your arm round my shoulders, my dear,' she told her. 'I will support you and take you to that house yonder, where we shall soon have you in front of a good fire.'

The shipwrecked girl, a pretty brunette with intelligent-looking eyes, seemed to come from a good family. She found the strength to murmur, through her deathly pale lips, with a faint smile:

'Thank you, Madame. You are very kind.'

'Here they come!'

A cry of hope went up at the sight of the white sails of the chebec and the cutter as they rounded Cerneck Point. The two ships made their way swiftly towards the wreck.

'Are there still many people left on board?' Angélique asked the young woman she was supporting.

'At least twenty of my companions, I think, and some members of the crew. Oh God, let's hope they're not too late!'

'No, they aren't! Look, our ships have already reached the wreck and taken up position on either side of it.'

Dawn had broken and they could now follow the stages of the rescue operation.

Le Gall, returning with his boat full of women, said that those still out there stood a good chance of being saved.

The wreck was certainly sinking, but slowly enough to allow time to get the survivors on board the chebec. Some of the Indians from the hamlet had also put out to sea in their canoes and were bringing some of the women back, no more chilled and terrified by their ordeal than by these redskinned faces and befeathered heads. They also brought in a cabin boy with long hair.

Then suddenly the masts began to go under, rapidly dwindling from sight as they plunged beneath the waves. The white sails of the two Gouldsboro ships could be seen tacking back and forth like birds hovering over the doomed ship in its death agony. On the shore, the women refused to leave the beach and stood with their eyes riveted upon the last moments of their ship.

When it had completely vanished they began to sob and wail and wring their hands.

CHAPTER 75

Dame Petronella Damourt—'with a *t*', she insisted—the fat woman whose life Angélique had saved, laced into some of Madame Manigault's spare clothes—the biggest they had been able to find in the place—was sitting facing Count Peyrac and Colin Paturel, trying to explain to them in a series of long speeches interrupted by equally prolonged bursts of weeping, what their exact position was.

She had been entrusted with the task, she said—'for six hundred pounds cash,' she added proudly—of acting as escort to a contingent of some thirty 'King's Girls' being sent out to Quebec as wives for the unmarried settlers, soldiers and officers there, in order to people the colony.

'But your ship was not making for Quebec, my good lady,' the Count remarked. 'You are in fact a very long way from it.'

'Is that so?'

She turned to Colin whose simple features intimidated her less than the Spanish-looking gentleman who had saved their lives. Colin seemed to her more likely to understand the torments of an ignorant and simple heart.

He confirmed what Count Peyrac had said:

'You are not on the route to Quebec.'

'But where are we then? The lights of a town had just been sighted when the ship went aground.'

She looked from one to the other, her face full of terror and incredulity, and tears streamed down her fat cheeks.

'Whatever will the Duchess of Baudricourt, our benefactress, say when she hears this? . . . Oh, but I was forgetting, she has been drowned. How dreadful! Oh no, she can't be! Our dear benefactress. A saint! What will become of us?'

She began to sob still harder, and Colin handed her a handkerchief as big as a duster, for sailors are prepared for all eventualities. She dabbed her eyes, and at last succeeded in controlling herself.

'Poor dear lady! She who so longed to give her life for New France!'

She resumed her story from a much earlier point. For her the adventure seemed to have begun when she became a chambermaid in the service of the Dutchess of Baudricourt d'Argenson. A few years later the Duke of

Baudricourt had died at the age of seventy-five after an extremely debauched life, having nevertheless contrived to leave his widow a handsome fortune.

The noble widow, Dame Ambroisine de Baudricourt d'Argenson who throughout her married life had patiently borne the affronts, vexations and infidelities of her husband, found that at last the time had come when she could do what she herself wanted to do, namely to retire into a convent of her choosing and there to await death in prayer and mortification, and also, under the guidance of learned men and astronomers, to give herself up to the study of mathematics for which she had a decided gift.

So it was that she entered the convent of the Augustinians in Tours as a canoness. But two years later her confessor persuaded her that her considerable fortune should be used in the service of the Church rather than in the pursuit of mathematics, and persuaded her to leave. He it was who had fired her with enthusiasm for the welfare of New France and the conversion of its savages.

However, the widow had continued to hesitate, until one morning when she was already fully awake, a tall woman dressed in a white serge dress appeared to her and said quite distinctly:

'Go to Canada. I shall not forsake you.'

She was convinced she had seen the Blessed Virgin, although she had not been able to make out her face, and from that time on she had dedicated herself to the succour of these distant territories. Having a good head for business and being fully conversant with the ways of the world, she was able to contact various ministers, obtain authorizations and form a company called the Society of Our Lady of the St. Lawrence, which had the advantage of being partly a commercial venture, partly a religious one, and which, by placing its services at the disposal of the King, the Governor and the Missionaries, ensured its own subsistence.

Dame Petronella, who had become very attached to the good lady and had even followed her into the convent, wished to remain in her service in spite of the increasing hazards associated with the Duchess's projects.

The inevitable had to be faced. One cold morning in May she had clambered on board that shifting world of planks and canvas known as a ship, and loaded her sixteen stone of flesh into the monster's hold—there to die a thousand deaths, less on account of the stormy seas than the peevishness of the girls in her charge. But how could she have left the poor Duchess alone and unaided to face the unknown with all its dangers? For the Duchess of Baudricourt, after enquiring what were the colonies' most pressing needs, had learned that wives were wanted for the colonists.

Indeed, all young men in the colonies were required, by order of the King, to marry before reaching the age of twenty. Failing this, the fathers of the recalcitrant young men were to pay a fine and present themselves every six months before the authorities to justify their sons' non-compliance with the regulations.

Recently the administrator of the Province, Carlon, an energetic man, had ruled that all unmarried Canadians should be forbidden to hunt, to fish, to trade with the Indians or to move inland into the forestlands under any pretext whatsoever. From Europe the Minister of the Crown, Colbert, had added to this ordinance the decree that any man objecting to marriage would have to pay a special bachelor tax. These men would be ineligible for any kind of distinction or honour and would be required to wear, prominently sewn to their sleeve, a special badge as a mark of this disgrace.

Following the publication of this decree, out of the thousand bachelors living in Quebec, eight hundred had taken to the woods.

Peyrac was familiar with this situation since he was acquainted with Nicholas Perrot, Maupertuis and his son, and even l'Aubignière, who were among the immediate victims of these laws.

As for the two hundred faithful men who had remained in Montreal and Quebec, resigned to their fate, they needed wives, and Madame de Baudricourt had wished to add her contribution to this noble aim. She herself took charge of a convoy of young women known as 'the King's Girls,' gave them all dowries, and, in emulation of the royal 'gift' which the administration was expected to give each of the girls, undertook to pay their expenses to the sum of one hundred pounds apiece, namely ten pounds for recruitment expenses, thirty for their outfits, and sixty for their fare. In addition to this she had given each girl a small trunk with a lock, four chemises, a full set of clothes—cloak, skirt and underskirt —shoes and stockings, four neckerchiefs, four mob-caps, four bonnets, two pairs of cuffs, four pocket handkerchiefs, one pair of skin gloves, one coif, and a black taffeta square, not to mention a brush and comb and other small items of haberdashery.

In this way they would all be well equipped to please the submissive bachelors awaiting them on the quayside at Quebec, formed up in two lines, wearing their best clothes and their heavy shoes, for the ladies to process between.

After a small reception and some refreshments to smooth over their first meeting, they were to be housed in a convent in the city—of which there was no lack— where, during the following days, they could receive the young men in the parlour, watched over and advised by the priests, nuns, and lady benefactresses.

'As you must know, Monsieur Colbert is very exacting about the women chosen to come to Canada,' Petronella Damourt stressed. 'And like him, we took great care about recruitment. The girls we have brought were all born in wedlock; some are orphans and the others come from families that have fallen upon hard times.'

In addition to all this, Madame de Baudricourt had chartered a ship; the King had donated a banner decorated with his monogram and the Queen had given holy pictures, statuettes and the like to adorn a church.

Dame Petronella burrowed in her pockets for documents to prove to these alarming strangers how piously and carefully the expedition had been organized.

She wanted to show them her precise accounts, for she herself had itemized every article for every girl, had had the document countersigned by a commissioner for oaths, and had kept it carefully filed away in a waterproof envelope together with the letter from Monsieur Colbert. . . .

When she remembered that the clothes she was wearing were not her own and that all these goods and chattels were now at the bottom of the sea, she burst into floods of tears once more.

They could not get much more out of her beyond the fact that, having embarked early in May on a small 150-ton ship sailing for Quebec, she found herself shipwrecked in these first days of July on the coast of Maine in Frenchman Bay.

'And what was the name of the captain of the wreck?'

'Job Simon. So charming and gallant a man!'

'But a poor navigator, it would seem,' Peyrac interjected. 'And where is your captain at the present moment? Where are all the crew? I know the ship was only a small one, but it must have had about thirty men on board to man it. Where are they?'

It soon became only too clear. The sea began to wash up bodies mutilated from being dashed against the rocks. They were found in every creek and inlet, and the Indians brought them in on their backs, and laid them out on the sand in Blue Creek. Joffrey de Peyrac set off to identify them with the ship's boy, a Breton lad who knew only a few words of French. The boy considered himself lucky to be alive and still in possession of his carved wooden spoon, the sailor's most important possession. He told how he had heard the hull split open on a reef. Then the mate had launched the longboat with a number of men and women on board, intending to seek help from the harbour of the nearby city.

'What city?'

'We saw lights, and we thought we had reached Quebec.'

'Quebec?'

'Yes, of course!'

CHAPTER 76

MEANWHILE ANGÉLIQUE had worked ceaselessly throughout the day to bring some comfort to the poor survivors from the shipwreck in Blue Creek. First it had been the survivors of the battle in the harbour, now it was women.

Then it had been the tanned, hairy flesh of the pirates she was obliged to deal with, now it was soft, smooth white flesh. But this difference apart, she would always remember the period of confusion that had followed her first return to Gouldsboro as one reminiscent of a visit to the infernal regions where Dante had described the damned writhing in torment, their naked bodies intermingled.

First it had been wounded men, now half-drowned women. After the groans and oaths of the men had come the tears and whimpers of the female sex.

Angélique began to think of her quiet, pleasant life in Wapassou as if it were some unattainable paradise.

The 'King's Girls' were aged between fifteen and seventeen. Some of them were peasant girls, but most came from Paris, where they had been chosen from among the inmates of the State Orphanage. Angélique recognized their lively, cheeky style of speech, which brought these remote regions of America the flavour of the narrow winding streets behind the Chatelet or the Quai aux Fleurs, the smell of the Seine, the whiff of cook-shops, and butchers' stalls, and made one remember the rumble of coaches over the round cobbles.

There were among them four 'young ladies' of good birth, intended as brides for officers, a Moorish girl with skin the colour of burnt toast, and one called Julienne who was manifestly a whore.

From the outset this girl boorishly refused all help from Angélique although she was evidently in pain, and dragged herself to a place away from the others. Her companions gave her the cold shoulder, for she was quite out of place in this convoy of brides-to-be, who, according to the directives of Monsieur Colbert, were always to be 'biddable, attractive, hard-working, industrious, pious young women'.

Delphine Barbier du Rosoy, the attractive, plucky brunette, stressed this fact by way of explaining that Julienne should never have found her way into their company. Madame de Baudricourt's over-generous heart had been taken advantage of in this case.

'You can talk, you young ladies,' shouted Julienne, who had overheard her, 'you can talk when it comes to

452

generosity! . . . You must have satin at twenty pounds a length for your clothes while we girls from the orphanage have to make do with Troyes cloth at thirty sous a time.'

In spite of her vulgar outburst, her attempt to create trouble misfired, since all the other orphanage girls were in fact affable, modest and well behaved in spite of their poverty, for they had been brought up by nuns in the orphanage, and the shipwreck had drawn them closer to their more distinguished and better-off companions. It was Delphine du Rosoy who had had the idea of building a raft and had encouraged and sustained them throughout the worst of their ordeal.

Angélique had no other means of housing her protegées than to install them in their turn in the grain store, now vacant against since the release of the prisoners who had gone back to their quarters on the *Heart of Mary*.

And now the men were on the prowl around the barn, examining the lines hung with petticoats and bodices flapping in the wind.

Lieutenant de Barssempuy appeared carrying a pale, inert form.

His eyes shone with feverish excitement.

'I found her,' he explained, 'I found her over yonder, there among the blue rocks, like a wounded seagull. She is just like in my dream. It's her, I'm sure. I have often seen her in my dreams; look how pretty she is!'

Angélique glanced at the bloodless face dragged back by the weight of its long blonde hair heavy with seawater, sand and blood.

'My poor fellow, the girl is dead . . . or as good as dead.'

'No, no, I beg you, save her life,' implored the young man. 'She is not dead. Do something for her, Madame I beseech you, you who have miraculous hands, care for her, bring her back to life, make her better. . . . She cannot die, she is the one I was waiting for.'

'That's Marie,' said several of the 'King's Girls' bending over the inanimate, blood-stained body. 'Poor girl! It would be better if she did die. She was the maid-in-waiting to Madame de Baudricourt and looked on her as her mother. What will become of Marie without her?'

While Angélique, assisted by old Rebecca, did her best to bring life back to the poor battered body, the other girls discussed how the Duchess had lost her life, and came to the conclusion that it must have been when she went back to the 'tween-deck to fetch Jeanne Michaud's baby boy who had been left behind there.

Jeanne Michaud was weeping in a corner. At the age of twenty-one she was the oldest of the women. She was the widow of a coppersmith and had so moved Madame de Baudricourt's generous heart that she had encouraged her to come to Canada with her little two-year-old son, Pierre, where she would find it easier to obtain a new husband than in France. She had a certificate from her parish priest stating that she was of good character and had no husband alive in France. She remembered nothing save that she had been woken up in the midst of darkness and the sound of shrieks and wails and searched in vain for the child that had been sleeping beside her.

She went on, moaning:

'It's all my fault. My child is dead and our benefactress lost her life trying to save him. She was a saint, and died a martyr's death!'

'And I think you're making a devil of a fuss of that damned Duchess,' Julienne shouted coarsely. 'That benefactress of yours, let me tell you, was nothing but a boring old bitch! Let the angels in heaven have her, if they want her, say I; I put up long enough with her and her mean ways.'

'You're only saying that because she made you go to Mass,' Delphine said severely, 'and made you say your prayers and behave yourself.'

The girl burst into a raucous cackle, then gave Delphine a sly glance.

'Oh I see. You let her harpoon you, too, Miss du Rosoy. She got you too in the end with her paternosters. And yet you didn't like her any more than I did at the beginning. But she got round you all right.'

'Julienne, you loathed her from the start because she tried to save you, and you hate all goodness.'

'Her kind of goodness? I'll say! I'll have nothing to do with that. Shall I tell you what sort of a woman she was, your Duchess? . . . She was a baggage, a trollop.'

The end of her sentence was lost in a chorus of shouts and cries while three or four of the 'King's Girls' hurled themselves upon Julienne in a paroxysm of indignation.

Julienne struggled with them, gesticulating wildly, and biting the hands they tried to place over her mouth to keep her quiet.

'I'll damn well say what I think . . . it's not the like of you that are going to stop me, you bitches!'

Her voice grew faint, and faded away, and she collapsed on the ground in a faint.

Her assailants were disconcerted.

'What's happened to her? We hardly touched her.'

'I think she was hurt when the ship went down,' Angélique intervened, 'but she wouldn't allow anyone near her. Now she will just have to let us attend to her.'

But no sooner had she bent over the unruly girl, than the latter sat up again with her eyes full of hate.

'Don't touch me, or I'll kill you!'

Angélique gave a shrug and left her, and Julienne went off into a corner, where she remained cowering like a wild animal.

'A girl like that ought never to have been included in a convoy for Canada,' the girls repeated once more. 'Because of her, people will think we're like those good-for-nothing thieving wenches they send to St Christopher Island. . . . We may be poor, but we aren't convicts.'

Marie opened her eyes, lovely periwinkle-blue eyes between golden eyelashes, now filled with unspeakable dread.

'Demons,' she murmured, 'I can see them, I can hear them screaming in the night. . . . They are striking me . . . demons! . . . Demons! . . .'

CHAPTER 77

THAT EVENING, when Angélique was down on the beach again, her mind running once more on the mystic prophecy and its relation to Gouldsboro, she sensed a presence behind her.

She turned round and felt her knees grow weak.

It was the mythical animal!

The unicorn.

It was standing erect, proudly arching its gilded neck, and its long nostrils 'glittered like crystal in the light of the setting sun'.

The beach was a tiny one, shaped like a half-moon, hemmed in by clumps of trees whose roots extended boldly down to the very edge of the seaweed. It opened into the narrow inlet known as Anemone Creek, because of the fact that multicoloured anemones bloomed there throughout the summer. And now, above the smooth white sand, rose the long neck and head of the unicorn.

Angélique thought that she must be dreaming and could not summon up the strength to cry out for help.

Then a hairy creature, bellowing like a seal, loomed up out of the water, and rushed forward, his shrieks filling the bay and echoing around the cliffs. He swept like a whirlwind past Angélique and threw himself down before the unicorn, with arms extended.

'Don't touch her, you wretches! Don't touch my beloved. I thought she was gone for good. . . . Don't touch her or I'll kill you all! . . .'

The man was huge. Blood and water streamed from his hideous, bearded face and trickled off his ragged clothes, while from his eyes shone an elusive, terrifying fire.

The men who had come running from the direction of Gouldsboro, their attention attracted by the shouting, clutched their knives or swords in their hands and watched the man apprehensively.

'Stand back, you wreckers, or I'll strangle you.'

'We'll have to shoot him,' said Jacques Vignot who was carrying a musket. 'He has gone mad.'

'No,' Angélique intervened, 'leave him. I think I understand. He is not mad, but he is in danger of becoming so.'

Then she went up to the unfortunate man who towered over her like a crazed giant.

'What was the name of your ship, Captain?' she asked the man gently. 'Your ship that was wrecked on the rocks last night.'

The sound of her voice penetrated to Job Simon's

456

befogged mind, and tears began to pour down his shaggy face. He fell to his knees clasping the gilded wooden figure-head from his lost ship—a figure that was almost as tall as himself.

'It was *The Unicorn*, Madame,' he murmured. 'My ship that went down was called *The Unicorn!*'

'Come, I will find you some food,' she said to Job Simon, laying one hand on his arm with a gentleness that soothed the wretched man's troubled mind like a balm.

'And what about her, what shall we do with her,' he stammered, pointing towards the gilded wooden figure-head rising out of the sand. 'No one must hurt her, my Unicorn . . . she is so beautiful!'

'We shall move her somewhere else. . . .'

'We shall move her to where she will be safe from the sea. . . . Then later you can put her on the prow of another ship, Monsieur.'

'Never! Never! I am ruined, I tell you . . . but at least I have her, my unicorn! Isn't she lovely? Real gold leaf on her, that was! I put the horn there myself on her head, that beautiful horn from a narwhal that I harpooned myself. Beautiful pink ivory just like a corkscrew. . . . You should have seen the way it glistened in the sun. . . .'

He talked on, unburdening himself to the unknown woman who guided him, quite unaware of what was happening around him. He let himself be led like a child.

When they reached Madame Mercelot's house she sat him down at a rustic table. In every settler's house in America there is always a pan of broth or soup simmering on the hearth, and Angélique gave the man a bowl of mashed pumpkin and stuffed oysters.

The man began to eat voraciously, sighing as he did so and picking up visibly at each mouthful.

'Well, there it is. I'm ruined,' he concluded on reaching the bottom of a second bowlful. 'At my age, I might as well say I've had it. A graveyard's the nearest thing to a ship I'll ever find to rest my bones in. I said to the Duchess: "I don't give much for our chances, in all this," but nothing doing! She does exactly what she wants to, that woman! I was sure that no good would come of this voyage, but at my age you take whatever comes along, don't you? Girls for cargo, that was what I was reduced to, settlers' girls for America.'

'It can't have been easy, a voyage like that with so many women on board!'

Only the whites of the captain's eyes were visible.

'It was hell!' he sighed. 'If you want my opinion, madame, women shouldn't exist at all.'

He stuffed a huge hunk of bread into his mouth, along with a piece of cheese she held out to him, and, as he chewed away vigorously, he watched her with his little sharp eyes.

'And all that to lose one's ship on a strip of coast full of wreckers,' he growled. 'And yet you don't look like a bandit, do you! You look to me more like a good, honest woman, you do. You ought to be ashamed of yourself. Allowing your men to become wreckers and murderers.'

'What do you mean by that?'

'I mean drawing ships onto your filthy rocks, and bludgeoning to death the poor wretches who try to escape, do you call that an honest livelihood? God and the saints in Heaven will punish you.'

Angélique felt quite incapable of showing indignation at this outrageous accusation. She had had her fill of madness during the past three days from all the despairing and hysterical men and women about her. It was all understandable, coming from people who had also lost their lives at sea.

So she replied without any sign of anger:

'But you are wrong, my good man. We are just ordinary settlers, making our living from trade and the work of our hands.'

'Well then, why would I have run the blasted ship onto that reef of needle-sharp rocks,' he roared, leaning towards her, 'if I hadn't seen those lights flashing through the night? I know perfectly well how wreckers go about it—how they wave lanterns about on the cliff tops to sink ships by making them think there is a port there.

'Ushant's the port I hale from, at the tip of the Breton Peninsula.

'So little was I expecting to run aground that I was thrown into the water. Then when I reached the shore and began to clamber up, "they" struck me there, and there . . . look. It was no rock that did that.'

And he tossed back his shock of hair, which was like that of a sea god, all sticky with salt and seaweed.

Angélique's eyes widened and her heart missed a beat. 'What do you say to that?' the man asked in triumph, delighted to see her so pale and dumbfounded.

But Angélique was less concerned by the wound she saw on the man's skull than by the appearance of a large red birthmark which Job Simon had revealed on his temple.

'When you see a tall captain with a red birthmark, your enemies will be close at hand! . . .'

Who had said this to her? . . . It was Lopez, the little Portuguese buccaneer on the *Heart of Mary*, when they had been together on Maquoit Point.

But where was Lopez now? He had been killed in the battle on board the *Heart of Mary* . . .

CHAPTER 78

SHE LOOKED at herself in the mirror. Night surrounded the cold surface of Venetian glass with its dark shadows, while the last glimmer of the sunset, coming in at the window, cast a pallid light on the mirror itself. Her face appeared to her like that of a ghost with flashing eyes.

Her hair, that lay like a silvery halo round her head, seemed to have gone mad. The wind had tossed it and entangled it when she walked up and down the beach and had encountered the unicorn, and she had grown tired of its endless flapping round her temples, which by now were throbbing with pain.

'I shall plait my hair,' she decided.

So she took it in great handfuls, twisted it, divided it, and brought some order into its gold and pearly sheen. The rich, heavy tress now lay across her shoulder like a shining fur. But she threw it back again, undid it, made it up once more, lifting it and knotting it at the back of her head after twisting it three times around itself. The weight of it against the nape of her neck, just above her shoulders, made her head feel heavy, but it did bring her a sense of relief. She ran the tips of her fingers over her forehead.

Who was it who had said to her: 'When you see a tall captain with a red birthmark, your enemies will not be far away?'

Earlier on she had remembered who it was. Ah, yes, it was the Portuguese half-caste, Lopez, back at Macquoit Point in Casco Bay.

But young Lopez had died in the battle on board the *Heart of Mary*.

Angélique threw herself down fully dressed upon the cold bed but failed to get the rest her exhausting life required. When all the sick and wounded had been attended to, she had retired for the night as Abigail had entreated her to do, for she was the only one who seemed to care about the exhaustion resulting from Madame de Peyrac's exertions of the past few days.

Had she even caught sight of her husband in the course of the day? She no longer knew. She no longer had a husband. He had become a stranger, indifferent to her suffering. She was alone as she had been before, in an alien world, with an invisible menace slowly advancing towards her. She was all alone, struggling through a chaotic heap of naked bodies, men and women covered with blood, with open wounds, their repulsive flesh tangled inextricably together as in Dante's Inferno, a vision from which the stench itself had been eliminated, shot through from time to time by terrifying *symbols*: the gilded figure-head of the Unicorn, the captain with the portwine stain gobbling his food, and the light-coloured wooden houses along the dawn-tinted shore.

Had Joffrey been there, she would have told him of her wild thoughts, and he would have made fun of her and reassured her.

But she was alone. . . .

'. . . It seems to me as if the stage is now set,' she would have said to him, 'and that terrible things are about to happen.'

'What terrible things, my love?'

'I don't know, but I'm frightened!'

She could hear Father de Vernon's voice saying: 'When diabolical things begin to happen . . .'

She turned over on the cold bed, longing for some haven, some warmth. She would get up and seek him out and would say to him: 'Forgive me! Forgive me! I did not betray you, that I promise, but please, please don't go on rejecting me. . . .'

But she could see him, implacable, sombre and distant, as in the days when he had been Rescator, and she found it impossible to imagine that he had ever been capable of caressing her as he had done, or that their life together, every moment of it, could have been so precious and intimate.

'Oh my love! We were such gay lovers, such serious lovers. All those fantastic nights . . . so much laughter, so much unclouded joy, when we could look upon one another ceaselessly, distractedly, without shame.

'And at the time of the smallpox epidemic, you remember? And especially . . .' at this point her eyes filled with tears, and she could see him, his tall figure bowing before the minute little creature that was Honorine, whom Cantor had offended. 'Come, young lady, let us find some weapons for you.'

'I used to think then that our love would last forever. . . . Fool that I was! Watch therefore, for ye know neither the day nor the hour. . . .'

Angélique began to toss in her sleep. She dreamed that her golden plait had grown to a monstrous size and was sliding down her body, binding her fast. All the signs of the zodiac writhed and twisted about her like her plait, suffocating her. Then a demon appeared with a cruel grin on its face which reminded her of Wolverine's.

She gave a horrible shriek, and awoke with a bitter taste in her mouth.

The sound of her cries still rang in her ears. And yet her body was still transfused with a sensation of voluptuousness, for she had dreamed that she was making love with some hazy creature, both frightening and strangely gentle.

She remembered her shriek, but it was not she that had given it.

For now she heard it again, piercing the early morning mist, the sharp shriek of a woman.

Angélique leapt out of bed, ran towards the open window and leaned out.

A mist still lay over the ground, like trails of pink smoke, a sea mist that hid the early beginnings of a July day that would undoubtedly be stifling hot. Even the silence of those first hours had something about it that was opaque and crushing.

Angélique's heart thudded irregularly in her breast, unable to resume its normal rhythm. So complete was the silence and so clammy the mist that once again she thought she must have been dreaming.

But then a third cry rang out; it came from the barn where the shipwrecked girls were sleeping.

'Good God!' she exclaimed. 'What ever is going on now?'

She rushed out of her room, shook the drowsy sentry and got him to open the gates of the fort, summoning one of the Spanish guards in a postern-gate outside to accompany her. The ground in front of their feet was barely visible.

Outside the barn a crowd of people moved aimlessly about like so many souls in limbo.

Angélique reached them just in time to position herself between two stalwart men armed with cutlasses who, notwithstanding the fact that it was impossible to see an adversary at a distance of three paces, were about to set about one another in single combat.

'Have you gone mad!' she cried. 'What are you doing fighting here? You should be on board your ships!'

'It's because of them as are trying to steal our wives,' one of the combatants explained, and she recognized him as Pierre Vanneau, the quarter-master of the *Heart of Mary*.

'What do you mean, your wives?'

'Blow me, the ones inside the barn there.'

'And what gives you the idea that they are your wives, since they only got here yesterday?'

'Blow me, because the Good God sent them specially

for us, didn't he, for us folks on the *Heart of Mary*. It was in our contracts, and Father Baure told us to pray, so we prayed, and . . .'

'So you know all about God's intentions for you, do you? And you imagine that all He has to do is to work miracles on your behalf? And under this pretext you consider you can dispense with any sort of respect for the poor unfortunate girls whom the storm has thrown up on our shores. . . . That's pitching it strong! I am astonished, you hunchback there,' she went on, staring him full in the eyes, 'that you had the nerve to lead your men into an escapade like this. When the Governor, your captain, hears about this, you'll be for it.'

'But, Madame la Comtesse, I would like to point out . . .'

'Nothing!' scolded Angélique. 'What are all these crazy notions running through your heads? . . . It will be the cat for you, Vanneau, let me tell you, not to mention the loss of your command.'

'But Madame, it was because of the others.'

'What others?'

The mist was beginning to disperse, and Angélique noticed a group of men from the *Fearless*, Vanereick's filibuster ship, consisting of the most sinister-looking members of the crew. The fair Ines, wearing yellow satin, with a coral necklace round her gold-brown neck, seemed to be urging them on to fight.

'When I learned that those scum from the *Fearless* were trying to pester our . . . well, those ladies, I and some of my companions came to their rescue,' Vanneau explained. 'We couldn't let those pirate pigs, those ginger-bread filibusters, those gallows-birds, lay hands on them.'

'What's it got to do with you, you great lump of pickled pork?' his adversary retaliated, still holding his long, shining dagger in his hand, and speaking with a heavy Spanish accent. 'You know the privateers' law: in the colonies all women belong to sailors passing through. By all means let us fight over them, but we have just as much right as you to that particular booty.'

Vanneau made a threatening gesture, which Angélique quelled with a single look, without a thought for the sharp blade that whistled through the air only a few inches from her face.

Grumbling and growling, two groups of men surged angrily around her, exchanging threatening glances, muttering insults between their teeth in every language under the sun.

Ines began to incite her troops to rebellion in Spanish, but she too was promptly reduced to silence by Angélique, who suspected her of having led the men on this expedition in order to create trouble for her, Angélique, through childish jealousy. The insolent air of the little Spanish woman did not impress her. She knew the type and how to handle her. They were not really bad at heart beneath their fiery exterior, the only danger lay in the way they might incite men to do all kinds of stupid things.

Her intelligence lay in her senses; beyond that she had the brains of a humming-bird. Angélique knew exactly how to deal with bold creatures of that kind.

With a single look she checked Ines's harangue in full flight, then tweeked her pretty ear with its gold ear-ring, giving her a mocking, indulgent smile. Finding herself treated in this almost maternal manner, the girl lowered her head, for she was in fact only a young half-caste who had been taken away from her Indian background and had never received any other form of attention than what men offered her, always through self-interest. She was in fact a rather pitiful courtesan from the islands, and Angélique's haughty but friendly condescension caught her so much off her guard that suddenly she became nothing more than a somewhat baffled child.

Deprived of the support of their hot-blooded champion, who had persuaded them that they ran no risk whatever in embarking on this adventure and that she would see that everything was all right with their captain, Vanereick's men began to waiver, to exchange glances and to appear far less cock-sure.

At that moment the last of the mist cleared and the scene was revealed in all its brilliance, including fat Petronella Damourt, her scant hair uncovered and both eyes blacked, for the poor lady had done her courageous best to defend her charges. And if she was not exactly lively on her legs, at least she had weight on her side. Behind her, two or three of the more curious girls, in their petticoats, stared anxiously round the door, while the others had sought refuge at the farthermost end of the barn.

Delphine Barbier du Rosoy, very pale, her naked arms black with bruises, was trying to cover her bosom with the torn shreds of her bodice. It was her terrible cry, on being brutally seized by a pair of lewd hands that had awakened Angélique.

A man lay at her feet—one of the sailors from the *Gouldsboro,* who had been placed on sentry duty at the barn door that night, and whom the men from the *Fearless* had knocked out before battering down the door. This dastardly action, which bore full witness to their evil intentions, put Angélique in a fury of indignation, all the more so when she noticed among the ruffians some of 'her' wounded who, in spite of their dressings, their wounds, and the state of their arms or legs, had nevertheless found the energy to participate in this gay expedition.

'This is too much!' she exclaimed, beside herself with anger. 'You all deserve to be hanged. You are nothing but a lot of scum. I've had enough of you. Enough, I say! If you carry on like this any more, I shall wipe my hands of the lot of you, for all your blind eyes and spilled guts, your pus and your pox! You can all rot as far as I care. . . . You can die of thirst under my very eyes, and I wouldn't give you as much as a drop of water!

'How dare you behave yourselves like this in our country? Have you no sense of honour? Not a shred of it! You're nothing better than vermin, scarcely worth feeding to the cormorants . . . and I'm sorry I didn't do just that when I had the opportunity.'

They were subdued by Angélique's wrath and the violence of her language, intimidated by her gaze, which was like that of an angry queen, and by her imperious air, emphasized on the present occasion by the severity of her hair style, and her dark violet robe of heavy silk and the ways she had of drawing herself up to her full height and wrapping her sealskin cloak about her—as she looked them up and down like so many clodhoppers which, after all, was what they were. Thus cut down to size—and pretty poor specimens of humanity they were—the men from the *Fearless* found themselves tongue-tied, and Hyacinth Boulanger and his friend Aristide began to sidle away.

'Monsieur Vanneau, you were quite right to intervene,' said Angélique. 'Would you be so good as to go and fetch Father Baure and the Abbé Lochmer whom I can see over there, probably on their way to say their first Mass.'

When the priests had come up and Angélique had told them of the sailor's behaviour, she went on:

'I leave them to you, Fathers. Try to make them understand that they have behaved as no Christian should, and that they deserve a severe penance. I must now go and inform Monsieur de Peyrac of what has happened.'

The Breton chaplain called down curses upon them all, warning his flock that all the torments of Hell awaited them, and the Recollect Father decided to take both the crews off to Mass, after hearing their confessions.

Then the sailors bowed their heads, sheathed their knives, and with heavy, repentant hearts and dragging footsteps, followed the two priests to the top of the hill.

CHAPTER 79

In the cabin on the *Gouldsboro*, Joffrey de Peyrac had just concluded a business discussion with John Knox Mather, his assistants and the English admiral. Colin Paturel was in attendance as well as d'Urville, Berne and Manigault. Gutting candles bore witness to the fact that they had been at work since before dawn, for the ship for Boston was sailing on the tide.

Angélique got Enrico to announce her. She had had some difficulty in finding out where her husband spent his nights. Now she knew it was on board the *Gouldsboro* in the den he had occupied in his Rescator days.

On the whole she felt pleased that events were forcing

her to act, and resume her position in their male lives. Since he had not cast her out, she would take her place once more, and he would have no choice but to speak to her again. This would enable them to have matters out and to clear up their misunderstandings. In those early morning hours Angélique felt at her best and ready to take control of her own destiny once more.

On seeing her, all the gentlemen stood up, wondering and silent, for each one of them in his own particular way had a place in his most secret thoughts for this uncommon woman, and each time she appeared she brought a new savour to their lives.

After greeting them she told them in clear and even tones about the incident that had brought the two crews to blows, one group having decided that the women were their legitimate booty the other taking the view that the Lord had sent the girls most opportunely to become their lawful, wedded spouses.

'What a splendid idea,' Peyrac exclaimed, turning towards Colin. 'Of course the miraculous presence of these women could well provide the solution to the discontent of some of your men who feel frustrated on this score. Governor, that is a decision which you must take. We cannot entertain the idea of sending those girls on to Quebec, even if that was supposed to be their destination. We have neither the time nor the means at our disposal. I had thought of sending them to Port-Royal, but isn't the solution your men have in mind probably the wisest and best for all concerned? It was a private company that sponsored them and it is quite possible that none of the French settlements of Acadia—which in any case are impoverished—would feel inclined to assume responsibility for them. If they would like to stay here, good, we shall welcome them as wives for our French settlers. I leave you to work out the details of the agreement.'

Colin Paturel stood up, rolling up maps and pieces of parchment which he packed away into the huge pockets of his jerkin. He saw now dressed with a sobriety and correctness that did not exclude a few concessions to finery demanded by his new position. His jabot and the frills at his wrists were extremely neat and the cuffs, collar and pockets of his russet-coloured coat were picked out with embroidery, the coat itself being cut away to reveal a pearl-grey under-jacket of brocaded linen. With his trimmed beard and his grave, intent expression, Angélique had difficulty in recognizing him. He had already become another man, whose broad shoulders seemed to carry lightly the responsibilities laid upon them.

He tucked his round beaver-skin hat with the black feather beneath his arm.

'For my part, I am also in favour of keeping the girls here,' he declared, 'but Quebec may take umbrage at our welcoming their expected guests, and the powers that be may regard it as a seizure. Are we not running the risk of still further poisoning your relations with New France, Monsieur de Peyrac?'

'Leave that to me. If they complain, I will point out that they ought to entrust their convoys to pilots who don't lose them in the Antipodes. And in any case, our relations with New France are already so strained that one incident more or less isn't going to make much difference. Anything, at any time, may serve as a pretext for war, or for peace. But one thing is certain: that now I no longer fear them, and that it is for me to decide whether or not to remain on good terms with them; and my view is that if the winds of fortune blew this charming cargo in our direction just when we needed it, we ought to regard it as a sign from heaven. I am in entire agreement with your men on this matter.'

'By the way,' Angélique remarked, 'I wish that man Gilles Vanereick, his Ines and all his crew would get to the devil out of here. They are causing endless trouble and if they have nothing better to do than to amuse themselves at our expense . . . I managed to put them under the charge of the chaplains. I suppose they won't get up to any mischief for the time it takes to say Mass, but what after that? . . . I am terribly sorry, Captain,' she went on, realizing that Vanereick was present, 'I am sorry I spoke so bluntly to your face, but you know as well as I do that your Caribbean seamen are no choir-boys, and that a little of them goes a long way in well-ordered communities. . . .'

'All right! All right!' the privateer groaned. 'I shall go, I have been struck to the heart,' he added, resting an agonized hand on his breast.

'Let us go back on shore,' said Peyrac with finality.

Angélique, walking up the beach beside Vanereick, tried to soften the effect of her blunt remarks.

'At any other time, believe me, Monsieur, I would be delighted by your company, for you are most charming. And I know that my husband values his friendship with you. You stood with him in many a battle, and only just now again. . . .'

'In the Caribbean, we were Brothers of the Coast. That is a thing that binds men together for all time.'

Angélique, examining the somewhat portly although extremely agile figure of the French adventurer, thought that here was yet another man who had been part of Joffrey's unknown life. The two of them shared many memories, from which she was excluded. He also knew Cantor and often spoke affectionately of him as 'the lad' or 'the boy'.

Of course at some other time, as she assured him most sincerely, she would have been delighted to chat with him about her husband and her son's past life, but now she just could not cope, she had to admit it.

'I am worn out from nursing all those people. I am deeply concerned about their fate, and live in constant dread lest some fresh quarrel should still further swell the list of the wounded.'

He gave her a knowing glance.

'And you might add that your little heart has been wounded and that's what's upsetting you, isn't it? Yes! Yes it is! As if one couldn't see. . . . Come, come! I know women. Tell me, young woman, aren't you and your husband soon going to make up your quarrel? Come, come! What is so terrible about a little bit of fun like that? That Swiss fellow blabbed, that I agree! If he hadn't happened to be there at the wrong moment the whole thing would have blown over in a trice. It's no more than a peccadillo, if you think of it. So you tore a little hole in the marriage contract? . . . Well, so what! What a fuss! You are far too attractive, my lovely lady, to be able to prevent things like that happening from time to time, here and there. You ought to go and see him and explain matters to him.'

'How I wish,' Angélique replied bitterly, 'that my husband shared your serenity of feelings. For it's true that he is dearer to me than anything else in all the world, but he is not a confiding man and even I . . . sometimes feel frightened of him.'

'It is perfectly true that where you're concerned he is as dour as an Englishman and as jealous as a Saracen.

'Although you are suspicious of me, I would like you to know that I am a good friend of yours to the extent of having tried to convince Monsieur de Peyrac how ill-founded his anger is, or rather how unreasonable it is where you are concerned. I have tried to get him to see that there are certain kinds of women whom men, even men of honour, must needs forgive. "Take my Ines for instance," I said to him. . . .'

'Oh, come,' Angélique protested with some annoyance, 'don't confuse me with your Ines.'

'And why not? I know what I'm talking about. For all that you are a fine lady and she is nothing but a little pest, popped out of some sea-shell in a sultry sea, you both of you belong to the exquisite strain of women who on account of their beauty, their skill in love, and that mysterious something known as charm, are capable of making men forgive the Creator for the aberration of mind He suffered the day He decided to make Eve from Adam's rib.

'"Now you must realize," I said to him, "you must realize that there are some women to whom we men must forgive certain lapses, for if we do not we run the risk of finding ourselves even more harshly punished than the guilty woman herself. The point is that when one is lucky enough to have been dealt an ace in the game of Love, one should make the most of it and thank the gods that be. For so many others go through life with nothing but second-rate cards in their hands. . . ."'

'I can imagine how my hot-tempered husband must have generated your specious and immoral arguments,' Angélique replied with a melancholy smile.

A little while ago, back in the cabin on the *Gouldsboro* he had once again pretended to ignore her, and by adopting this attitude, she felt that he was striking her still harder than he had previously done. This encounter had taken the heart out of her and already she was feeling exhausted; what would it be like by the evening, after a day that brought her no relief, and when all her fears assailed her.

It was all so much more serious than Vanereick imagined.

What he did not know was that she could never endure being rejected by Peyrac. She would die of it. And the fear of this risk checked her spontaneity.

'But whatever have you done to him to have got under his skin like this?' Vanereick cried, scrutinizing her with his shrewd, coal-black, sparkling eyes. 'It's inconceivable! . . . I would never have thought a great pirate like him could be so vulnerable, with all his experience of life, of science, of philosophy and of the ups and downs of fortune! He made a terrific impression on us all in the Caribbean on Tortuga Island and in the Gulf of Mexico, and the women were all the keener on him because he never seemed to care a jot for them. But I can see that, as soon as he laid eyes on you, he succumbed. Making love to you must really be something . . . unforgettable, prodigious. . . .'

'Captain, please keep your imagination under control,' Angélique interrupted, laughing. 'I am only an ordinary mortal, alas!'

'Too much so! Too much of an ordinary mortal. Just what we men need. Good! I have managed to make you laugh. All is not lost. Now listen to my advice. Say no more about all this business, think no more of it! Go to confession. It is a good thing to begin by seeking God's forgiveness. And as for your husband's, just slip into his bed one night without warning him, choosing the right moment, and I guarantee your absolution.'

'I am beginning to think you really are a true friend,' Angélique told him, feeling much more cheerful. 'Now, having said that, my dear Vanereick, if you have nothing better to do round here than to repair broken hearts, once again I would suggest that you set sail. There is a

471

good wind, the fog has lifted, and I for one have had enough of spending my days from dawn till dusk dressing the wounds of men bent on cutting one another's throats. If you don't sail on the next tide, there will be more bloodshed caused by your hotheads from Tortuga.

'Those of your crew who were wounded are well on their way to recovery and I can safely hand them back to you now, quite fit enough to join in your future expeditions.'

Dame Petronella Damourt came rolling rather than running towards them, her hair still tousled and her eyes full of tears.

'Ah, Madame, please help me, the girls have gone mad! I simply can't control them. They are talking of running away from here and of setting out across the forest on foot, goodness only knows where to!'

CHAPTER 80

'WELL NOW, girls, do you or do you not want to get married?'

Colin's voice, booming out as his tall figure appeared on the threshold, put a sudden stop to the weeping and lamentations that filled the barn. Had not Angélique been beside him the more excitable girls would have died of fright. As it was they rushed towards her and clustered in a group round her, finding reassurance in her female presence.

'Well, my dears, whatever's going on? Why all this noise?' Angélique asked with her most conciliatory smile.

'Tell me everything,' said Colin, striking his broad chest. 'I am the Governor here and I promise you that the wretches who frightened you, gentle ladies, will be punished.'

They immediately launched out into a description of their impressions, all speaking at once, which went from 'I didn't hear anything. I was asleep' to 'A beastly man grabbed me by the wrist and dragged me outside . . . I don't know what he wanted from me. . . .'

'He stank of rum,' Delphine Barbier du Rosoy ended

up with a grimace of disgust, for as bad luck would have it she, one of the 'young ladies', had been the most roughly handled in the scuffle. Her dignity obliged her to fight back her tears of humiliation.

Angélique drew a comb from her belt and did her best to tidy the poor girl's hair. Then she wiped swollen noses and eyes, smoothed folds on neckerchiefs and bodices, and decided to call for a large pot of broth and some good wine, which, in the eyes of the French is the best panacea of all ills.

Meanwhile, Colin Paturel continued to question them and listen to their complaints, stooping his tall frame down towards the young creatures as they spoke. His rough, kindly appearance coupled with the attention he paid towards them eventually reassured them and even Delphine, although offended that he should have included her among the 'girls' when he first addressed them, looked up trustingly at him.

'Oh, please sir, please have us taken to Quebec, we beg you!'

'But it must be by land! We never want to set foot on board a ship again, never in our lives. . . .'

Poor girls! It was obvious they had no idea of the sort of place Canada was, any more than they had ever heard mention of Acadia or Nova Scotia, even supposing that a single one among them even knew that the earth was round or had ever set eyes on a map.

Bearing these things in mind, Colin, after promising them that all the unpleasant characters who had pestered them that morning would have left the neighbourhood before dusk, began to tell them about the settlement of Gouldsboro to which the Lord seemed to have guided them by some inexplicable miracle—but everyone knew that miracles were by nature inexplicable—at the very moment when a number of worthy French sailors, having decided henceforth to lead the healthy, courageous lives of settlers, were lamenting the fact that they had no valiant wives at their sides to assist them and make their lives more pleasant.

It was a lovely part of the country, never frozen up in the winter, and the climate was far less severe than that of Canada.

And when they learned that the 'King's gift', which they were so distressed about losing was a mere pittance compared with what this kindly Governor of such handsome appearance was prepared to offer to newly-married couples in the settlement of Gouldsboro—nor would they need to set sail again across the fury of the deep, nor journey through forests infested with Indians and wild beasts—their smiles returned and they began to exchange glances, tempted to accept the offer. There were, however, a few protests, more for appearance' sake than anything else.

'My three friends, and I had been promised officers,' Delphine said with grave modesty. 'In the convent we were taught how to run a house, how to receive important guests, how to make conversation and curtsy to royalty. I feel sure that the husbands intended for us in Quebec didn't reek of rum.'

'Yes, you're probably right,' Angélique agreed. 'They would be more likely to smell of rye or maize whisky. An excellent drink, be it added, especially welcome during the long, hard winters. Come, ladies,' she added with a laugh, 'if you're going to make a fuss about every trifle here in America, how will you ever face the Iroquois, the storms and the famines, and all that awaïts you in the New World? And that's as true of Canada as of here. In fact, if anything, it's worse there, as it's a more remote and less civilized place.'

'And what about me,' the Moorish girl enquired, 'won't I be treated like a slave as in the West Indies, as I was warned that people with dark skins are treated there? I was brought up in a convent at Neuilly where a great lady came regularly to pay for my board and lodging. I can read and write and embroider on silk.'

Colin took hold of the girl good-naturedly by the chin.

'You'll find a taker, my pretty one, if you are as gentle and sensible as you seem to be,' he assured her, 'and I myself will make sure you get properly settled.

'In any case we shall allow you plenty of time to think over these proposals and to discuss them with your chaperone. And if they don't suit you, Monsieur de Peyrac will have you sent on without any further ado to one of the Acadian settlements on the other side of

Frenchman Bay, where you will certainly be well received.'

Dame Petronella was in a dreadful quandary. She was much better informed than her companions and far more level-headed than she appeared, and she was well aware that these French settlers, interspersed as they were with a fair number of Englishmen, without being wreckers as Job Simon alleged, were hardly among the King of France's most devoted subjects. Moreover, she too found it hard to grasp her precise geographical situation, and the maps Colin and Count Peyrac had unrolled in order to convince her that Quebec was not just next door had only succeeded in adding to her confusion.

'Oh, if only our dear benefactress was here!' she sighed.

'Then we'd be able to set up a regular whore-house!' Julienne rasped out in her vulgar voice. 'She was as well up in the running of whore-houses as she was in saying prayers and that. . . .'

Antoinette, her sworn enemy, grabbed her by the hair, and when they had been separated, Colin turned to Julienne and said:

'You, girl, come here!'

She was the only one to whom he had spoken with such familiarity, showing that he was under no illusion about what kind of a girl she was.

'I can't keep you here,' he told her after he had taken her off into a corner. 'Not because you're common, but because you are unwell, and I don't want any of that for my men.'

Julienne immediately began to shriek her head off in protest without worrying in the least about creating a scandal.

'Me, not well? It's not true! Not so long ago I was examined by a doctor at the Chatelet who told me that I was as fresh as a rose. And since I spent all my time after that locked up in the orphanage, what men do you imagine I could have caught anything from, you and your illnesses! Madame Angélique, come and help me! Listen to what he says. . . . He says I'm rotten!'

'This woman is unwell,' Colin reiterated, calling Angélique to witness, 'just take a look at her.'

475

Indeed, the girl's chubby face was an unpleasant waxen colour and there were dark rings round her eyes as if she had blackened them with kohl. Moreover, the excessive brightness of her eyes indicated that she was running a high temperature.

'I don't think that she is sick,' said Angélique, 'but I'm sure that she was hurt in the wreck. But she has consistently refused to allow me to treat her, and her wound is getting worse. Come on, Julienne, let me attend to you, or your life could be at stake. . . .'

'Oh go to hell . . .' the girl replied coarsely.

Angélique slapped her twice across the face, sending her tumbling to the ground. In fact the unfortunate creature could scarcely stand anyway.

'Let yourself be seen to,' Colin concluded, 'otherwise there'll be no quarter. I shall pack you off this very evening with the men on board the *Fearless*.'

Lying there on the ground Julienne looked vanquished, a pitiful sight. Her wild eyes darted hither and thither in panic, seeking a way out.

'It's that I'm frightened,' she moaned, unable to think of any better argument. 'You'll hurt me when you cut me up.'

Aristide Beaumarchand's grating voice was heard suddenly behind them, for somehow or other he had managed to sidle into the barn.

'Not with her, you won't, my lovely! She won't hurt you, that I guarantee. There isn't anyone who'll make you better with a lighter hand. Just cast your peepers on this piece of handiwork. Hand-stitched, I assure you.'

With deft fingers he undid the laces of his breeches for Julienne, fascinated by his authoritative manner, to examine his wretched pale belly traversed across its full width by a long purple scar.

'Just take a look at that! Well, it was her, Dame Angélique, who sewed me up with a needle and thread, yes, that's exactly what she did, my lovely. All me guts was lying on the sand. I'd had it, and that's a fact.'

'It's impossible!' cried Julienne, accompanying her exclamation with many a heartfelt oath.

'It's as I say. Well now, look at it today. And what's

below *that* is still in good trim and at your service, my lovely!'

'Enough of your broad jokes,' Angélique interrupted, seeing the turn the demonstration was about to take. 'Aristide, you are a good-for-nothing, and I wouldn't encourage the devil's daughter herself or the lowest trollop on earth to have anything to do with you. It would still be too good for you and too bad for her.'

'You are offending me; I have my dignity,' said Aristide, slowly lacing up his breeches again. . . . 'I'd even go so far as to say you are insulting me.'

'That's enough,' Colin intervened, moving the man away. 'You've no call whatever to be in here.'

And he seized him by the collar and propelled him in the direction of the door.

'Upon my word, you're harder to shake off than vermin. I shall have to drown you with my own hands in the end.'

Julienne was roaring with laughter, greatly cheered up. 'I likes him, I do! He's a rare one that, a real man, I calls him.'

'Well, I'm pleased to hear you think so. But I warn you that he's the worst scoundrel in the two hemispheres.'

She knelt down beside the miserable, limp creature who nevertheless still managed to summon the necessary cheekiness to crack jokes and distribute insults. A typical child of the Court of Miracles in Paris.

'I know why it is you don't want me to dress your wound,' she whispered to the girl.

'You can't possibly know,' the girl protested with a hunted look.

'Yes I do! I can guess. . . . It's because you have been branded with the fleur-de-lys! . . . Listen, I promise to say nothing to the Governor, but on condition that you behave yourself and do exactly as I say.'

The terrified expression on poor Julienne's face was tantamount to an admission.

'Honest, you won't tell on me?' she whispered.

'I swear it,' said Angélique.

Then crossing two fingers and spitting on the ground,

she twice repeated the secret sign of recognition used among members of the Paris underworld.

Completely dumbfounded, Julienne never so much as made a squeak, allowing Angélique to lay bare her swollen ribs, and apply poultices to them, and she docilely swallowed potions and drinks of herbal tea, so preoccupied by the deep mysteries that awaited her in this land of America, that she even forgot to wail. Reassured about the girl's condition, Angélique propped her head up and tucked her up comfortably in her corner, giving her a friendly tap on the cheek before leaving her.

'That man Aristide you've taken such a fancy to, I bet he has a fleur-de-lys branded on his back too, just like you. Get better quick, my lass. We'll have you married too . . . and what a fine pair you'll make! . . . That I'll swear.'

Julienne's eyelids were beginning to droop over her fiery eyes which, through sheer weariness, were at last losing some of their fierceness. Calmed by the medicines she had been made to take, she was falling asleep.

'What a funny lot of people you do have here,' she whispered, 'and who are you, Madame? Lady of America . . . you can see things that are hidden from other people. That plait of hair suits you. . . . You look like those holy queens you see . . . on missals. Surely a poor rough girl like me could never be *that* lucky. . . .'

CHAPTER 81

THE FLAGS were flapping in the wind and the sails ready to catch the breeze.

Once again everyone was down at the quayside.

'Won't you even kiss me goodbye?' asked Vanereick, holding out his arms to Angélique. 'Not even when I'm going away?'

She ran to him and kissed him on both cheeks, feeling the comfort of his manly arms about her, and utterly heedless of the presence of the entire population assembled along the harbour side watching their demonstrations of friendship.

Let them think what they wanted, jealous lot that they were! She had the right to kiss anyone she liked.

'Keep your courage up!' Vanereick whispered in her ear. 'You will win! But remember my advice. First to confession, then to bed. . . .'

He waved his big, feathered hat and jumped aboard the boat that was to take him out to his ship.

The *Fearless* stood quivering with the surge of the tide, its yard-arms black with sailors ready to spread the sails, tugging at its anchor like a thoroughbred horse at its halter.

Cheers and bravos mingled with the terse words of command that came from the bridge in Gilles Vanereick's voice.

'Prosper Jardin, are you standing by?'

'Aye aye, sir,' the quarter-master replied.

'Miguel Martinez, are you standing by?'

'Aye aye, sir,' the quarter-master replied.

And when he had been through the whole list, 'Stand by. Cast off ship!' he cried with a sweeping gesture.

The ropes were released, the sails filled out, billowing and dazzling white against the blue sky, and slowly the *Fearless* began to get under way, tacking between the islands, escorted by the fly boat and the small cutter which Count Peyrac and Colin Paturel had boarded to escort their guests as far as the exit from the narrow channel.

On the poop-deck, the fair Ines stood waving her fan and yellow satin scarf in Angélique's direction. Reassured about her Vanereick's feelings towards her, now that she was setting sail with him again, the little half-caste adventurer felt able to show her friendship towards the woman whom she had considered her main rival.

When the ship was no more than a distant white triangle on the horizon Angélique returned to the fort. On the way back she met the herb man and his Caribbean slave, sitting side by side on the sand chewing cloves. For some complicated reason they had asked to stay on for a while. There had been a certain amount of swopping after the sharing out of the loot: precious stones, bolts of cloth and merchandise, in which—a unique case in the annals of privateering—the captain of the prize ship, Paturel, formerly known as Gold Beard, had himself participated. In exchange for two priceless emeralds, Vanereick had agreed to take on board the buccaneers regarded as undesirables. Despite their idleness and untrustworthiness they would serve as replacements for the men he had lost in battle, provided they were kept up to scratch with a touch of the rope's end.

So it was that Hyacinth Boulanger had been parted from his Barbary Coast brother, Aristide, who, claiming that his stomach was still weak and swearing by all that was holy that he would behave himself, had begged to stay on in Gouldsboro. 'And I've made a hit, you see,' he whispered in Hyacinth's hairy ear; 'a smashing girl called Julienne. When I've got where I want with her, I'll let you know and you can come back and fetch me. . . .'

So it was no good thinking they were done with the *Fearless* for good! They would see her back again with her cargo of black patches, wooden legs, toothless grins and breath reeking of Jamaican rum; they would see the gay dogs from Tortuga once more, with their feathers, their ribbons, their print turban, their belts stuffed full of cutlasses, daggers, sabres, pistols and frightening-looking hatchets.

The summer was only just beginning.

And they would also be seeing again the English and Bostonian ships which had sailed at dawn, and the Acadian sloops that had set off full of Mic-Macs and—purchased with some of the proceeds of the sale of the cattle they had brought—a selection of luxury goods to delight the hearts of the ladies of Port-Royal over on the other side of Frenchman Bay: lace, velvet, trimmings, soap and perfume, arms and ammunition for the defence of the French fort, embroidered banners, and a magnificent windfall in the form of a ciborium and monstrance of silvergilt seized from the Spanish booty of a converted pirate. Surely God would be doubly honoured in the poor church of the oldest of the French colonies founded by Champlain?

A strange calm seemed to fall on the village, whose inhabitants dispersed in silence to their wooden houses.

'Oh look!' young Séverine suddenly exclaimed, 'there are only two ships left lying at anchor in the bay, the

Gouldsboro and the *Heart of Mary*. After that great forest of masts swaying about there these last few days, how empty it looks!'

'Two ships lying at anchor in the bay' . . . whispered the voice of the visionary nun in Angélique's ears.

CHAPTER 82

'I SHALL go to you my love. I must go to you . . .' she kept on repeating to herself. 'I am frightened. You are a man; your two feet are firmly on the ground; your sleep is deep and nothing can trouble its mystery; whereas I am a woman . . . and because I am a woman, I can read the meaning behind symbols. And what I see there is terrible! I can no longer sleep.'

In spite of the fact that peace had returned once more, in spite of the songs the sailors hummed as they hung about in the vicinity of their promised wives:

> Ten maids one day I chanced to spy
> When o'er the meadows I did hie
> One was Dine and one was Chine
> One Claudine and one Martine . . .

In spite of the more relaxed atmosphere that had followed upon the days of distress and anguish, a change of which all the settlers in Gouldsboro were conscious, Angélique found that she could not share in the enjoyment of it.

July came sizzling in, rising to the surface of the world in a puff of scorching heat. It made people's heads swim with the chirping of crickets, the buzzing of bees, the heavy scent of flowers, resin, and overheated sap. The tall candelabra of pink, blue and white lupins, rising up thickly in banks of fairyland beauty, vied with the splendour of golden rod, monuments of pure metal carved into a thousand arabesques, that stood along the edge of the woods. Wild eglantine mingled with the roses against the houses, and clouds of delicate poppies covered the river banks right down to the sea.

The sea birds, in their long, white lines, glided through blue air tinged with pink.

The bay, too, was pink like an open flower, like surrendered flesh. . . .

Catherine and Cath'rinette
Comely, dimple-cheeked Suzette
The Duchess of the Maine,
And Montbazon, I saw them plain . . .

For Angélique alone the fabulous languor of each dazzling day, with its evening full of mauve clouds fringed with fire, was like slow poison.

The day after the departure of the ships, after yet a further sleepless night, she decided to get herself some weapons, for she had lost her pistols at the time of the attack on the English village.

Yann le Couennec used his key to open the door to Count Peyrac's study in the fort, for Angélique had met Yann near the armoury and he had told her that the *Gouldsboro* had brought in a large stock of pistols, arquebuses and muskets, and that the Count had had the best and most up-to-date models placed in his study so that he could examine them at his leisure.

Yann took the guns out of a chest where he had put them himself, and spread them out on the big table on which lay goose quills and ink stands; then he opened the narrow window to let the light in. The little narrow room was fully to Joffrey's familiar smell, the smell of tobacco and sandalwood oil, an Eastern perfume with which he impregnated his clothes. It was a strong yet subtle perfume, somewhat disconcerning in its originality which did not seek to please but was in perfect harmony with the distant yet seductive personality of its user.

'When you see Monsieur le Comte, would you please tell him what I require,' Angélique asked Yann. 'I have not seen him yet this morning.'

Would he respond to this appeal that she was making to him in everyday words, but with a trembling heart; would he come?

She bent to examine the handsome new weapons, and absorbed in their contemplation forgot her cares. Some of the English gunlocks showed interesting improvements. The gunlock was the mechanism by which the charge was ignited and varied in its details according to the country of origin. In these English pistols the battery was combined with the cover of the pan which admittedly increased the risk of accidental discharge, but was compensated for by a little catch at the bottom of the hammer known to initiates as the hammer-lock or dog-lock.

But in spite of this undoubted advance, Angélique still preferred the French type of lock—no doubt because it was familiar to her. Her eye was caught by a long-barreled Scandinavian gun with an ivory stock set with amber, the elegant appearance of which pleased her. Its firing system was rather antiquated but it did have the advantage that it could be armed with any flint picked up at random, whereas other types of locks required carefully cut and calibrated flints which were too complicated to produce in a more-or-less uncivilized land like this.

She was busy turning the pistol over and over in her hands, examining the cocking mechanism, the capacity of the magazine, when she sensed that Joffrey de Peyrac had entered the room and was standing behind her.

'I came to select some pistols,' she said, half turning her head in his direction; 'I lost mine at Newehewanik.'

She could feel the weight of his glance on the nape of her neck and once again she realized just how weak she felt, how in spite of everything a secret joy rose up within her at his very presence.

From behind he had almost failed to recognize her, although Yann had warned him that Madame de Peyrac was in his study.

The deeply pleated, violet taffeta dress and the pale gold plait she wore in a coil at the nape of her neck made her look different. He had thought for a moment that some unknown noblewoman, some great lady must have arrived . . . but where from? . . . Still, so many people kept on disembarking at Gouldsboro these days, that anything was possible!

A fleeting impression, but how piquant! But it was by the dexterity with which the 'stranger' handled the pistols that he had recognized HER. There was only one woman in all the world who could do so with such utter familiarity—Angélique.

Likewise there was only one woman in all the world with such beautiful shoulders.

He drew closer.

'Have you found anything that suits you?' he asked her in a voice he sought to make neutral, but which to her seemed icy.

'Actually,' she replied, forcing herself to remain calm, 'I cannot make up my mind. Some of them seem excellent for shooting, but are cumbersome; others are elegant but have defects of design that could be dangerous.'

'You are hard to please. These arms bear the seal of the best workmen in Europe: Thuraine of Paris, Abraham Hill of England, and this ivory pistol comes from Maestricht in Holland. Look at that warrior's head carved into the end of the butt. . . .'

'It is certainly handsome.'

'But you don't like it.'

'I had grown accustomed to my old French pistols, with all their bits and pieces—screws, keys, flints—that one had to keep in one's pockets and that could easily go astray but that allowed for quite a lot of finesse.'

She felt that they were like two actors speaking their lines in a play. Neither of them had their minds on what they were saying but they still went on working away at it.

Count Peyrac seemed to hesitate then turned and walked over to the half-open chest. Returning, he placed before her a long box of inlaid mahogany.

'This was what I got Erikson to bring back for you from Europe,' he said briefly.

In the centre of the lid the letter A had been inlaid in gold, its scrolls and curves forming a medallion of intertwining enamelled and mother-of-pearl flowers. The same flowers formed a posy on either side of the letter, the craftsmanship being so fine that she could make out the minutest detail of each flower, down to the delicate pistils in silver or gold filigree work, and the veins on the green enamel leaves.

Angélique laid her fingers on the ironwork lock. The lid opened to reveal a green velvet-lined case containing two pistols and their accessories—powder horn, a pair of tongs, a priming box and a bullet mould.

Everything was made of the finest materials and bore the same stamp of elegance, delicacy and beauty.

At a glance Angélique could see that these weapons had been conceived, designed, and made for her.

Executed with minute care, every detail pointed to the fact that the gunsmith, ironsmith and engraver who had worked on these beautiful weapons had striven to delight the woman for whose use they were intended. And that woman was she, Angélique, a woman on the other side of the world.

They had doubtless received special, carefully prepared instructions and must have worked from detailed plans and drawings prepared by Count Peyrac, which had been taken over the ocean and been given to them in their workshops in Seville or Salamanca, or Rivoli or Madrid. And inasmuch as the instructions were accompanied by leather purses bulging with gold doubloons, they had been careful to give their wholehearted attention to the execution of this unusual order—pistols for a woman's hand.

'Such a lovely gift,' thought Angélique, 'which he had thought of specially for me . . . with love . . . with love! A present he intended to give me this spring in Gouldsboro! . . .'

Her hand trembled as she lifted out the magnificent pistols one after the other. It would have taken days to take in all their refinements. They had been designed not only for her to fire in self-defence with the maximum speed and the minimum of discomfort—loading a firearm with delicate fingers was not always a simple matter—but also to appeal to her particular tastes.

How could she fail to be delighted by those inlaid bunches of flowers that likewise decorated the shining butts, fashioned out of wood the colour of red amber.

The barrels were long, of Spanish steel, an extremely rare product, given a bluish tint by the addition of oil so as to eliminate tell-tale flashes of light when the user was waiting in ambush. Inside they were rifled to ensure accuracy of fire but were smooth at the mouth.

'How well he knows what I like, how well he knows what gives me pleasure!'

And as for the lock, it was a marvel! By combining the battery and the cover of the pan in a single part, it was possible to eliminate four moving parts, thus simplifying the mechanism and ensuring that the touch-hole could only open at the precise moment of impact of the flint on the battery. Hidden between two silver scrolls lay the main spring, and the fact that this was fixed outside the gun and not, as previously, inside, was bound to make it exceptionally powerful. The difficulty of setting the spring was offset by the presence of a ring on the threaded screw that regulated the vice. Not only was this ring exactly the size of Angélique's index finger—this she verified there and then—thus enabling her to set the main spring without effort, but she could also adjust the vice by hand, obviating the necessity to carry around a cumbersome screwdriver or similar tool, which was often liable, as she had had occasion to note, to go astray.

Finally the cock had a little projection at its base against which the spring acted directly without need for an intermediate tumbler, thus eliminating one further part. And behind this assembly, which had been designed and put together with clockwork precision, there was a sliding bolt, which very few gunsmiths had had the daring or skill to make up to that time, enabling several shots to be fired one after the other quite safely and without re-loading.

Behind the quality of so handsome a present Angélique had a picture of her husband bending over his files last autumn, secretly, just before the ship set sail, dashing off rapidly and peremptorily with his customary inspiration outline drawings complete with calculations and masses of figures that compressed the essential points of this masterpiece into a few strokes of the pen.

He must have wondered what material to use: metal —copper or silver—ivory or bone? . . . He had opted for wood, which was lighter than metal and less brittle than ivory, and it must have been he who had specified the Turkish-style curved butt, which grew narrower on the curve to give a better grip to the fingers and enable the pistol to be held firmly without fatigue.

She recognized his hand in the double action of the 'vice' which, stripped of its flint and suitably tightened, could serve as a hammer with which to strike, in a specially constructed cavity, a charge of gunpowder, the secret of whose manufacture was known to the Count alone, and which constituted a completely new method of firing.

As for the ornamentation and the inlaid work, IT WAS FOR HER that he had chosen flowers.

A lump rose in her throat, and she asked herself why he had chosen to give her this gift that morning? Was it a mark of reconciliation? Did he want her to understand that the period of ostracism he had imposed upon her was coming to an end?

Standing before the window, Joffrey de Peyrac, with a look he could have wished to appear less avid, sought to read Angélique's thoughts in her sensitive face.

A pink wave had mantled her over-pale cheeks as she raised the lid of the box, followed by an expression of wonder on discovering the beauty of the pistols. He had been unable to resist giving her this pleasure. He so longed to see her happy on his account, even if only for a brief moment!

She was biting her lower lip and he saw her long eyelashes flutter.

Then at last she turned and looked at him with those admirable eyes and murmured:

'How can I ever thank you, my lord?'

He gave a start, for the words reminded him of the first occasion he had made her a gift in those far-off days in Toulouse—an emerald necklace—and she had possibly thought of it too.

He replied dryly, almost haughtily:

'I don't know whether you have noticed that the lock is of the Miquelet type. The exterior spring gives considerably more force to the shot, and the hand is protected by a special flange.'

'So I see.'

The flange was decorated with a salamander, or a long-tailed lizard, whose tongue of golden filigree shot out towards a red enamel poppy on the butt. Actually it was definitely a salamander, for the creature's ivory body was dotted with spots of jade. At the back, the metal of the gun-lock was embossed with a round posy of May flowers, of incredibly delicate workmanship, and the hammer, know as the 'dog', which the craftsman had carved with the same minute care into the shape of the snout of a fierce-looking little pug, was adorned with an eye of gilded glass which blazed with light.

But beneath all this prettiness and refinement lay hidden the responsive, implacable tension of the mechanism.

And while with her deft fingers, and the familiar light touch she brought to the most unexpected tasks, she handled the different parts of the gun-lock, he was rapt in contemplation of her beauties, and the contrast between her femininity and the business-like way she handled the guns made him catch his breath.

Through the open neck of her bodice he glimpsed her pearly skin, all the more luminous for being surrounded by shadows and for melting so softly into a warm, dark hollow full of mystery.

The milky softness of this woman's flesh, this fragile, smooth, swelling corolla, it was in this that he saw the symbol of her weakness, the vulnerability of her sex.

A tender-breasted woman, that was what she was, that was what she remained however formidable she might appear with a gun in her hand.

'She has borne my children within her,' he thought, 'my only sons. I never wanted to have children by any other woman.'

The spell of her charm emanating from her entire being overcame him, intoxicated him, made him grow numb, filled him with the desire to clasp his hands around her slender waist, to rest them on her hips and feel her warmth through the amethyst-coloured taffeta of her bodice. For too long now his arms had been empty of her.

He drew closer and said in a slightly hoarse voice, pointing to the pistol she held in her hand:

'Load it! Cock it.'

'I am not sure I would know how. I am not familiar with this kind of lock.'

He took the gun from her hands and promptly loaded it with bullets, gunpowder and primer. She followed the movements of his brown hands, longing to stoop down and kiss them.

He handed the gun back to her, saying: 'There!'

And added with a caustic smile:

'You could kill me now . . . and be rid of your troublesome husband.'

Angélique turned deathly pale. She felt as if she would never recover her breath, and she had the greatest difficulty in laying the pistol back in its case with a trembling hand.

'How could you say anything so foolish!' she at last managed to say. 'You are incredibly unkind!'

'Ah! So you think you are the victim?'

'At the moment, yes. . . . You know perfectly well that in saying things like that you are tormenting me appallingly.'

'And undeservedly, no doubt?'

'Yes . . . no . . . yes, more undeservedly than you think. . . . I have not done you as great a wrong as you want to think . . . and you know it well. . . . But you are insanely proud.'

'And you are fantastically dishonest and impudent!'

And he felt, as he had that other night, an insensate desire to pummel her, to strike her down, and at the same time to luxuriate in her perfume, in her warmth, as in some heady incense, and to lose himself in the brightness of her green eyes, now flashing with anger and love, with despair and tenderness.

For fear of succumbing, he made off towards the door.

'Joffrey,' she cried, 'are we going to allow ourselves to fall into the trap?'

'What trap?'

'The trap our enemies have set for us.'

'What enemies?'

'The enemies who have made up their minds to separate us in order to strike us down more easily. And now it has happened. I don't know how it was all contrived at the beginning and what tricks were used to bring about our downfall, but I know that it has happened. You see, it has happened. *The fact is that we have been separated.'*

She glided over to where he stood and laid one hand upon his heart:

'My love, are we to allow them such an easy victory?'

He drew away from her with a violence that betokened his fear of giving in too quickly.

'That's rich. You behave in a completely senseless manner and then accuse me of acting illogically. For example, at Houssnock, whatever gave you the idea of setting off for the English village?'

'But you yourself sent me orders to do so.'

'I! Never on your life!'

'Well then WHO did? . . .'

He stared at her speechless, suddenly struck by a terrifying presentiment.

Although of very superior intelligence, Peyrac nevertheless was typically masculine in his approach to the world. Men proceed by leaps of the intellect, whereas women are guided by an instinct of cosmic foresight.

Men bound forward like the big cats. For a long time they remain motionless, sometimes stagnant, causing anxiety by their refusal to move, then suddenly they leap forward, rending the skies, discovering, in a single flash, all that the eye can see, and penetrating still further, pushing back the limits of the horizon.

That was how Peyrac felt as Angélique's voice unleashed within him a series of passionate impulses, and he saw everything about him transformed, taking on a new significance, a different aspect. Yes, they were faced with a grave peril, and yet his male logic rejected the onslaught of the occult.

But Angélique was not mistaken. She had a greater feeling for the mystical than he, and he was well aware that *that mattered too*.

He kept up the struggle.

'Stuff and nonsense, all these feelings of yours,' he grumbled. 'It would all be too easy.

'All adulterous women would have to do would be to claim that demons were involved. Was it they, Madame, who were our enemies, or was it chance that brought your erstwhile lover to Casco Bay, ready to fold you in his arms? . . .'

'I don't know. But Father de Vernon said that when diabolical things were afoot, chance was always on the side of evil, that is to say on the Devil's side, on the side of destruction and unhappiness.'

'And who is this Father de Vernon?'

'A Jesuit who took me in his ship from Maquoit to Pentagouet.'

At this remark Joffrey de Peyrac seemed thunderstruck.

'You fell into the hands of the French Jesuits?' he cried, in a strange voice.

'Yes! At Brunswick-Falls I only just avoided being taken off to Quebec as a prisoner.'

'Tell me about it.'

And as she briefly described her adventures since her departure from Houssnock, he saw in his mind's eye Outakke, the great Iroquois chieftain, saying to him:

'You have a treasure! They will try to take it from you. . . .' Had he not always feared that it would be through her, Angélique, that they would attempt to strike at him? She had spoken rightly.

Enemies were lurking about them, more cunning, wily and subtle than the 'Cowardly Ones', the spirits of Air.

Could he deny that he had suspected this himself, inasmuch as he still had in a pocket of his doublet the anonymous message an unknown sailor had brought him on the evening after the battle with the *Heart of Mary*, a scrap of parchment on which the following words had been penned:

'Your wife is on Old Ship Island with Gold Beard. Land on the north side of the island so that they do not see you, and you will be able to catch them in one another's arms.'

Infernal spirits, without a doubt, but spirits which, lurking among the islands, were capable of taking pen in hand to ensure that such a damaging denunciation reached the intended quarter.

He drew a deep breath. Everything semed to have changed, to have taken on a different aspect, and in the tumult, Angélique's infidelity no longer appeared to him to have been so odiously calculated. She had been

491

caught up in a web of plots, further complicated by a series of coincidences. It was inevitable that so feminine a woman should reveal the vulnerable side of her nature, but beneath her weakness he had seen evidence of an extraordinary courage. He thought back to that night in the island, when he had watched Colin and Angélique from afar and had seen clear signs of their struggle against temptation.

Of course, it was not pleasant for him to have to admit that she could be tempted by another man, but in this he knew that he was behaving as unreasonably as a young boy.

What did remain was the loyalty towards him which she had shown that night. And as for what had taken place on board the *Heart of Mary*, he did not particularly want to know the precise details, although various things that Colin Paturel had said had hinted at what had occurred.

Sometimes he even thought he would more readily forgive Angélique for giving her body than for a single passionate kiss, for he knew by heart every aspect of her responses. For her, a kiss had always seemed to commit her entire being more completely than the impersonal surrender to physical intimacy. That was how she was, his unpredictable goddess! She would more willingly give her body than her lips. And he would have been prepared to bet that with 'the others', it had always been thus. He would have liked to think that his were the only lips she enjoyed, but once again, in his demand that this should be so, he was displaying ridiculous, adolescent feelings. This was what she had brought him to, after a life in which, on grounds of well-considered policy, he had sought to give women an attractive and important place, but one which should never be allowed to affect his own inner being.

But what was the point of dwelling on what had been?

Far more serious were the risks she had run, the traps which had been laid for her, and this must all be sorted out.

He paced up and down in front of her, glancing at her from time to time, looking at her, as she thought, somewhat more gently, then his eyes would harden again under the influence of his thoughts, his fears and his suspicions.

'Why do you think Father de Vernon allowed you to go free?' he asked.

'Indeed, I have no idea. Possibly because, during the three days we spent at sea, he had become convinced that I could not be the She-Devil of Acadia as everyone seemed to imagine.'

'And what about Maupertuis and his son? Where are they?'

'I imagine they have been taken back forcibly to Canada.'

The Count exploded:

'This means war!' he cried. 'I've had enough of their underhand methods! I shall send my ships against Quebec!'

'No, don't do that! We should be wasting our strength and I would be accused more bitterly than ever of spreading misfortune. But we must not be parted! Do not let them prevail against us by tearing us apart, by hurting us. . . . Joffrey, my love, you know that you are everything to me. . . . Do not reject me or I shall die of grief. Now and henceforth I am nothing without you! Nothing!'

And she held out her arms towards him like a lost child.

She was in his arms and he was crushing her to him. He still had not forgiven her but he did not want her to be taken from him. He did not want anyone to threaten her, to make attempts on her life, her precious, irreplaceable life.

His iron embrace crushed her and she trembled, overwhelmed with joy, her cheek against his hard cheek. The sky reeled, dazzling bright.

'A miracle! A miracle!' cried a voice from afar off in the distance of space. 'A miracle! A miracle!'

They could hear the sound of voices outside, growing louder and louder.

'A miracle! A miracle! My lord, where are you? Come quick! A real miracle!'

It was Yann Le Couennec's voice in the courtyard beneath the window.

Count Peyrac released his grip on Angélique and drew away from her, as if regretting the impulsive gesture he had made in opening his arms to her. He went over to the window.

'What's going on?'

'A real miracle, my lord! The benefactress . . . the noble lady, the patroness of the "King's Girls", who we all thought had been drowned . . . well, she wasn't. Some cod-fishers from Saint-Malo picked her up on an island in the bay with her secretary, and a sailor, and a boy whose life she had saved. They are coming by boat. . . . They are just arriving in the harbour.'

CHAPTER 83

'DID YOU hear that?' Peyrac asked, turning towards Angélique. 'The benefactress! It looks as if the sea found the honourable duchess and her pen-pusher too much of a bellyful.'

He glanced at her, hesitant and perplexed.

'We shall see one another again later,' he said, looking away irresolutely. 'I think it's my duty to go out and welcome the poor woman thrown up by the sea like Jonah by the whale, on our lawless shores! Will you accompany me, Madame?'

'As soon as I've put away these guns, I shall join you down at the harbour.'

He went off.

Angélique stamped her foot.

That girl Julienne was right. This benefactress was an unqualified pest. After being deemed drowned for three days, she could at least have waited a few more hours before surfacing again! Instead she had to choose the very moment when Joffrey de Peyrac was opening his arms to Angélique, but when he had still not lowered all the defences of his proud heart.

She had sensed his impulse of concern for her but was also aware that his pride still bristled. Then suddenly fate seemed to have turned against her once more.

In spite of the memory of that all-too-brief embrace, a

deathly chill crept in Angélique's veins, and dashed her spirits.

She felt like rushing after Joffrey, to call him and beseech him to return.

Her feet felt heavy and she could hardly move them, like in a nightmare.

She staggered against the doorway and almost fell. There on the floor sat a demon, with grinning jaws and flashing eyes, looking up at her.

Her flesh crept and she suddenly felt sick.

'Oh, it's you, Wolverine! How you frightened me!'

The wolverine had not followed Cantor up the Kennebec but had been prowling round the village, his body heavy, supple and snakelike, like a giant weasel.

He stood looking up at her.

'Go away! Go away!' she whispered with a shudder. 'Go away! Go back to the woods!'

Then a huge, hairy shape, moving among the silky green leaves of a tree, caught her eye.

Once again it was only a mirage of threatening danger: it was only the bear, Mr Willoughby, waddling along, sniffing the scent of fruit on the soft, warm wind.

With one paw he turned over a stone, revealing a swarm of ants which he lapped up with a few rapid licks of his tongue.

Angélique strode mechanically down to the beach, guided by a distant babble of voices that sounded farther off as she moved towards it. The stifled voice of a white ghost-like figure called to her as she went by.

'Madame de Peyrac! Madame de Peyrac!'

'What are you doing there, Marie? Be careful, now! You should not have got up with your wounds. . . .'

'Let me lean on you, please, dear lady, so that I may go to meet my benefactress.'

Angélique put a sustaining arm round the frail, supple waist of the girl with the radiant face. Her feet seemed to carry her forward in spite of herself, and from time to time she turned round to see the bear and the wolverine still following her, and shook her fist at them, saying:

'Go away! Go away, you dreadful creatures!'

495

CHAPTER 84

EVERYONE HAD gathered on the beach. That beach! It was a theatre facing a stage to which each day brought some new spectacle.

Now a boat was making its way up the harbour towards them, and over the sea of heads Angélique could hear shouts, sobs, and cries of joy and devotion.

'She's alive!' Marie kept on saying as she wept. 'May God and all the saints in Heaven be praised!'

Angélique stood back a little, at the point where the ground began to slope down towards the water; in this way it was possible to get a better view of what was going on, and she saw the boat reach the shore and Yann wade out into the water to steer it in and prevent it jolting as the stem touched the bottom.

Straight away all the 'King's Girls' raced towards it screaming hysterically.

In the midst of all this activity Angélique failed to identify the Duchess, although her eye was caught by the unexpected presence of a very young woman whose elaborate costume gave a touch of colour to the prow of the boat.

In spite of the distance that separated them Angélique could see that she must be quite exceptionally beautiful. In contrast to her dark hair, her complexion was as bright as a lamp, or rather reminded one of an exotic flower—a camellia or magnolia—brilliant in the shadows with all the delicacy of a perfumed petal, pure white tipped with pink.

A flower. Or a bird if you thought of the brilliant colours of her costume. Although this was as daring as the latest fashion allowed—her peacock-blue coat-dress opening over a short yellow satin skirt, with a paler blue bodice above, inset with a scarlet modesty-vest—it formed an astonishingly elegant ensemble that suited her to perfection.

The only discordant note was the wretched-looking child she was holding in her arms.

496

'You have saved my boy's life! God bless you!' came Jeanne Michaud's trembling voice rising above the hubbub, as she stretched out her arms and took her Pierre into them.

Relieved of her burden, the woman in the bright clothes laid her hand on that of one of the bystanders and sprang nimbly ashore holding her yellow satin skirt high to prevent it getting wet.

At that moment, what Angélique noticed was to remain engraved in her memory for a very long time, assuming a disproportionate importance, incomprehensibly so, in fact, until the day when, haunted by these unconsciously registered memories, she was finally to discover the key to many a mystery.

She noticed the young woman's scarlet stockings and her dainty little clog-shaped shoes of carmine velvet, trimmed with white leather and decorated with golden satin rosettes.

Angélique heard herself asking:

'But . . . who is that woman?'

'It's SHE,' Marie replied with a sob. 'Our benefactress! Madame de Baudricourt! . . . Look at her! Isn't she lovely? Adorned with all the virtues and graces! . . .'

Slipping free from Angélique's sustaining arms, Marie mustered all her strength to make her way towards the newcomer and fell to the ground at her feet.

'My dearest lady! . . . You are alive!'

'Marie, dear child!' came the reply in a soft, deep voice—a moving contralto—as the duchess bent down to Marie and kissed her forehead.

A man dressed in dark clothes, somewhat corpulent, with a pair of spectacles on his nose, had managed to climb down from the boat without anyone paying the slightest heed to him and was vainly attempting to bring a little orderliness into the effusive exchange of greetings.

'Come, ladies, come,' he urged them. 'Please, ladies, please allow the Duchess to receive the respect of the lord of these parts.'

Joffrey de Peyrac stood waiting a little higher up the beach, his brocaded cloak flapping in the wind, and if he too had been surprised at the unexpected appearance of the duchess, this was revealed only by a faint touch of irony in his smile.

'Make way, ladies,' the bespectacled gentleman insisted, 'have some consideration for Her Grace's fatigued state.'

'Monsieur Armand!' all the girls cried out, finally deigning to recognize him too. Friendly and welcoming, they clustered round him, and Madame de Baudricourt was able to move a few paces towards Count Peyrac.

Now that she could see her closer to, Angélique realized that the duchess's clothes were stained with sea water and torn in places, and that her feet, in their delicate white leather and velvet shoes, seemed to be having great difficulty in walking across the sand, whose shifting surface added to her problems, and that, in spite of their gracefulness and the slenderness of her ankles, thrown into relief by a gold band round one of them, those feet seemed heavy and weighed down, just as Angélique's had been shortly before when she made her way down to the harbour.

Either those feet were lying shamelessly, or else it was her face that lied. She was less young than she had seemed from a distance but still more beautiful. In fact the Duchess Ambroisine de Baudricourt must have been about thirty, and possessed all the ease of manner, the assurance, and the verve of youth—at once animal and refined—of that splendid age.

And yet it was becoming more and more obvious to Angélique's practised eye that this dazzlingly beautiful woman who strode boldly up the beach was at the point of collapse. Was it exhaustion, or fear . . . or some overwhelming emotion?

And Angélique could not understand why she herself found it quite impossible to rush forward towards the exhausted woman to welcome and sustain her as she would have done to any other human being.

Joffrey de Peyrac swept the ground three times with his plumed hat, bowing low as he did so before the beautiful woman, and kissing her outstretched hand.

'I am Count Peyrac de Morens d'Irristru . . . a Gascon by birth. Welcome to you, Madame, welcome to my American settlement.'

She gave him a warm glance through her eyelashes.

'Oh, Monsieur, what a surprise! You wear your cloak more elegantly than any courtier at Versailles.'

'Madame,' he replied gallantly, 'allow me to tell you that there are more gentlemen of noble birth on this beach than in the King's antechamber.'

Then he bowed low over her white, ice-cold hand, and turning to Angélique who stood motionless a few paces away, went on:

'And this is the Countess Peyrac, my wife, who will see to it that you are given whatever refreshment you may desire after your cruel journey.'

Ambroisine de Baudricourt turned towards Angélique, her eyes now as dark as night in her lily-white face. A smile full of pain flitted across her lips that had suddenly become drained of all colour.

'And surely, in the whole of the palace of Versailles, there could not be a lovelier woman than your wife, Monsieur de Peyrac,' she graciously added in her deep voice that almost seemed to sing as she spoke.

She grew still paler and her eyelids began to quaver. Then a sigh, a faint moan, escaped her lips.

'Ah! Please forgive me, Madame,' she murmured, 'I am dying! . . .'

And there, in all her dazzling clothes, like some magnificent bird struck down in full flight, she fainted away and slid gently to the ground at Angélique's feet. For a brief instant Angélique had the sensation of being alone in a strange, unreal place.

Her mind petrified and seized with some unspeakable fear, she asked herself: 'Is this she? Is this the woman who is to rise from the sea? . . . The woman who is to come amongst us in the service of Lucifer?'

ABOUT THE AUTHORS

ANNE and SERGE GOLON, actually husband and wife, have collaborated to write the novels which bear the name of Sergeanne Golon. Sergé Golon acquired a background as an engineer, prospector, chemist, and geologist prior to turning full time to writing. Anne Golon, the daughter of a French naval officer, became a journalist. The pair met while pursuing their separate careers in darkest Africa and married shortly thereafter. After their return to France in 1952, they had devoted themselves largely to recording the adventures of their fascinating heroine, Angélique, who has become one of the world's most famous fictional personages. Serge Golon died after writing *Angélique and the Demon,* but his widow is already at work on a new novel.

Catherine Cookson

For years a bestselling author in England, Catherine Cookson's readership today is worldwide. Now one of the most popular and best-loved writers of romantic fiction, her spellbinding novels are memorable stories of love, tragedy and courage.

☐	A GRAND MAN	2233	$1.50
☐	THE INVISIBLE CORD	2350	$1.75
☐	THE LORD AND MARY ANN	2432	$1.50
☐	THE MALLON LOT	6323	$1.50
☐	THE DWELLING PLACE	7246	$1.25
☐	FEATHERS IN THE FIRE	7289	$1.25
☐	OUR KATE	7599	$1.25
☐	THE MALLEN STREAK	7806	$1.50
☐	THE GLASS VIRGIN	7962	$1.25
☐	PURE AS THE LILY	8079	$1.25
☐	THE FIFTEEN STREETS	8174	$1.25
☐	THE MALLEN GIRL	8406	$1.50
☐	KATE HANNIGAN	8646	$1.25
☐	FENWICK HOUSES	8656	$1.25
☐	KATIE MULHOLLAND	8678	$1.25

Buy them at your local bookstore or use this handy coupon for ordering:

Bantam Books Inc., Dept. CC, 414 East Golf Road, Des Plaines, Ill. 60016

Please send me the books I have checked above. I am enclosing $_____ (please add 35¢ to cover postage and handling). Send check or money order —no cash or C.O.D.'s please.

Mr/Mrs/Miss_____

Address_____

City_____ State/Zip_____

CC—7/76

Please allow three weeks for delivery. This offer expires 7/77.

ANGÉLIQUE

Seldom has there been a woman in historical fiction who has captured the imagination of so many people as has Angélique. The most dazzling beauty of her time, her thrilling adventures in the flamboyant world of the 17th century enrapture readers everywhere.

Angélique's colorful life takes her from the Paris sewers, where she scratches and claws her way upward to wealth, all the way to King Louis XIV's bedchamber. Although she knows many lives and many lovers she is always haunted by the fevered dreams of her first love, Joffrey de Peyrac. At times proud and arrogant, at times a bold gutter wench, Angélique is always a captivating creation whose endless search for happiness leads her into fascinating encounters in exotic lands.

Read one book and you will want to read all of them. They are published by Bantam Books and listed below:

Bantam Book Catalog

It lists over a thousand money-saving best-sellers originally priced from $3.75 to $15.00 —bestsellers that are yours now for as little as 60¢ to $2.95!

The catalog gives you a great opportunity to build your own private library at huge savings!

So don't delay any longer—send us your name and address and 25¢ (to help defray postage and handling costs).

BANTAM BOOKS, INC.
Dept. FC, 414 East Golf Road, Des Plaines, Ill. 60016

Mr./Mrs./Miss_____
(please print)

Address_____

City_____State_____Zip_____

Do you know someone who enjoys books? Just give us their names and addresses and we'll send them a catalog too!

Mr./Mrs./Miss_____

Address_____

City_____State_____Zip_____

Mr./Mrs./Miss_____

Address_____

City_____State_____Zip_____

FC—9/75